the SCARAB

Catherine Fisher writes, Argelin has killed the Speaker and destroyed the Oracle, but who among mortals can silence the words of the god? In the steeliest of men there is always one weakness, which may be his downfall or his deliverance. And Mirany knows that beyond the desert and the tombs lies the Underworld where the dead wait. But if one of the dead should return, chaos might overwhelm the world. And perhaps not even the gods could survive it.

Catherine's first novel, *The Conjuror's Game*, was shortlisted for the Smarties Book Prize, and *The Candle Man* won the Tir Na n'Og prize. Her acclaimed fantasy series *The Snow-Walker's Son* was shortlisted for the WH Smith Mind Boggling Books Award. As well as the critically acclaimed *The Oracle*, Catherine's latest books include *Darkhenge, Corbenic, Darkwater Hall* and *The Lammas Field*, of which Jan Mark wrote: 'This is strong, passionate writing, deep and quite unsettling . . .'

the SCARAB

Catherine Fisher

Hodder
Children's
Books

a division of Hodder Headline Limited

To Sheenagh, with thanks and because of the cats.

For more information on Catherine Fisher, please visit:
www.geocities.com/catherinefisheruk/

First published in Great Britain in 2005
by Hodder Children's Books

A Catalogue record for this book is available
from the British Library

ISBN 0 340 84894 0

Typeset in Bembo by Avon DataSet Ltd,
Bidford-on-Avon, Warwickshire

Printed and bound in Great Britain by
Clays Ltd, St Ives plc

The paper and board used in this paperback by
Hodder Children's Books are natural recyclable products
made from wood grown in sustainable forests. The manufacturing
processes conform to the environmental regulations of
the country of origin.

Hodder Children's Books
a division of Hodder Headline Limited
338 Euston Road
London NW1 3BH

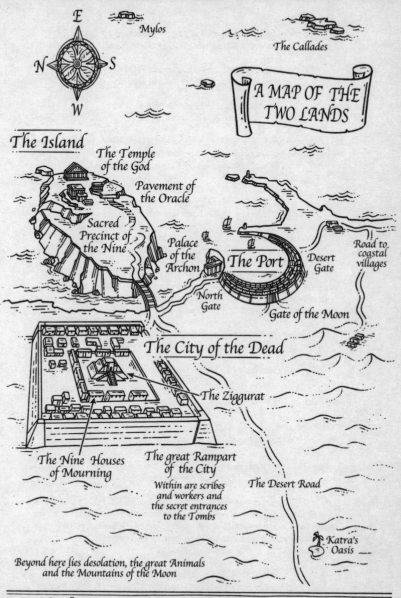

A MAP OF THE TWO LANDS

E

N — S

W

Mylos

The Callades

The Island

The Temple of the God

Pavement of the Oracle

Sacred Precinct of the Nine

Palace of the Archon

The Port

Desert Gate

Road to coastal villages

North Gate

Gate of the Moon

The City of the Dead

The Ziggurat

The Nine Houses of Mourning

The great Rampart of the City

Within are scribes and workers and the secret entrances to the Tombs

The Desert Road

Katra's Oasis

Beyond here lies desolation, the great Animals and the Mountains of the Moon

The First Gate
Of Skulls

Between the grains of sand are tiny spaces.

I hid in one while an insect crawled towards me, a vast beetle, its carapace shiny and black, its claws stubbled with hairs.

I felt it pick me up and roll me over. I tumbled, giddy, wrapped with other rubbish, dung and dust, dead ants, fragments of leaf. We became a ball of small beings, and the creature manoeuvred us all clumsily into darkness.

It buried us.

But we were the sun, and we burst the earth's crust, and scorched across the sky.

She hears the thunder of the Rain Queen

She could only squeeze in if she went sideways. Even then
the axle stuck out through the wooden wheel and she had
to hold her breath and drag herself past it, her infuriating
black veil snagging on the wall.

But behind the cart there was a space.

Once in, Mirany reached up and caught hold of the
boards; putting her foot on the axle she pulled herself
carefully higher, and peered over the top.

The cart was piled with oranges. Their smell was
mouthwatering, a sharp juicy sweetness that made her
hunger worse and her dry lips sore. She hadn't eaten a
whole orange for weeks. Maybe she could have sneaked
one out, but three of Argelin's guards were sitting in

the dust of the square, gambling, and the risk was too great.

Dice rattled.

Mirany bit the nail of her thumb, then noticed and stopped herself. It was a habit she'd had when she was small; lately it had come back. There was still no sign of Rhetia. Where was she? An hour must have passed since the time they'd arranged to meet, when the afternoon gong had chimed from the City. Now the hottest part of the day held the Port silent. The market had closed and everyone was indoors. Only stray dogs snoozed in the baking streets.

'What is she *up* to? Do you think she's been caught?'

She asked out of habit, but there was no answer. Maybe there never would be an answer again.

'And where are you, Bright One?' she thought angrily. 'Where are you when I need you!'

The piazza was high in the Fullers' Quarter. Rhetia had chosen it because it had five different exits, and the streets around were a maze of doorways and alleys and steps hung with drying cloth. At this hour it should be deserted.

But it wasn't.

There were more soldiers across by the shuttered wine shop. And as she watched in dismay an entire phalanx of Argelin's new mercenaries marched in, pale-skinned men who dressed in foreign clothes and spoke some guttural language. Their bronze greaves and corselets and spears glittered in the sunlight.

6

Something was going on.

Crouched, her bent knees aching, she watched the men halt in the centre of the square, below the statue of the Rain Queen.

The officer yelled a curt command; the column fell out, mopped sweat from their faces, brought up mules, unpacked equipment. Echoes rang in the enclosed space. All around them, from the white buildings, the sun's wrath blazed.

Mirany sucked her parched lip. If she could work back under the shadow of that striped awning she might make the nearest alleyway, and slip away without attracting more than a few glances.

But if they stopped her . . .

And what if Rhetia turned up?

A commotion jerked her head round. A man had come running out of one of the buildings, a small, oldish man. He was shouting in alarm and holding his hands above his head, racing straight at the soldiers.

Instantly the nearest one grabbed a spear and swung; the old man stumbled over it, then fell with a painful thump.

The mercenaries laughed. One made some comment.

The man was pleading with them; he scrambled on to his knees, and Mirany heard his breathless, barely intelligible gasps. 'You mustn't do this. Lords, please! This is a terrible thing. This is a desecration.'

They probably couldn't understand a word he said.

Almost casually, one of them gave him a kick in the chest that took the breath straight out of him; then they turned back to their task.

In sudden horror Mirany realized what they were doing.

Ropes and tackle were being dragged from mules. Efficiently the fair-haired men swung weighted loops; the ropes soared up and round the shoulders of the Rain Queen, her neck, her outstretched arm.

'No!' Mirany breathed.

The statue was vast, higher than the houses. It had been carved from a single piece of sea-green stone, a veined agate. Ancient beyond memory, the calm face of the Rain Queen had looked out over the Port for centuries, over the white houses to the endless azure semicircle of the sea. In the thousand pleated creases of her dress crystals glinted, embedded by the sculptor, and the blue lapis lazuli of the collar she wore glimmered with linked scorpions of gold, and scarabs of coral and amber. She held out one hand, and in her fingers a bronze bowl burned in the sun. Once a fountain had cascaded from it, splashing, diamond bright, into a white marble shell at her feet. But during the drought the fountain had been dry, and even now the river ran again it had not been restored. Lizards basked in the hot curve of the shell, among rubbish and a broken pot.

Ropes rattled.

Mirany gripped her hands into fists. 'Do something!' she demanded.

But the god did not answer. He had not answered for two months. And in that time her world had fallen apart.

Suddenly the gambling soldiers were scrambling up, thrusting dice into helmets, grabbing spears. Even before they could get themselves in order, the first rank of the bodyguard rode into the square.

Mirany ducked lower, hissing one of Oblek's worst swear words.

Among the armed men was a litter. She stared at it grimly. Litters were no longer allowed in the Port, except for this one. It had no flimsy curtains but stiff blinds of papyrus, reinforced, she'd heard, with metal against any sudden knife-thrust. Instead of windows, small slits were dark; eyes moved behind them. And she knew whose.

Since the destruction of the Oracle, Argelin rarely rode out openly. He travelled enclosed, protected by armed riders. He needed to. Every statue of the god and the Rain Queen in the Port was being systematically destroyed by his men, every image confiscated and smashed. Instead, paintings of Argelin decorated walls and squares; vast statues of him were hastily being constructed. All day she'd seen them – Argelin seated, his hands on his knees; Argelin standing astride, grasping a spear; Argelin in a war-chariot striking down his enemies, his deeds written in hieroglyphs on shining new obelisks and pylons.

There had been unrest. But then the longships of Argelin's new army had arrived, and terror had cowed people. After the chaotic riot in the harbour last month, when fifty men had been rounded up and beheaded, and their wives sold to slave traders, the General had become a figure of hatred and dread.

And if he found out she was still alive . . .

She smelled a heady jasmine scent, and glanced round anxiously. In the wall behind her was a small door; now it was ajar, an eye peeping out at her through the dark slit.

'Please,' she breathed. 'Let me come in.'

A pause. Then the door opened.

Instantly she slid inside. The bolt clicked behind her. The darkness smelt of cats and incense; she sensed a woman near in the dark passageway. A hand caught hers, and led her up some twisting stairs. Cobwebs hung against her face, and under her feet sandy dust crackled. Mirany guessed this was some sort of storage cellar, little used now there was nothing to store. She wrapped the black veil hastily round her face and shoulders, so that only her eyes showed. There was no knowing who these people were.

A curtain was pulled aside.

She climbed into a sunlit room, its shabby walls patterned with bright rays that streamed through latticed shutters. It was full of women. They turned to look at her briefly, then clustered again about the windows, as if unwilling to miss a moment of what was happening outside.

The girl who had brought her in was little more than

Mirany's age, her face painted with kohl and rouge, her dark hair tangled and unkempt. A small toddler clutched at her skirt.

'You shouldn't have been out there,' she said quietly.

Mirany nodded. 'What's happening?'

'They're going to destroy the statue, what else?'

Mirany glanced round. The room had couches, frail hangings. Three cats slept in the sun. There was an image of the Rain Queen in one corner; small sticks of sandalwood burned before it. The girl shook her head. 'He's insane,' she whispered.

As Mirany moved to the window, the women edged back. They were mostly young, garishly made up, flimsily dressed. All at once she realized what sort of house this was, and blushed under the veil.

Then she saw Argelin.

He had climbed out of the litter and was looking up at the statue. She had not seen him since Hermia's death, and was shocked at the change in him. His beard was still sharply razored, his breastplate glinting bronze, but the eyes that stared up at the Rain Queen had sunk and seemed duller; his face was haggard, its expression a cold loathing.

He stepped back; gave a curt command.

The men hauled on the ropes. Around Mirany, hands went to lips; someone breathed a prayer. The Rain Queen swayed. Very slightly, her hand moved against the sky, her remote face shifted in the sunlight. Dust fell from her ledges and shoulders; one of her fingers cracked where the rope held it, and a knuckle of marble, big as a man's hand, crashed to the ground.

There were people in the square now. They had emerged from the houses, gathered in the shade. They were silent and ominous; Argelin snapped something and the soldiers formed a hasty double formation round the work, facing out, spears crossed. The old man sat stunned in the dust; he seemed unable to believe what was happening. He had probably known the statue all his life, Mirany thought, and the fountain too.

In her mind she said grimly, 'Gods are supposed to see what happens on earth. You must be able to see this. *Do something.*'

As if in answer a gong chimed. All the women looked to the right.

'Who is it?' one breathed.

A procession was entering the square from the archway down to the harbour. Mirany pushed to the front. 'Officials.'

'From the Emperor?'

'From the City of the Dead.'

She recognized them easily. The Chief Embalmer, in white; the Overseer of the Tombs; five of the top scribes; the Archon's Steward; the Mistress of the Sacred Cats.

'They'll stop him.' One of the older women folded her arms. 'They have to. He just can't go on pulling down everything.'

'He can do what he likes,' the girl next to Mirany said quietly. 'He killed the Speaker. The god has cursed him, and all of us with him.'

Mirany edged the shutter open slightly. The dignitaries came forward. Just below the window, Argelin turned to face them. After a moment all of them bowed, the Embalmer's white robe sweeping the dust, the bareheaded scribes sweating.

'What's this?' Argelin sounded more amused than annoyed.

The Chief Embalmer licked dry lips. He was a fleshy man, his thick fingers heavy with rings.

'Lord General . . .' he said hesitantly.

Argelin smiled a smile like steel. 'Lord *King.*'

A fraction of silence. Then, 'If you wish it, sir.'

Argelin stepped forward. 'I more than wish it. I have ordered it. You saw me crowned, Parmenio.'

Mirany had heard about that. Kreon had brought news down into the tombs that Argelin had crowned himself king with the silver diadem from the god's statue in the Temple. She remembered how appalled Rhetia had been. And how furious.

The Embalmer had an attendant with a feathered fan. Argelin waved the boy away. He backed quickly as his master stammered, 'Lord King. Yes. Indeed. But I . . . we . . . the Servants of the Dead. There is something we wish to say.'

He had nerve, Mirany thought. Now he extended a plump hand, and a slave came forward with a casket. The Embalmer opened it.

The women gasped, as one.

Even from here the contents blazed. Diamonds, almost certainly. Their brilliance threw tiny rainbows across Argelin's face. His eyes narrowed, but he showed no surprise. The Embalmer took a small scroll out and his gilded fingers held it tight. 'Lord King.' His voice was high with tension. 'Your actions are your own. But we cannot stand by and see them without pleading with you . . . without supplicating you . . . to show mercy, and desist.' He gave a nod; at once the officials knelt, clumsy in their cumbersome robes, the Mistress of the Cats in her whiskered mask, the scribes in saffron and red. They bowed their foreheads to the ground.

The crowd murmured.

Argelin watched, unmoved.

'For a mortal to make war against the gods is to invite disaster,' the Embalmer went on. 'You will bring the god's wrath and the Rain Queen's anger on all of us, on the people, on the slaves and the children. We, the Officers of the Land Below, beg you to spare this last image. There has been enough terror. You are too generous, too wise to refuse us. In return, accept this token of the people's gratitude.'

Terrified, the slave laid the casket at Argelin's feet. The

General looked down at it. When he raised his face Mirany saw his eyes were cold.

'What about my anger, old man? What about my wrath?' Like a striking snake, Argelin reached out and grabbed the Embalmer by the neck of his robe, heaving the fat man's sweating face close to his. 'This Rain Queen of yours took Hermia's body out of my arms, blinded me into murder. I swore I would tear down every image of her for that and I'll do it. And I defy you, and the stinking dead, and the god himself, to stop me!'

Viciously he kicked the casket over. Diamonds hissed out. He ground them into the sand with his boot heel.

'My Lord,' the Embalmer gasped 'think again. When the Archon returns . . .'

'*I am the Archon*. I am the Oracle, and the Nine, and the god himself. Get that into your head, Parmenio, and make the City understand it too. Because when I've finished with the Port I'll be coming to you, and if I want the riches of the tombs I'll take them, with my own hands.'

There was a terrible silence.

And then a shriek. It was so eerie and unexpected that even Argelin's head shot up; he turned, and the soldiers gripped weapons.

On all the housetops around the square, the town baboons sat watching. As if the noise had wakened them from their siesta, the monkeys stared down, desert wind ruffling their fur. Mothers held babies; the males prowled, anxious. Another screeched, then another, and suddenly the whole square was a cacaphony of panic; the animals rising and beating their chests, grabbing jutting stone and jabbering furiously, their white teeth wide.

Out at sea, thunder rumbled.

Argelin dropped the Chief Embalmer. The man staggered, said: 'Lord King, she will send plagues—'

'Enough!' Without another word Argelin turned on his heel. He gave one yell; the mercenaries took up the ropes. The pandemonium the baboons were making must have been terrifying and strange to them, but they ignored it, their hands grasping the rough thick cables.

'Hear me, Rain Woman!' Argelin yelled. 'Take this for your worship!'

He jumped back.

The soldiers heaved.

With a crack like lightning, the statue snapped. Black fissures shot up from its base; the sea-green dress shattered. Fingers and curls of hair and an ear rained down. Rocking as the soldiers heaved and yelled and heaved again, the Rain Queen toppled. She jolted forward, her calm face fragmenting, and for a moment Mirany was sure the goddess would turn her head and shimmer into life, that she would shrivel Argelin with one touch of her crystal fingertip. Instead, with a shudder that shook the house and the world, she fell, and all that crashed into the stones was a mass of agate, a heaped tumble of broken slivers and glistening shards.

Dust rose in a great cloud, billowing in through the windows. The girls coughed, covered their faces. Objects fell from shelves. The baby woke and screamed.

Slowly, the huddled monkeys fell silent.

The officials stared, appalled.

After a moment, his boots crushing rubble, Argelin crunched over to the broken face. It lay on its side, one eye and half a nose, and as they watched he crouched and laid his hand almost tenderly along the cracked brow.

'So, Lady,' he whispered, 'destroy me now, if you can. Do your worst. Because we are enemies, you and I.'

Crystals glinted all round her. In the corners of her eyes.

Argelin snatched his hand away. He turned his palm up, and behind the window shutter Mirany drew in her breath, because in all the blazing heat, his skin was wet.

And in her ear a breathless voice said, *Look at him, Mirany. Does he really think he's me?*

The beetle begins its flight

Astonished, Mirany gasped, but before she could answer a hand caught her by the chin and jerked her head round.

'So! An intruder in the Palace of Delights.'

The woman was fleshy and had small black eyes. She wore a loose robe of dark linen and round gold earrings that jangled. Her grey hair was cut very close to her head. Behind her, discreetly, a hefty slave waited.

Mirany swallowed. 'I'm so sorry. I was outside. In the square. I thought—'

'How very clever of you to think, my lovely.' A plump finger stroked her hair. 'And how did you get in?'

Mirany glanced round, confused. The girls were almost

all gone. 'Someone opened the door. I don't know who, but I'm grateful.'

The woman looked at her closely. 'So you should be.' She reached out a hand heavy with gold rings and pulled the thin veil from Mirany's face. Hot, Mirany stared back.

Shrewd eyes looked her up and down.

The dress was ragged enough; Kreon had bought it from a woman in the City. And after two months of living in the darkness of the tombs, dirt had ingrained itself into her skin, and her hair was tangled and unkempt. She was thinner, but not thin enough, not starved, and she could never hide the smoothness of her hands. She had no sores, no rickets, no suppurating ailments.

And the woman saw that.

'Something of a lady.' She touched the dress lightly with long red fingernails. 'In hiding.'

Mirany pulled the robe tight. She had to get out, straight away. She made a step towards the door but the woman jerked her head and the slave moved smoothly to block it. He grinned at Mirany.

'Which is interesting.' The woman went to the window and closed the shutter, looking through its lattice. 'Because there are notices all round the City, for those who can read them, proclaiming a tempting reward – *highly* tempting, for a poor businesswoman like me – should anyone happen to discover the whereabouts of the Nine. Those still alive, that is.'

Mirany thought quickly. She and Rhetia were surely presumed to be dead; after the flooded Draxis had gone down, the caves would have been searched. Argelin may have thought their bodies washed out to sea. But the other priestesses, Chryse, Gaia, Tethys, Persis, Ixaca, Callia, where were they? Had they fled? Had Argelin found them?

'I'm not what you're looking for.' She kept her voice firm.

The woman looked over and smiled. 'Then you won't mind me inviting one of the General's men up here to find out, will you?'

I think she means it, Mirany, the voice said sadly in her ear.

Where are you? Where's Seth? Are you back in the Port?

Oh, we've had such adventures in the desert, Mirany. What animals we saw, what mountains we climbed! And Oblek has his songs again!

Fine. While we've been through hell.

The woman must have thought the frown was for her. 'Of course, I'm open to offers. Though I doubt you have as much as the dear General will pay.'

Through the lattice, Mirany saw the litter being carried away, the ranked bodyguards marching behind it. In the square the hammer and tap of stone smashing began. She said, 'Who are you?'

The woman smiled. She spread her arms in a theatrical

gesture, and her robe was iridescent and patterned like wings. 'I am the queen of the night. My name is Manto.'

'You own this house?'

Manto studied her. 'You don't ask the questions you want answers to. Yes, I was once a hetaira. Now I supply girls to those who can pay.' She glanced out at the stonebreaking. 'Business is good. There are a lot of new men in the Port.'

Mirany swallowed. She was sweating, and desperate to get out. The room which had seemed a haven a few minutes ago was closing in round her. And she had to get back to the tombs before the curfew.

'Help me,' she said to the god in her mind. But he was gone as swiftly as he'd come.

Manto turned leisurely, and sat at a small table. On it were strange objects; a set of sandalwood boxes, a mirror, a mummified paw reflecting in twisted glass. She picked up herbs and began to crumble the dry leaves between her fingers; the rich scent of wormwood filled the room.

'I also have a certain reputation as a worker of magic. A maker of charms and potions to summon spirits.' She looked up. 'Of drugs to quiet the soul and body.'

Mirany went cold. Then, like a silent whisper from the god, an idea came. She folded her arms.

'If you're threatening me,' she said quietly, 'perhaps you should know that I am very good friends with a certain . . . desert scavenger.'

The woman's eyes slid to her, amused. 'That would be a vulture?'

'That would be a Jackal.'

Shock. That was what she saw. And avid curiosity. It was quickly covered; the woman laughed and made a great play of arranging her dark robe, but Mirany's heart sank. A thread of terror chilled her; had she made some hideous mistake?

Manto turned; she picked up a circular silver mirror with a green-eyed snake coiled round it and gazed into its depths thoughtfully.

'Now, that *is* interesting. And there was I thinking you a precious little priestess innocent of everything but the Island. But the one you speak of, the Lord of Thieves himself, is a myth, is he not? Half man, half creature of the dark. A haunter of tombs and waste places. My girls tell their children stories of his exploits, in tales at bedtime. Even should he exist—'

'He exists,' Mirany snapped.

In the mirror she saw Manto's knowing smile. 'Yes, sweetie. I know he exists. But I've heard a rumour that he's disappeared from the alleys and opium lairs of the Port.'

'Perhaps he's back.' Mirany glanced at the slave.

Manto laid down the mirror and looked up. Her voice darkened; the playfulness went out of it.

'Then tell him he would do well to be careful. In Argelin's new regime, thieves are tortured without trial.

But if he is back, I'm delighted.' She put her crimson nails to her mouth and blew a kiss into the air. 'Give him this from me,' she said quietly. 'Tell him I will soon extract the payment of his debt.'

Mirany stared. Something flew from the woman's mouth or hand; a shining blue and gold insect, carapace raised, wings buzzing. It landed on her tunic, clinging; she leapt back, beating it off, but the thing clattered and fell on the floor.

Slowly, she picked it up.

It was a scarab beetle, wide-winged in enamel, blue and scarlet. Above its head was a disc of gold, representing the ball of dung it rolled, the sun crossing the sky.

Looking at it, she said, 'You know the Jackal?'

'Oh yes. Tell him: Manto.' She smiled, putting her red-nailed hands together and gazing at Mirany over them. 'He'll remember.'

Behind her, Mirany heard the slave unlatch the door. Trying not to look shaken, she gathered up her veil and strode towards the stairs, head high, as Rhetia would have done. On the first step the mocking voice arrested her.

'Such a waste. If you ever need a job, sweetie, look me up.'

Despite herself, Mirany shuddered. Then she ran.

The slave let her out at a different entrance, in the street. Siesta time was long over; a train of donkeys was trudging past her, the beasts' warm dungy smell comforting. She let them clop by, then squeezed out behind the last, jumping from its irritable kick, and walked hurriedly, head down, towards the North Gate.

She had to get out before curfew. Since he had made himself King, Argelin had closed his grip on the Port. The gates were locked now an hour before sunset, and anyone found on the streets after dark was arrested. Everyone had papers with their name and description, and though hardly any of the guards could read, scribes had been posted to assist them. She fingered the grubby square of parchment in her pocket. Kreon had forged it, with ink and papyrus stolen from the workrooms. He had laboured over it carefully, his weak eyes close to the script, but the hieroglyphs were complex, and she couldn't read well enough to know if there were any mistakes.

Seth would know.

She smiled. *She was so relieved they were back*. Now things would surely be better. The cobbled roadway radiated heat. She slipped under a white arch and through the loggia of the small theatre, then round the corner and into the maze of streets that clustered behind the wall.

At a small dolphin fountain the usual queue of slaves and women carrying amphorae waited in the dimming light; a dog lapped thirstily at the splashes on the sand. Water and food were tightly rationed; Argelin's mercenaries guarded every well. She hurried past the ruin of a garden; scents of myrtle drifted over, and though every lemon and fig had long been stripped from the trees she sighed, because it reminded her of the Island, its orchards and groves. No one went on to the Island now. The bridge was barricaded and guarded, and the gardens of the Precinct must be dry and parched, the swimming pool empty, the Upper House a home for scorpions and spiders. Only the Emperor's elephants were corralled there, half-starved; Argelin held them hostage because they were sacred, and their trumpeting blares of woe rang out nightly over the sea.

The granaries must have been emptied. And worst of all, in the Temple, the god's statue stood uncared for. About the Oracle she dared not think. It scared her, made her hot with anger.

There was an even longer queue at the North Gate. Anxiously Mirany scanned the people, but couldn't see Rhetia. A group of nomads clamoured to get their goats through, and workers for the City, scribes and cleaners and artists and shabti-makers, waited patiently in the shelter of the walls.

Argelin's men were everywhere.

'Please,' she breathed. 'Let Rhetia come.' This was only the second time she'd dared to enter the Port, and she'd never gone through the gate without Rhetia. The tall girl was good at bluffing. She could change her voice and say things that made the soldiers laugh, or she'd flirt with them, oblivious to their crude remarks. Mirany could never do any of that. She knew with a sinking terror that she looked just how she felt, small, scared, guilty.

Shadows fell on her. Looking up she saw, impaled on spikes, the rotting heads of those who had protested at the harbour, some picked almost clean by the birds, others unrecognizable shreds of flesh hanging from eyeless skulls. The smell was sickening. Flies buzzed and rose in clouds about them.

Mirany wrapped her veil over her nose and mouth.

The queue shuffled forward.

Through the archway opposite latecomers were crowding in; a waggon load of salt from the mines, a phalanx of mercenaries. Those without papers were thrust back out into the desert; everyone else was checked against the lists of the denounced, posted on mudbrick pillars.

The nomads went through, droppings from their goats littering the road. The scribe beckoned Mirany closer. 'Next!'

Keeping her face covered, she handed him the parchment.

He read it carefully, then looked at her. 'Why are you going out?'

'My father is an artist in the tombs. I live there.'

'Why enter the Port?'

'To visit my aunt. And buy things.' She showed him the small bag under her robe; he tugged it open, inspected the dried figs, the linen bag of salt, the few copper coins. Then he pulled out the scarab. 'What's this?'

She'd forgotten it. She licked dry lips. 'My aunt gave it to me. For a present.'

In his hand it looked cheap and garish, the sort of thing they sold in the market. She must have been mistaken about the gold; it was brass, the enamel poor quality glass.

The scribe turned and spoke to the soldier. He turned the trinket over; together they watched the low sun catch its colours.

Was it some sort of secret symbol? Suddenly Mirany was sure the hetaira had betrayed her.

'Who's your aunt?' Something in the scribe's voice had changed. It was subtle, but she heard it. The guard too, stepped closer.

'Sappho. She lives in the Potters' Quarter.'

'Does she?' He checked the list quickly then looked up. 'I think you're lying to me, darling.' As he tossed the scarab back to her he smiled an oily smile. 'I think you'd better come down to the guardhouse.'

Appalled, she stared at him. 'But . . . my father . . .'

He caught her wrist. 'Can wait. Come with me.'

'No!' She jerked free, horrified. At the same time a horn blared, high on the wall, the signal for the Gate to be locked. People behind her surged; one yelled angrily and the echoes rang in the confined gatehouse.

Before the guard could grab her again he was thrust aside.

A man had come stumbling through from the desert. He was well-wrapped against the hot winds, and he wore one of the loose robes the nomads wove, of pale striped cloth. A stick was gripped in his hand, and on his back hung a battered pack.

Only the man's eyes were visible in his face; dark eyes, the skin around them sunburned, sand in the creases of his forehead. He spun the scribe round.

'You,' he said.

The guard's spear came up; he ignored it. 'Are you in charge here? Why are scribes at the gates now?'

'Argelin's orders.' The scribe scowled. As if annoyed at himself for answering he barked, 'And where are your papers?'

'I haven't got any papers.'

The simple statement silenced everyone. People were pushing past Mirany; in the dimness she risked a step backwards.

'But the new regulations . . .'

'Stuff the regulations.' The man's voice was husky with thirst. 'Leave this rabble and take me directly to Argelin. *Now*. I have news he'll want to hear. But first, get me a drink.'

For a tense moment the scribe didn't move. Then he nodded to the guard, who lowered the spear and fetched a jug of water and a dented cup. Mirany tried another step back. The traveller's eyes glanced at her, then flickered to the gate. He poured the water slowly.

Her heart thudded. For a moment she had thought he knew her, that a message had passed between them.

The archway was black with shadow, stinking with dung. One of the gates had already clanged shut, the other was being heaved by three mercenaries, the vast bronze-nailed construction creaking as they put their weight behind it.

The traveller said, 'Argelin will reward anyone who brings me straight to him. He's been expecting my news for months.' He loosened the cloth around his face, drew it away and drank.

And Mirany stared.

Because it was Seth.

Bronzed, burned, weary, his eyes red-rimmed, his face stubbled and drawn with hunger, but Seth. Again he flicked an urgent glance at the gate, and this time she stumbled back, silent and stunned, unable to take her eyes off him.

Why on earth should he want to go to Argelin?

And where was the Archon?

There was no time. She turned and fled through the slit of the closing gate, dodging a soldier's hand, ignoring the scribe's yell; then she was running, racing as fast as she could along the desert road towards the brooding darkness of the City of the Dead. Her veil fell off; she grabbed it.

The bag bumped against her hip but she didn't slow, even when a stitch pierced her side and made her gasp for breath. Only as she came under the ominous shadow of the seated Archons on the City wall did she glance back, clutching her side, dragging in air.

No one was following.

The gate was closed, the road empty. She crouched, tugging off the veil and bundling the hateful thing in the bag. Then, silently, she turned into the bushes.

The path led through scrub and spiny spindlewood; an animal trail under the wall of the City. Far above, the stone Archons kept their eternal watch, their jewelled eyes gazing across the desert to the eastern horizon, dim now with the first stars.

Mirany glanced behind, then up. She slipped into the darkness of a jutting bastion, the fifth along. Bushes screened it; gently she pulled them aside. The wall was immense; each block huge as a house, tight-fitting, overgrown, but near this corner a small section had been cleared. She groped for the secret mechanism, deep in its hidden crack.

Stone swivelled, with a hoarse rasp.

Crouching, Mirany crawled into the hole. Inside was darkness; she slid the stone shut and blackness closed round her, tight. Her breathing became huge, and the small noises as she groped for the lamp and the tinderbox echoed in the unseen spaces around her.

When the flame cracked she saw at once what she had dreaded. The other lamp, Rhetia's, was still here. So she hadn't come back.

Mirany lit her own with a shaky hand, then straightened. As the light strengthened to a yellow glow, it revealed the labyrinth of mummies.

This place always unnerved her. Kreon had showed her many secrets of the tombs; there were several entrances that led outside the City, and though this was the easiest, it was the one she liked least.

The mummies were not of people, but of cats.

Thousands of them, maybe millions; the population of cats in the tombs was unguessable. Now she picked her way between the rigid bundles, some in great stacks of boxes, some loosely wrapped, gnawed by rats, sawdust innards spilling, some with intricate criss-cross bandaging still in place, their tiny doll-like heads fashioned of wax or clay, studded with green glass eyes, painted with whiskers and nose. Desiccated bodies were piled to the painted roof, they lay on biers and caskets and elaborate sandalwood boats. Many – probably the Temple cats – had amulets and scarabs woven into their wrappings, were heaped haphazard in golden boxes, the boat of the Rain Queen incised on the sides.

Holding the lamp high, Mirany walked through the aisles and vaults of small distant deaths, and from under her feet shadows slunk, the living animals nesting in the dead.

Kittens squealed; she glimpsed a beautiful tortoiseshell with a gold earring reflecting the lamp for a moment in its eyes.

At the far end was a staircase; she descended it and opened the door carefully. It wasn't locked, and the key still hung on the wall. She left it there, hurrying from the stifling musty airlessness down into the levels below.

Darkness no longer bothered her. Here, in Kreon's kingdom of shadows, she had grown used to not seeing the sun, to sensing time by the faint breath of underground breeze, the shifts and trickle of sand, the tread of the living far above. But running down the stairs now to the Third Level, and then the Fourth, she felt all the old doubts cluster round her, about the god, about Seth. Why was he going to Argelin? What had happened to him? What had happened to all of them at the Mountains of the Moon?

For two months, since that terrible day when the river had resumed its course and Hermia had died, she hadn't heard a word that the god had spoken. Only silence and echoes and darkness, until today. But maybe she had imagined those words, had heard what she wanted to hear. Because Seth couldn't have been sure that she had rescued his sister and father from slavery. Perhaps he had despaired. Perhaps the rewards Argelin had offered had been too great.

Perhaps he had killed Alexos.

She stopped dead; shook her head. She wouldn't believe that.

She wouldn't.

At the door to Kreon's chamber of copies she rubbed her face clean and knocked the secret knock. For a moment no one came, and then she heard his light limp, the patter of Telia's feet behind.

'It's Mirany,' she whispered.

The door opened. The albino's colourless eyes narrowed; he put his hand up against the lamplight.

'Mirany!' Behind him Telia danced a dance of delight. 'You'll never guess . . .'

'Where's Rhetia?' Kreon's voice was anxious.

'I don't know.' She pushed past him.

And saw Oblek. He sat with his feet up, gulping down water. As she gasped in astonishment he gave a great ugly guffaw of laughter. And a voice behind her said petulantly, 'I did tell you we were back, Mirany. I don't know why you get so upset about things.'

She turned.

Alexos lay on his stomach with his feet up, a pile of Telia's toy bricks stacked in front of him.

And behind, lounging on a couch of fake mahogany, his strange eyes watching her sideways, was the Jackal.

33

He dares the lair of the wounded beast

Seth marched down to the harbour between two soldiers. He wasn't sure if they were escorting him or arresting him, but he kept his head up and strode out confidently. The pretence began here, as the Jackal had said. There must be no looking back.

But seeing Mirany had nearly finished him. The temptation to take her arm and run with her, to flee out through the closing gate, had swept over him like a heatwave, and sweat had broken out down his back.

He was so scared.

That morning, lying under the tamarind tree watching the Port walls, he'd been calm and assured. The plan, devised in the long tramp back, had seemed within his ability; easy lying, cool bluster. He had boasted to Oblek and the Jackal, and believed it. Now, with no one here to impress, he knew he had fooled himself. He was alone. And even if he succeeded, even if Argelin believed him, there was no knowing what would happen after that.

The streets were darkening. He saw women snatch up their children and hurry indoors. The smoke of cooking fires purpled the air; he breathed it in, the mingled smell of lemon and rotting vegetables and washing and fish and cinnamon that he had known all his life.

Small red geraniums bloomed in a pot. As his sleeve brushed one it released its scent; then the moment was gone, and they were descending the tangle of steps and twisting lanes, into the darkness of huddled houses.

Through a gap in the roofs he saw the sea.

Its dark splendour made him draw in his breath; the salt breeze and the cry of one gull stung surprising tears to his eyes. In the burning days of the desert he had had waking dreams of the sea, had stumbled through visions of its blue water, rising and falling, its fish and dolphins. Now, hurrying down the street that led to the harbour, its seaweedy stench rose up and astounded him; he slithered on scales, and a net someone had left out to dry.

The guard glanced at him. He pulled upright, quickly.

Argelin's headquarters had changed. For a start, there was a whole new defensive structure around it; hastily built stone bastions, a gatehouse, three trebuchets and another stone-throwing device mounted on platforms and facing out to sea. In the harbour itself a great chain, huger than any metal-work he had ever seen, hung dripping across the entrance, and the fishing boats were overshadowed by the half-built hulks of seven – no, eight – vast triremes, men still hammering and banging on them even now, by guttering torchlight. A row of strange dragon-prowed vessels lay at anchor.

And there were mercenaries, everywhere.

Tall foreigners, from the cold lands beyond the Empire. Their eyes were blue, and their hair like straw. Fascinated, he stared at their swords, odd leggings, swirling serpent brooches. They spoke a language of curled snapped words. He wished he could see it written down, imagined it in hieroglyphs and demotic, to keep his fear away.

It took half an hour of arguing to get through to Argelin. Once he threatened, and twice he bribed, with a few staters the Jackal had given him. Some things didn't change. He was searched twice, then marched to a small holding cell and locked in, with a crazy woman and a man who held his head in his hands and groaned and said nothing.

Seth didn't sit. He paced the cell, planning his words. They changed from moment to moment; by the time the guard came back in a big hurry and ushered him out, he was so mixed up he knew he could never do this.

Argelin would smell his lies like dung in the sun.

They took him to the optio Seth remembered, a small

harassed grey man, now slightly more important, it seemed, because his bronze breastplate had a few curls of decoration and a gorgon head in its centre.

'You!' The optio stared. 'Thought you were dead!'

'Not yet.' Seth licked his dry lips. 'Does the General know I'm here?'

'His Holiness the King-Archon, the Bright One, the Son of the Scorpion, has been informed.'

'*Holiness?*' Despite himself, Seth breathed in in horror.

The optio shrugged wearily. 'You've been away too long, scribe. The world's flipped upside down.'

As if to echo him, a roar of rage erupted behind the closed door of Argelin's room. Something crashed into fragments. The optio, grim faced, said through it, 'For your sake, I hope it's good news.'

'The best.' He rubbed his rough chin, feeling the sand grains on his skin.

The door opened.

Two of the Northern men dragged out a slave. His feet scrabbled on the floor; his face was a welter of blood. As he passed Seth heard him murmur; odd, sobbing phrases.

'Wait here.' The optio went in. In the stillness, the dim passageway flickered in the flames of a torch that guttered in the niche. The statue of the Rain Queen that Seth remembered once standing beside it was gone.

He could run. Right now. He could turn his back and go. As the fear came up into his mouth like vomit, he managed one step. Then the optio came out.

'You next.'

His voice was colourless, and when Seth looked into his face there was nothing but a carefully cleared stare. Seth turned, straightened his back, and walked in through the door.

The chamber was more or less as he remembered it; the opulent couches, round table with its brilliant majolica bowl of lemons, rich hangings, huge red-figure vases. Lamps that hung from the roof lit shadowy corners with flames reflected in bronze and gold. But it was a mess. Rolls of papyrus were heaped in vast stacks, their tags tangled. Stele, incised with wedge-shaped letters, tumbled from boxes. The tigerskin rug was stained and trampled, heaped with a pyramid of rusted armour, and maps were everywhere; pinned on walls, propped in the arms of statues, obliterating the half-eaten remains of meals mouldering on plates of pewter.

Argelin was bent over one, tracing something with his fingers. When he turned his head and saw Seth, a feverish light lit his eyes.

'I was beginning to think you were bones in some dry wadi.' He straightened, leaning his back against the table. He wore a leather breastplate over a dirty red tunic, and his arms were bare, their scarred skin muscled.

Seth said, 'It was a long journey.'

'So I see.' The General smiled coldly. 'It's marked you.'

And you, Seth thought. Something in the man's eyes chilled him. Alexos had told him how Hermia had died; now he wondered what else Argelin had killed in that moment.

'I presume he's dead, the little crazy Archon? You would not have come here if you'd failed.'

'He's dead.' The lie came easily. His own steady voice pleased him.

'The gold?'

'We found none.'

'And his magic Well?'

Seth shrugged. 'We reached the Mountains. The boy was obsessed with climbing them. At the top of the highest there was a cave with a pool of water in; he made us drink from it. It was cold and tasted of metal.' He paused, then walked to one of the striped day couches and sat on it, stretching his legs out. Argelin watched, saying nothing.

'That night there was a storm. Lightning, vast rain clouds. The boy danced and sang in it. He seemed to think he had caused it to come. Streams began to run; the river bed of the Draxis flooded. You know about that.'

Something strange happened then. Argelin's composure flickered and, for an instant, was gone. Seth went on hastily.

'Next day, as we were descending on a rope, I was last. The boy was climbing down a sheer cliff. Let's just say he fell.'

'You cut the rope?'

Seth smiled sourly. 'You were right. It was easier than I thought.'

'Indeed. You seem to have overcome your scruples without difficulty.'

Keeping the smile on his face was hard. So he let it fade. 'I found myself without a choice.'

Argelin watched. Then he nodded. 'The others?'

'Two men the boy had picked up from somewhere. One a drunkard, the other a thief. I left them at Katra's oasis.'

'Then they know too much.'

'They know if they open their mouths they answer to you.' Again, he shrugged. 'One murder was enough for me.' He tried to put hidden agony in the words, remorse crushed down and trampled, an edge of fear.

Maybe he succeeded. Argelin watched him for a long moment, then went over to a silver jug and poured two cups of wine out of it. He handed one to Seth.

'To the death of the god.'

Seth took it. Though he was appalled to the depths of his soul he raised it without a pause. 'To the death of the god.'

The wine was sour and bit at the back of his throat, but he was grateful for it. Now he had to stop himself thinking the worst was over. Because the hardest part was still to come.

'Of course,' Argelin was saying, wandering through the

heaped papyrus, 'there is *always* a choice. I presume you've discovered that your father and sister escaped from my . . . custody. You know where they are?'

It was hard, then, not to betray himself. The muscles of his mouth tightened; he said, 'I know now. I didn't know then.'

'Tell me where they are.'

'Staying with friends.'

Argelin smiled. 'Friends. How useful. You want your reward.' He pulled out a scroll and glanced at the tag, then flattened it on the table. Even from here Seth could see it was crammed with wedge-shaped letters, intercut with occasional cartouches circling the blue-gold hieroglyphs of the god and the Rain Queen.

'I think we spoke of a quaestorship.' Argelin took a stylus from the table and dipped it in ink. His eye travelled down the writing; savagely he slashed out the sacred names and wrote his own, the nib spattering ink. 'I keep my promises. I could have you killed, but you might be useful again, and I think money will ensure silence just as well. I knew the first time I saw you you could be bought.' He didn't bother to hide his scorn.

Seth stood, and put the silver cup down. It clinked on the stained inlay of the table.

'*I don't want a quaestorship*,' he said quietly.

The stylus stopped, mid-letter. Argelin turned his head; he had stepped back and had whipped a long blade into his hand before Seth could get another word out.

'No . . . no, I don't mean—'

The General strode up close to him. He raised the knife to Seth's face, the bronze blade jagged-edged, catching the flamelight. Its tip was an inch from Seth's right eyeball.

'A blind scribe is a worthless scribe,' he said. His voice was oddly breathless, his knuckles white on the hilt.

For an instant Seth was giddy, as if the ground had moved, the world had spun. Argelin's madness was a buzzing he could hear, a saltiness on his lips. It clogged the dark air.

Then a single drop of water plipped from the ceiling. It splashed on the General's wrist; he gave a gasp and flung it off, scrubbing wildly at his skin, screaming up at the rocky slabbed roof. 'You! Is it you again?'

Seth jerked back. Argelin seemed not to notice; he was holding the knife out defensively, turning, staring up. 'Where are you?' he snarled. 'You creep and drip and trickle but I'll find you. Don't think my revenge has even started yet, waterwoman, slut, witch! I'll smash and burn every statue of you, hack out your name from a million stele, rip up every papyrus that even breathes of you! Not only will you not exist, you'll never have existed. Men will learn that water is my gift, channelled and irrigated by my workmen, controlled by the sluices and pumps I devise. There is no Rain Queen.' He lowered the knife, his voice sinking to a sudden hiss. '*I am the only god here now.*'

The chamber was silent. From the harbour the hammering of the shipwrights rang faintly.

Argelin was sweating, his face grey.

The optio and the three men who had rushed in stood awkwardly inside the door. Their weapons were drawn. They glanced swiftly round the room.

Seth peeled himself off the back wall.

'What do you want?' Argelin said hoarsely.

The optio was sweating. 'Someone shouted, lord. I thought . . .'

Argelin laughed, a hollow, empty sound. He seemed to realize he was holding the knife, glanced at it and then dropped it with a clatter on the table top. 'Get out. Out!'

Just for an instant, the optio glanced at Seth. Then he muttered something, and the men backed through the door.

Argelin ran a hand over his beard. Its razored perfection seemed to calm him; he went and took another sip of wine, and when he spoke again his voice was as icy as if nothing had happened. 'If not the quaestorship, then what?'

Seth's heart was still hammering. A lump of something seemed stuck in his throat; he managed to swallow it and said, 'Not money. Power.'

'I won't be blackmailed, scribe.'

'No . . . It's just . . .' He shrugged, took a step forward. 'I helped Alexos because I thought he would be powerful and I'd be someone. But he was just a boy, capricious and silly.

My father always told me that I should have joined your staff, because one day you'd make yourself the real power in the Two Lands. He was right. Out there, in the desert, I saw he was right.'

Sweat was trickling down his back. He clenched a fist, then opened it. 'I want to work for you. Personally. I want to run things for you – you need someone, look at it, all this paperwork is a mess. I don't want to spend my life buried in the tombs or threatening old women for pennies. I want to be at the heart of things.'

Silence.

Had he said too much?

Argelin tapped one finger on the topmost lemon in the bowl. It was green with mildew, Seth noticed.

'The heart of things. How interesting.'

'You need someone efficient.' He had to be bold, he saw. 'The people are rebellious, the negotiations with the Emperor must be complex. The river has to be controlled if you want to profit from it; there are plans to draw up, levies, contracts for the irrigation work. Ships have to be provisioned, their crews recruited. Your new mercenaries have to be paid.'

'I have a thousand scribes.'

'And they all report to you. Waste your time with tiresome, petty matters. You need to be overseeing the fleet, the defences. Your business is war. Let me run things for you.'

The General smiled. 'You make quite a tempting case,' he said quietly. 'But I am not such a fool as not to know a few years of bribes and influence will make you dangerous. I might have to start looking over my shoulder.'

'I would be loyal.'

'Indeed you would. I would make certain of that.' He turned, paced. Seth waited. He had done all he could. Another word, another movement, would be too much. His throat was dry, his legs weak. He longed to sit down. But he waited.

Finally Argelin turned.

'I agree. You will be my personal Secretary. You will have rooms here, and be under no one's authority but my own. I will expect your attendance at any hour of the day or night. Your wages will be a thousand staters a year. However, your sister and father will be handed over to me and will live in a house of my choosing. They will not be allowed to leave the Port. Should you fail me, they will be killed.'

He came up to Seth, his eyes hard as steel. 'Because I think I will need to watch you, Seth. The fat musician is dead and the girl is dead and the Archon is – apparently – dead, but still you remain.'

Seth shrugged. 'I'm on no side but my own,' he said gruffly.

Argelin raised an eyebrow. 'Let's hope so.'

★ ★ ★

Outside, he wanted to collapse, to gulp in air as if he was stifled, but the optio who'd been sent to fetch him was watching, so instead he allowed himself to be marched down a network of corridors and some dusty stairs, to a warren of storerooms and chambers and barracks.

'Is he putting me in the cells?' he muttered.

'Cells are two more levels down.' The optio stopped, flung a rickety cedarwood door open and looked inside. 'This is it.'

Tiny. Airless. Dim. A hard bed with one blanket and a cracked wooden bowl on a table. Seth looked around. 'Right,' he said. 'I want the floor swept, two rugs, a chair, fresh cotton sheets, writing materials, as many lamps as you can find. A silver bowl, some cups, two shelves up there for storage. I want someone to clean the place every morning. Food and water. And what the hell is that smell?'

'Patchouli.'

'What?'

'It's some sort of fancy scented oil. Prince Jamil has his back rubbed with it by slave girls most days.'

Seth said quietly, 'His cell is near here then?'

'Cell!' The optio went to spit, and stopped. 'Suite, more like. The Emperor's precious nephew is the best bargaining card Argelin's got – him and the bloody elephants. Do you know those beasts are considered sacred? Without Jamil as hostage the Emperor would have reduced the Port to cinders weeks ago.'

Seth nodded. Despite himself, he sank on the bed.

'Get all my possessions sent over from my house,' he muttered. 'Right now.'

The optio went out. 'Another bloody arrogant scribe to lord it over us.' And this time he did spit.

Seth rolled over and lay still, dropping the pack on the floor in exhaustion. He closed his eyes and the darkness swam.

He was in.

He had done it.

Oblek had said it couldn't be done; the Jackal had silkily doubted he had the nerve, but here he was.

At the heart of things.

He opened his eyes, and saw a beetle crawl across the wall and into a tiny hole. He saw the gate and the way the girl in the black veil had stared at him, astonished, glad, wary.

He saw how she'd slipped through the gate and not looked back.

'Oh, Mirany,' he whispered, into the silence. '*What have I done?*'

The Second Gate
Of Ashes

There are Nine Gateways on the road to the Garden of the Rain Queen. That's what the people tell themselves. Each gate is an obstacle and a test, a danger and a delight.

Only the dead and the god can walk that road, and it trickles and runs like a stream bed.

On the Day of the Scarab every year, my statue and the Queen's are carried through the streets, through gateways the people make, and around me the crowds mass like insects, swarm like fish, hold up their hands to me.

I cannot speak to them, because my lips are marble, but I smile because they seem so small and weak, because they want me so much.

I feel something that might be fear.

If a god can be afraid.

She sees the underground sun

'How could you let him *do it?*' Mirany whirled round on the Jackal. She was torn between relief and disbelief.

'It was his own idea, Holiness.'

'He's full of stupid ideas!' She sat, stunned, on one of Kreon's spread-winged thrones.

'What did you think he was doing,' the Jackal said slyly, 'when you saw him?'

'I don't know!'

She did know. She didn't want to think about it, but the tomb thief watched her with his animal eyes and smiled.

'You thought he might be betraying us. It seems to me that that unspoken doubt lies behind all our young friend's heroics.'

His voice was mocking; she turned away from him. 'Archon! You could have stopped him!'

Alexos had piled the bricks to a wobbling height. Now, frowning with concentration, he placed another on top of the pile. 'Gods can't stop people doing what they want, Mirany. And we had to get someone on the inside.'

Helpless, feeling tears come, she looked at Oblek. The big man leaned over. To her surprise his voice was a growl of kindness. 'What they're not telling you, girl, I will. Seth took the risk because of that time with the Sphere.'

'The Sphere?' She was baffled.

'The moment you first gave it to him. On the journey back through the desert, one starry night when just he and I were awake, he told me about it. He said he wanted the Sphere, was greedy to have it, snatched it from you, and you saw that. Afterwards, he was ashamed. He wants you to think well of him, Mirany.'

She felt numb. When Kreon pushed the cup of warmed milk into her hands she drank it without tasting it. Something cold seemed to have embedded itself in her, a shard of dread. Finally she whispered, 'He'll be killed. If he believes him, Argelin will silence him.'

'Perhaps not.' The Jackal stretched his legs out lazily on the couch; the movement caused a draught that toppled the pile of bricks. Alexos gave a wail of dismay; a faint shiver rippled through the walls and roof.

Oblek looked round anxiously. 'Did you do that, old friend?'

Alexos scowled at the pile of bricks. 'I'm sorry, Oblek. I won't do it again.'

As he re-sorted the bricks, the Jackal and the big man exchanged glances. Then the Jackal brought his feet back, carefully. 'As I was saying, Argelin is cunning. He may seek to use Seth for himself. Especially if he suspects him. It's a dangerous tightrope, but the scribe can walk it. Seth is a master of self-preservation.'

He took a cautious sip of Kreon's wine and pulled a face. 'Now, what's been going on here? How long has this curfew been in force?'

'Two months.' Mirany linked her fingers together round the bent cup. 'Since Hermia's death, Argelin has ruled by terror. He's destroying every image of the god and the Rain Queen, and replacing them with his own. He crowned himself king, closed all temples and theatres, and arrested anyone who objected. Taxes are up, traders keep away. People are angry, but scared to say too much, because his mercenaries, the Northerners, are arrogant and brutal. There have been executions, public maimings, confiscation of property. All this news we've had to get through Kreon's contacts, the cleaners and scribes and slaves, because Rhetia and I only dare go up into the City after dark. The Port is just too dangerous. I've only been there twice.'

'And the war?' Oblek muttered.

She shrugged. 'It seems to be a stand-off. Rumour has it the Emperor's fleet has occupied the Callades, and Mylos, and all the islands.' Briefly she thought of her father, and put the cup down. 'The Port is blockaded; nothing gets in or out. Soon there'll be famine.'

'No trade, and a thousand mercenaries to pay!' The Jackal sipped the wine thoughtfully. 'Argelin must be nearly bankrupt.' He eyed Kreon. 'While the Shadow waits in darkness.'

'As he has always waited.' The albino crouched, his lanky knees folded up. 'Because the Shadow guards the tombs, the places of sleep. And yes, Argelin will come here next.'

Oblek scowled over the rim of his cup. He was only drinking water, Mirany noticed with a dim surprise. 'Surely he's not crazy enough to rob the dead?'

The Jackal glanced at him sourly.

Kreon smiled his crooked smile. 'Riches beyond counting lie below us. He's abandoned the gods and is hungry only for revenge. The wrath of the Archons won't deter him.' He gave a sidelong glance at Alexos. 'But now my brother has returned, Argelin will learn what the god's anger can be.'

'You have plans,' the Jackal said smoothly.

Kreon shrugged. 'Certain . . . contingencies are being put into place. Traps and pitfalls, tunnellings and constructions. Argelin's men will discover that key maps are missing or are oddly misleading. Any searchers who enter the tombs using them will find themselves lost. Already there are rumours that the god's Shadow prowls, his outline lean and deadly.'

'What about the river?' Alexos said suddenly. He sat up, his dark hair in his eyes. 'My river! I said I'd bring it back and I did!'

Kreon glanced at Mirany. She said, 'Argelin has the banks patrolled. At certain allowed places the people have to pay for water. There's some sort of irrigation scheme being built, but we don't know what.'

Alexos scowled. 'He shouldn't do that. *And all my statues, Mirany. So old and of such workmanship.*'

His voice rang in the dark corners of Kreon's chamber. Small scatters of dust drifted, something slid and fell with a clatter.

'Old friend,' Oblek said earnestly, 'we will make him pay.'

'How?' Mirany stood up and began to pace. 'None of us can do anything against his army! We're safe down here, but if he knew we were alive! And then there's Rhetia! Where *is* she?'

'Would she talk?' the Jackal said quietly.

'Of course not.'

'Might she have gone to him with some plan of her own?'

That made Mirany pause. You never knew what Rhetia was planning. Being cooped up in the tombs for two months had almost driven her mad. She had gone to the City alone twice, refusing to say where she'd been. And today she had been very anxious to make the trip to the Port.

'Maybe,' she said, her voice reluctant. 'But she wouldn't betray us.'

'In that case,' the Jackal swung round and sat up, 'I have idled in this Kingdom of Cobwebs too long. It's time the Jackal returned to his lair and Lord Osarkon to his tumbledown palace. You may all be dead and in your graves, but so far, I'm not.' He leaned forward, his fair hair hanging down, his almond eyes moving to each of them in turn. 'But first I will tell you my plan.'

'What makes you think you're running things?' Oblek growled.

'Quiet, Oblek.' Alexos crossed his legs. 'I want to hear.'

'So you shall, little god. Our aim is to restore the Oracle, the Archon and the Nine. To defeat Argelin for ever. Agreed?'

They nodded, silent.

'Then first we need the rest of the Nine. My people will find out where they are.'

'They may be dead,' Oblek muttered.

The Jackal ignored him. 'Secondly, Prince Jamil must be rescued. That's Seth's task, as he knows. But we need to be careful – Jamil has to be rescued but not set free. We, like Argelin, need him as a hostage against the Emperor. Meanwhile, all through the Port, the thieves and pickpockets, con men and forgers, will be working. Weapons will be stolen, ammunition accumulated, spears hoarded. Argelin will find himself being robbed blind.' He picked up one of the building blocks and held it out to Alexos, then made it disappear into his empty hand. 'As if by magic.'

Alexos grinned, but Mirany said, 'What then?'

He leaned forward, his sharp face close to hers. 'We re-take the Island and hold it against him. We rebel, Holiness.'

She held his gaze. 'As Speaker, I won't agree to that, unless you promise me there will be as little bloodshed as possible.'

Oblek snorted. The Jackal didn't waver. 'You ask miracles. But I'll try.'

She nodded. She knew it would be hopeless, and surely he did too, against Argelin's forces.

But all she said was 'Why?'

'*Why?*'

'Yes. Why are you doing this?' She looked at them all, suddenly puzzled. 'Why isn't Oblek drunk? Why aren't you making plans to sell Argelin arms, to profit from the food shortages, to set up some racket smuggling water? What's happened to you?'

They were silent. The Jackal shrugged, elegantly. Oblek scowled.

'They've drunk from the Well of Songs, Mirany,' Alexos said, stacking the bricks.

If it was an answer, it meant nothing to her. But Kreon smiled, and in the warm darkness she felt the god move into her mind and whisper, *I'll tell you all about it one day.*

'What's my part in this grand plan?' Oblek demanded.

'To guard the Archon and the Speaker and to remain underground until I send for you. You *don't* go up.' The Jackal stood and looked down at Mirany. Then he said, 'In fact, Holiness, I do intend to prosper. I intend to be Lord Osarkon in truth; to regain my lands and my family's honour, to remind Argelin of my brothers' blood and my mother's agony.' The darkness lay across his face; then as he moved back into the flamelight she saw his expression flicker; he turned quickly to the crowded, cluttered depths of the chamber. 'Who's there?'

'Me.' From between the heaps of fake furniture a man emerged holding a little girl by her hand. He was thin and grey, his hair and face smeared with dust, his arms filthy to the elbows. He dumped a pile of tools, and Telia ran to Mirany and wrapped her arms round her waist.

'She told me you were back.' Pa pulled himself upright with an effort. He glared at Oblek, then eyed Alexos. 'You must be the Archon.'

'That's right,' Alexos said gravely.

60

Pa snorted. He looked at the Jackal, at Kreon, then around, into the shadows. 'So where's Seth? Where's my good-for-nothing son?'

Later, lying in the bed of parchment that creaked and shifted every time she turned over, Mirany thought of the way his face had kept so rigid when Kreon had told him. Utterly still, as if a movement or a word would have broken his composure.

Telia had said crossly, 'But Seth's supposed to be bringing me a present,' and the words had cut the silence like knife slashes.

Pa had turned and walked into the clutter of dark furniture. Oblek had watched him go, then muttered, 'He will, girlie. Don't fret.'

Mirany lay wide-eyed, unsleeping. It was warm down here, the eternal never-varying temperature of the kingdom of the dead, and its silence was complete.

Rolling over, she stared at the rocky ceiling. Seth was doing this for her. That was what Oblek had said, and yes, it was true she had read his flash of avarice, and that he had known that. But to run this sort of risk! Had he succeeded? Or was he already dead? The thought was such a sliver of dread it made her sit up; she pulled the coarse linen tight in her fingers.

'Well? Is he dead?' she asked the god.

The darkness took the words, hummed and softened

them. They echoed in cracks and crevices, and Oblek's distant snores broke and resumed, as if in his sleep, he'd heard them.

'Not him.'

At first she thought it was the god who had answered, and then she saw Pa.

He was on the other side of the curtain Kreon had rigged up for her privacy; a flimsy ragged purple.

'Come through,' she breathed.

Dust swirled as he ducked under; the bed creaked as he sat on it. Mirany swung her feet out and caught hold of his hands. They were calloused and gritty with dust; he and Kreon had been working long hours on their secret contraptions. 'You shouldn't have heard that,' she breathed.

'It's only what I think myself.' His voice was sombre. 'I asked Alexos. He said Seth was where he wanted to be, *at the heart of things.*' He looked up. 'The boy is the Archon, so . . .'

'Yes.' Mirany nodded. 'He would know.'

Pa's face was pale, as if the months without sun had drained him of vigour. His grey hair was cropped, his skin leathery and dry. 'The musician said Seth does this for you, Mirany, but that's only part of it.' He shrugged. 'My son and I have never been close. After his mother died there was Telia to care for, a tiny scrap of a thing, a sick baby. Times were hard. I fell from the scaffolding and couldn't work – I was a mason, Holiness, a good one. Seth had to provide for us.' He shrugged. 'I was ambitious for him. Get a position with Argelin, I said. Go to the top. When he went to the City instead, I was scornful. Fourth assistant Archivist in a swarming anthill of scribes and scribblers. What good would that ever do him! We argued every time he came home. So he never came home.'

Mirany shredded the edge of the sheet. 'He's just like you,' she said.

Pa raised his head. 'You think so?' He sounded surprised.

'Oh yes. Stubborn. Thinking he knows better than everyone.'

She was trying to cheer him but her voice came out all wrong. She cleared her throat. 'My father is just the same, you know. He planned and bribed for years to get me on to the Island. He must be distracted with worry.' It was something she tried not to think about, the large draughty house above the harbour at Mylos, the old servants, her father in his library of scrolls. 'I wish I could get a message out to him. Just to say I'm alive.'

'No chance, with the blockade.' Pa rubbed a grimy hand over his face; the sound it made was a rasp in the darkness. 'Anyhow, that's what I came to say. Don't blame yourself. My son is arrogant and always has been.'

'But you love him,' she said quietly. It was almost a question.

Pa took a breath. 'I love him when he's away,' he muttered. 'If he was here I'd call him a bloody fool.'

It made her smile.

Pa turned suddenly, as if he'd made up his mind. 'Holiness, I want to show you something. Right now, while the others are asleep. I found it yesterday, when I was alone in the Sixth Dynasty tombs. Will you come?'

Surprised, she nodded. She couldn't sleep anyway.

He waited while she dressed and then they tiptoed out through the clutter of fake furniture and unbolted the door of Kreon's kingdom. Kreon was out somewhere on one of his food gathering expeditions; Oblek slept noisily near the fire, Alexos a small heap in the bed. Telia must be in the separate room Pa had made for her out of heaped coffin-cases.

Pa trimmed the lamp and led the way into the labyrinth of passageways and stairs.

Mirany followed, one hand on the wall.

He went down several sets of stairs into the levels below, then turned along a corridor that immediately divided into seven. He chose an entrance she had never explored. In the lamplight she could see that this corridor had once been painted white, and that along its length gateways had been constructed at intervals, vast edifices of marble and stone, rising into the hollowed darkness of the roof. As she walked under them she felt their weight, saw glimpses of statues; the eyes of cats that might have been crystal or alive; a myriad cut hieroglyphs of lost histories. The corridor led downwards at a steep angle; in places fragments of a handrail were left in the wall, and great slabs of stone blocked the way more than once, as if they had crashed down centuries before.

Between the third and fourth gateway Mirany paused, looking back. Utter darkness closed behind her, as if it was solid. A hollow whisper of sound came out of it.

'What was that?'

Pa looked back. 'Who knows? The workers above call it the Shadow. Kreon says it's the breathing of the dead, but when I asked him how the dead can breathe he gave me that lanky shrug. It comes often, that sound. When we first came down here, it terrified me; I used to wait and listen for it, but you get used to everything, I suppose. Now I don't even hear it.'

There were nine gateways, each different; each more imposing. Marble and gilt trees had been carved in them, baboons in their branches. Mirany and Pa were dwarfed by the arches; then Pa helped her scramble over a crack in the floor and she felt under her feet the crisp dryness of petals, desiccated millennia ago, still lying here undisturbed.

Pa ducked. 'The entrance is low. Watch your head.'

At first she thought the corridor was a dead end. Then she saw a tiny opening, no higher than her waist. He got down on hands and knees and crawled into it, and the light went with him, so that for a moment she was completely alone in blackness. She felt that it would smother her, catch in her throat, and the terror she had known when she was shut in the sealed tomb came back like a shudder of sweat.

She knelt quickly, and crawled after him.

The tunnel was longer than she'd expected. It seemed bizarre that the vast corridor should lead only to this, she thought, feeling lumps of grit embed themselves in the palms of her hands and bruise her knees. Until Pa turned his head with difficulty and murmured, 'All right?'

'Is it far?'

'Just up here.' He wriggled the lamp back. 'Do you see what you're crawling in?'

It wasn't grit. It was gems.

The tunnel was littered with them; onyx and opal and jasper, fragments of turquoise, shards of chalcedony. She gasped, seeing how the walls were studded, not an inch of rock bare, how the facets of a billion diamonds turned the weak light into rainbow brilliance.

She was inside a fortune; it scraped her back; as she lifted her head, her hair snagged on encrusted amethysts, and under her fingernails the dust of rubies cut like glass.

'It's incredible!'

'Wait till you see what's at the end.' He turned and laboured on, his voice coming back distorted and breathless, the lamplight sparkling and jagged. 'How they got it in here is beyond me . . . well, they couldn't have. The whole tomb must have been built around it.'

Suddenly, he was gone.

Ahead of her the tunnel burst into a golden glow. She

saw a square entrance, and beyond it a brilliance that made her close her eyes instantly, as if the sun had risen there, in that underground chamber. Golden radiance lit her hands and face, made the tunnel of gems a crystal river, running and moving.

Mirany hauled herself out into the chamber.

She stood on the petal-littered floor and stared up.

It was enormous. A vast disc of beaten gold, perfect, untouched, an underground sun. It hung from the ceiling, took the frail light from Pa's lamp and shimmered it to a soft warmth that was breathtaking, that filled the air like sound or the note of a gong.

And when Pa whispered, 'See how delicate it is, Mirany,' the words immediately hummed and chimed around the disc and along its concave surface, dissolving into syllables and esses.

Amazed, she walked round it. Fine as eggshell, the metal had been beaten thin. Somehow its makers had then smoothed it; it had no marks, no dents. It was perfection. And Pa was right; this could never have been brought down the corridor, let alone the tiny tunnel. How on earth had it got here?

It rose here, Mirany. Like the sun rises.

The god's voice was close and so clear she glanced instinctively at Pa, but he was staring up at the disc, his whole face golden.

'That doesn't explain . . .'

67

The real sun is much bigger. Bigger than the desert, wider than the sea. All the world could fit into the sun, Mirany, and yet I roll it across the sky with a finger. And in people too there is a sun. Deep in the darkness, like this one. Fiery and golden.

She wanted to ask him about Seth, but Pa was saying, 'If Argelin knew about this! There are wonders down here undreamed of, Mirany, and he must never get his hands on them. Kreon tells me there are endless labyrinths of tombs, that it would take lifetimes to explore them all. It makes you wonder how old the albino is. How long he's lived down here.'

He held up the lamp. 'I wanted you to see it, because Seth says you can hear the god. And I want you to tell him, Mirany, that my son is working in his service now, and that he must look after him for me. Will you ask him, Mirany?'

'He hears you,' she said quietly.

'Yes, but what does he say?' He turned to her, and she saw then, in the golden light, his terror, the fear that the disc's radiance revealed. 'You're the Speaker now. You have to tell me what he says.'

Gods make no promises. The voice sounded uneasy. *Does he think the events of the world revolve around his concerns? You people are so self-centred, Mirany.*

She chewed her lip. Then she said, 'The god has heard your request.'

'And?'

'He says he'll watch over Seth.'

Pa nodded, gratefully.

In her ear, the god laughed. *You are beginning to see how it was for Hermia. Tell me, is there a difference, Mirany, between lies and tact?*

Annoyed, she turned. Then she screamed and jumped back.

The walls of the chamber were an iridescence of beetles. Millions and millions of them, scarabs and earwigs and hornbugs and armoured woodborers. They crawled and shimmered, massed and clung in swarming clots on the ceiling, dropping and flying back up, their emerald and black carapaces glinting in the disc's golden light.

Mirany put both hands over her mouth and shuddered.

'The light must attract them,' Pa remarked.

She didn't answer. Because like a stab of remorse, the memory of Manto's brooch had swooped into her mind.

She had forgotten all about it!

She had forgotten to tell the Jackal.

He asks the way of a painted prince

The sun blazed in the blue morning sky.

Walking in from the street, Seth paused gratefully in the shade of the loggia and wiped sweat from his face with the back of his hand. It was cooler in here, and though his expensive new tunic stuck to his back there was a sort of breeze from the sea. Shifting the scroll under his arm he gazed out over the rooftops to the blue horizon.

Nothing. Today the blockading ships were too far out to see.

That was good, and bad. Lack of trade was starving the Port, but the Emperor hadn't attacked, and probably wouldn't while Argelin held his beloved nephew prisoner. Rumour had it that an emissary disguised as a camel trader had come alone to negotiate for Prince Jamil's release, but if that was true, Seth hadn't seen any sign of him.

There was a climbing shrub with pink flowers growing over the arches of the arcade; bees swarmed from its scented blossoms. He had no idea what it was called. Mirany might know. He reached out and touched one of the flowers. Too many hours with books and scrolls. Too many years buried in the tombs.

Beyond, on the open spaces of the palaestra, men and boys and a few girls were exercising. As he walked the cool arcade he watched them wrestle, their oiled bodies gleaming, their muscles firm. Shouts and swearing rang in the hot air, gasps and giggles echoed. Near the bathing rooms taller men were practising combat, and he saw the glitter of bronze swords, recognized the guttural language of the Northerners.

Seth strode out into the heat and crossed the training yard, the sun burning his bare arms.

'Hey,' he said.

The mercenary sitting on the stone bench looked up into the glare. He was drinking water from an earthenware jar; as he put it down tiny drops splashed in the dust.

'You speak our language?' Seth snapped.

The man shrugged. Then he stood up, and Seth took a step back. The Northerner was muscular. And extremely tall.

Seth licked dry lips and kept his voice steady. 'I have

orders here from the Gen—, from His Holiness the King, to your leader . . .' he consulted the scroll, 'Ingeld. Do you know where he is?'

The blond man folded his arms. When he spoke, his accent was so strange Seth barely understood it. 'I am Ingeld.'

For a moment Seth didn't know whether to believe him. But the man's stare was blue and clear.

'Right. Well . . . that saves time I suppose.' Seth fished among the heap of scrolls. 'The Lord Argelin sends this. Details of his scheme of irrigation of water from the Draxis to the fields on the south bank. Work is already underway, but . . .'

The mercenary took the scroll. Then he threw it on the ground. 'I did not lead my warriors here to dig in the mud,' he said calmly. He looked at Seth appraisingly. 'I've heard of you. People speak of you. They say you are a man who would do anything for power.'

Seth took a breath. 'Do they, now.' He glanced down at the scroll, then picked it off the hot stones. 'You are not being ordered to dig. There are slaves to dig. Your orders are to guard the work. There are dissident elements in the Port who will try to steal water.'

The Northerner gave a gruff laugh and sat. 'Old women. Children with buckets.' He gestured at the fighters, grunting and slashing in the sun. 'These are men with honour. Argelin promised us gold, and warfare. But we see very little of either. Instead we grow fat in the luxury of olives and figs, of sherbert and cinnamon. We break statues. We stand on the walls and look out and see only desert, and sea. On the sea, no ships. In the desert, no armies.'

'The armies will come soon enough,' Seth said sourly.

'Will they?' Ingeld turned his blue gaze on him. 'While Argelin holds the foreign prince? And meanwhile your General makes war on his own gods. That is not something we like.' He reached out and plucked the scroll from Seth's grip, holding it upside down. 'More pretty marks on parchment. You people are good at those.' He touched a blue cartouche with his thick finger. 'This one. What does this one say?'

'Son of the Scorpion.'

Ingeld nodded. 'Ah, yes.' He seemed to consider it for a moment; then he studied Seth. Seth looked away and snapped, 'Where is Jamil?'

'In the bathing halls. His Excellency is not a wrestler.'

'You should be guarding him.'

'We are.' His eyes narrowed. 'They say you are the one who killed the god on earth. The Archon.'

Seth was silent.

'A ten-year-old boy. It is spoken of with awe, but it seems to me a coward's act.'

It was a challenge, pleasant and deadly. Seth didn't move. The man was twice his weight and superbly fit. He wouldn't last half a minute. Instead he said calmly, 'We all do what the Lord King orders. We are all in his pay. And the boy was the god.'

Ingeld's shadow stretched over the parched ground. Contempt was clear on his face.

'Then it was also the act of a fool,' he said. He spat at Seth's feet, turned, barked a word at his men and stalked under the colonnade.

Seth breathed out. Sweat was chilling his face and neck; he wiped it away. Then he turned quickly into the bathing halls. The more people that despised him the better, of course. As Argelin's Secretary, it came with the job. And what a job it was.

As he walked through the marble doorway he reviewed his first week. It had taken two days of solid work to get to grips with the mountains of scrolls and stele. Orders, invoices, lists. Warrants for arrest and execution. Spies' reports – he wasn't supposed to see those, but the chaos was such that baskets of them had come into his office. Wage payments. Argelin had promised a fortune in gold to the Northerners and didn't have it. A hurried search late one night in the private letters made it clear that the General had sent an expedition to the Mountains of the Moon to mine gold. Nothing had been heard of it. Under the flickering lamp, Seth had shaken his head. He knew enough of that road not to be surprised. Had the Animals devoured them, or the bird-people's god? Or had the desert taken its due?

Then the Nine. Or rather, the remaining Seven. Two of them, the girls called Tethys and Persis, had been arrested two weeks ago trying to buy passage in a salt caravan. Now they were being held somewhere in the headquarters building. Seth allowed himself a tight smile. Maybe the others – Chryse, Ixaca, Callia, Gaia, the new one – were there too.

Ignoring the slave at the door he strode through the warren of hot rooms and massage chambers, glancing in at the groups of men gambling, being scraped down, sweating. When he came to the main bath hall he stopped, looking round cautiously.

This was the first time he'd managed to get out alone. Argelin had told him to take guards, but once in the streets he'd dismissed them. It was a risk. Now it was known he was the Archon's assassin, he'd be a target for any discontent.

The hall was vast and echoing. On the far wall the faded image of the Rain Queen held her arms out over the swimmers, moist algae smothering her, lichen growing over her robe. Her face had been freshly hacked away. From her fingernails condensation ran, and the small green lizards that inhabited the wall flashed through holes into the heat outside.

The pool was marble, its water warm and clear. As soon as the river had begun to flow Argelin had had it piped here, though he never came himself. Seth had been sure of that, after only a few days of watching the General, and that was why this had to be the place to make contact.

Argelin would not touch water.

It was insane, but true. Discreet enquiries among the slaves and officers confirmed it. Since Hermia's death Argelin had not washed with water, nor drunk it. He drank only wine and milk, washed with the squeezed juice of limes and lemons. Not one drop of water was allowed in his rooms. He had declared war on the Rain Queen, and it was total.

Seth crossed the wet pavement. Swimmers splashed and called, and from the adjoining halls the giggles and high shrieks of women echoed. Under the white colonnade that ran the length of the building a group of men was seated at a table gaming with coins and cards, servants at their backs. Behind them two hetaira in white dresses watched the swimmers.

Seth frowned. Where was Jamil?

A great wave of water splatted on the stones, soaking his feet. He stepped away, scowling, and walked down the colonnade past a row of sphinxes. How long before they all had Argelin's features? Under his feet in intricate mosaic the great Animals of the desert were formed in tiny tesserae; the Lion, the Beetle, the Monkey. Seth glanced at them, and a secret pride grew in him. He had seen them, the real beasts. They had allowed him to pass. He had drunk from the Well of Songs. He was Seth. He must hold on to that.

The men at the gaming table turned and he eyed them. Then he stopped.

There were six of them, well-fed, gleaming with oil, dressed in expensive robes. The one at the back had long fair hair.

These were the rich, pampered people. Once they had ruled. Now they turned up at Argelin's parties, applauded his processions. Seth envied and despised them. So he folded his arms.

'I'm looking for the Prince Jamil, my lords. Is he still here?'

The nearest, rolls of fat stomach oozing from his bathing robe, studied his cards and waved a jewelled hand. 'Try the Room of Roses, scribe.'

Seth kept very still. Then he said, 'My title is Personal Secretary to the King-Archon.'

It shook them. One even staggered to his feet, clutching his towel. The prettiest girl pulled a flimsy veil up over her face and stared at Seth through it.

The fat man had paled. 'I beg to apologize. I had no idea . . .'

'You will next time we meet, Lord . . . ?'

'Malchus.' The word dropped like a reluctant plop of moisture in the echoing hall.

'Where is this Room of Roses?' He was demanding it of the tall fair-haired man in the green robe. Elegant outlines of kohl edged the man's eyes; the strange unreadable eyes

Seth had come to know so well.

'I believe,' Lord Osarkon said languidly, 'that it lies in that direction.'

'Show me.'

After the barest hesitation, the tall man stood. He moved out and spread a courteous hand; Seth walked beside him.

'I congratulate you on your promotion, Secretary. I hope you find the work interesting?'

'Very.'

No one was near. Under the splash of a diver, the Jackal said sharply, 'You shouldn't have spoken to me.'

'I've spent a week living in fear. It's a relief to speak to anyone. Is he guarded?'

'Always. But only two men.'

'Mirany?'

'Is well. Worried for you.' The Jackal turned smoothly into a corridor. 'Argelin may have you watched. Don't take any more risks. Make contact with Jamil. Then wait for a man with red hair who sells wine; he will bring and take messages. Don't speak to me again and don't go out into the Port without guards.'

Seth said, 'He's got two of the Nine. Tethys and Persis. The others too, maybe.'

'Where?'

'I haven't found out yet.'

'Then get on to it.'

'He goes nowhere without his bodyguards. Except

twice he's been out at night. Alone. I don't know where.'

The Jackal said, 'We must find out.'

'One more thing.' He bit his lip. 'He's going to destroy the statue of the god. The one in the Temple. Warn Mirany.'

The Jackal flashed him a glance. But all he said was, 'Thank you, Secretary. And here is the Room of Roses.' He swung the door open and bowed out, elegantly. Before Seth had a chance to mutter another word, he was gone.

Spears clashed across the door.

Patiently, Seth took out his new identity papers and held them up. The blue cartouche of Argelin's name was clear. One of the guards said something in the guttural language. He was searched for weapons, then the spears opened.

Before him Seth saw a room of wonder. It was trellised with honeysuckle, sweet with climbing roses. They clambered on all three walls, smothered the ceiling, their flowers scarlet, their scent so rich he felt it lay heavily on the air, a velvety taste. The fourth side of the room was open on to a small garden; sunlight slanted across the shallow pool clotted with petals, across the ungainly man lying face down on the wooden table, being pummelled by a small, determined masseur.

Seth walked over. 'Lord Jamil?'

Awkward, Jamil turned his head. 'Yes?'

He looked wary, glanced behind Seth at the Northern

guards. Seth kept his voice level. 'I've been sent by His Holiness the King-Archon. Perhaps we could speak alone?'

The Pearl Prince looked him over. Then he said to the small man, 'Thank you, Malek. That will be all.'

As he sat up, Seth saw that he was overweight and heavy, but well-muscled. Not a man to move quickly, though. After the masseur had wrapped a robe of gold thread around him and bowed out, Jamil crossed to a table and poured orange juice from a jug into two glasses. He added cinnamon and sherbert, then waved Seth over.

A bench surrounded the pool. It was tiled with tiny blue squares, edged with a key pattern. Seth sat and took the drink gratefully. It was sweet, almost sickly, but he was very thirsty.

'Thank you.'

'You're the Secretary.' Jamil leaned back, his elbows on the marble. 'I remember you.'

Seth nursed the cup between his fingers. 'Listen to me, Prince Jamil, please. You wish to be free?'

The Pearl Prince was very still. 'That's a question that needs no answer.'

'Indeed.' Seth glanced around, nervously. The room was empty, the garden peaceful. The guards didn't understand the language. He lowered his voice. 'It may be that a way can be found.'

Jamil said nothing.

'We need you with us.'

'Us?'

'The opponents of Argelin.'

'You work for Argelin.'

'I've infiltrated his headquarters.' Suddenly he was unsure this was wise. Would Jamil betray him? Certainly the foreign prince seemed unmoved, tipping the last trickle out of the jug, then yelling for more. As if she had been waiting, a tall servant girl strode in with another, exchanged it swiftly, and went out into the garden.

Jamil poured. Finally he said, 'To exchange one prison for another is not freedom.'

'Once Argelin is overthrown you'll be free to go.'

'You seem very sure he will be.'

'We are sure.'

'How? He holds power. The Oracle is destroyed. The Archon is dead.'

Seth bit his lip. Then he said quietly, '*The Archon is not dead.*'

The door behind him crashed open.

Instantly he jumped up. Jamil rose ponderously but Ingeld filled the doorway, his men behind him. They wore their bronze helmets with the strange cheekpieces, and Ingeld's eyes were icy blue behind the eyeholes.

'Time to go, Prince.'

Jamil gathered his robe about him with dignity. He turned to Seth. 'I will consider this. We will speak again.'

As the soldiers escorted him out he didn't look back, but Ingeld did, one swift hard stare.

In the empty room, Seth sank on the bench and breathed out. Had the Northerner heard? His hand shaking, he picked up his cup and drank the rest of the sweet liquid. It was as he was pouring out more that he saw the note.

It must have been meant for Jamil, a grimy scrap of parchment, hastily stuck to the jug with what looked like honey. He tugged it off and opened it, glancing out into the empty garden. From the bathing halls the noise of splashing swimmers covered his indrawn breath. The note said, BEWARE THE SCRIBE. HE HAS BETRAYED US. TELL HIM NOTHING.

It was signed. RHETIA.

His mouth is stopped

'I don't give a dog's fart how dangerous it is!' Oblek raged. 'I don't care if ten thousand mercenaries are lined up outside the door with axes and scimitars. I am *not* staying cooped up in this bloody black pit of hell for another day!'

Arms folded, Kreon glared at him. 'You were grateful for it once, fat man.'

'I still am. But I need to *do* something! Anything!'

Mirany had seen this coming. Oblek had been pacing the tunnels for a week, getting more and more frustrated and reckless, creeping up into the City more often. Seth's note had brought things to a head.

Sitting cross-legged among an ornate heap of wooden slave models she read it again.

HE WILL DESTROY THE STATUE
TOMORROW. SIX OF THE NINE ARE HERE.
RHETIA IN CONTACT WITH JAMIL. PA AND
TELIA MUST COME. HE'S ASKING FOR THEM.

It was so very short. What did he mean about Rhetia?
Had he seen her? Mirany wanted more, a word about
how he felt, but that was stupid. Underneath the
Jackal had scrawled: *We're not ready to act. I'm afraid
the statue will have to be sacrificed. Send his father up and
stay below.*

'How did you get this?' she muttered.

'Someone shoved it into my hand.' Kreon shrugged. 'I
was sweeping in the Arches of the Shabti-painters and a
crowd of slaves went past. It could have been any one of
them.' He smiled his lopsided smile. 'The tomb thief is
indeed a Lord of the Underworld. You're sure it's Seth's
writing?'

'Certain.' Mirany folded it absently. The news that
Persis and Tethys and the others were in captivity was
bad; that Argelin was going to desecrate the Temple even
worse.

'It seems there's nothing we can do.'

'Rubbish.'

'He says . . .'

'Forget what he says!' Oblek heaved a pile of Telia's toys
off the table and sat on it. It creaked alarmingly, and he got
up again fast. 'Tonight, we go. Me and you, Shadow man,

and you, Mirany. Out through one of the secret doors and across the Bridge . . .'

'The Bridge is guarded,' Kreon said.

'Then we'll swim then. On to the Island. We remove the statue and get it to a place of safety.'

Kreon paced lankily. Finally he said, 'The Jackal is right. And yet I agree we must take the risk. You go, both of you. I will not leave the tombs. This is my realm and I must guard it. And there's my brother to think of.'

'Oh no there isn't.'

Alexos' voice came muffled from behind an elaborate screen decorated with waterlilies.

Oblek swore.

'Yes, Oblek, I'm here. I've been here all the time. I don't know how you think you can do these things without me, my son.'

He wriggled under it and came and sat on the table, legs dangling, looking at the big man ruefully. 'I'm coming too.'

'Absolutely, totally and utterly NO!' Oblek roared.

Alexos sighed. His beautiful face looked over at Mirany. 'People don't think, do they? They just don't. You're the Speaker. Explain to him, Mirany.'

The Speaker.

She remembered Hermia's cold fingers fitting the mask on her face, that hard, vengeful look. Hermia had hated her. And now Hermia was among the dead, and powerful. It chilled her. She came and sat by Alexos. 'Sit down, Oblek.'

He wouldn't. He just glared at her. So she said, 'It's true. The Archon has to come. First you say, get the the statue to a place of safety, but you're one of the few who've seen the statue, so you ought to know how difficult that will be. It's marble, and life size. Any ideas how we move it?'

That took the bluster out of him. He muttered, and Kreon grinned. The albino pushed a chair closer with his foot; Oblek sank into it. 'Go on.'

'A place of safety, you say. Well, nowhere is safe. We can't get the statue off the Island and anyhow, I have no idea how things are there. There are possible places in the Upper House or on the cliffs, but it will take the god's power to help us.'

'Alexos is supposed to be dead,' Oblek said stubbornly. 'If he's seen and it's reported to Argelin, the General will realize that Seth has lied. Seth will be tortured for what he knows and then killed. You know that, Mirany.'

She did know it. It was a scorched place in her mind; if she touched it, it burned her. She circled round it, warily.

'But I won't be seen!' Alexos said impatiently. He drew his knees up and hugged them. 'I have to go up, Oblek. I have to. It isn't right that the god should be under the ground. My place is in the air, in the blue sky, like the sun. Already things are going wrong in the world. Insects are gathering, out in the desert. The Animals are anxious, the birds wheeling and crying. Deep in the oceans, the fish and the whales and the mermen sense the disturbed currents. *The sun cannot be buried underground, Oblek. It must rise, and burst through the darkness.*'

There was a light from somewhere.

A faint golden glow. It was in the darkness, all around him.

Mirany thought of the vast sun disc down in the tomb, of how it would be shining now, even in the dark. Then Oblek scratched and scowled. 'All right. All right! You're the god, old friend, you should know. When do we leave?'

'Tonight.' Mirany scrambled up and the slave images tumbled and slid. She held the note tight in her fingers. Reluctant, she said, 'After I've told Pa.'

Alexos looked unhappy, and Oblek dragged the water flask over and poured from it, down to the last precious drops. Kreon said quietly, 'I could tell him, if . . .'

'No.' She brushed dust and cobwebs from her dress. 'No, I will.'

Pa was eating with Telia in their screened-off room.

Mirany ducked her head under the hangings. 'Can I come in?'

'Oh yes! Sit by me, Mirany.' Telia's hair had grown while she'd been underground. It was long now, the straight dark fringe almost in her eyes. It was much darker than Seth's.

There was a chest, one of Kreon's parchment creations, painted with peacock feathers, green and blue, iridescent in the faint lamplight. Mirany sat on it, hands between her knees. She said quietly, 'We've heard from Seth.'

Pa put down his knife.

His silence made her nervous. 'Through the Jackal. A message that the Nine are found. And . . .' She was clutching the thin linen over her knees, so she smoothed the creases out and looked up. 'He says you have to go to him. You and Telia. Argelin wants to know where you are.'

Pa's grey eyes did not flicker.

'Oh good,' Telia said happily. 'I like Kreon but I'm sick of the dark.'

Mirany looked at Pa and Pa looked at Mirany.

'Will there be other children?' Telia swallowed a mouthful of rice. 'And a big house with lots of windows?'

'I'm sure you'll be very comfortable,' Mirany said. 'Seth is probably earning a lot of money.' She wished Pa would say something. Anything. Swear, get up, stamp about. But he didn't. He gave one small, noiseless sigh and then laughed.

A dry, sour laugh.

'So that's how it is,' he murmured.

The red-haired man said, 'Are these all, master?'

Stepping aside to avoid the mercenaries tramping up the

corridor, Seth glanced at the tally. 'All. Next time don't send that disgusting Chian. More of the red.'

The wine seller nodded, heaved the two empty amphorae on his broad shoulders and struggled out, sideways. At the door he was stopped and searched; Seth watched as the man put the huge pots down and raised his arms, was turned round, impatiently waved through. Then he walked back to his room and sat on the bed.

The notes were being carried inside the smaller amphora, stuck with wax under the dregs. He had started to write them in code; it was safer, and the Jackal would work it out. Now he lay back and thought wearily about the message he had dug half-burned out of Argelin's room; the one a huge slave had brought and that had sent the General prowling so impatiently.

Do not forget what I have promised you. The Nine Gateways through which the beetle rolls the sun.

He had passed it on. But he had no idea what it meant. Or who it was from.

The three of them left when Kreon told them night had fallen.

This time they took the way up through the trapdoor that opened under the Thumb of Assekar, an Archon who lived so long ago he was all but forgotten. The Thumb was the only remaining part of a colossus that might once have stood above the City gates. Now it lay unnoticed behind the Western Pylon, a dusty digit bigger than a palace.

Oblek leaned down and pulled Alexos out, then grasped Mirany's hand. Pa handed up a bag of tools which was so light that Oblek scowled. Then the big man said, 'Good luck.'

Pa shrugged. 'I'll survive.'

'If anything goes wrong,' Mirany said hastily, 'find the Jackal.'

Pa smiled grimly. 'If anything goes wrong I doubt I'll have the time.'

Below, in the darkness, Kreon was a shadow, a glimmer of pale hair. He said something in the strange syllables of the gods, and Alexos answered, a whisper of sound that moved out into the vast windy spaces of the desert.

Then the trapdooor slammed shut.

Oblek pulled Alexos close against the brickwork of the Wall. High above, among the seated Archons, sentries paced.

'Careful. Keep in the shadow.'

They wore the black robes that Kreon and Pa had made, dyed with ink stolen from the Hall of Records. Mirany felt as if she had brought the darkness up with her, but the breeze was warm and scented with the pungent herbs of the desert, and she breathed it in delight. Far to the west, over the cleft summit of the Mountains of the Moon, the vanished sun had left a blush of redness, fading into twilight.

The stars glittered and shone, the wide constellations that bestrode the Two Lands; the Hunter and the Scorpion, the Running Girl, the Lyre and the Curled Cat. They sparkled over the grey desert, on the white mass of the Archon's palace, the gates and wall of the Port. Their light made the road a path of light, a million tiny chips of quartz reflecting in dazzling pinpoints.

Looking up, Mirany breathed, 'What's that sound?'

Oblek said, 'The desert.'

Barely a murmur at first. Then, as they listened, a gathering of whispers, of faint creaks. As if all around them the earth relaxed from the scorching heat of the day; as if tiny creatures emerged, their minute limbs dislodging crumbs of soil. As if insects slid and slithered and zigzagged, seedpods cracked, carapaces creaked, flowers unfolded. As if the land breathed and woke.

Alexos raised his head.

Dark things in the darkness, he whispered.

A slave shook Seth awake. Bleary, he mumbled, 'What? What?'

'It's sunset, Secretary. The King's asking for you.'

Seth rubbed his rough face. He had to snatch sleep when he could and the lack of it was wearing him out. Argelin never seemed to rest, as if his thirst for revenge consumed him. Seth slid feet into sandals, splashed his face with water, and hastened up through the corridors.

Prisoners were led past him, slaves and scribes hurried by, an ephebe, running.

Something was happening.

He opened the door into Argelin's chambers and stopped dead.

Ingeld stood with the General. He was fully armed and wearing a breastplate with some ferocious dragonish creature emblazoned on it in enamels. A sword glinted on his thigh, a great oval shield leaned by the door.

Seth took one breath of terror. Then Argelin turned.

'About time! We're not waiting. We act now.'

'Act?' He felt stupid with anxiety and lack of sleep.

Argelin smiled, steely. 'Rumours seem to have got out about my plans to destroy the statue. If we wait for morning there may be some foolish attempt at a riot.' He took a step closer. 'Any idea how that could have happened, scribe?'

Shocked awake, Seth managed to shrug. 'People talk. Why should it bother you, Lord King?'

Argelin's eyes scrutinized him. They were red-rimmed, and his normally smooth olive skin was rough, his beard very slightly ragged. 'It doesn't. Come on.'

He pushed past Seth; Seth turned. 'You want me . . . ?'

'My Secretary accompanies me.' He paused in the doorway. 'I've cleansed the Port of the Rain Woman, and now the boy-god will be smashed to atoms in his own sanctuary. I will have no other god here but me. And when that's done, my assault on the Shadow will begin.' He wrapped the dark red cloak around his shoulders and stalked out.

Seth shot a sidelong look at Ingeld.

The Northerner scowled. 'You heard him,' he said.

The Bridge was guarded, but they'd expected that.

Two of Argelin's men sprawled by a makeshift shelter in the desert, one asleep and the other shuffling his feet to keep awake.

'Leave him to me,' Oblek said with a certain relish.

'No, Oblek.' Alexos frowned. 'We don't want them to know we've been here. Have patience. He'll fall asleep soon.'

They waited.

The guard sat, drank, cleaned his fingernails, nodded, jerked upright, drank again. Crouched in scowling temper, Oblek muttered, 'Can't you do some magic on him, old friend?'

Alexos scratched sand from his hair. 'It's not fair, Oblek. A god has to be fair. And there's only so much sleep in the world. If I give some to him I have to take it from someone else.'

While Oblek was puzzling over this Mirany said, 'I think we can go now.'

The guard was a snoozing huddle by the sinking fire. They crept past him noiselessly, through midges and night mosquitos, Mirany's sandals sending sand slithering. Once on the Bridge they were in the open, and flitted across it like shadows, the faint thud of the woodwork under Oblek's weight terrifying.

'This way.' Mirany ran up the road. The processional way seemed narrower, until she saw in the starlight that the bushes had encroached on it. Sandalwood and spiny myrtle had tangled across; she was amazed at how weeds had sprouted in a few months. Lizards ran from under her feet; a scorpion skirted Alexos' bare toes and rattled into a hole.

At the doorway to the Oracle she paused.

'I'll wait here,' Oblek said gruffly.

'I want you to come with us, Oblek.' But she didn't move. Under the great stone lintel moths gathered; there was a taint in the air of burned wood, which she surely must be imagining. She didn't want to move. She was afraid to see the destruction.

A small hand slid into hers.

'Come on, Mirany,' Alexos said kindly. 'It will be better after we know.'

He led her up the curved path. The smooth stones were the same, and for a moment she thought her fear was foolish, but as they emerged on to the stone platform she gave a cry, and stopped, one hand to her mouth.

It was worse than she had dreamed.

A great heap of ashes and burned wood had been

dragged wide by jackals and night-beasts. Under its intense heat the stones had cracked and splintered; the leaning monolith that had stood here for centuries lay smashed in three pieces, the biggest toppled down the cliff. Black charred boughs had been thrust into the pit that had once been the Oracle; as Mirany stepped carefully over the mess, grit crackling under her feet, her shadow fell over the opening, and she saw the cracked edges, the rammed stones that filled it, the furiously piled soil that stifled it. The god would speak no words here. His mouth was stopped.

So how was it that he whispered to her over the sea?

Mirany. The desert has eyes and they look towards us!

Oblek swore; Mirany turned quickly.

All along the road from the Port, men were marching. Torches glinted in their hands.

Seth thought fast. There was no way he could save the statue. Already they were nearly at the Bridge. On the opposite seat of the litter Argelin sat with his eyes closed as if he slept, but every muscle in his face betrayed tension, and at each jolt in the road he shot a glance through the slatted blinds.

Seth whittled the tip of the stylus sharp. It gave his hands something to do.

'I want an inventory,' Argelin said suddenly 'of everything left in the Temple coffers. The gold and grain are gone but there will be papers, scrolls. I want anything and everything that refers to the Rain Queen, her garden, the Nine Gateways, all copies of the Way of Guidance. You will be personally responsible for that. I want it all out, boxed up and carried to the Port. Got that?'

Seth nodded, puzzled. Then he said, 'The statue could be sold.'

'No.' The General drew on his black gloves; as Seth looked up he fixed him with a hard stare. 'Don't speak of it again.'

The Temple doors were open; as Mirany raced in she smelt the familiar tang of incense, and that wasn't imagination. Someone had been here. As Oblek brushed past her she saw with surprise the remains of dried flowers, a scatter of rose petals, sweet iris, honeysuckle, round the base of the statue.

She looked up.

The white marble face of the god smiled his sad smile at her. The garland on his hair was withered, but his smooth limbs and hands were clean and cared-for. He wore a tunic of white linen and that was clean too, and a bowl of wine and offerings of food were laid at his feet. Puzzled, Mirany crossed to them. Not soft bread, but a few dried figs.

'Who left these?' she whispered.

'We'll never do it.' Oblek stared up hopelessly. 'It

would need tackle and a hoist, at least six men. It's not big, but it's heavy.' He turned. 'I'm sorry, Mirany, he's been too sudden for us. The statue is lost.' Already the trudge and clank of armed men was clear and ominous up the processional way. He grabbed her arm. 'We've got to get out before they find us here. Alexos!' Around them the temple was dark and empty. Tall pillars rose into its roof, and in the breeze from the open door dust drifted in ripples like the sand in the desert.

'Archon?'

Nothing moved in the scented spaces.

'Where the hell is he!' Oblek hissed.

Alexos' voice came close and clear. 'I'm up here, Oblek.'

He was on the pedestal. He had one arm round the statue's knees and was straightening. The marble seemed to shift.

'Alexos!' Oblek hovered in agony. 'Get down!'

Concentrating, wobbling, the Archon stood upright. He held his own hands. He looked into his own face.

'How beautiful I am,' he said.

Seth had never been on the Island.

It was forbidden, and as the litter was hauled up the sacred road he felt some mysterious anger close round them; a warm gathering of scents and dreams, omens and secrets. This was the god's place, the Precinct of the Nine, a place of holy words and ancient ritual, and they profaned it by even being here.

If Argelin noticed, he didn't show it. As soon as the litter stopped he jumped out, and beyond him Seth saw the facade of the Temple, a vast white glimmer in the starlight. The great bronze doors were forced wide, one almost twisted off its hinges. Before them a row of fluted columns rose, and a flight of weed-strewn steps led up.

The night was silent.

Even the sea hardly breathed. Then, from their enclosure nearby, one of the elephants trumpeted, a bizarre blare of sound. Ingeld's men halted, their eyes in the helmet slits uneasy.

They fingered strange amulets, muttered words to foreign gods.

Argelin turned. 'I want the statue toppled before dawn.'

Ingeld said, 'This god. His power is broken?'

'I have taken his power.' Argelin snapped at Seth, 'Follow me,' and climbed the steps. Seth thrust the stylus into the basket of scrolls, shouldered it. The smell of artemisia was heavy, almost cloying. He felt sick. 'Do something,' he pleaded, silently. 'Do something!'

For a moment as they walked into the dark interior he thought he saw the god in its depths looking at him, a hurt smile. He stopped.

Ingeld's voice, like a guttural echo, rang in the blackness. 'Something is wrong.'

Argelin turned. 'Afraid, Northerner?'

Instantly the building rippled. Movement passed through it, a deep sound rising from stones and slabs. It grated, and Seth felt the ground shift under his feet, a trembling vibration. He flung his arms out to keep balance. Somewhere in the dark a slab fell, with an enormous crash.

Slowly, the echoes died. The world seemed tilted, the air thick with dust. Then Ingeld steadied himself and spoke, and his voice had an odd flatness, as if the building's acoustics had cracked.

'When the earth shakes, it is a message from immortals. We will leave this place, Lord King.'

Argelin was white with rage. 'There are often earth tremors here, and they mean nothing! You will do as I say. You will break the boy's stupid grinning face!'

He turned, and stared up, and behind his sudden stillness, Seth gasped.

Because the pedestal was empty.

The Third Gate
Of the Devouring Hunger

The doors into death are tiny and open suddenly.

They lie in a snake's fang, the tail of the scorpion, wolfsbane, the flight of a spear. Any one can enter them, at any time.

Death is simple, but people make it complex. They design roads to it, and load themselves with goods. They make myths about kings and sorcerers and babies.

All over the desert, creatures die. They die silently, billions of them, every hour, every second, without fuss. But the people don't think about this.

I have been an insect, and a cat, and a baboon. Last night I became a mouse taken by a hawk. Before I could squeal I was devoured, and the place I went was dark and red.

I could tell them, if they asked me.

I could tell them that there is no way back from the Garden.

Well, just the one.

The earth shakes under them

They heard Argelin's roar of fury, even in the Lower House.

Mirany flung open a door and dragged Oblek in. 'Down here! The kitchens!'

He was through in seconds, Alexos limp and white in his arms. There was a bench, littered with gnawed bones; Mirany swept them off and they laid the boy down, his head rolling to one side.

'What do we do?' Oblek groaned.

She had no idea. When they had seen him climbing the pedestal, when he had embraced the statue and become it, when its stone had softened into his skin, when its calm smile had turned to her, it was almost as if she and it had changed places, she was frozen so still.

And then the earth had shuddered, and he had fallen, crumpling into Oblek's desperate grip.

She touched his lips, his forehead. He breathed, was warm. 'Alexos!'

Oblek turned. 'They're searching.'

'They'll strip the sanctuary. There are hundreds of store rooms.'

'Where, then?'

She took a breath. 'The Upper House. Quickly.'

But Alexos was moving. In the darkness he coughed, murmured, opened his eyes. For a moment their blue was clouded, as if some memory of marble chilled them; then he smiled wanly. 'Carry me, Oblek. I'm so tired.'

The big man scooped him up with an oath of relief. In Mirany's mind the voice continued.

Stone, Mirany. So dense, so dark. So cold in its hollows! That must be what death is like.

A door crashed, outside. Mirany grabbed Oblek. 'This way.'

They ran through the deserted kitchens and stillroom to the courtyard, then into parched gardens, where the pale moon lit the white facade of the house of the Nine. Mirany took the steps to the upper loggia two at a time, Oblek gasping for breath behind her. She raced along the corridor, past the still beauty of dead Speakers to the room at the end. On the door was the Scorpion, and the word, BEARER. Her old room.

She flung the door open.

The room was the same, a small bed, a stool, two windows, edged with moonlight. Some of her dresses were probably still folded in the chest. But that wasn't what made her stop and stare in astonishment.

It was the girl sitting in terror on the bed, clutching a blunt bread-knife in both her hands.

At the same instant, Oblek shouldered in. 'What in hell is she doing here?'

The girl jerked the trembling knife to her own throat. Moonlight gleamed on the blade. 'Don't come any closer!' she screamed. 'Or I'll kill myself!'

Mirany's heart thudded with shock. 'Chryse?' she whispered.

Seth stood very still.

He had never seen such fury. Argelin had raged and stormed round the Temple, striking out at anything, even the walls. He had hurled oaths and threats, turned himself in circles, screamed at the emptiness of the vast roof.

Now, as suddenly as it had started, it was over. The General was breathing hard, clutching his arms round himself before the empty pedestal of the god.

Seth shot a glance at Ingeld. The mercenary's face was set.

'Get out!' Hoarse, Argelin turned. 'Get out there and find it.'

The Northerner went. Argelin looked at Seth, a cold, reptilian stare. 'They must have known. It would have taken time to move it. Equipment. I know who's responsible.'

'You do?' Seth could barely keep the fear out of his voice.

'There is a man. His name has always appeared in rumours, in the gabbled lies of informers. A scavenger of tombs, the lowest of the low. A creature that the beggars of the gutters fear, that prowls the Port and the City, half-human, half-beast. They call him the Jackal.' He took a lamp and lit it, and his voice was matter-of-fact, changing instantly.

'You've seen the reports. Crime is up in the Port. A consignment of weapons from Milonos was stolen yesterday, from under the noses of my guards. The receipt papers were forgeries. Every spy I use to infiltrate opium dens and brothels has been found beaten half to death in a back alley, too terrified to talk. Whoever this Jackal is, he's real, and he's organized, and he's getting more daring.'

Pacing now, he scratched the ragged edge of his beard. 'Do you know anything?'

'Only what I've read.' Seth licked dry lips.

'And you didn't bring it to my attention.'

'My report is ready for you, Lord King. It's on your desk.' It was, deliberately under the highest pile of maps Seth could find. To deflect suspicion he said, 'Why would this thief take the statue?'

'As you said, it can be sold. But this is a plot. They want to bring me down.' He turned, and his face was as calm and amused as Seth had ever seen it. He strode to the vast doors and watched the noisy, systematic search of the Precinct.

'Go and organize these Northmen. Take the documents now, straight to my headquarters, with any valuables. Then send Scarpia out here with another phalanx and some carts.' He gazed across the olive groves to the dark outline of the City of the Dead, a rampart in the desert.

'Gods or thieves, it makes no difference. I will take my revenge on them all.'

'I'll kill myself! I swear I will!'

She was filthy. Her hair, once bright blonde, had darkened and was knotted in a careless tangle in a piece of blue ribbon. Only her clothes were as gaudy as ever, though the lemon silk dress seemed too big, and Mirany recognized it as one of Persis'.

'Chryse! Chryse, listen. It's me. Mirany.' Carefully, as if not to startle a terrified bird, she unwrapped the black veil and took it off, showing her face.

She had expected relief, but Chryse's wail was so shrill Oblek swore in anger.

'How can it be you, Mirany! You're dead! And so's that boy!'

'I'm not dead.' She took a step forward and reached out carefully for the knife. 'You're always so keen to think me dead, Chryse. What on earth are you doing here?'

'There's no time for this,' Oblek snapped. 'We need to get down the cliff.' He went to the window and began wrenching off the nailed planks. Alexos came and sat by Chryse. 'Hello again,' he said sleepily.

She stared at him. Then, silently and helplessly, she began to cry. Tears broke out from her, spilled through her fingers as she clasped them over her face. Gently, Mirany took the knife out of her hand and gave it to Alexos. Then she sat down and put her arms round the girl, and Chryse sobbed on her shoulder.

'Oh, where have you *been* all this time, Mirany! I waited *and waited* but no one came! And I ate all the food until there were only berries and grain, and I wore everyone's clothes till they were all dirty . . .'

'You've been hiding out here? Alone?'

'Ever since that terrible day he killed Hermia. I ran, Mirany. All of us did, but I didn't know where to go because there's only my aunt and she's so stuck-up she'd hand me over to Argelin straight away, to save her precious olive garden and her jasper necklaces! So I came here, because Argelin's men don't like it, and there are only the elephant keepers. If they came I hid. There are lots of places. They were scared and jumpy. I made noises and they hurried away. But I was so afraid, Mirany! Every night, all by myself!'

Mirany drew away. She looked at the girl's pale skin, her

kohl-streaked eyes. 'Were you?' she said quietly.

Chryse felt it. She tugged herself back, blue eyes wide. 'You don't believe me!'

'No, it's not—'

'Yes it is, Mirany! You don't believe a word! You think I couldn't have stayed here by myself, not silly spoiled Chryse. You think I went to Argelin, that he told me to come here and wait for you. Well, you're wrong!' She stood up, and her face was flushed with an anger Mirany had never seen there before.

'This is all your fault, Mirany, don't you see that! We were all happy, Hermia and Rhetia and all of us, living here, being the Nine, and I know Argelin was a tyrant but it didn't affect us! And then you started all this meddling. Finding that boy and the scribe and that fat man there. Stirring things up, saying Hermia was lying. Starting a war, Mirany, a whole war! And now Hermia's dead and the Oracle is ruined and none of us are safe, and you did it! I can't believe what you've done! And all for *nothing*.'

In the dark warmth of the room only the flimsy bedcurtains moved, as the breeze came in through the window from the sea.

Even Oblek was still a moment. Then he said gruffly, 'Mirany. Come on.'

She couldn't move. As if the words had pinned her down, hand and foot. Because for a moment she knew it was true, that she had done this, opened a rift in the world, imagined a voice she called a god's.

Then Oblek had her arm and was dragging her roughly to the window. 'You're not stupid, girl. None of us started this. Don't lose your nerve now. Out, quickly!'

A slam stopped him.

Below, in the Lower House, the doors were being thrown open.

There were more store rooms than Seth had imagined, and they were all full. The Island was littered with documents, and the written records of every oracle pronouncement for a thousand years. Seth rubbed a hand through his hair and gave orders quickly. He had five scribes on site, and more were due.

'Sarvo, the far rooms. You, and you, begin in the treasure chambers.' Leaving them to it, he hurried back up the stone steps.

The litter was still outside, so Argelin was here somewhere.

Seth turned, and went quickly back into the Temple. Night had thickened; the building was even darker now, except for the small oil lamp Argelin had left. Picking it up, Seth crossed to the pedestal.

Curious, he knelt and examined the dust around its base, looking for drag marks, the indications of heavy hoists, but there was nothing. Nothing but a few smeared footprints, that might be anyone's. How could the Jackal have got here in time?

Then he saw the lettering. It was tiny and cramped and ancient, but he blew the sand off and read it, holding the guttering lamp close.

Below, the Nine Gateways through which the beetle rolls the Sun.

Looking round, listening, he watched the shadows of the building. Then he turned back, and placed his thumb in the small hollow that had been hidden by the god's foot.

It sank. A slab swivelled, hoarse with grit. He looked in, and saw a box.

It was crude, painted badly, flaking with age. Carefully he put his arms in and heaved it up, and it was heavy. Something slid inside it. Breathing hard, Seth hefted it to the ground beside the pedestal.

A draught of air on his cheek.

He raised his head, quickly, blew out the lamp.

The Temple was black. One slot of moonlight slanted between its pillars. Dust still hung in the air, and as he breathed in he could taste it in the back of his throat. Dust and fear.

And then a voice whispered, '*Seth.*'

For an instant of terror he thought it was the god. And then he saw her. She was behind the furthest pillar, wrapped in a dark cloak.

'Mirany!'

Taking one quick look behind, he ran. 'What are you doing here! Argelin's here!'

'I know. Oblek's with me. And Alexos.'

His stare of terror frightened her. 'Alexos!'

'We had to save the statue. We got your message.' She looked pale. As if something had stunned her, knocked her sideways. Perhaps the earth tremor. He grabbed her arm and pulled her into the shadows. 'How did you do it?'

'I can't explain. We have to get off the Island, Seth, but there are guards everywhere. They're—'

'—clearing the place. Argelin's orders.'

She had tears in her eyes. To his amazement he heard her whisper, 'Is it all my fault, Seth? That the Oracle is destroyed and everything's lost? Chryse says—'

'That little cat! You've found her?'

'She was hiding here.'

'Well it's rubbish, Mirany!' He gripped her hands, and as he did so thought how little he really knew her, how far apart they still were. 'Argelin has done that, not us. You're the one who's Speaker, Mirany. You hear the god! We're doing what he wants us to do.'

She was looking at him with a kind of distance, as if somehow she'd stepped back. But still he held her hands, until he realized and awkwardly let go.

They glanced away from each other. Mirany said, 'I wanted to speak to you at the gate. What you're doing . . . it's too dangerous, Seth.'

He couldn't answer for a moment. Then he took her hand and pulled her towards the statue.

'Take this with you.' He shoved the box into her arms, closed the stone gap. 'Get the others to the courtyard at the back of here. Where the carts are.'

She nodded. 'It isn't . . . because of me?'

He shrugged, that annoyingly arrogant shrug. 'Of course not. Why you?'

She didn't answer. He knew she wouldn't, so he went on quickly. 'Keep hidden, and watch for my signal. Don't let Alexos be seen.'

She was looking at the box. When she glanced up she said, 'I'm sorry I ever got you into this.'

'I'm not.'

'You're just saying that. Showing off.'

'That's right.'

She managed a smile. 'Pa and Telia have left for the Port.'

A cold sliver of dread slid down his spine. He ignored it. 'I trust the god, Mirany.'

She looked at the empty pedestal. 'Do you, Seth? Once I didn't believe he existed. It was easy then. But now I know him, and he's a person, and like all people he's . . . unpredictable. He does what he wants.'

'But he's on our side, isn't he? He's never let us down.'

She smiled then, as if he was a child, had said something innocent. He thought, for a cold moment, she would deny it, but when she spoke her voice was wistful.

'It must have been wonderful, to drink from the Well.'

'It was.'

She drew the dark cloak round her. Outside, the night was paler. She said, 'Goodbye, Seth.'

Then she was gone.

He turned on his heel and marched out into the dawn, not knowing why he was angry, where this fear had come from. It took ten minutes of barking orders to have everything as he wanted, the scribes scared and confused, the slaves loading goods with bowed heads and hunched backs. Halfway through filling the cart he saw Argelin come out of the Upper House and stand on the terrace, looking out to sea. The General's face was bleak and hard.

On the horizon, the sun was rising red through veils of mist.

The first cart stood ready; from her sprawled cover under the sandalwood shrubs Mirany saw Seth come out and snap an order. A slave followed with a great bale of cloth; she recognized the yellow silk that Jamil's merchants had brought a few months ago and spread at Hermia's feet like an offering. Now the slave dumped it on the half-full cart.

'That's enough. Get a covering.'

The slave said, 'It can take more, lord.'

'I said, *that's enough!*'

'Listen to him,' Oblek whispered in her ear. 'Giving orders suits him.'

'That's not fair, Oblek,' Alexos said.

The big man grunted. 'Something a man can get used to, Archon. That's all.'

Mirany didn't answer.

Why you? he had said. It had made her feel foolish. And yet she had come to realize he always did that cocky act when he was threatened.

The slave brought a rough cover, and fastened it on.

'Now get back there and fetch me the sphinx.' Seth was checking his list; the stylus made small scrapes. 'The onyx one. Quickly.' The slave wiped sweat away and trooped into the Temple.

Seth looked round. 'Mirany!'

They moved, slithering out into the dawn mist. Oblek hoisted the Archon up, and Chryse slid under the cover so fast Seth barely had time to say, 'Watch her.'

'We will.' Oblek grabbed the box, then Mirany. 'Quick, girl.'

Under the tarpaulin it was unbearably hot and stank of cinnamon. When Oblek heaved himself in, the whole cart swayed and something made a crunching sound under the axle. The musician swore, but Seth's face appeared briefly in the opening. 'Shut up. Keep still. If you're found, we fight. There's—'

He jerked away, fastening the ties.

Heavy breath. Mirany heard the slave say, 'Don't forget this.'

'I'll carry it. Get up and drive.'

Noises. The muffled snort of an ox. Lurching.

Then movement.

She had her face against a sack of something metal and Chryse's hot bulk against her back. Down at her feet Alexos lay curled. It was stifling and hard to breathe.

The cart swayed, heading downhill, and she knew they had reached the ceremonial road to the Bridge. It seemed an age until the wheels ran on wood; the heavy rumble was deafening where she lay, one ear to the wooden planking. Through a tiny slit she saw the road, its grit casting long shadows in the horizontal shafts of the rising sun.

A pause. Voices. Seth said something in reply and the cart rumbled on, now over the hissing layer of blown sand that covered the road.

They were across the Bridge. How would he get them into the Port? She wanted to ask Oblek, but even moving was dangerous. Under the rumble of creaking wood she ventured a whisper.

'Can we jump out?'

'No chance.' Oblek's throaty breath was just to her left. 'Unless we kill the slave.'

Shadow.

It fell across the covering. Voices yelled. The cart lurched violently, crunched to a halt. Mirany tried to breathe but fear choked her. They couldn't have reached the Port gate. Not yet.

And then, with a terrible tearing that made Chryse screech, the tip of a knife stabbed down inches from Mirany's eyes and ripped through the cloth. A hand worked its way in, grabbed and tore.

The slit showed daylight.

Through it, one cold eye peered down into hers.

The pyramid underground

The thief turned and yelled. 'Tie them up! Now!'

Two of the five men threatening Seth and the slave with curved swords sheathed theirs, and took out rope. Seth was hauled down; he hit the desert with a thud.

'This is an outrage,' he roared. 'The lord Argelin—'

'Stuff Argelin.' A filthy gag stifled him. His arms were pinned back; he kicked and struggled. At least, while the slave was looking he did.

Rolled into a patch of spiny growth, he cursed, wriggling, but everywhere the needles of the plants stabbed him. Then a long shadow came down; the Fox's single eye watched him through the wrappings on his face.

'Comfortable?' he said quietly.

Seth squirmed, furious.

'That's it, scribe. Make lots of fuss. Some interesting passengers you're carrying. The slave's not in on it?'

Seth shook his head. He made an urgent jerk; the Fox looked over, then reached down and loosened the gag.

Seth spat. 'Get them to the Jackal,' he whispered. 'I don't know what Mirany's done with the god's statue. Tell him the box has something to do with the Nine Gateways.'

'What the hell is that supposed to mean?'

'I don't know, but Argelin does. I'll find out more. Just don't leave me in these spines.'

The Fox grinned. 'Sorry. Got to make this look authentic, ink-boy.'

Before Seth could gasp, the gag was between his teeth; he groaned, but all the Fox did was roll him over with his boot further into the thicket.

Stabbed in wrist and thigh and chest, Seth hissed.

He couldn't see anything but sand. But he heard the cover come off the cart, scuffles and whispers, goods hastily unloaded. They were silent and efficient. Once came a clop of hooves, once a murmur that might have been Mirany's voice. Then only silence, and the insects of the desert, whining and gathering over him in clouds. He squirmed under their bites, and the spines stabbed him.

He cursed the Fox with long, silent, venomous curses.

★ ★ ★

They walked a long way. They were blindfolded, and Chryse kept hanging on to her and dragging annoyingly at her skirt, but Mirany knew they were in some tunnel. Not ancient, like the tombs, but recently dug, a thieves' ratrun, smelling of garlic and dung. At some point it must have scraped under the Port wall, because the Fox gripped her elbow and rasped, 'Crawl here, Holiness. Hands and knees,' and he kept his hand on her head, holding it down, so she knew the roof must be only just above.

Behind, Oblek hissed and squeezed his bulk through.

'I suppose they don't have many fat thieves, Oblek,' Alexos murmured, consolingly.

The big man groaned. 'Thanks, Archon.'

The Fox grinned. 'The boy's right. Thieves are lithe and skinny and athletic. They need to be. You'd make a good one, Holiness.'

Alexos sounded thrilled. 'Would I? Really? Did you hear that, Mirany?'

She nodded, but she was thinking of Seth, tied up back there in the unbearable heat. Perhaps the Fox knew, because he put his rough face close to her ear and said, 'Don't worry about the scribe, lady. Argelin will tear him off a strip, but he won't suspect anything. We've been robbing him blind all over the Port for days.'

His hands helped her up. Behind, she heard Chryse shriek, 'Oh god, something furry touched me!'

'A cat.' Fox sounded amused. 'This way, honoured guests of the Jackal.'

He led them along a stone surface, and through a door into some courtyard. Mirany felt the sun's heat briefly, and then a faint breeze and the smell of washing.

'You could take these things off our eyes now,' Chryse said crossly. 'I'm sure we haven't a clue where we are and we'll never tell anyone.'

'Rules of the Lair.' The Fox sucked his teeth. 'Besides, I'm not sure you, pretty lady, can be trusted at all.' His voice changed to a leer. 'Think of it as being better than having your eyes gouged out.'

Chryse was silenced.

Steps. More corridors, a stone passageway, three doors. At the final one, a knock, and quiet words. Then Mirany felt the Fox take her arm and guide her round a corner and under a low arch. Noise swept over her, a cacophony of voices, hammering, echoes, smells of cooking, the sweetness of opium.

'We're here, Holiness.'

Her blindfold was undone. As it came away she blinked and stared, her sight blurry.

It was a pyramid of light.

That was her first thought; a vast pyramid of air and sunlight, and she was inside it. It rose to an apex so far above that she couldn't see the roof for smoke, and down here the great space made the people thronging it seem tiny.

There were hundreds of them. Beside her, Oblek swore in surprise and Chryse said, 'Who are they all?' but Mirany could see at once that these were the beggars and pickpockets of the Port, its mountebanks, jugglers, hetairas and laundrywomen, drunks and addicts, its ropetrick men and illusionists who did conjuring on street corners. In the vast echoing spaces of the hall they drank, talked, slept, swapped stories of good pitches and easily conned marks. Nearby was a man she'd seen a hundred times in the market, with no legs and a pitiful tin bowl for coins, and yet here he was with both feet up on a table, drinking wine. There were scribes, a group of women painting themselves with henna sores, gangs of dirty children, and in one corner a whole menagerie of tame marsets and hawks and hooded owls that made Alexos cry out with delight.

Cauldrons sent the steam of stewing meat up into the roof; as her eyes followed it Mirany saw structures up there, hanging nets, ropes and intricate walkways, a stairway that zigzagged high along one sloping wall all made of stolen joists from the tombs, their coloured carvings still visible, their gods and Archons crazily processing upside down.

'Follow me,' the Fox said over the noise.

He led them down some steps, then around benches and a forge where oiled sweating men were hammering dies of metal. Oblek scooped up a handful of the coins and whistled.

'So you make your own money.'

'With dear Argelin's face all over them. The latest design, with his crown.' Fox ducked under drying racks of cured leather, and Alexos jumped down beside him. 'Look at the cats!' he said happily.

Chryse shuddered. 'I hate cats.'

They were everywhere, curls of fur sleeping on tables, under chairs, on the precipitous ledges high on the walls. They had to be stepped over and walked round, and each time small eyes opened, and pierced ears flickered crossly.

'The trouble with thieves is that they're superstitious.' The Fox waved a hand. 'Cats are lucky. At least to us they are. The Chief puts up with it, though I sometimes think the stink gets to him. He'll be in here.'

They saw a small square doorway, one of many around the walls, as if the pyramid led to a warren of rooms and cellars on each side. 'How can all this not be seen from outside?' Oblek demanded.

'We're deep below the streets of the Port and the tip is all that's visible. It looks different from outside. You've seen it. It's . . .' He stopped. 'Well, never mind what it is.'

Oblek scowled, but Mirany had ducked under the doorway.

Into a chamber of bronze.

Swords, scimitars, falchions, spears. Blades of all shapes hung from the walls, or were heaped in slithering piles. Armour spilled from chests: bronze greaves, breastplates, a lot of it old and rusted but some new and ornate, foreign in style. It was being cleaned, the whetstones rasping in intolerable chorus as twenty men polished and whetted, oiled and sharpened.

Behind them was another doorway, and the Fox swept aside the curtain over it. 'Surprise for you, Chief,' he said gruffly, and held it open.

Mirany walked in.

The Jackal was leaning against a table, arms folded, surveying a bedraggled figure who looked like a prisoner. 'Not now, Fox!' he snapped. Then he saw who they were. A flicker of astonishment lit his strange eyes.

But it was the girl behind him everyone stared at. Ragged, greasy, her hair in ratstails and her hands tied with rope. Despite that, unmistakably arrogant.

Unmistakably Rhetia.

After Seth's stammered explanation, Argelin said nothing.

His silence was unnerving. Seth gazed down at the tigerskin, and the beast's glassy eyes stared back.

Finally, the General said, 'Did you have time to examine the papers?'

'Very briefly. Temple levies, old prophecies, Oracle records, nothing to interest thieves.'

'You seem sure.'

'The thieves were after any treasure.'

'And got it.' Argelin's voice was icy. He stood and poured lemon juice from a silver ewer and drank it thoughtfully.

'I told you to take men with you.' But he sounded preoccupied, and Seth just shrugged. Then Argelin said, 'You found nothing about the Garden?'

Seth felt his spine tingle. 'The Garden?'

'The way . . . That is . . . It is said there are scrolls in the Temple, ancient parchments, that tell of a way . . . a road back . . .' He stopped, seeing Seth's stare. Then he slammed the cup down.

'We need to deal with this Jackal. Come with me.'

He strode out into the corridor and Seth hurried after him, relieved and thirsty and still sore from the mosquito bites that were tormenting him. Argelin put his head into the optio's room.

'Two men. Discreetly armed. Now.'

'Right away.' The optio glanced at Seth and hurried out.

'You're not taking the litter?' Seth asked, cautiously.

'No. Get a cloak.'

Quickly, Seth obeyed. His heart thumped with tense excitement. Now he'd find out where Argelin's mysterious journeys led.

When the men were ready, Argelin wound a dark red cloak around his body and face, and led them out through a small door to the side of the Headquarters building. It was nearly noon, the sun an unbearable furnace overhead, and the stink of fish from the wharves of the harbour as pungent as ever. Out in the bay, work on the triremes went on

127

without stopping, exhausted slaves and workmen changing shift at the blast of a horn.

The General walked swiftly. He led them up through the streets, and his silence and urgency cleared the way. A few people glanced at them. No one spoke.

Halfway through the Silk-Weavers' Quarter he said, without turning, 'Your father and sister arrived this morning.'

Seth didn't miss a step, though his heart lurched. 'Where are they?'

'I've had them taken to a house.'

He ducked washing. 'Can I see them?'

'They're not prisoners.' Argelin gave him a sideways glance.

They were well up among the highest of the steep white alleys before they turned into a quiet piazza. Houses surrounded three sides of it; on the fourth, over a mudbrick wall, the tops of olive trees sprouted.

The General snapped, 'You men, stay here. Don't come in unless I send for you.'

Turning away, Seth caught a wink and a leer from one guard to another. It puzzled him, until he saw who answered Argelin's quiet knock on the door in the wall.

She had to be a hetaira. A girl with a painted face. Her clothes were so flimsy, Seth turned his eyes away in hot embarrassment. Was this the General's secret?

Argelin said nothing but pushed past; after a second Seth

followed, into an antechamber hung with red silks and stinking of cheap scent. Behind them the girl closed the door. She had said nothing, as if she recognized him, and it was obvious Argelin knew his way, striding up some stairs in a corner, and barging open the doors of a room without knocking.

Over his shoulder, Seth stared.

An enormous man had instantly blocked the doorway, drawing a curved knife. Behind him, standing before a mirror that distorted her features to a slanting shrewdness, a woman waited. In the warped metal her eyes, small and black, watched calmly. As if she'd known they were coming.

Argelin swept into the room. 'Send your ape out, Manto,' he said, sitting on a carved chair near the window. 'We need to talk.'

'Have you any *idea*!' Mirany raged. 'Of the worry I've had about you?'

'You know her?' the Jackal said.

'Of course I know her! This is Rhetia. The one—'

'—who started the war!' The Jackal's long eyes narrowed. 'So this is the one. What a pleasure to meet at last, Holiness.'

Rhetia glared at him. 'Untie my hands! *At once.*'

He didn't move; Mirany turned on him. 'Has she been here all this time?'

'My men dragged her in this morning. She was spying on them in the palaestra.'

Rhetia's back was straight. 'Mirany, I don't know who these scum are, but if they don't untie me straight away I'll—'

'Oh, shut up, Rhetia.' Suddenly Mirany felt bone weary. She sat as if all the energy had gone out of her.

The Jackal looked at her closely, then turned and yelled at Fox. 'Food. Now!'

Alexos had curled up on the bench with his head in Oblek's lap, and immediately gone to sleep. A small marmoset he had brought from the zoo in the pyramid chattered as it picked through his hair.

Mirany put her hands together, trying to think. Oblek handed her something. When she picked at it she found it was fruit, but she could barely swallow it.

'Why are you out of the tombs?' the Jackal said sternly. While Oblek told him about the statue Mirany glared at Rhetia, and Rhetia glared back. In the stunned silence as the men gazed at the sleeping boy, she said quietly, 'We know you've been in contact with Prince Jamil.'

Rhetia shrugged. 'I had to *do* something. Why wait for a crazy child and a scribe? Time was wasting. I decided to make my own plans.'

There was silence.

'How?' Oblek spat a pip into a metal jug; it rattled inside.

'Untie me, or I won't say another word.'

'Holiness, you don't seem to realize who rules here,' the Jackal said.

She eyed him imperiously. 'The god does. Not you.'

He smiled his cold smile. But he jerked his head and Fox took out a knife and sliced the bonds. Rhetia rubbed her wrists. Then she said, 'First I got work. In the palaestra.'

'You?' Mirany couldn't imagine it.

'Why not me?' Rhetia shrugged. 'I can get on my knees and scrub floors, if I have to.'

Chryse, sitting just inside the door, stifled a giggle. The tall girl stared at her in disbelief.

'So that little trollop's back. I wish I could say I was glad.' Ignoring Chryse's scowl, she turned back to Mirany. 'Jamil goes to the baths most days. It's the only place we'll have a chance to snatch him. Argelin never does. He's got this hatred of water, they say he doesn't even drink it any more, and thirst is driving him mad.'

Mirany said, 'But—'

'Let me finish, Mirany. I've spoken to the Pearl Prince. He trusts me. He thinks I'm providing a ship to get him out of the Port, to his uncle's fleet out there beyond the islands.' She gave a satisfied smile. 'I've arranged to be warned when he's next coming. Then I get him.'

Mirany looked at the tomb-thief. But it was Oblek who growled, 'All by yourself?'

Rhetia shrugged. 'I have an ally. A powerful one.'

'Who?'

'I have no intention of telling a fat drunk and a gang of thieves.' She picked up a strip of meat, sniffed it suspiciously, then put it back down. 'But my plans are laid.'

Mirany stared at her angrily. Rhetia had been a worry when she was missing, but her turning up here made everything more complicated. Heavily she said, 'Seth is working for us. Didn't you realize that?'

Fingers poised over a peach, Rhetia paused an instant. Then she said, 'Is he? I had no idea.' Her voice was flat, but the Jackal looked at her closely.

'Your plan will put him in danger.'

'I don't see why.' She bit into the peach, hungrily.

'Mirany's fond of him.' Chryse's voice was sly.

'I am not fond of him!'

Silence. Oblek grunted, and the Jackal watched them all. She felt ashamed suddenly, as if she had betrayed him. Or herself.

'I just don't want him hurt,' she whispered.

'No.' The Jackal stood up. He went to Rhetia and looked at her calmly. 'And that's why there will be no attempt on Jamil. You'll stay here, Lady Rhetia, just to make sure. As my guest.'

'You can't keep me prisoner.' Almost as tall, she glared straight back. 'Who the hell are you anyway?'

He smiled. 'I am the Jackal. The leader of the Speaker's army of resistance.'

'This thief-rabble!'

'As you say. This thief-rabble. Which will kidnap the Pearl Prince from under Argelin's nose, and make him vanish as smoothly as a dolphin into dark water. You, lady, will not be allowed to ruin that with foolish amateur heroics.'

Furious, she turned her glacial look on Mirany. 'You must be mad, trusting this scum.'

Mirany looked up. 'They're my friends.' And in her mind the god breathed, *I don't think she knows much about friends, Mirany.*

'There is still the problem of the other priestesses.' The Jackal watched Fox come in with the box from the Temple; as it slammed down on the desk tiny clouds of dust rose from its cracks, 'Only Seth can get them out.'

Fox looked at Mirany. 'What about his message, Holiness?'

'What message?' Oblek muttered.

Mirany stood, and crossed to the box. Looking down on its painted lid she repeated the words he had whispered, and for the first time she felt like the Speaker, with the truth on her tongue.

'*The Nine Gateways. Where the beetle rolls the sun.*'

Alexos cried out in his sleep. His eyes snapped open; he gave a great gasp of fear. Oblek grabbed him.

'Archon! It's all right.'

'No, Oblek, it isn't.' He struggled up, shuddering, and

they saw with shock that his dark eyes were filled with tears that broke and ran down his cheeks. 'The Rain Queen is sending her revenge. It's coming!'

High above, as if on the apex and sides of the pyramid, tiny patters grew louder. Oblek put heavy hands on the boy's shoulders.

'It's just rain. Rain is good, old friend, isn't it?'

Alexos whispered. '*It may be rain, but it isn't water, Oblek.*'

A scream from outside. The Jackal stepped to a door in the wall; when he jerked it open, light poured down an alleyway, light flecked and dulled, its colour coppery and ominous, and even as he stood there looking up, it faded and a darkness like night fell on his face.

He looked appalled.

In Mirany's ear the god sighed very quietly. *Please don't blame me, Mirany. Argelin broke her statues. What else could he expect?*

134

He glimpses joy and heartbreak

When the slave had scowled out, Manto turned.

Seth saw she wore a dark robe and a priceless necklace of blue scarabs linked across it. Her cropped hair surprised him; most women kept it long, and would have dyed its greyness.

She returned his scrutiny. 'So this is the young Secretary from the Tombs.'

'Never mind him.' Argelin leaned forward. 'Am I facing insurrection?'

The sorceress smiled. She picked up her mirror and cast a puff of powder into a flame beside it; scents of sandalwood and gum sizzled. Seth glanced rapidly along the rows of objects on the shelf, and his skin crawled. Pieces of mummified animal; paws, a monkey's head. Green stones and a dried hand. A skull carved of crystal. Then he saw she was watching him in the mirror, so he leaned back against the wall, folding his arms, trying to look arrogant.

'You must know, Lord King, your policies make you enemies.' The woman gazed thoughtfully into the bronze disc. 'I sense many stirrings in the Port, much unrest. Someone is taking a stick to our nest of ants.'

'Someone. This Jackal.'

Seth kept very still. Manto smiled. 'Ah yes. As you say, this Jackal.'

'Who is he?'

'No one knows. Or they choose not to say.'

Argelin frowned. 'Can you find out?'

The woman turned. She paused a moment, tapping her fingernails on the mirror. 'I will discover him for you. He is clever; his people are organized. But I will find out his name. Because I believe, Lord King, he is someone you know. A creature with two lives, one bright, one dark.' Her eyes flickered to Seth, and she smiled, calmly.

'And your price . . .'

'You know my price. I must become Speaker.' She moved to the latticed window. Hot slants of sunlight fell across her, and the musky smell of the room seemed to have become a faint mist that caught in Seth's throat, so that he had to clear it nervously.

'And to prove my loyalty, let me also tell you this. *I have seen one of the Nine.*'

Argelin stared in surprise. 'Impossible. I have them all. Where was this?'

'In this very room.' Her black eyes watched him. 'A small girl, with brown hair. A nervous, yet intense manner. As if she believed she heard not my voice, but also a voice beyond.'

Seth drew his breath in sharply, but Argelin didn't notice. He stared grimly at Manto. 'Are you telling me Mirany is alive?'

She shrugged. 'I do not know her name. But her fear, that I knew.'

'And you let her go!'

'She told me she knew this Jackal, so I had her followed. She went to the Desert Gate and was nearly apprehended, but slipped out. She will be hiding in the tombs. With him, doubtless.'

They both watched his silent fury, how his hands clenched on each other. Then he nodded.

'Tomorrow I take my men down there, and strip every tomb of every Archon back to Sthretheb. And let the Dead do what they can.'

A baby cried somewhere in the building. An odd hush had fallen outside. Seth realized the usual clamour of gulls had stopped.

Argelin leaned forward over the table. 'How much

progress have you made in . . . that other business?'

'I have consulted ancient scrolls and communed with the demons I summon, and have discovered that it can be done.' She was watching him closely, and Seth saw it too, a sudden flicker that came and went on the General's face. A flicker of hope.

Manto smoothed her robe with plump fingers. 'It can be done, but it will not be easy. Blood will need to be spilt, animal and human . . .'

Argelin shrugged. 'Blood's cheap. What else?'

'Certain costly ingredients . . . powdered gold, diamond, ambergris, rare spices. The organs of animals. For the Fourth Gateway the venom of scorpions; for the Fifth the skin of a dolphin; for the Sixth the unborn offspring of a hare.'

Argelin stood impatiently. 'I don't want to know details. Gold and diamonds I'll get you. But are you sure, woman, *sure* it can be done?'

The desperation in his voice chilled Seth. Manto went up to him. She said, 'Lord King, Holiness, hear me swear this. I will bring her back. Through the Nine Gates I will cause her to come back to you, despite the god and the Rain Queen's anger. Secret and forbidden, there are ways to leave the Garden, ways to return from death. Give me what I asked, and I'll do it.'

Seth was sweating; his hands shook. He hoped his appalled horror was not showing on his face. *Did she mean what he thought she meant?*

Argelin looked haggard. For a moment exhaustion seemed to wash over him, as if something he could not forget tormented him and was unbearable.

'She comes to me in my sleep. Shadowy. I can't see her, can't touch her. She rebukes me and cries out to me—' He choked over a word. 'So it is easier not to sleep.'

'I could show her to you,' Manto said slyly, to his back.

Something was dimming the light; perhaps it was the mist of incense, perhaps the drifting gauzy red curtains around the room. Argelin was rigid a moment; when he looked round, his look had changed; it was charged with wild astonishment.

'Now?' he whispered, hoarse.

Manto said, 'Why not?' She glanced at Seth. 'Lock the door.'

Seth crossed to it and slipped the latch, then stood with his back against it. The warm wood felt solid and reassuring. Fear was gathering in his chest; it seemed hard to breathe, to get air.

'Do you think this is right?' he murmured.

Argelin did not even hear. Manto had taken his hands and drawn him to the mirror; carefully she placed him at an angle to it, and he was submissive, and still. Seth saw his eyes were fixed on the polished bronze, searching, anxious.

'Be patient.' Manto closed the shutters. In the muffled darkness they heard her move softly, caught a crack of flame, a glimmer of metal. The scarabs at her neck gleamed with an iridescent sheen. She slipped on a robe of black, picked up a small staff tipped with a moon-crescent, and came back.

'Now. Don't move, don't speak. Not even a breath. She cannot be touched or spoken with. A glimpse I can give you now, no more.'

'A glimpse will be more than I deserve.' Argelin's voice was raw with pain. Manto glanced at him sidelong; Seth caught her small smile. It was amused. Even mocking.

'Keep still. We begin.'

Nothing happened. Seth had time to know he was so tense his muscles were clenched and aching; he forced his shoulders to relax in the darkness, and then, abruptly, froze again.

A tingling in the air. Charged blackness closed round him, became a solid, crackling thing; terror swooped and bewildered him. He wanted to back out, but he couldn't move.

Because in the mirror an image was forming, a distant, barely lit quiver. It swam eerily, as if it was underwater, had dragged itself from aquatic depths, was struggling towards them out of obscurity. It rippled and changed, grew, solidified. It became a woman, her dark hair elaborately dressed, her robe white and many-pleated, her arms bare.

Seth choked back a cry. He knew her. The tall confident walk, the angular face.

Argelin's whisper was pure anguish. '*Hermia.*'

Her eyes turned to him. Through currents of air and mist she lifted her hand towards his face, and opened her lips.

'Find me,' her voice whispered. 'Find me!'

Desperate, he grabbed at her; his fingers clunked against metal, and instantly, as if he had caused it, blood filled the mirror, a red trickle that ran down its surface, down the white dress, her hands, his own.

'No!' he roared, snatching back. But with a scream that cut Seth like a knife, the apparition vanished.

'Hermia!'

The mirror was sticky and empty. With a roar of fury Argelin flung it on to the floor. He turned like a cat. 'Show yourself! Tell me you forgive me, Hermia! *Tell me!*'

Seth was cold as ice. Manto watched, a silent shadow. 'She's gone, Lord King. As I said, this was only a glimpse.'

Argelin stood a long moment as if he gathered control. The sorceress went up to him, and to Seth's astonishment she held his arms from behind, laying her cropped head sideways on his back. 'I feel your agony, Holiness. It runs deep into you. Trust me. I will bring her back. All I ask is to be Speaker. A new, dark Oracle.'

In the silence something tapped against the shutter. Then Argelin turned, pushing her away. His voice was raw. 'If this is a trick I will cut you into pieces myself.'

'And I wouldn't blame you. But it's no trick. You saw her.'

'Find out who this Jackal is. And prepare for the spell. I'll send whatever you need.'

He turned and strode towards the door but at the same time something fell through the grid of the lattice. It landed on the floor with a peculiar crackle; Seth glanced down at it. He saw a large insect, its back legs jointed, its mandibles twitching. In disgust, he went to stamp on it but the General grabbed his arm before he could move. 'Wait.'

Slowly, Argelin knelt and looked at the thing. Then he turned towards the shutters.

They crackled. Soft thumps blurred outside them.

'Open those.'

Manto moved, but Seth was quicker. He strode over and wrenched the windows wide, desperate for light and air, but he found neither. With a howl of fear he whipped his head back in, scrabbling and dragging from his neck and hair the insects that were swarming all over him, the huge locusts that came spatting and smacking into the walls, that clung to the ceiling, crash-landed on the table.

Argelin stood up.

Outside, the sky was dark with deadly rain.

Panic.

As he raced through the streets Seth heard it rise, in screams, curses, sobs. Children were snatched inside, people beat on the doors of houses for admittance. Swirling in the narrow slots between the buildings, the swarm was a vast living thing, blackening the sky, clotting the air with its crackling hiss. A rain of insects smacked into him, bouncing off walls, clustering in heaps on anything that grew. Houseplants were stripped of leaves before he ran by them, olives trees eaten alive in seconds. Dogs howled and tore at their ropes, maddened by the crawling masses that swarmed over them. Ducking under cloth that was already a web of holes, Seth felt the locusts rain on him, fly into his face, crack under his boots. Wrapped in the cloak he had snatched from Manto's, only his eyes exposed, he ran breathlessly after Argelin down steps thick with jerky, jointed movement, slithering on the smeared slicks of bodies, grabbing at walls coated with clinging wings.

The locusts ate every leaf and fruit. They stripped window boxes, devoured fabric. In the market Seth fought his way through merchants who cursed and swore and raged among the turmoil as the swarm fell on pomegranates and grapes and chomped everything down to the stalk. People crawled under the ruins of stalls, tore down cloth to wrap themselves, spat out insects, tripped over the cats that screeched for cover.

Hurling himself under the arch Seth slammed into a patrol of the foreign mercenaries. They were staring, appalled, at the destruction.

Argelin grabbed one. 'Get to the irrigation scheme. Beat the things out of the crops!'

'Lord King . . .'

'*Do it! Now!*'

They ran. Argelin spun on Seth, but before he could speak a woman threw herself at him, screaming with panic. 'You did this! You've cursed us! Enemy of the gods!'

He flung her to the floor and hauled Seth round the corner. 'The ships!' he yelled.

Through the stinging rain Seth could hardly hear. But as they leapt the last few steps down to the harbour he thumped into the General's stillness, and understood.

All across the water, filling the caldera of the drowned volcano, the air swarmed. There was no sky, and no sea, nothing but maddened gulls and a hideous crust of living green on the waves and wharves. Beyond, where the ships had been, timbers rose, crawling with a skin of ravenous insects. Billions of mandibles chewed and gnawed. As Seth watched ropes snapped, masts and spars fell without a splash into the choked sea. Sails shredded in seconds into vast holes, and were rags. Men dived, yelling in fear, struggling and choking in the rustling foam.

Argelin watched, silent.

He watched until the last half-built deck was smothered.

Then he turned and stormed into the building.

The locust swarm lasted for three days.

No one went out unless they were desperate for water. In the Port the streets were left to the heaps of gorged insects, and only Argelin's men, faces heavily wrapped, kept up their patrols. But the thief-world did not waste the time. The Jackal mounted two lightning raids, on the armoury store by the Tower of Daron, and a heavily guarded warehouse in the Potters' Quarter where Argelin kept spare ropes and timbers for the artillery.

The Fox had found each of the three priestesses a room to herself, and Mirany was very glad of the chance to sleep and wash. As she combed her hair and stared at her face in the piece of glass that served for a mirror, Chryse put her head round the door.

'Oh, there you are!' She came in and stared round the dingy chamber gloomily. 'It's just like mine. Absolutely nothing nice. They must have some stolen jewellery, or some perfume. I'm certainly going to look.' Then, before Mirany could stop her, she picked up the scarab brooch from the chest.

'Oh, that's pretty.'

Mirany took it. 'It's not mine.'

'Are these people safe, Mirany?'

'I think so.'

'But they'll never defeat Argelin.' Chryse rubbed a finger along her bottom lip. 'Don't you think we should sneak out, and go to him? Tell him where they are, and about Rhetia? He might—'

'I'm going to pretend you didn't say that.' Mirany's voice was hard. 'Now come on.'

They went down into the Lair and crossed to the Jackal's

room. There were no guards here or anywhere in the complex, so Mirany knocked and opened the door.

The Jackal was working on the box. He had turned it up and was testing every part of the underside with a metal implement. Tools and delicate probes littered the floor. He looked at them over it, and then tossed the blade down in disgust.

'Mirany, I have encountered many fiendish devices of the Archons but this beats them all! I've been working for hours at it. No lock, no secret compartment, nothing but a solid block. And yet something moves inside.' He sank wearily on to a stool and folded his arms.

Chryse touched the box curiously. 'It might be magic.'

The Jackal snorted.

Mirany said, 'Chryse, I want you to fetch Oblek.'

'That drunk! Oh, Mirany, he smells!'

'He doesn't drink now. And musicians are touched by the god.' She turned. 'Go on.'

Chryse went to the door and lingered. She looked uneasy. 'These horrible, dirty people . . .'

'. . . Will not harm a hair of your empty little head.' Politely the Jackal rose, ushered her firmly out and shut the door. Then he put his back to it. 'Or is it so empty? You still don't trust her, do you, Mirany?'

His sharpness always surprised her. 'She says she was on the Island all that time. I don't know what to think.'

'But you want it to be true.'

Instead of answering she took out the scarab brooch, crossed the room, and put it in his hand. He stared at it, and his face darkened.

'I should have given it to you as soon as you came back,' she said. 'It's from—'

'I know who it's from.' His voice was cold and hard. He looked up. 'How did she get hold of you?'

'She didn't. It was an accident.' Quickly she told him of the destruction of the statue, how she had taken shelter in the House of Delights. He clicked his tongue once in dismay, but said nothing till she'd finished. Then he put the scarab down on the bench and stared at it grimly.

His silence scared her.

'Is this woman so bad?'

He managed a cold smile. 'Worse. Her message?'

'She said soon she would extract payment for your debt.'

The Jackal began to pick up his tools, and slot them back in the leather holder. His fine fingers moved quickly. 'That is what I feared.' Then abruptly he put the tools down and looked at her.

'Like you, I met Manto by accident. Several years ago. With two others I had made a misguided attempt to break into one of the Fifth Dynasty tombs, but we'd been seen digging and Argelin's men chased us into the Port. We split up, but three of the soldiers followed me. I turned into an alleyway and found it was a dead end.' He shrugged. 'I drew my sword, ready to fight, prepared to die but not to be taken.' He was silent a moment. Then he sat on the table, his feet on the stool. He looked at her sidelong. 'I have killed in my time, Mirany. I know death well, but I have never tortured or enjoyed cruelty. Manto's slaves swooped out of the shadows like vultures; they stripped the guards of their weapons and beat them. Then she came. She wore black, and carried a wand tipped with a moon-crescent. She said, 'I saw you in my magic mirror, Lord of Thieves. Your life is mine now.'

He shook his head, his fair hair shining. 'I am not used to fear, Holiness, but I felt it then. Before my eyes she killed them slowly, and I will not horrify you with their agonies. Her magic requires blood and pain. Her soul too, I think.'

Rigid, Mirany said, 'You said nothing?'

He looked up. 'Was I that much of a coward, you mean? In fact I insisted she stop, but I might have been a fly on the wall for all the notice she took. I was held tight and weaponless. When it was over she came up to me, and as my face was wrapped she tore the hood away and saw my hatred and disgust. She smiled. Then she said, 'You owe me a debt. Pay me.'

He flipped the scarab. 'This was in my pocket. It was the only thing we had found in the sand, deep, on the steps to the tomb entrance. So I gave it to her.' He shook his head. 'It was not enough. They held me tight, took three drops of my blood, some hair, a clipping of my fingernail. In all these years I have dreaded what she would do with those things. Now it seems the time has come when I will find out.'

Mirany stared at him. She had no idea what to say.

Putting the beetle down, he said, 'She would have had you followed.'

'What!' She thought back, panicking. 'She couldn't have! I got through the gate. No one else did.'

'That's good.' The Jackal stood as Oblek's heavy voice came through the door. 'Say nothing to the others. This is my problem.'

The door crashed open. Oblek came in with the Archon on his back, and on Alexos' head a marmoset from the pyramid, chattering with glee. Alexos jumped off as Oblek collapsed on to a seat.

'Well, what's in the box?' the big man asked.

'You tell me,' the Jackal muttered.

Oblek glanced at him, catching the sourness in his voice, but Alexos came and ran his small hands over the painted wood.

'I remember this! It belonged to me when I was Hastris. How long ago was that, Oblek?'

'No idea, old friend. Centuries, probably.'

Alexos smiled. Then he took his hands off the box and put them on his hips. '*Open, box. The god commands you.*'

With a click the painted lid unlatched.

The Jackal allowed himself one small groan.

The Fourth Gate
Of the Crooked Sword

Once, they say, the Rain Queen loved a man.

His name is lost. Even I can't remember it.

She was besotted with him, taught him her wisdom, took him to the green orchards and crystal fountains of her paradise.

I think the man grew lonely there. Because he found a way back.

She wept storms for him. But then she killed him with her lightning, because he had seen too much.

She does not forgive. Tempest and deluge, what mercy do they show?

How can they know what it is to drown?

She enters the heat of the sun

The house was big. Someone's confiscated home. A guard leaning on the wall outside hastily stood upright as Seth got out of the litter, ankle deep in the desiccated crusts of dead locusts. The streets should have been swept, but the workers obviously hadn't got this high yet. Seth had had to give the order himself; Argelin had hardly stirred out of his room for days.

Seth surveyed the man. 'Everything quiet?'

'Yes, lord.'

He wanted to say more. Instead he took a step away from the litter and its slaves, and pulled a small purse of staters out of his pocket, pouring the coins carelessly into his palm. The gold discs tinkled; the guard's eyes fixed on them, intent. Seth flicked a glance at the slaves; one at least would report back to Argelin, so he didn't want this seen. He gave the guard an insolent glare.

'Give me some of that water.'

It was the man's precious tiny supply, but after a hesitation he dipped the cup in and held it out. Seth drank. It was sun-warmed and brackish, probably days old. Discreetly he dropped five staters in, so that none but the guard saw them. Handing the cup back, he snapped, 'My father and sister are not to be molested. If they have any complaints I'll hear them, and you'll pay with your head. Understand?'

'Yes, lord.'

'If they require protection, you'll protect them. Get it?'

'I understand you, lord.' A hefty man, his face weatherbeaten and stolid. Seth sighed, then waved him aside and stalked in. It was probably useless. But it was all he could do.

The house was airy. In the whitewashed walls open windows allowed breezes to drift through, and from the terrace floored with coloured marble he found he could look down on the Port, all its bustling streets, and beyond the roofs, the harbour. The triremes were already under repair, but the damage had been enormous. There was little timber; wharves had been torn up to provide it. Ingeld had ordered that, after one stormy row with the General. All

Argelin seemed to think of now was Hermia. His obsession was eating him alive.

'So you've turned up at last.' Pa was standing under the vine that grew round the wall; Seth turned and faced him. To his surprise he found he was taller, saw a man grey and shrivelled, his face pale from lack of sun.

'Pa. You're looking well.'

'Liar. But you are, *Lord* Seth.'

He knew that. His hair was oiled and curled, and he wore a new tunic of scarlet with narrow borders of woven gold. The harrowing hunger of the desert was gone; now he ate well. Fine gold chains hung at his neck.

He shrugged, feeling the marble balustrade hard against his back. 'Where's Telia?'

'Asleep.' For a moment they confronted each other, silent, then the strain in his father's face seemed to crumple; he sat wearily on the marble bench and said, 'I hope you know what you're doing, son.'

Seth sat beside him. 'Any listeners?'

'No. I searched the house for passages and hiding holes as soon as we came. Argelin provided a slave girl but I sent her back; she would surely have spied for him. So far no one else has come. He leaves us alone, except for the guard. By the way, you wasted your money there. The patrol changes every week. He doesn't want them getting fond of Telia, in case they have to cut her throat.'

It turned Seth cold. Pa nodded down. 'That sausage

seller on the street corner with the dirty apron is one of the Jackal's. Someone else keeping an eye on us.' Then he said, 'How did we get involved in all this? That girl . . .'

'The god. It was the god, Pa, not Mirany.'

His father raised an eyebrow at him. 'You've changed. You and the fat man and the thief. What was out there in the desert that hardened you into a man?'

He didn't know what to say. 'The sun. That was all that was out there. The sun, and ourselves.'

Then he said, 'I'm sorry. This plan was my idea and I should have realized it would bring you into danger.'

Pa laughed sourly. 'It was me that always nagged you to get on Argelin's staff.'

In the silence Seth felt the heat burn his bare arm. It was a new silence. Not the cold hostility he had been prepared for. Then it was broken by a squeal of joy.

'Seth!' Telia ran in and jumped up at him, heavier and drowsy with sleep. 'Where's my present, Seth? You promised!'

'I promised, and I never forget my promises.' He put the wrapped parcel down on the floor and grinned as she fell on it and tore the cloth away.

'Is it from the Archon's Palace?'

The Palace, he was sure, was a stripped shell, but he said, 'From a palace of delights.' In fact he had bought it that morning from a woman in the market, one of the last with anything to sell, and at a vastly inflated price.

Telia's eyes went wide. 'Look, Pa!' she gasped.

A chain of finely carved monkeys tumbled out of the sacking. Their jointed paws and limbs were linked in curious ways; as Telia held them up they danced and somersaulted, untangled and clasped again as if the wooden fingers lived. Their droll faces had eyes that slid and mouths that opened; deep in their bodies, tiny rattles made chattering noises.

Watching her fascination with it, Pa said, 'Will he go into the tombs?'

'Soon. He's bankrupt. All the money has gone to pay the mercenaries and they want more. There's no harbour tax, and with the Emperor's fleet out in the islands, trade is shattered. He needs men, ships. The tombs are a treasure house.'

The monkeys stretched, a long line, then concertinaed into a sudden squashed heap. Telia giggled.

'Take care, if you're with him.' Pa's voice was acid. 'The Shadow is waiting.'

'I have to be with him, Pa.'

'You had a choice. You chose this.' Then, as a gull cried low over the terrace, he stood and looked out to sea. Far away, barely seen in the hot shimmering of the horizon, the ships of the Emperor lay at anchor, a threatening line.

'You've found Jamil?'

Seth looked down at his sister and the monkeys. By tonight she would be tired of them, he thought. 'Yes. The trouble is, Rhetia's found him too.'

Within the box was another box. And then another.
Nine containers littered the table, each smaller. Inside the
painted wood, blue lapis. Then alabaster, papyrus,
silver, sliced thin jade. Nestled in that was a cube of
ebony, completely black, and when Alexos had made it
divide in half, another of alligator skin, dried almost to
desiccation. The final box, small and perfect, was of
rock crystal.

'Open it,' Mirany breathed.

Alexos reached out and lifted the lid. Instantly his face
was lit with an unmistakeable glow; the Jackal smiled and
Oblek said, 'Is it gold, old friend?'

'Oh yes, Oblek. A great treasure.'

He lifted it out. Mirany saw a flat disc of beaten gold, at
its centre a stone of glowing red, a carnelian perhaps, or a
ruby of unusual fire. Under the stone a scarab spread its
wings, and radiating from the sun sign nine beams burst,
raised in gold, each ending in a single hieroglyph.

That was all. Its perfection silenced them.

'Pretty,' Oblek growled.

'More than that.' The Jackal reached out and took it
from the boy. 'This is unique. In all my years of turning
over tombs I've seen nothing like it.'

'I have.' Everyone looked at her, so Mirany said, 'In the
tombs. Deep down. A huge sun, buried underground. But
where did Seth get it?'

'From me.' Alexos sat down on a stool, pulling his knees up and hugging them.

Catching the Jackal's eye, Oblek said carefully, 'You, Archon?'

'My statue, Oblek. Well, that's me now. He found it underneath my feet. I can't remember how long ago I put it there, but it was made by a man whom the Rain Queen loved. He made it to show others the secrets of the Way. Whoever owns it can do amazing things.'

'Such as?' the Jackal asked smoothly.

'Well, walk through walls. Find their way in the dark. Go to the Garden and come back.'

The tomb-thief stared at him. Then, with the disc in his hands, he walked to the wall of the room and softly collided with it.

'That would be every thief's dream. But I'm afraid you may have been misled, Archon.'

Alexos looked cross, but Mirany said, 'Wait a minute.' She turned to the boy. '*What garden?*'

He folded his arms sulkily, but she came up to him and caught hold of him. 'What garden? Tell me!'

'You know what garden, Mirany.'

'The Rain Queen's?

'Far beyond the world. Where the water drips from the trees.'

Mirany glanced at the others.

'Do you mean, old friend,' Oblek said carefully, 'that

whoever owns this disc can go through . . . I mean can really . . . die . . . and then come back?'

Alexos re-tied his sandals with great concentration. Then he said, 'I think I mean that.'

The Jackal raised an eyebrow. 'But who would be insane enough to put it to the test?'

Mirany said, 'Seth's note—' but before she could finish, the door was flung open and the Fox crashed in, Chryse looking hot and smug behind him.

'Chief. She's gone!'

'Who?'

'The priestess. Told a pack of lies to Moret and got through the outer guards.'

'Rhetia!' Mirany gasped. 'She's going for Jamil!'

'She'll ruin everything.' The Jackal dumped the disc in Mirany's hand, grabbing his robe.

'Oblek, Fox, with me.' At the door he turned. 'Holiness, stay with the Archon.'

Before she could object, they were gone.

In the abrupt silence Alexos swung his legs under the table. 'You might not have to be insane, you know, Mirany,' he said thoughtfully, as if nothing had happened. 'You might just have to be very, very unhappy.'

The palaestra was quiet.

As Seth walked in he saw the mercenaries out in the shade, cleaning spears. Two were wrestling aimlessly. No one else seemed to be about. He headed straight for the Room of Roses, but when he opened the door the place was empty. Rose petals lay on the floor, and a few stray locusts rustled on the wall.

He backed out, looked round.

The hot room. As he strode down the corridor a cat ran past him, tail up, and he wondered why the guards weren't in here. He stopped and listened. No splashes from the baths. Where was everyone?

Suddenly he felt nervous. Even the outside of the hot room door was warm, its greened bronze latch smooth with use; putting his ear to the metal, he heard Jamil's deep bass inside. And a woman's voice.

Instantly he heaved the door wide and stepped in.

The girl at the low window swung round and glared at him. She was tall and dressed as a slave but he knew her now, had seen her haughty stiffness before behind the mask of the Cupbearer.

'You're Rhetia.'

She scowled. Prince Jamil looked uneasy. 'Is he with us?'

'Apparently.' Rhetia shrugged. 'Get out of here, scribe. There's no time to explain. I have to act now, and I don't need your help. Get out of here before Argelin thinks you were involved.'

Her insolence infuriated him. 'Is this the Jackal's idea of security?'

'The Jackal's got nothing to do with it,' she snapped.

'I'm risking my life . . .'

'Then go! Now!'

When he didn't move she shoved past him and looked up and down the corridor. 'Come on, Prince. Quickly.'

Jamil took one step. His hefty body was clothed in an embroidered robe, stiff with pearls. He glanced sidelong at Seth. 'Come with us,' he said.

'I can't.'

'As you said, your life—'

'—Belongs to the god. Don't trust her. This isn't how it was planned.'

The Pearl Prince shrugged. 'So there are factions. But escape is escape.'

Seth caught his arm, desperate. 'There are guards outside. The mercenaries.'

Halfway through the door, Rhetia smiled an acid smile. 'I don't think we have to worry about them,' she said.

Alexos slipped restlessly off the table. 'But I want to go too, Mirany! I don't like Oblek going into danger by himself. He roars and shouts and fights too recklessly.'

She had put the gold disc back in the crystal box; now she looked up at him in surprise. 'The Jackal said—'

'The Jackal is very clever. But he told you to look after me, and that's silly. Because I'm much older than you, Mirany.' He came over and took her hand. '*And Seth is in danger.*'

For a moment she was still. Then she opened the door

and glanced out into the teeming pyramid. Three men sat on a bench outside. One nodded at her mildly, but after Rhetia's escape she knew they would be alert, and there was no time for heated argument. Instead she came back in, ran to the small outer door and tugged.

It was locked.

She thumped on it in fury.

Alexos was watching her.

'Do something!' she hissed.

He said patiently, 'You were the one who put it away, Mirany.'

For a moment she had no idea what he meant; then she flung the box open and snatched out the sun-disc.

'This? But what—?'

'Just walk.' His voice was sad. '*Oh, Mirany, the way through the Gates requires only courage.*'

His small hand took hers. The door was copper-sheathed, dusty, spider-creviced. She felt its smoothness, pushed her palm against it, knew it would never open for any power she had. And then she held up the disc.

Dawn. Pale light. Growing in the room, strengthening until its heat was the heat of the sun at noon, the infernal, burning furnace of the desert, the metal door incandescent and white, scorching, running down in dribbles, its rivets loosing, its shape quivering like mirage.

A golden gateway melted in its heart.

They walked through, into the street.

With a shock, Seth understood.

Alone in the room after they had gone he realised that the building was never this silent, and only the mercenaries could have kept people out. Could Ingeld be in the plot with her? Was that possible?

He flung the door wide and ran after them, headlong, knowing only panic and a sudden sense of certainties collapsing under his feet like oubliettes.

It was a trap and Jamil was the bait.

The marble corridors were cool, the walls faintly gleaming with moisture. He raced by bath suites and changing rooms, through slants of hot sun that striped the tiles, past urns of red geraniums wilting in the heat. Hurtling into the palaestra, he stopped dead.

Ingeld was waiting. Rhetia was running towards him, Jamil behind her. The Pearl Prince stopped, looking confused, and wary.

Rhetia turned. 'It's all right!'

'These are Argelin's men.'

'Not now. Now they work for me.'

'You've paid them?'

She shrugged. 'They fear the god. They're simple men. I've told them—'

'You fool.'

Her face flushed with anger, but he was angry too, a cold, massive wrath.

'They have tricked you, priestess.' He looked over her head at Ingeld. The tall mercenary wore his bronze helmet, the cheekpieces slicing his face into angles; his ice-blue eyes watching coldly. 'Do you not see?'

She looked. Ingeld's sword was in his hand. 'The Prince is right, lady,' he said. 'Now, where are the others?'

'Why not go straight in?' Oblek put his foot into the Fox's clasped hands and heaved himself up. The roof tiles of the bath suite were almost too hot to touch; he yelped and went to wrap his cloak round his hands but the Jackal snapped, 'Because this place is far too quiet.'

The tomb-thief slithered swiftly to the gable and peered over, only his eyes visible in the dark wrappings round his face.

'Come on.' He gave signals; his men on the opposite roof ducked and vanished. Oblek clambered on, tiles wheezing and creaking under his weight. Fox came last, knives drawn, wary.

The buildings were silent. Over flat roofs and tiled ridges the Jackal led them, a lean figure, his shadow small in the noon sun. Around deserted courtyards they scrambled, past cisterns to catch precious rainwater, the soft lead scorching under their hands. Lizards flicked away; basking snakes hissed. Under Oblek's boot a black scorpion raised its menacing sting. When they reached the ridge of the pediment, the Jackal stopped and crouched.

'Listen.'

They heard distant noises from the Port, hammering on the breeze. And very close, voices. Carefully, the breeze drying their sweat, they climbed to the stone parapet, and peered over.

'There are no others!' Rhetia drew herself up with a glare of pure hatred. 'Did you think I couldn't plan this myself?'

Ingeld shrugged. 'Women can't plan.'

Ignoring her fury he glanced over her shoulder down the colonnaded loggia; Seth jerked back instantly into the shadows.

Jamil folded his arms, resigned. 'She's right. I have seen no one else.'

'You would say that, Prince, but I'm afraid none of the Nine are to be trusted.' Argelin stepped out from the alcove where he had been leaning and walked up to Rhetia. He looked at her, a careful, cold scrutiny. Then he said, 'I had been sure you were dead, you and Mirany. I see now that the hateful Queen preserved you. She and I fight our war through small mortals like you, people who think they are important. But I have you now, and there will be no more escape.'

Rhetia's face was white. She must have been devastated, but Seth admired her icy calm. 'Then kill me like you killed Hermia,' she said, defiant. 'Because I'll never stop working against you.'

Argelin didn't move, didn't breathe. Then he held out his hand; Ingeld put a sword in it. Seth went cold. He had to do something. The General's face was rigid with a purpose that terrified him. He leapt up, and at the same instant, among the pillars of the colonnade, he saw Mirany.

And Alexos.

'No!' he hissed. 'Go back!'

Mirany had something in her hand, a small disc. Breathless, she gasped, 'I thought you were in trouble!'

'Not until you brought him! Get him out of here!'

Too late. Argelin had heard the echoes, had barked an order; now he and Ingeld were striding down between the pillars, the guards fanning out on each side. Seth swore viciously, turned and flattened his back against the rounded pillar. 'Go, Archon, please! If they find out you're alive, we're both finished!'

The boy looked as if he would cry. He stepped back. 'I'm sorry, Seth. I forgot that.'

But in Mirany's ear his words were different.

Unseal the Oracle.

She turned, aghast. 'All those stones . . .'

I mean speak my words.

'Show them I'm alive? But why?'

You do not question a god.

Argelin yelled, 'Seth?'

Mirany moved. She grabbed Seth's hand and twisted her own arm up behind her back. 'Get hold of me. Now!'

'Mirany . . .'

'It's the only way.' Before he could answer she screamed and ran out, kicking and punching him. Appalled, he hung on, gripping her tight as Argelin raced round the pillar and caught hold of her chin, tugging up her face to stare at it with grim joy. Mirany twisted and fought. 'Let me go!' she screamed. 'Let me go!'

And Seth heard his own voice. It was cocky and pleased with itself and he hated it. It said, 'Just look who I found spying on you, Lord King.'

Blood for a spell

Chaos erupted.

There was a yelled command from the roof; as the mercenaries stared up weighted nets were flung on them, the mesh spreading as it fell. Ropes dropped; beggars and thieves slid down, well-armed men in ragged cloaks, only their eyes visible.

Argelin grabbed Mirany, dragged her back. 'Get hold of Jamil,' he raged.

Ingeld ran, shouting in his guttural language, but his men were already mired in nets, hauled off their feet, swung and tangled, swords and greaves and spears spiking out of the struggling bundles. Seth saw Fox skid down a rope and grab the Pearl Prince; Rhetia whipped a dropped sword from the paving and backed, slashing it efficiently in front of her. 'Mirany,' she screamed, 'come on!'

Mirany stood very still. She was breathing hard but made no attempt to move and Argelin had a firm grip on her hair. 'Very wise,' he hissed in her ear.

Seth glanced behind. The shadows were empty. Alexos had vanished.

Expertly the thief-army cut down the remaining soldiers. A row of swords and sharp spearpoints held Ingeld at bay; he snatched out a small horn and blew it, three urgent notes. Behind the pillars of the colonnade Seth glimpsed Jamil being hurried away: he wondered how the Jackal would get the well-known figure of the Pearl Prince through the streets.

Argelin was looking up at the roof, white with wrath. Very quietly, almost to himself, he said, 'At last.'

The Jackal stood, perfectly balanced, on the vast stone pediment. In the high wind a few long fair hairs streamed from his dark scarves; his animal eyes looked down at the General and Mirany far below. Under his feet, ancient carvings of the Nine enacted rituals; a procession of fluteplayers and flower girls and priests from the City paced in silent stone along the frieze.

For a long moment tomb-thief and King surveyed each other. Then Argelin thrust Mirany into Ingeld's grip, and stepped forward.

'Who are you?'

The Jackal folded his arms. After a moment his voice came, clear and mocking.

'Your shadow. Every god should have one.'

Noises. Shouts, running feet.

Go! Seth thought desperately. But the Jackal didn't move.

'We can come to an agreement.'

Argelin's laugh was sour. 'The girl stays here. And I will tear apart every hovel in this port until I find you and that bitch, Rhetia. Your head, thief, will drip from the Desert Gate.'

The Jackal nodded. 'And I say this. You will not enter the tombs. The god forbids it. Any man that enters the halls of Shadow will find the dead awaiting him, and the revenge of the dead is beyond horror, and beyond the nightmares of men, Lord King.' He raised his voice. 'You, ice warriors, listen to me. Has he told you there are a million tunnels down there where a man might wander till he prays to die of thirst, a labyrinth of rooms and tunnels, traps and killing devices? The Shadow guards his kingdom with crawling creatures and insects that eat men alive. Cries echo down there, the trapped whispers of the lost who have never found the Garden. Above all there is darkness, unbroken since the god was born. That darkness is madness. Stay out of the tombs, Northern men.'

Half a phalanx came racing into the palaestra. Argelin

yelled, 'Kill him!' and twenty spears whistled into the air in seconds, but the pediment was empty, and they bounced and rattled on the hot stones.

Argelin was still. Then he turned, ominously slowly, on Mirany. She faced up to him, not once looking at Seth behind him.

The General folded his scarred arms. His bronze armour was tarnished, his scarlet cloak unwashed. Dark hollows lay under his eyes; new wrinkles in his skin were grey with dirt.

'It certainly seems to be possible,' he said coldly, 'for the dead to come back.'

He reached out and took the gold disc from her fingers. Turning it over, he looked at it carefully. 'What is this?'

Mirany managed a smile. 'A gift the god sends you, Lord Argelin.'

As he looked down at it, a small insect crawled out from under it, a jewel-blue thing like a gnat, tiny as a pinhead.

It bit him.

'I've got to find him!' Oblek thrust a spare knife into his belt.

The Jackal said, 'You heard Argelin. He'll tear the Port apart. We're evacuating.'

The Lair was swarming like an upturned hive. They must have done this before, Oblek knew, because even the furniture was being dismantled round him, weapons shifted, coin-making devices boxed, nets of stolen goods lowered and passed swiftly along efficient lines of men. He had run back through the streets, shoving everyone out of his way, had searched the whole pyramid, yelling the boy's name, been sworn at, ignored. But Alexos wasn't here.

'He'll come back.' The Jackal thrust some papers into the fire.

'What good will that be if we're on the Island? I have to look for him.'

'He's the god.' The Jackal turned to face him. 'He can look after himself.'

'He's a ten-year-old boy. He'll be scared.'

For a moment they were silent in all the uproar. Until Oblek sank on to a stool and growled, 'What the hell was he doing, coming after us! What was Mirany doing?'

'She did it for Seth.' Rhetia had come in, with Chryse behind her. 'Don't you see that?'

The two girls looked very different. Chryse hefted a large bag stuffed full of what looked like dresses, probably from the tomb-plunder. Scarlet silk and jewelled collars spilled out from it; thin chains of gold and malachite hung at her neck, fine clasps glinted in her hair. Rhetia wore a simple red tunic, the sword belted round it, a bow slung on her shoulder. Her hair was tied back severely and she looked tense with self-disgust.

She went up to the Jackal. 'I'm sorry. I'm the one who's

brought all this down on us, before you were ready. Jamil was right; I was a fool to trust Ingeld.'

He looked at her hard. 'It was a costly mistake.'

'Let me do something. Let me fight.'

'There'll be no fighting.'

She stared at him, appalled.

Oblek growled, 'Of course there bloody will be.'

'I promised Mirany to take the Island without bloodshed.' He looked up. 'But there is one thing you can do, if you have the courage.'

She glared at him. 'Name it.'

'I need someone to sail out to the Emperor's fleet. Jamil will write a message.'

Her eyes were bright. 'I'll go.'

Oblek said, 'And what's to stop her tearing up the letter and telling him just what she wants? Which is war, and her as Speaker at the end of it.'

The Jackal watched Rhetia. 'Nothing,' he said quietly. 'Except her respect for the god's wishes.'

'I'm not going,' Chryse said hastily. 'I'm going to the Island. I don't like boats.'

A crash echoed from somewhere in the building. Oblek heaved himself up. 'They're close.' He turned at the door. 'I'll find Alexos. But don't wait for me. Take the Island and hole up there.'

Rhetia said, 'Is there a ship?'

'A harbourful, Holiness. How you will steal one . . .'

She smiled, haughtily. 'Don't worry, I'll have no trouble.'

When she was gone the Jackal raised an eyebrow. 'No,' he said quietly. 'I doubt you will.'

Suddenly the pyramid was empty, sunlight shafting through its crystal apex.

'Just us,' Chryse giggled, nervously. The Jackal nodded. Then he sat down and looked at her.

She stared. 'Come on! Everyone else has gone!'

He didn't move. Instead he scratched his cheek with one delicate finger. 'Explain why I should take a spy to safety.'

'I'm not a spy!'

'Mirany feared so. I agree. You did not spend two months alone on the Island, Holiness.'

Shockingly loud, a door crashed in; two of the merceneries charged through, sweeping axes before them. Seeing the vast space they stopped in amazement. The Jackal caught Chryse's hand and pulled her back into his room, sliding a bar across the entrance.

He turned, and his voice was hard. 'I'm leaving you here unless you tell me the truth.'

Chryse's pretty face reddened. It crumpled into a sort of wailing cry, but he just shrugged and went to the outer door.

'Oh, *wait*!' she screamed. 'All right! All right! It's true. I gave myself up to Argelin.'

'He kept you prisoner?'

'In that horrible Headquarters. He's quite mad, you do know that? He's obsessed with Hermia. All he thinks about is getting her back.' Another crash. She looked in terror at the door. 'Don't leave me with those men,' she breathed.

'How can he get her back?'

'Sorcery. He sent me to the Island in case Mirany came. Or it would have been my blood.'

The Jackal drew a sharp breath. '*Blood? For a spell?*'

'Oh yes. There's a witch called—'

'Manto.' His voice was bleak.

Chryse pouted. 'Well, if you already knew! Oh, look, please can we go! Manto has magic. He took me there but she said I wouldn't do. She wants the blood of a Speaker to raise a Speaker. Mirany escaped at the Island, but he's got her now.' She shrugged, a little smugly. 'I'm really, really sorry of course, but then Mirany's always been so—'

He was across the room and grabbing her arm; she gasped breathlessly.

'She knew Mirany was alive? Does this Manto see anything else in her mirror? What about Seth? *Does she know about Seth?*'

'I don't know!'

The door shuddered; she stared at it white faced. In seconds the Jackal was at the outer door. He wrenched it open, wondering for a puzzled second how Mirany could have got out. Then they were racing up the alley, twisting and turning down the network of lanes and steps until

Chryse was lost and breathless. At the next corner the Jackal peered round. He swore, jerked back and looked at the bag. 'Open that.'

'What?'

'Get that stuff out!'

Five minutes later a tall lord in a green robe stumbled drunkenly up the street, followed by a slave girl carrying his half-empty luggage. Staggering past the mercenary patrol, the Jackal slurred, 'Hello, good men.'

Eyes like blue ice through the slits of bronze, the tallest of them lingered behind. 'Get into your house, painted prince, if you still have one. Tonight we tear this place apart.' He took a step nearer. 'Your slave girl is pretty.'

Chryse shrank away; the Jackal scowled. 'She has a shrill tongue, friend, believe me.' He went to lurch on, but the Northerner stepped in front of him. He looked at the Jackal's fair hair. The flicker of doubt was barely in his face when the Jackal's blow doubled him breathless; another on the back of the neck delivered with both hands laid him in a crumpled heap in the doorway. Glancing towards the vanished patrol the Jackal stripped sword and knife.

'Take this,' he said, giving Chryse the knife. She thrust it into the bag quickly. 'Now move!'

'Did he recognize you?'

'Maybe.'

'Shouldn't you kill him then?'

He looked at her strangely. Then he said, 'Once I would have thought so.'

Round the next bend they dodged into a side lane. Chryse said, 'This isn't the way to the island!'

'Down here first.' Tall in the shadows of the alley he walked to a wooden door behind an upturned pigsty and thumped on it.

She looked round. 'Oh, hurry up!'

Smoke and a cloud of eerie blue gnats was swirling down the street. Somewhere houses were burning. From the North Gate, cries and shouts rose. A woman screamed in terror.

The Jackal stepped back and kicked the flimsy door down. Over his shoulder Chryse saw a wine seller's shop, stacked with dusty amphorae. The red-haired wine seller was lying on the floor among smashed shards of his wares. A dark pool spread under him, and it wasn't a fine vintage.

His throat had been cut.

Seth ran a hand through his hair in despair. He had no idea where Mirany had been taken or what was happening in the Port. But he could guess.

From the roof of the Headquarters building he stared up at the steep white streets. Smoke blurred the stars, its acrid stink rising in black columns above the harbour. He could see roofs on fire, mostly the rich palaces of aristocrats, and the streets seemed full of Ingeld's men, carrying gold and booty, kicking down the barred fronts of wine shops to loot the contents. Beside him, the optio stood in silent disgust.

'Does he know?' Seth muttered.

'If he does he doesn't care.'

'I hope . . . my father and sister . . .'

'They've a guard outside, scribe. Most people haven't. The shopkeepers, the merchants.' The optio chewed the corner of his mouth. 'This has been simmering for weeks, and now they have their excuse. Ingeld could take this whole Port if he reached out for it, like a ripe peach it would fall into his hand, and he will, mark me. You've seen the General. He's sliding into madness.'

Seth shivered. Then he said, 'Where is he?'

'Don't even think of it. When he gets these dark moods you leave him alone. I've seen him kill men for disturbing him.' The optio slapped his own cheek. 'And damn these bloody gnats! Another plague from the Queen.'

Seth turned and hurried down the stairs, the sand under his boot soles crackling. The corridors of Argelin's Headquarters were oddly silent, the usual bustle of scribes and soldiers subdued. In places the lamps had gone out, as if no one had bothered to refill them, and the few people that passed Seth kept their heads down, or carried their swords openly in their hands. He knew that the General's power was seeping away; he could feel fear and uncertainty oozing from the walls like slime. For years Argelin had ruled here and they had hated his tyranny, and yet now a new threat had sprung up, to him and the whole of the Two Lands. A foreign army already inside the walls, looting, killing, out of control.

He'd had the keys copied two days ago. Now he ran down to the lowest row of the cells and saw the guards here had gone too, maybe to join in the looting. The door was dingy and low and there were voices behind it. He unlocked it quickly and stepped in.

The priestesses sat or leaned around the walls, looking at him. They had that numbed look of prisoners who were losing hope, and one glance showed him Mirany wasn't here. The nearest – Persis, he thought – leapt up. 'I know you,' she hissed.

He flung them the keys. 'Get out. Get to the North Gate. You'll find a man called the Jackal; he'll get you on to the Island. Tell him I've gone to find Mirany.'

They moved quickly. Halfway out, Persis gasped, 'Is it rebellion?'

He shrugged. 'Only if it succeeds.'

Outside Argelin's room the empty niche of the Rain Queen was a dark hollow. Seth breathed a prayer to her and opened the door cautiously. 'Lord King?' he whispered.

The room was in darkness. One tiny nightlight flickered on the desk heaped with new orders and counterorders, the confusion he struggled with daily. It glinted on the glassy eyes of the tiger, the tarnished gold of the fruit bowl full of rotten pomegranates, a grey mass of soft mildew.

Seth moved across the littered floor. Ahead, in the dark, a murmur stopped him. It was a muttering, rapid, like a man in a fever. Edging round the zebra-skin couch, he saw where it came from.

There was a small door in the far wall that he had never seen open. He had assumed the General slept in that chamber; now he realized that the door was ajar, and a slit of light glimmered out on to the wall nearby, a red, ominous light, like flames.

Seth stepped silently up to it. He put his hand on the timber, felt its strength, the double thickness of metal bars welded across it. Then, barely breathing, he peered in.

It was a room of flame.

A room with every wall red as fire, glinting with veneers of sliced ruby set in faceted slabs. The floor was red too, trodden with the strange blood sand of the Pits of Kalessar; powdered remains of monstrous bones, more ancient than the mountains.

Argelin was crouching on the floor. His back was to Seth, and the murmur came from him, and he was rocking slightly as he spoke, head down, arms tight around himself. The mantra he chanted was a single word, breathed so quietly it was almost a wash of sound, a quiet wave lapping on a shattered beach.

'*Hermia*,' he whispered. '*Hermia. Hermia.*'

And all around him, lit by a thousand candles, she was there. Images of every size, of stone and terracotta and ivory and sandalwood stared down at him in unchanging accusation. Carved in jet, blue-faced in lapis, green in malachite, Hermia gazed from the shelves and tables of the fiery room; she stood tall, striding forward in white marble, sat on painted thrones, held out wooden arms over the sea, stood masked and regal before the Oracle. In the flicker of flamelight she was a glitter of angry eyes, a robe moving in a draught.

Seth couldn't move. He wanted to back out, but dared not. He thought he was silent, but his heart thudded and his breathing sounded enormous in this stricken place.

Argelin stopped praying. He raised his head, and Seth took one pace away but it was too late. Very carefully, with a terrible control, Argelin turned.

Red light played over him. He said nothing.

Seth wanted to gabble, to invent excuses, an apology. The silence was hard to breathe, charged with threat. Then the General stood, took a crooked bronze sword that lay on the table, and with one vicious deliberate crack smashed Seth back against the wall, pushing the tip deep into the skin of his neck.

Choking, dizzy, Seth kept still. He could feel the sharp point in his flesh, warm blood running.

'I'll never speak of this to anyone,' he whispered.

Close up. Argelin's eyes were black. 'You'll never speak of anything again.'

The blade felt huge. He couldn't breathe. Darkness

184

loomed before him; he wanted to fall into it, but some courage from deeper than he knew made him say, 'Ingeld's men are rampaging through the Port. People are dying.'

'Let them die.'

It was now. This was it.

He closed his eyes to stop the pain, said to the god, 'Help me.'

To his shock a voice answered him. It was not the god's; it was cold and laughing and it said, 'My dear Lord King, you seem to have found us the wrong victim.'

Slowly, Argelin released him.

Seth collapsed, pain throbbing in shoulders and forehead, clutching his throat where the blood seeped over his fingers. Huddled choking at the foot of the wall, he looked up.

Manto wore her black robe and carried her moon-crescent wand. She smiled calmly at Argelin, and he turned to her. He said nothing, but she nodded as if in answer.

'Yes, lord, the time has come. Everything is ready.'

Like a child, he said, 'Will I . . . be with her?'

'Oh, yes.' She put her plump hand comfortingly on his sleeve. 'You will be with her soon. I promise you that.'

They learn the nature of their enemy

I think you should answer, Mirany. It's not as if you can't hear me.

She sat without moving, against the wall.

Sulking is hardly becoming for the Speaker.

The wall was oddly warm, and rough. It was probably tufa, she thought, the soft rock mined deep into the extinct volcano. The whole Port was built of it. Argelin had put her in his strongest prison.

The voice sounded peeved now. *I know what it is. You think I should apologize.*

She smiled in the dark.

Would you like some light, Mirany? I can make it for you.

'Don't bother.'

For a long time, so long she thought he had gone, there was no sound. Then, far in the shadows of the cell, a child's contrite whisper.

All right. I'm sorry.

She didn't move; then she shook her head. 'No, you're not. Being sorry means wishing it had never happened.' Angry, she looked up into the dark. 'Is there a reason for me being here? Or is it all just some whim, some game you're playing with our lives like Alexos plays with his pets and his toy soldiers?'

She had annoyed him. She knew it, but she didn't care.

'You lied to me! Seth wasn't in any danger till we got there. And if you're sorry, get me out of here! Blast the world open, break the walls wide and pluck me out in your fingers. You're a god, aren't you! You can do that!'

Her voice echoed in the vaulted spaces of the cell. Out of the crevices a mouse peered, then came and sat by her knee, a small, shivering, terrified thing.

To have the god possess you is frightening, I know. Look how this creature is almost dead from fear. I can feel its tiny heart, Mirany, beating so fast. I can feel your heart. And Seth's.

'Seth's?' She scrambled up.

He's coming. Don't be afraid. Trust me.

Footsteps. Not just his but someone else with him; a low rumble of voices. Then the rusty slither of the chain, and the door was forced open, its swollen frame shoved wide.

An oil lamp slipped in, held by a shadow. At first it

187

seemed so bright she had to shield her eyes with her hand.

'Get up.'

It was Seth, but the roughness of his voice warned her not to speak. She scrambled to her feet, dusting the soft rock from her hands and clothes; he came close and grabbed her arm.

'Don't try anything,' he muttered.

She let him lead her to the door. As she passed she glimpsed the other man; he was enormous, shaven-headed and carrying a bent bronze sword, its edge wickedly sharp. He looked like an executioner, and for a moment dread turned her cold, but then she remembered where she'd seen him before.

At Manto's.

Manto's?

They hurried along strangely deserted corridors and dark stairways. She wanted to ask where everyone was but couldn't, so she asked the god, but when he answered he sounded preoccupied and a little concerned.

I'm afraid sand has been in our eyes, Mirany. We have been blind.

Then they went through a doorway. The big slave was first; in her ear, Seth breathed, 'Take this.'

A cold sliver of metal slid into her fingers. She slipped the knife into her sleeve.

They hurried through a room, a tumbled mess of luxury, then into a blood-red chamber that filled her with fear.

Because Argelin and Manto were waiting there, and behind them clustered a thousand images of the Rain Queen, but in each the face had been expertly remodelled as Hermia's; the proud shrewd features she had known so well.

'What is this?' she said in horror.

Argelin didn't speak. He looked tense, arms tight around himself. But Manto motioned the slave closer and came over. With the tip of the moon-wand she lightly touched Mirany's cheek.

'This is your death-chamber, sweetie,' she said.

Oblek climbed down the wall and crouched in the parched garden.

The fountains were dry, the undergrowth crackling with heat. Strange jewel-blue gnats crawled on his skin; he scraped them off, irritably. Then he drew his sword and crept into the inner courtyard.

'Archon?' he whispered.

The Palace was a white ruin. Everything of any value must have been taken long ago. Wandering through the warren of broken doorways and loggias, he stepped over the spilled cages of the Archon's pets, the trampled remnants of toys. In the jungle chamber the trees had grown wild; a few stray parakeets chattered, rainbow flashes in the green, but the monkeys had gone, looping down into the Port after food, and only a solitary tortoiseshell cat slumbered in the deserted halls.

'Archon!'

The boy must be here. Where else could he go? And the Port was in uproar; Oblek had only got through the streets by violence and threats and breaking a guard's nose.

In the kitchens rats scraped for spilled corn, and in the Room of Sapphire the thin-sliced precious stone of the walls had been prised away, leaving bare mudbrick. Oblek paused under the window. He recognized the small chest, painted with scorpions, lying on its side. He righted it, and after a moment without hope, opened it.

The lyre was still there.

Not valuable enough to steal, obviously.

He reached in and took it out, slid off the oiled cloth and turned the pegs. Small, wobbling notes hummed under his fingers. He dropped the sword and sat heavily, sliding his bulk down on to the floor. When he had it tuned to perfection, he began to play.

The North Gate was a battleground.

Hurtling round into the chaos, the Jackal saw that Fox's men had taken the gate and opened it wide. The thief-army was already streaming out through it, but more and more of Ingeld's men were running from streets and alleys, dumping their plunder, hurtling into the fight.

Grabbing Chryse he said, 'Use that knife if you have to,' and dragged her into the fray, slashing his way through. Surprise and ruthlessness got them halfway; then the

Fox's men swooped around them, a tight shield of bodies. Breathless, the Jackal wiped sweat from his face and said, 'Is Oblek here?'

'No, and we can't wait. Nearly everyone's out. Sifa's sent word they hold the Island; the Bridge is being cut right now.'

The Jackal nodded. He pushed Chryse towards the gate. 'Go to the Island, Holiness.'

She turned, then swung back. Her pretty face was dirty, her blonde hair tangled and she still clutched the half-empty bag.

'The others! The rest of the Nine. You said they'd be here . . .'

'Seth's job. It's too late.'

'But you have to wait for them!'

The Fox dodged a flung spear. 'Lady, we can't hold this gate for ten more minutes!'

Chryse glared. 'You have to! What use is the Oracle without the Nine! Without a Speaker.'

The Jackal's smile was almost admiring. 'Oh I'm sure you can think of someone as Speaker, Holiness.'

He drew her back into the rumbling arch of the gate. Through it the thief-army was streaming, some driving waggons loaded with food and weapons. Beggars and hetairas, street urchins, painted women were running, and among them terrified families fled the town's sack. Traders raced with their goods; corn sacks, pots, amphorae of precious water. Donkeys brayed, slaves sweated under heavy loads. The road was littered with dropped and trampled possessions. Beyond, over the pitiless desert, the City loomed, its dark Archons frowning, the gates locked, the walls lined with the hastily armed servants of the Dead.

A big man in a ragged coat was discreetly escorted by. He turned, amazed. 'Holiness?'

Chryse stared. 'Lord Jamil!'

'Take her with you.' The Jackal pushed Chryse. 'Hurry.'

'But . . .'

'We'll wait as long as we can!' He turned back to the seething streets. 'But if they don't come soon, they'll never come.'

'Too right, chief.' Fox spat, then looked up. He turned his scarred face to the wind, as if something sweet drifted under the clash of bronze, the stink of sweat. 'Can you hear music?' he muttered.

She was led to a chair; her legs felt weak and she was glad to sit. Manto stood beside her.

Over her short grey hair the woman had put on a mask, and Mirany shivered because the sorceress's eyes gleamed now through the fixed death gaze of a Sphinx, its long dark hair cut from a dozen corpses and plaited in a thousand tiny braids. On the forehead a scarab in blue and gold spread its wings; small hanging crescents of silver tinkled and clinked as the woman turned.

In a voice of echoes the mask said to Argelin, 'Her throat must be cut.'

Mirany swallowed. She gave a desperate glance at Seth; he was shadowy in the darkness.

Argelin nodded. Then he said to the slave, 'Get out.'

The man glanced at his mistress.

'I need him.' The murmur whispered from the hideous lips.

'Then let him do it, quickly.'

Manto sounded as if she was smiling. '*You* require Hermia from the dead. *You* must do it, Lord King.'

Mirany lifted her eyes and looked at him; he stared back. He was beyond appealing to, she knew, caught up in the torment of his remorse. He would kill her like an animal, without feeling.

Is this what you want? she screamed at the god. Aloud, she said, 'This is folly! You don't really believe she can do this! No one can bring back the dead!'

Argelin turned to Seth. 'Hold her.'

Seth came forward. He stood behind Mirany and brought her arms round; slipped the knife down her sleeve into her hand. She felt him grip her wrist and give it the smallest firm shake. His hand was warm and slippery with sweat.

Argelin turned for the crooked sword. In that moment the slave was behind him; Manto gave a nod; Mirany gripped her knife. She would fight. She would sell her life dearly, she swore.

But the god's command thundered in her ear, and shook the room and the Port and shattered all her certainties. *Not Argelin. Save Argelin.*

Astonished, disbelieving, she saw the slave, the gleam of bronze, in an agony of despair screamed, 'Behind you!'

Despite himself Argelin turned; then Seth was sent sprawling, the slave's brawny arms flung tight round the General, hugging him in a bear grip of bronze. They roared with fury, raged and fought; furniture toppled but the slave held on, and as Seth crawled up from his dizziness he saw Manto raise the sword, ready to slash down, to cut into Argelin's heart.

The woman's eyes gleamed through the mask; her voice rang in triumph. 'Give my love to Hermia, Lord King!'

Then she froze.

She froze so still she seemed not even to breathe. Because behind her mask, the tip of Mirany's knife pressed very gently into the vein under the ear.

Oblek played a song.

It was a song of battle, of death and treachery. He sang the eternal exploits of the Archons, their loves and fears. The music moved through rooms and deserted halls, across slants of moonlight on the wrecked floors. It hummed and echoed down stairways; in courtyards spiders slid into the corners of webs; mice crept out, quivering, to listen. As he made the song his own he wove words into it, closing his eyes and letting his deep voice soar, creating an incongruous beauty from the lips and throat and fingers of a fat sweating man, scorched by the sun, scarred by violence. The song was the god's own song, a dream of rain, of its soft patterings in the desert, of tiny craters plopping into the sand. It soothed heat and itches, slaked the throat, ran and trickled, gathered in pools on the marble floors.

Oblek knew the whole palace listened; he heard the slitherings of snakes, oozing out of their cool holes, the minute scuffles of scorpions scuttling in ungainly nervous rushes towards him. He heard the music draw them, all the god's tiny fevered life; sensed as he sang the words the slight creak of the door, the thin dark figure that slid in and stood hesitantly behind him.

He didn't stop. Not until the boy had padded over and sat down next to him, warm against his body. Not until the song had reached its end, dying into a trickle of sound like a spring bubbling in the desert. Then, in the aftermath of the soft chords he raised his head and said, 'I knew you were here, Archon.'

I'm not sure that I am, the boy whispered.

'We have to go to the gate, old friend.'

Alexos sighed, a small sadness. He slid his thin arm around Oblek's thick elbow.

All the gates, he said. He put out a hand and stilled the

strings and in the sudden silence asked, 'Are you afraid of dying, Oblek?'

'All men are, Archon.'

'But if I asked you, you'd come, wouldn't you? Even to the Land of the Dead?'

The big man put his arm round the boy's thin body and hugged him. 'Through all the Gates of the Underworld, old friend.'

'Hey! You!'

The Jackal turned. He saw a brown-haired girl helping an old man. 'You're the one. Seth sent us . . .'

He yelled, 'Fox!' Then in the same breath, 'Where are the others?'

'Coming.'

Dodging across the square he saw a huddle of released prisoners, among them six girls.

'Which are you?'

'Persis. Watcher-of-the-Stars.'

'Then get yourself through the gate, Holiness.' His long eyes scanned the group anxiously; then he caught her arm. 'Where's Seth?'

'Gone after Mirany.' She shook her head, fretful. 'Listen! Ingeld is bringing his whole force up through the Port. You should get your men through the gate and barricade it. If you do it now you might still make it to the Island. Otherwise you'll all be cut to pieces here.'

He nodded, pushing her on; she ran hastily after the others.

In the uproar the clash of armour was loud; behind it grew a new, sinister rumble, the tramp of an army, the unmistakable tread of a thousand men marching. The Jackal yelled an order; at once the thief-gang broke off the fight and paced back, a rag-tag of bristling spearpoints. On the far side of the square the alleys and streets were a sudden mass of gleaming bronze.

'Everyone out!' The Jackal raced up the steps to the rampart; he stared down grimly over the row of rotting heads.

'*Where are they?*' he breathed.

The Fox spat. 'Even if they come, Chief, only a god could get them through.'

For a moment the Jackal hesitated; the wind caught his fair hair, a scatter of blue gnats drifted down on him.

He glanced up at them.

Then, his voice grim, he said, 'Barricade the gate.'

'Manto is plotting with Ingeld.' Seth's voice was rapid, panicky. He fought to steady it. 'She was going to kill you while Ingeld took the Port. Don't you see! She's been using your . . . your desire to see Hermia.'

'And now I never will.' Argelin turned; with a sudden savage fury he drove the sword into the belly of the slave. The man had stepped back; he collapsed with a strange airless gasp of amazement and pain; fell forward in a twitching, bleeding heap. Mirany clamped both hands over her mouth in horror.

Manto stood perfectly still. They had taken the knife and wand from her; now Argelin whirled on her and snatched the mask away. Her face was flushed, but her black eyes were cold with contempt.

'Ah, General.' She smiled, calmly. 'What a fool you are. To be led by the nose and tricked with mirrors and incense. Yes, I would have killed you and the girl; been Speaker to a new Oracle under a new King, who is even now conquering your realm because all you can think about is Hermia, your own victim picked to bones long ago by the sharks.'

She stepped forward, ignoring his shuddering anger, the bloodstained blade.

'There is no way back for the dead, Lord King. You murdered her and you will never forget her cry. Despair will drive you deeper into madness. All your life, for months and years you will suffer that remorse, dripping like snake venom into your mind until it eats your reason away, corrodes every thought and memory, poisons every night. You'll dwindle to a tormented old man, despised by the people, hated by the gods.'

She was close to him, her small eyes fixed on his. 'End it now, Argelin. Turn the sword on yourself. Go to her quickly. What use is your kingdom to you, your people in riot, your gold spent on soldiers who betray you? No one loves you, Argelin, no one cares for you. Soon they won't even hate you any more. You will be a laughing-stock.'

In the silence of the scarlet chamber, the General's face was fiery. He raised his eyes and looked at her, and his voice was a whisper. 'Seth . . .'

'I'm here,' Seth said, but Manto laughed.

'Even your Secretary betrays you. Who else gave the girl the knife? Surely you knew he is a spy for the Jackal.'

Argelin didn't move. Then he lifted the sword, but at the same moment Mirany ran across the room, grabbed the gold sun-disc from the table, and held it out to him. 'Wait! Don't use the sword. Use this.'

He looked at it as if he could not focus. Then his voice cracked, hoarse.

'What is it?'

She didn't know, but the answer came without knowledge.

'The way to Hermia. The god sends it to you. The god says this. *Enter my realm, Lord Argelin. If you dare, go down into the Underworld and find her. You have until the Day of the Scarab. Journey through the Nine Gateways. Defy the anger of the Rain Queen, and bring Hermia back. Alive.*'

She felt strange. Her voice was speaking the god's words, but it wasn't her voice, it was a boy's voice, high and clear, and they could all hear him, they were all turning and watching him, as he walked forward from the darkness of the room, Alexos in his dirty white tunic with a scab on his knee, the Archon returned from the desert, the beautiful young god stepping down from the pedestal in the Temple.

Argelin stared; then gave Seth one icy look. 'I should have known you were a liar,' he said. He turned, and took the sun-disc from Mirany's hand, held it up.

'Another trick?'

'No trick.'

'Then show me how to use it, Archon,' he said.

And then Mirany knew that what she had cried out for in the prison had come true, because Alexos spread his hands and the world split wide, and the walls of the flame-red room cracked and splintered. They opened, to show a wide tunnel running into darkness, and without a word, without a single look behind, Argelin strode into it, Alexos running beside him.

A shape detached itself from the darkness and took Mirany's elbow; Oblek whispered, 'Come, Holiness. Our place is with the Archon.'

He led her into the dark hollow. At the brink she turned. 'Seth . . .'

'Don't go without me!' Terrified, Seth flung himself forward. 'Wait. Mirany. *Wait!*'

He reached out for her, saw his own face reflected grotesquely in the scarlet stone of the wall, slammed his palms against it, thumped it and kicked it, flung his whole body against it in a bruising shock of despair.

'Mirany! Archon!'

It was solid. It had never opened. It could never have opened.

He turned, heart thudding.

Manto had fled. From the streets rang the cacophony of a city torn apart.

The Jackal waited. He stood alone on the Bridge, staring back up the Desert Road. From the distant gate, axes pounded; fire rose in columns above the burning Port.

On each side the desert lay dark under the stars, swarming with blue gnats. He could see them rising like a cloud from the Port, imagined their bites, the irritation, the second plague of the Rain Queen.

Behind him, Fox said, 'There!'

A figure. Exhausted and still running, falling and running again. Coming from the Palace, where the defences were broken. Behind it, in a sudden outpouring of dark bronze, the gate was breached, a mob of soldiers roared out.

The Jackal said, 'Cut the ropes!' He flung down his sword and ran, fast as a sand cat, out along the road, grabbing Seth and dragging one arm over his shoulder, hauling him along. Arrows slashed around them, slicing into the sand. Breathless, barely able to see, Seth staggered on, the Bridge shaking before him; the wood hollow under his feet, moving and slithering even as he was dragged across, shaking wider and wider until, as he collapsed on the green cliffside of the Island, there was one terrible crack and the whole immense timber construction crashed down behind them, plummeting into the waves with a vast upswoosh of water.

The Jackal was bent double, gasping for breath; it was Fox who had to ask, 'Where's the boy? Where's Mirany?'

Seth shook his head. He was drained, lost.

'Gone,' was all he could say.

The Fifth Gate
Of the Triple-faced Dog

Once I entered an ant hill. The creatures were busy; they hurried past, intent on their work, a million scurryings of food bringing, egg laying, war, repairs. They crawled by me and over me as if I was not there.

People are like that most of the time, but then they go to sleep and they dream. And when they dream they step outside the hurrying world. They see the mermaids and the naiads and the monsters. They understand the intricate plot, and are satisfied.

It doesn't last. Only poets and madmen glimpse it in the daylight, and they can spend lifetimes finding the words to explain.

A god does not explain.

It would be far too tedious.

People must muddle through for themselves.

He is chosen to hear fear's voice

Unlike the locusts, the jewel-blue gnats did not fall from the sky. They hatched out of crevices in brick, out of drains and sewage holes and roof tiles. The smoke of the burning houses seemed to enrage them; they drifted in clouds, through the smallest crack. Their bites inflamed quickly; a few scratches and the arm or leg was sore and red. Soon the sores stung.

Pa bathed Telia's ankle with a few drops of water and muttered under his breath. Then he tied a clean silk bandage round it.

She looked up at him resentfully through her dark fringe. 'It hurts.'

'Don't scratch it. Play with the monkeys.'

Thank the god for the monkey toy. During all the terrible night and following day of the Port's sack he had hidden with her in the cellar of the house, the door barricaded. Outside, terror raged. Arms tight round her, he had listened to the smashing, the screams, the running feet. Telia had cuddled the monkeys and tipped them upside down, taken them apart and put them back together obsessively. Finally she had slept with them.

Late in the night he had unbolted the door and climbed fearfully to the roof, and seen the Port burning, the harbour blotted out by smoke, strange lights on the Island. The house had been ransacked, most of the food taken, whether by the mercenaries or anyone else he didn't know. Picking up a chair and righting it he had prayed then for Seth, remembering Mirany's promise. Surely a god would not lie. The boy was under his protection, whatever happened.

It was he himself and Telia he should worry about. The guard on the door had vanished at the first sign of trouble; Pa scowled at the thought of the wasted gold coins. They had three amphorae of water in the cellar; that might last two weeks. He had no idea what was happening at the public wells, and didn't want to venture out. Now, sliding the shutter of the high room open lightly, he peered through the crack.

The street was hot and empty. A dead rat that had been lying there for a few hours was being picked clean by gulls, fighting and squabbling over the scraps of flesh. There was no other sound; the air stank of scorched wood. By creaking the window open a little further he could see the harbour, where the triremes lay in pieces, and out at sea the green misty bulk of the Island. Bronze glinted there, possibly near the Bridge.

A movement below disturbed the gulls; looking down he saw a girl wrapped in a dark cloak slinking up the street, and for a moment his heart thudded with the idea it was Mirany. Then she glanced up, and he saw she was thin and starved, her face painted with dark kohl around the eyes. That sort of girl. He drew back, but she cried out, 'Water! Please! Do you have any water? I have a child . . .'

Pa scowled.

She had come under the window, was gazing up. He cursed himself.

'Please! A tiny drop. Just a cupful.'

He looked down at her. 'Go away,' he said in a hard voice.

'We're desperate!'

'Go home. It's not safe.'

'I can pay. Gold.' She reached her hand up to him; it was dirty and thin. 'Or if you like . . .'

'NO!' Horrified he looked round, but mercifully Telia wasn't there. Then he sighed and cursed himself again. 'Wait there.'

He went to the cellar, filled a small jar of brackish water and brought it up, taking the barricades apart cautiously and opening the door barely enough for the container to slide through.

'Here,' he said.

It was snatched from him. 'May the god bless you and your family. May the Rain Queen watch over you.' A small hot kiss was pressed feverishly on to his palm; he shook her off, embarrassed.

'I don't want that. I want news. What's happening?'

She came close to the crack of the door; he heard the rustle of silk, smelt her sweet perfume.

'The Northern men have taken the Port; they've killed many and burned and rampaged. I'm so afraid! People say the Headquarters is crammed with stolen treasure, and that they have murdered Argelin!'

Pa's spine went to ice. 'Is that true?'

'No one has seen him. No one knows where he is.'

'And his people? His staff?'

'Killed or fled.'

Pa chewed his lip.

'There is resistance.' The girl's voice was quiet. 'A man calling himself the Jackal. You've heard of him?'

Pa nodded sourly.

'They say he's captured the Island, and the Nine priestesses are with him. They say he will reopen the Oracle and speak to the god, but Ingeld's army are encamped all round, and though the gnats torment them, the people on the Island are not bitten.'

'Pa? Who is it, Pa?' Sleepily Telia tugged at him. 'Is it Seth?'

'No.' But she had pulled the door open a fraction before he could grab it, and the hetaira saw him, and glanced quickly at Telia.

Annoyed, Pa growled, 'Go home now. And don't come back here.'

He slammed the door, bolted it, dragged the bar across and then heaped up more of the splintered furniture.

'She was pretty,' Telia said quietly.

Pa looked at her. Then he took her by the arm and led her back into the cellar.

The hetaira drank the water round the next corner. She threw the small jar down and pulled her cloak around her and then ran swiftly down the narrow streets, ducking under arches and past the smashed doorways of ruined buildings, expertly dodging approaching footsteps. Once, when one of the blond Northerners leaned out of an opium den and caught her by the waist she bit him, and as he yelled she stepped back and held up her hand, thrusting the scarab sign right in his face, because they were stupid, these ice men. Strong, but stupid.

He stared at it and said something in their language. Not waiting, she turned and ran on, under the wrecked lanes of fullers' cloth, across the piazza where the rubble of the Rain Queen's statue was still heaped, to the small door in the wall. She gave the knock and it opened. Upstairs, the room was dim and smoky. Manto stood gazing out through the latticed window.

'Well?' she said sourly, not turning.

The hetaira took down her veil and arranged her hair. 'I found them. Just where you said they would be.'

Manto nodded.

Then she smiled.

'It was an illusion. A trick.'

'I'm telling you, no! I saw her. Hermia. She spoke to him, said, "Find me."'

The Jackal shook his head. Turning to Fox he said, 'Get Phaedro up here.'

They waited in silence. Seth was drained and weary; though he had slept for hours in one of the servants' rooms he felt as if the strain of all the days in Argelin's madhouse had fallen on him at once, crashing down with a weight of misery and terror. And Mirany was gone, walking into an Underworld he could not even imagine, a tunnel that had appeared and vanished in a solid wall! He pushed the hair from his eyes and glanced up at the Jackal, standing tall on the terrace of the Upper House.

Across the harbour the Port lay silent and white in the sun. No one moved on its quays or streets and only a few small twists of smoke still rose among its buildings. But like a glimmer of movement in the blue hot sky, a barely seen myriad of glints, the gnat plague danced over the baking houses.

Fox came back with a small grimy man in a blue tunic. The Jackal said, 'Tell him,' and so Seth explained it all again, the vision Manto had made of Hermia in the mirror, the darkness of the room, the blood that had filled the glass.

When he had finished the Jackal said, 'Well?'

Phaedro sucked a tooth. 'Fairly standard, Chief. She set him in one place, right, and told him not to move?'

Reluctantly, Seth nodded.

'Then it was done with angled mirrors, and lights, probably behind a curtain. The vision would be an accomplice, maybe masked, certainly her face painted. The blood would have been in a small bladder under the rim of the mirror. Lights, smells, all these things contribute to scaring the mark witless before you start. Sounds like some classy fortune-telling con.'

Smoothly the Jackal said, 'Thank you, my friend. How are your illusions down at the Bridge?'

'Oh, we can make them think there are hundreds of us, Chief. As long as they don't attack.'

The man went back down the steps. Seth stared at his back gloomily.

'An expert.' The Jackal poured water into a cup and held it out. 'Worked in the theatre for years and ran nearly every con on the east side of the Port.' As Seth took the water the thief's hand held it tight a moment. 'Manto is dangerous, Seth, but she cannot conjure the dead. We have to believe that.' For a moment he almost sounded unsure himself; but then the long eyes slid away. 'Argelin would believe what he desired, but you, Seth, I would have thought you would have seen through it.'

'I was scared.' Seth looked up at him. 'Don't you understand! Every minute. Every second. You don't know what he's like! I was walking on eggshells. The wrong word, the least slip, and he turns on me. Twice he nearly killed me. And now he's with Mirany. And Alexos! And *Oblek*!' The thought filled him with dread.

The Jackal folded his arms. 'Maybe the god is a being just as unguessable.' He was watching the entrance of the Temple. 'Ah. Here they are.'

There were only seven of the Nine but they still looked impressive. They had spent hours ritually washing in some of the precious water; from somewhere they had found white dresses and smiling golden masks, looped with lapis and discs of crystal. The Watcher-of-the-Stars, Persis, had taken the lead; she had ordered the Temple to be purified with flowers and incense and all night the girls had swept and cleaned it with their own hands, bringing to the empty pedestal of the god milk and roses and pomegranates.

Now they came and sat on the terrace and the chairs, and as the masks came off the serenity went too, revealing hot, weary faces, Chryse falling instantly on the remains of the food, Gaia brushing back hair from her eyes.

'Is it done?' the Jackal said quietly.

Persis shrugged. 'The Temple is pure but empty.' She looked at him, then around at the makeshift tents pitched in the gardens, the thief-rabble and the hordes of refugees with their campfires and water stashes, the donkeys eating the flowering creepers on the Upper House. To make it worse, from the far side of the Island came the throaty displeasure of a thirsty elephant.

She sighed. 'How long can we last out here, Lord Osarkon?'

The Jackal laughed. 'Holiness, until Ingeld builds a new bridge. There is no way we can withstand his army.' He sat on the marble balustrade, his feet on the bench below. 'But I don't think he will attack us, not as yet. We are not a danger to him. His next move, obviously, will be to break into the tombs.'

There was silence. Into it, Chryse said, 'Those North people are awfully superstitious. Do you think—'

'I think their greed will lead them there. After all, Ingeld is not interested in the Oracle. That's Manto's desire. He wants gold and plenty of it, and to get out before the Emperor finally loses patience or discovers that his nephew is out of danger.'

'The City is strong.'

'It looks strong. But it is defended by fat eunuchs and

artists and slaves and scribes.' He turned to Seth. 'How long will they hold out?'

'About ten minutes,' Seth said gloomily.

In the silence that followed only bird cries cheeped; the flapping flock of finches that had come out of the desert to prey on the billion gnats. Alexos would have loved them; with a strange dismay Seth realized he missed the boy's bright curiosity. It was Persis who asked what everyone was burning to know.

'What has happened to Mirany?'

They all looked at Seth. He shrugged, exasperated. 'I've *told* you what happened! Do you think I'm lying, Holinesses? The god took them. Argelin, Oblek, Mirany. He's taken them into the Underworld to fetch Hermia back.'

Their eyes – blue and grey and dark – looked at him, then each other. Finally, Persis stood.

'We've been discussing what to do, and we've decided to try the Oracle. Perhaps the god will speak to one of us there. We want both of you to come with us.'

Seth glanced at her in amazement; then at the Jackal. The tomb-thief raised a hand. 'Holiness, I do not feel at all worthy of—'

'You are defending his precinct, Lord Osarkon. Men are forbidden usually, but it has been known, in emergencies, for men to make up the number of the Nine.' Persis looked at the others. 'Agreed?'

One by one, they nodded. Chryse stifled a giggle. The Jackal glanced at Seth, and stood. 'We should be honoured,' he said.

Seth had only seen the path to the Oracle once before. Now, walking the coiled slabs worn smooth by thousands of years of suppliants and Speakers was strange, as if he was an intruder, clumsy and ignorant. The entrance was a lintelled slab; the path led under it and upwards, through artemisia that whipped against his legs releasing its aromatic oil, and lavender where thousands of drowsy bees fumbled and buzzed. In front of him the Jackal strode, his long hair lifting in the breeze; ahead the girls walked in their white tunics, barefoot on the hot stones. They climbed through heat and flies and blown gnats into a cooler breeze, and as they came out abruptly on to a smooth circular platform Seth gasped at the expanse of the world that lay before him. Far out on the blue sea the unmoving ships of the cordon hung above perfect reflections of themselves, becalmed and ghostly, and even to the horizon the salt ocean was blue-green and complete. Turning, he saw the steep white huddle of the Port, and beyond it the desert, a wilderness of sand and rock and the Mountains that lay at the edge of the World, that he had once climbed. Nearer, a dark fortress lined with the colossal seated Archons, the City of the Dead towered, a grim shadow.

'This is awful,' Chryse murmured.

Turning, he saw the destruction. Piled broken wood,

charred bricks, heaps of rubble. Once, in the centre of this platform, the Oracle must have opened, but now the very stones were cracked with heat, the standing stone smashed.

The Jackal tugged a black cindered branch away. 'I'll get help, and get this cleared . . .'

'No.' Tethys came forward. 'No one else comes here. We'll clear it.'

Chryse looked appalled but the Jackal nodded. 'If you say so.'

The priestesses looked at each other, then joined hands. Chryse smiled coyly at Seth and held her fingers out; feeling uneasy, he took them. With Gaia on his other side, and the Jackal incongruously tall in the opposite half of the circle, they surrounded the destroyed and crammed Oracle.

First, the girls sang. Even the words were unknown to Seth, though he recognized some from fragments of ancient script he had seen in the tombs. It was a slow, eerie song, and as it rose up, the hot afternoon seemed to slow with it. Butterflies came and settled on the stones, their bright wings flattening; with a rustle and scrape that sent Seth's skin crawling a green snake oozed from the charred wood and lay basking, its tail twitching very slightly. Alert, he watched for scorpions, until across the circle he saw the Jackal's amused glance.

The song ended.

In the silence the bushes around him crackled with heat.

Far off, the soft wash of the waves hushed at the cliff foot; hammerings came faintly from the Bridge.

Persis said, 'Bright One, our offering.'

Chryse let go of Seth's hand and went out, crouching by the burned kindling and putting down a handful of grain. Then she poured oil and wine from small flagons, and Gaia placed a wreath of laurel leaves on top. They walked back, and took their places.

Seth licked dry lips. Sweat was moistening his forehead, but he couldn't wipe it away. A small stone in his boot irked him.

'Bright One, Mouse Lord, Rider of the Chariot of the Sun.' Persis had a clear voice; it rang over the platform. 'Hear me now. Give us guidance. Speak to us from your journey through the Gateways. Do not leave us, Lord, without advice. Because this is your Oracle, and we are your servants.'

The breeze lifted her hair. It rippled the pleated edges of the white tunics, touched Seth like fingers on his hot skin.

What did they expect? There already was a Speaker, wasn't there? Each of them was looking at the others, Chryse slyly, Gaia alert, Tethys almost frightened. Which of them would hear the god in her mind, his voice which must be like thunder crashing in? Seth shivered at the thought of it. What must it be like, to speak with a god?

But you know that already, Seth.

He stood perfectly, rigidly still.

Then, barely opening his lips he whispered, 'No!'

Chryse turned; she stared at him. The Jackal noticed.

You've heard my voice before. Perhaps you thought it was the sand slithering, or the trickle of water. Or the creak of the pen on parchment, the murmur of hieroglyphs. Perhaps you thought it was you yourself, thinking.

He dropped Chryse's hand. 'No. It's not . . . Please . . . It can't be me.'

Why not? Gods have their whims like anybody else.

They were all staring at him now. Chryse backed, wide-eyed; Persis came over and the Jackal was with her.

'Seth?' the tomb-thief said.

Clear my throat, Seth. Open my voice so I can speak. Because the world of the Shadow and the world of the Sun are very close. Don't be scared. Mirany isn't scared, and she always thinks you're so assured.

He stared. Then whipping round he shoved the Jackal aside, and began heaving at the burned timbers.

'Clear this!' he snapped. 'Quickly, now, all of you. Get it clear.' He didn't want to think, to have any emptiness inside him that the voice might fill. He hauled the wood away, dragging it and dumping it to the side, clouds of ash rising and choking them all. After a second, Tethys joined in, then the Jackal, and suddenly all of them were working, even Chryse, in a swift, hurried line, pulling at the debris. The snake hissed away, scorpions scuttled out, charred wood crumbled into handfuls of soot and splinters.

The girl's tunics were swiftly smudged with black, their hands filthy; they tore away the wreckage of Argelin's hate, and as Seth heaved a huge branch up he gasped, 'Help me with this.'

It took four of them, staggering and heaving, to roll it and let it fall with a crash. Then they turned back.

The Oracle was a great split in the pavement. He had never expected it to be so big; had imagined a small pit, a hole of blackness.

Persis cried, 'It's not the same!'

'Explain, Holiness.' The Jackal crouched, his fine hands fingering the cracked edges. 'I see these are fresh.'

'The earthquake!' She stared around at the others. 'The earthquake or the fire! Something has split the Oracle wide!'

The Jackal flashed a glance of triumph at Seth. 'Is that so! Then maybe we can travel into the Underworld, too.'

In Seth's ear the god sounded amused.

Well done, Seth. Mirany would be so proud of you.

All dangers are reflections in her mirror

It was a corridor into a god's world.

Mirany knew that because it was too smooth, had no markings or doorways. The perfection of its curved walls made it seem like the swollen tunnel of some vast beetle, formed over aeons by the rolling of a fiery sphere. She had no idea how long she had been walking down it. Maybe days. Maybe only minutes.

It was dark, but not completely black. She could see Argelin in front, and looking back, the bulk of Oblek trudged behind like a hunchbacked shadow, carrying the Archon. She stopped now, and let him catch up.

Looming next to her his puzzled whisper echoed round the walls. 'Where the hell are we, Mirany?'

'Nowhere,' she said. Then she smiled. 'I'm glad you're here though, Oblek.'

He grunted, peering through the dimness. 'He's stopped.'

Argelin had halted before a massive structure. Hurrying down, Mirany saw how a great gateway rose to the roof, how the General spread his palms against its bronze doors.

Hearing them, he turned.

For a moment he and Oblek glared at each other; then in the big man's ear the Archon whispered sleepily, 'Put me down,' and the lumpy shape dissolved into two, a thin form sliding to the floor, yawning and scratching.

'So,' Argelin said quietly. 'Is this a nightmare? Or some spell?'

'Neither of those,' Mirany said.

'And I am not dead? Because I believed all of you to have been.' He laughed, harshly. 'Maybe death is not so much to be feared after all. At least I can assume the fat musician will not be trying to cut my throat at every turn.'

'Don't give me ideas,' Oblek growled.

Argelin smiled thinly. His smooth beard was ragged, his eyes dull with fatigue. He turned back to the gates, holding up the sun-disc like a lamp. 'These are locked.'

Mirany came up beside him. The entrance to the Underworld was made of bone; an ivory stack of criss-crossed femurs and tibias, as if all the displaced inhabitants of some lost tomb had been piled up here

223

in pieces, a ramshackle structure on which to hang the brass doors. It should have been fragile but it wasn't; when Argelin kicked the pillars they were immovable, and the row of skulls across the top stared down through dark sockets.

'The doors of death.' Argelin's voice was quiet. 'Hermia would have come this way and these doors would have swung wide to admit her. Your magic disc is not working, boy.'

'I expect you have to knock.' Alexos wriggled past him, put his fist up and knocked once, then again on the beaten brass. A tiny, hollow sound, it echoed oddly and for a moment Mirany was afraid that there was nothing behind the doors at all but a terrible emptiness studded with stars, so the sudden deafening crack made her jump back, grabbing Oblek's arm.

The doors split.

Dust fell. Oblek pulled Alexos away. Only Argelin did not move.

Shuddering, as if pushed from behind, the doors opened outwards. They grated over the smooth black floor, tall as the tunnel, softly creaking, and the triangle of light beyond them grew to brilliance, sending long spindly shadows streaming behind them, making Mirany put her hand up to her eyes and Oblek swear softly.

They saw a cave, and the light was coming from its depths. A hot, fiery light, as if they were facing into a furnace. Argelin took a step; before he could take another Oblek grabbed him.

'Wait.'

Furious, the General raised the bronze sword, but despite the point at his chest, Oblek stood solid.

'Use your brain, General. Remember the Way of Guidance. The entrance to the Underworld is always guarded.' He glanced at Alexos. 'Right, old friend?'

'Oh yes, Oblek. There's always a great dog with three heads. It's in all the stories I've heard. Or everybody would be trying to get their lovers back.'

Argelin glared at him. More cautiously, he turned to face the cave.

'Come out!' he roared. 'Monster, lamia, serpent, cyclops! Whatever lurks here! Come out or let us pass!'

Nothing moved. Mirany saw only a mist of drifting ochre.

Then, with a scrape of claws and rattle of pebbles, something woke, stirred from sleep; they heard it scramble up, panting.

Argelin hefted the sword. 'Are you armed, fat man?'

Oblek spat. 'With a lyre, *great king*.'

'I'm sure you have more than that. Girl?'

'A knife,' Mirany stuttered 'but—'

'Go for the eyes or the throat.' He turned as a shadow loomed in the entrance, vast, as if the eerie light magnified it. Something snuffled, and a low growl sounded in the mist, chilling the sweat on Mirany's back. She clutched the knife.

'Archon?'

Alexos was peering from behind Oblek. 'I'm sure it won't be too horrible, Mirany,' he whispered.

The dog slunk around the rocks.

Mirany stared. Oblek frowned. Argelin drew himself up.

The General faced a snarling night-black mastiff, yellow teeth dripping in its maw. As high as the cave roof, it turned its glowing eyes down on him, snaky tail whipping behind. Viciously it growled again, a terrifying threat, flattened itself ready to spring, small coils of darkness rising like smoke from its frosted skin.

Rigid, Argelin said, 'Be ready.'

'Against that!' Mirany snorted in disgust. To his shock she slid the knife into her belt and crouched, holding out one hand. 'Here, boy! Come on!'

The puppy made a rush towards her. It was tiny and sandy-coloured and foolishly playful. Nipping at her fingers it hurtled away, yapping.

'For the god's sake!' Oblek roared. The dog wasn't up to much but she shouldn't take risks. A desert cur, slinking and sly, half-starved. He'd seen plenty like it. It certainly had fleas and its bite would infect. Best to kill the thing straight. He took out his curved knife. The cur backed, head down.

'Oblek!' Mirany looked scandalized.

He glanced at her puzzled. 'Holiness . . .'

'It's just a puppy.'

'Hardly . . .'

'Will you fools be silent!' Argelin's hiss was edgy with tension. He watched the monster bare its fangs; it gave a great roar and snapped at him, and he sliced swiftly with the bronze sword, the vicious edge whipping past the beast's jaws. Saliva sizzled like acid on the smooth floor.

Mirany screeched. 'What are you doing!'

The puppy whimpered. It sat in a pitiful huddle, its tiny sandy back shivering. She took one step towards it, but Oblek had her in a grip of iron.

'What do you see, Holiness?'

'What?'

'I said, *What do you see?*'

She pushed hair from her eyes. 'The dog, but—'

'The same dog?' He turned to Argelin. 'Because I see a desert scavenger, thin and mean, scratching with mange.'

The General barely took his eyes off the creature. He was braced like a man in battle, the sword held ready, its point following the slinking hound. 'A drunk's delusion. Let me tell you what's really there, fat man. A creature out of nightmare. A mastiff of the Rain Queen, its maw huge, its tail a writhing of snakes. It will devour us all, unless we kill it.'

Mirany looked at Oblek. 'It's a little puppy,' she breathed.

The musician was silent. Then he looked accusingly at the boy. Alexos' perfect face flushed.

'I did *say* Oblek, that it had three heads.'

'But like this, old friend! Tell us which is the true one.'

Alexos looked unhappy. 'I don't know. Well, I do. All of them.'

Mirany gasped as Argelin swung again and the puppy yelped. 'They can't *all* be true.'

'Of course they can, Mirany.' Cross, he sat on the rocky floor, elbows on knees.

Then he said, sulkily, 'This is how it is for gods all the time. I mean with people and what they want. Everyone sees things differently. Now you can see how tricky it is.' He undid the lace on his sandal and retied it, patiently. Over his head Mirany gazed at Oblek in despair.

Heavily, he said, 'We kill it anyway. No choice, lady.'

Head down, Alexos muttered, 'The Rain Queen won't like that.'

'The Rain Queen and I are enemies,' Argelin snapped.

'Anyway, you have your lyre, Oblek.' Alexos sat back, his hands behind him, his feet crossed at the ankle. 'Play them to sleep. That's how it's done.'

The musician stared, then swung down the lyre from his back and took it out. Briefly he tuned it, and the bending notes vibrated in the fiery hollow of the cave.

Tightly, Argelin said, 'Be quick. This creature grows. Now its back brushes the roof.' He was alert, his eyes fixed on some horror Mirany could not imagine.

Watching the puppy curl up and lick its own tail as the

soft music entered the cave she said to the god, 'What does this say about me?'

That you are different from Argelin, he answered slyly.

The music was quiet. It wasn't a tune, more like a soft selection of notes, each far apart, so that she found herself waiting and longing for the next, and when it came it was the slow falling of water, a wobbling drop of sound that splashed her ear and fell on to the rocky floor, a tiny crown of harmonies.

And she watched the puppy curl contentedly and sleep, and she went over to it and sat beside it, rubbing its warm slightly tubby stomach, its ridiculously tiny tail, drowsy in the rain of small sounds, the delicate deluge of music. The cave dimmed, its redness ebbing, as if the song put out the fires she couldn't see, and there was a voice singing too, though she wasn't at all sure it was Oblek's, and it soothed her and she put her head down on her arm and closed her eyes to listen to it. But it went on, inside her, in her veins and heartbeat; it was the water singing, a song that went on for ever in the heart of the world, down into darkness, round and round, sweeping her into its whirlpool of sleep.

Mirany.

She sighed, turned over. The window was open in her room and she could hear the servants outside. They were setting out the blue and yellow dishes for breakfast on the terrace, and the breeze was wafting the flimsy curtains, blundering an irritable bee through drifts of gauze.

Mirany. Please wake up.

She was climbing the steps of the Oracle in sizzling heat, a procession of lizards following at her heels, each one masked with a tiny mask of red and gold. And through the mouth slit of the masks reptilian tongues darted, snapping at flies.

The Oracle was open. Someone had carried all the wreckage away; it was a vast crack now, and she knew that it would grow and grow across all the world, and the whole earth would be severed by it into two semicircles that could never meet again. One of the lizards climbed on her sandal, its small feet scratching her skin. *Mirany*, it said anxiously. *There is someone here.*

Her eyes snapped open.

The cave was dark. The fiery light was gone; a cold smoke drifted. Oblek was slumped against the rock, the lyre fallen to one side, Alexos curled beside him. Beyond, a dark huddle, Argelin lay as if he had fallen, one hand stretched out, the sword lying inches from his groping fingers.

The puppy snored. And beyond it, she saw the stranger.

He was a thin man, watching them. As she sat up she saw him step into the cave. His hair was black as night, and he wore a dark tunic to his knees, edged with silver. The mask over his face chilled her; it was the face of a jackal, the tall ears, the long snout. In the shadows, through its slits, his eyes glittered.

'Oblek.' She whispered it, but he woke at once. She heard the lyre string hum as he sat up.

Then his voice growled, 'Who are you?'

The dark figure did not answer. Instead it put out a hand and beckoned, one finger tipped with a claw of silver.

Unsteady, she climbed to her feet, heard the scrape of bronze behind her, saw Argelin's eyes open, his hand grab for the corded hilt. He stood clumsily, glancing round as if his sleep had been so deep he had forgotten where he was.

'What's going on?'

'Keep your voice down,' Oblek said. 'We seem to have a guide.'

Argelin eyed the strange figure coldly. Then he moved; Mirany saw how he circled around the sleeping puppy with careful steps, as if he saw the death dog as a great sprawled creature, and just for a moment, she wondered if she didn't see it too, a dark steaming heap, its fires dulled in slumber.

Alexos whispered, 'I've met you before . . .'

A voice said through the mask, 'Many times, Holiness.' The figure turned. Glancing back once to see if they followed, he led them deep into the cave.

Cavernous, it rose over them, its roof obscured by mist. Small pebbles dislodged under Mirany's feet; she could hear Oblek's loud breath and Argelin's step but the masked being made no sound, as if it walked without substance. Under a twisted pillar seamed with malachite it led them, and then ahead in the misty darkness they heard one small splash.

Argelin stopped dead.

Oblek muttered, 'Scared of water, General?'

Argelin ignored him. Glaring at the masked guide he said, 'What trap is this?'

'No trap, lord. You must cross the river. Everyone must cross.' Without waiting for an answer he turned and strode on and Mirany followed him. After three steps the mist wafted open and thinned, and the jackal mask turned to her. 'Don't touch the water unless you wish to forget,' his voice said, a silvery, amused voice. 'For this is the river of forgetfulness. It will take away all pain and anguish, all love and desire, all joy and inspiration.'

They saw a wide sea of scarlet. Mirany's eyes widened, because at first she thought it was blood, and then she realised that every inch of the surface was thick with the petals of red poppies. They lay as if they had fallen from an invisible roof, and the air was heavy with their scent, a sweet opiate that made her giddy.

Oblek's voice, a growl of discontent, was reassuring. 'How are we supposed to cross? Wade it?'

'There is a boat.'

'I see none.'

'He comes. Have your payment ready. For this is the only way to the land of the dead, musician.'

Oblek frowned, but Alexos pointed suddenly. 'There! Look, Oblek!'

Through the mist the boat was coming. It was black from stem to stern, its prow high, carved to resemble a serpent with eyes of chalcedony. Sitting amidships, his back to them, the single oarsman rowed steadily, the oars dipping into the red petals, lifting and dropping a row of splashes back into the hidden black waters.

The jackal-faced guide backed into shadow. 'I will return when you need me,' he said.

'Wait!' Argelin grabbed at him. But the General's gloved hand stubbed against rock; held a pillar of rough granite, gleaming with quartz. He cursed, glanced round wildly. But the stranger had gone.

Oblek came up behind him. 'Get used to it, General. In this land not everyone dances to your tune.'

Argelin shoved past him. Striding down to the beach he stood beside Mirany, watching the black ship sweep towards them. At his feet the wash rose and fell, leaving a scum of petals. He glanced down at it, then took one step back.

'You could let it touch you,' Mirany said quietly. 'And then you would forget her.'

For a moment he did not move at all. He stood silent, his face grim, his eyes dark with some torment she could only guess at. When he raised them, she almost quailed at their stare.

'There is no power in the universe that could make me do that,' he said.

Alexos wailed. He sat down on the pebbled shore and put a hand to his mouth and made a small choked cry.

'Archon?' Oblek crouched. 'What is it? What's wrong?'

'It's me, Oblek. *It's me.*'

As the oarsman turned to look at them he waved, and Mirany gasped, leaping back as the keel of the boat rasped with sudden power up the beach, the black wood seamed and ancient, a great eye painted on its prow. Throwing down the oars the rower stood a little stiffly and clambered over the seats; he jumped down into the shingle and flung his arms wide.

'My dearest Oblek! How wonderful!'

'*Archon?*' For a moment Oblek almost seemed speechless; then the old man grabbed him and kissed him on both cheeks, beaming at them all.

'Yes, Oblek, yes, it's me. And here's General Argelin, ah, good day, lord . . . and the girl from Mylos, who read my note all that time ago. You look so much more grown up, my dear.' He held her hand and they looked at each other. 'I'm so sorry I got you into all this.' Mirany managed a smile. He released her fingers slowly. 'And – ah indeed. The new Archon.'

He crossed to Alexos, and the boy stood up to meet

him. The old man lifted the boy's chin with one finger and looked into his face, a long look as if he gazed into some pool or mirror. The boy's beautiful face looked calmly back at him, his dark eyes taking in the wrinkled forehead, the deepset eyes, the salt-roughened skin.

'And so we meet as no mortals ever should meet,' the old Archon breathed. 'Youth and age, life and death. Each other and ourselves.' Very gently he leaned forward and kissed the boy lightly on the brow.

For a moment they were silent. Then he swung around and waved at the boat. 'Well, enter now, my friends. That is—'

He looked confused, a little embarrassed. 'That is, if you have the payment.'

Oblek fished in his pocket. 'Is it money, old friend? You know I never have—'

'Not money.' He glanced apologetically at Mirany. 'It has to be gold.'

She looked at Argelin. 'The disc.'

'Surely not. We need it . . .'

'When the god asks,' Mirany said quietly, 'there's no way of arguing. I've learned that.'

His hand went reluctantly to his inner pocket; when he brought the disc out, it gleamed. The scarab carved into its surface seemed to scuttle; as the old Archon reached out for it both their fingers grasped it for a moment. Then, very slowly, Argelin let it go.

'I fear this may be a mistake.'

The old man smiled wryly. 'Once you gave me up for sacrifice, Lord General. Do you fear I will do the same for you?' He glanced at Mirany. 'Climb aboard. We must go.'

She scrambled up and Alexos jumped in with her. The Archon said, 'If I might trouble you, old friend?' With a grin Oblek tossed the lyre to Mirany and put his shoulder to the keel, heaving the boat back into the scarlet sea. Just as it floated, he climbed aboard, taking a great leap to avoid even one splash of the invisible water.

Stranded on the beach, Argelin said, 'Give me your hand.'

For a moment, in the prow, Oblek hesitated. He said nothing, looking down at the General.

Then, from behind him, two voices chorused, '*Do as he says, Oblek.*'

Mirany smiled.

Annoyed, Oblek leaned over. 'Old friend, I love you dearly, but one of you was enough.' He gripped Argelin's hand; lightly the General scrambled up, but his foot slipped on the clinkered boards and he gasped and grabbed the gunwale, hanging over the scarlet water until Mirany caught his arm. Together they dragged him aboard.

Breathless, he glared at her.

'Now sit.' The old Archon settled himself at the steering oar. 'You can row, Oblek. You look as if you need the exercise. And you, General, if you would.'

The dark boat moved. Gently it turned and swung out on to the river of poppies, the oars dipping and rising, Oblek breathing hard, Argelin alert to avoid splashes. Into the mist they rowed, into a dimness that swallowed them, until the old Archon stood and clambered unsteadily to the prow, the disc in his hand.

'Behold,' he said softly. 'The land of the dead.'

With one swift movement he held the disc high. It glittered and flashed, and all the air scorched with its heat, and Mirany saw how the mist dried up as if beyond it, high and far beyond, a new sun had risen.

The sky was blue, the river was a blaze of poppies. And on its further bank she could see the Underworld.

He is stung by the wasp in the honey

Seth leaned on the white balcony.

From up here he could see the ghostly shimmer of the Emperor's ships, almost beyond sight. Only in the glaring brilliance of midday could they be glimpsed, tiny in the expanse of blue. Had Rhetia reached them? Was she a prisoner? Had his generals believed her, and even if they had, how long would it take for them to send word to the Exalted One that his nephew was held by rebels, on the Island itself?

'He'll come too late,' Seth muttered gloomily.

Since the god had whispered in his mind he had often found himself talking aloud, because his mind was no longer a private place. That cool voice had been like a sliver of unease, a calm shock; now he wasn't sure if he was ever alone, he felt an invisible presence and had to keep glancing behind. He hadn't heard the voice again, but there was no defence against it, was there; it could speak to him at any time, right inside him, and there was no way not to hear it. That scared him. If he thought about it too much it would drive him mad. How did Mirany cope with this? Was everything he dreamed and imagined laid open to the amusement of the god? Even now, at this very moment?

A shadow behind him. He turned; Chryse jumped back with a little gasp. 'It's only me!'

She was carrying a flask of wine and a bowl of rough bread and dates. She put them down hastily on the blue table.

'I thought you might be hungry. It was all I could find.'

Seth looked at her. 'Thank you.' He opened the flask and poured the yellow wine into a cup and tasted it. His eyebrows shot up.

'I knew you'd like it,' Chryse said smugly. 'There's a little secret stock up in the Speaker's suite. Hermia always liked a good wine.'

He had never tasted anything so fine, even in Argelin's Headquarters. Picking up one of the dates, he said, 'How's it going?'

Chryse frowned. 'Well, my nails are all broken.' Catching his grin she said hastily, 'But of course that doesn't matter at all. Only I don't understand why the

Nine have to labour like slaves. There are enough other people here.'

'He's given you as many as he can spare. And the Oracle is . . .'

She shrugged. 'Yes I know. It's our holy place. But the pit is full of rubble, packed right inside.' A hopeful look came into her eyes. 'That skinny man Kreon must be working at it from below?'

'Probably for months, but it's unsafe. The whole chamber was blocked.'

The god's order had seemed such a flash of revelation, but time was against them. Even from where he stood he could see the mounds of sand that Ingeld's men were raising outside the black walls of the City. They were digging, sapping the vast structure, probing for tunnels, eager to break into a tomb. Sooner or later they'd find one, and then the looting would start.

From the ramparts, missiles were being rained down on them; arrows and stones, hot pitch, pots and pans, poisoned darts. But the City was a place of the Dead, and despite its swarming workers, had no artillery, no real weapons. Except of course, fear.

An idea was coming to him; he spat out the date stone, grabbed two more and said, 'Where's the Jackal?'

'Oh, him!' Chryse shrugged. 'At the Bridge, I think.'

He strode past her down the loggia and its elegant images, but she ran after him.

'Seth.'

'What?'

Silence.

He stopped and looked back.

Chryse was staring at him angrily. 'You forgot to call me Holiness.'

For a moment he was astonished. 'I'm sorry.'

'Do you like me, Seth?'

'Of course I like you. Holiness.'

'As much as you like Mirany?'

Danger. He sensed it like a fire against his skin. Cautiously he murmured, 'I'm honoured by the friendship of both of you, Holiness. I'm just a scribe . . .'

'That's right, you are just a scribe, so don't get above yourself!' She folded her arms and he knew by the anger in her voice that he hadn't said enough, should have flattered her more.

'You know, none of the others really think you heard the god. Tethys said to me, 'That cocky scribe! He'd do anything to make himself important.'

Seth smiled wryly, and turned. So this was what Mirany had had to put up with. But the bitchiness of a few girls was nothing to him.

Until Chryse said, 'You must be *so* worried about your sister and father.'

He stopped. It wasn't just the words but her voice that made him turn back. He almost expected to see someone else there, an older, harder girl, bitter with sarcasm, but only pretty Chryse smiled at him, leaning her elbows against the balustrade, her rose-pink tunic rippling in the breeze.

'What are you saying?'

'Only that you don't know what's happened to them, do you? It must be terrible in the Port. It would be so much better if they were here.'

He still had a date in his hand; he flung it down. He wanted to grab her arm, but she was one of the Nine so he just said tightly, 'Holiness, I recognize a threat when I hear it.'

She smiled. 'Not a threat, Seth. At least, it needn't come to that.'

Mirany had warned him. She seemed so harmless, but there was a hard edge under all that blonde silliness and he felt it now, as if he had caught hold of a blade hidden in silk, and it had cut his fingers.

She straightened and stepped towards him. 'Am I pretty, Seth?'

He forced himself to say, 'Yes.'

'I'm prettier than Mirany. Mirany isn't pretty at all, is she?'

He shrugged. 'What do I know?'

'Well, she isn't.' She put her fingertips together and tapped them. 'And the thing is, Manto knows where they are, Seth. Pa and Telia, I mean. She's found out where they are, and she could get them any time.'

Then he did grab her. She smiled up at him, as if it was some victory. Instead of pulling away she stepped closer. 'You could kiss me, Seth, if you wanted.'

'What do you mean, *Manto*?'

'I suppose you never had a chance to kiss Mirany. She's always so prim.'

He had to play this right. He wasn't going to let her do this to him. He let her go and stepped back and made himself smile a thin cold smile like the Jackal's.

'Oh, I wouldn't say that.'

Chryse's eyes widened. 'She wouldn't!' For a moment a flush of fury suffused her face. 'I don't believe you.'

Seth shrugged. 'Don't you? You all thought Mirany was a quiet little thing but you were wrong, weren't you? She's got more brains than all of you put together. After all she's the Speaker now. Not Hermia, not Rhetia, not you. As for all this about Manto, I don't believe it for a minute. How would you know? A woman like Manto would never confide in you!' He let the scorn sound in his voice.

She was trembling with anger. She straightened up, glaring at him. 'Perhaps Mirany's not the only one with secrets. Do you know what this is, *scribe*?'

She lifted her hand and faced it at him, palm out, and he saw the scarab. It was tiny, a blue and red cloisonné beetle, the disc above its claws solid gold. For only a moment he saw it, and then she closed her fist and it was gone. She stepped closer.

'That's our symbol. Manto thinks it's fun to use one of the holiest devices of the god. She doesn't care. The scarab flies between us all, her and me, and Ingeld, carrying her words. You'd better believe me, Seth. Did you think I really spent two months cowering on the Island?' She laughed, a little unsteadily, and walked over to the balcony, looking down on the blue sea, leaning on her fists. 'Or in Argelin's dungeons? Do you think I'm that stupid?'

'No,' he stammered.

'Yes, you do. Fluffy, airhead Chryse. But I'm not like that, Seth, not at all.' She looked at him sideways, her reddened lips smiling.

'I went where I knew I would be safe. Manto is my aunt. She was the one who got me into the Nine in the first place; you'd be surprised how many influential people a hetaira knows.'

She stopped, studying him. He knew he looked devastated, defeated. His shoulders slumped; though he pulled himself together quickly, it had shown. So he shook his head in dismay. 'My sister . . .'

'Oh, yes. So pretty. I hope she likes that little toy you bought her. But nothing will happen to them.' She took a step closer. 'Unless—'

'Seth!' The shout was close, the Fox's harsh bark. 'Get down here!'

Chryse jumped back. 'Don't say anything about this,' she snapped. 'If I think you've told the Jackal, Pa is dead.'

Instantly, as if her words had conjured it, something came out of the sky and sucked the air from his lungs, exploding with a terrifying crash. Chryse screamed and was flung against him; the roof burst into a thousand fiery fragments. Seth was knocked sideways; for a moment the world was dark and tilted and then it came back upside down, a roaring inferno of voices and yells and the crackle of flames.

'Seth!' The Fox hauled him up. 'Holiness, get into the kitchens. Quickly!'

Without a backward look Chryse was gone, racing down the stairs. The one-eyed thief yelled orders, turned to Seth. 'Hurt, ink-boy?'

'What . . . what was it?'

'Firebombs. The Northern scum have set up a ballista.'

'They're attacking? But I thought you said—'

'We were wrong.'

Bewildered, still slightly deaf, Seth ran after him. The explosion seemed to ring in his ears and skull, and the aftershock of Chryse's jealousy numbed him all the way through the parched gardens to the processional way. As they ran the heat of the sun scorched down; lizards flicked away from under his feet, and the blue dome of the sky was perfect, a stifling lid.

Skidding past the entrance to the Oracle he heard the clatter and slither of shifting rocks; the Jackal's men had set up some sort of leverage system there. Then he turned the slope of the hill and saw the Bridge.

Its two broken ends jutted starkly into the sea. Between them he saw a terrifying sight. A group of the mercenaries were swimming over, light shields strapped to their backs to protect them from arrows. On the shore the defenders cowered behind hasty makeshift barricades as gobbets of fire hurtled over them, scorching the sandy ground and setting bushes of artemisia and myrtle ablaze.

'Get that trampled out!' The Jackal was armed; a breastplate was strapped over his tunic and two swords glinted in the shoulder holsters. He picked another weapon up and threw it to Seth.

'Time to fight, Seth.'

Seth caught it awkwardly. 'I'm a scribe. I don't fight.'

'Well, if you have any other suggestions, I'd be glad to hear them.'

He didn't. It was clearly an all-out assault. On the desert shore the ballista clattered; rocks and fireballs and small shot from slings whistled by, tore great skidding furrows in the holy soil of the Island. Next to Seth, a man was flung back with a scream of anguish; he lay crumpled, a bloody heap. Far off, the elephants brayed.

Jamil was running down the path, servants about him. He ducked down by the Jackal.

'Get back, Prince. There's nothing you can do.'

Jamil shrugged. 'I do not intend to be Ingeld's prisoner, Lord Osarkon.'

'Can't we fire back?' Seth muttered.

The Jackal's laugh was tense. 'With what?' He watched the mercenaries swim closer, then his long eyes slid to Seth. 'Unless the god can help us now, we're finished.'

Seth swallowed. 'Look. About that. I'm not even sure it happened. I don't want it to happen again.'

'We need him, Seth.'

'You don't know what it's like! A voice, inside me.'

An enormous crash took half the tipped waggon away in one blast. Cowering, he gripped the scrubby grass until the terror had stopped choking him.

Then the Jackal said calmly, 'Ask him.'

'I don't know how!'

'Ask him. Or die.'

The thief-lord's voice was grim; raising his head Seth gazed hopelessly at the warriors in the water, the parched defenceless shore, the ragged army of refugees and pickpockets, con men and thief-girls. He turned his back on them, put his hands over his face. Inside the darkness it felt safer, the sandy rasp of his palms against his rough chin.

'Listen,' he said. 'I'm not the Speaker. I can't be the Speaker. But help us!'

The voice answered. He had known it would answer. Inside himself he had known it had never gone away.

It said thoughtfully, *Did you know, Seth, the Underworld is not dark, like it says in the scrolls. You should see it! The river is red with poppy petals and the sky is blue. Mirany is so surprised.*

'Never mind that! Help us. Send earthquakes, thunder. Send terror! Do what gods do!'

There was something like a laugh. *You are quite capable of making those yourself.*

'This is your Oracle they're attacking.'

You are my Oracle.

'Mirany is!'

You are Mirany. Have you noticed? You and she have changed places, Seth.

Astonished, he took his hands away.

The Jackal was watching. 'Well?'

He stared ahead. Then he said, 'Thunder. Terror.'

Exactly. The calm voice came from a scorpion that was running into a hole. *And I didn't even have to tell you, Seth.*

He jumped up, shoving the Jackal aside. 'Hold them. Hold them as long as you can.' And then he was racing, running up the steep path in a skidding weave, head down.

'Where the hell is he going?' the Fox roared.

'No time to find out.' The Jackal turned quickly to the shore. 'A man possessed by the god is not sane, after all.' He turned to his men. 'Be ready!'

They drew swords. Some had spears, but if they made a shield-wall against this onslaught how long would it hold? He looked at them wryly, his rag-tag army, his rabble of the untrustworthy and the dishonest, the deceivers and the dregs. The last prince of the House of Osarkon would die in worthy company, it seemed. And how ironic that the god should choose such defenders.

'Fox.'

'Chief?'

'Form the line.'

As he said it the bombardment stopped; the mercenaries were wading out of the water. Bronze glittered; the sea streamed from their greaves and breastplates. Their long pale hair was tied back, their faces slashed with paint. Expertly they formed up and paced forward, clashing swords on shields, a rhythmic, ominous beat. The noise rang high in the cliff, echoed from the Temple facade. He could see some of the Nine up there, watching in terror.

'Bright One,' he breathed silently, 'accept our offerings of blood.'

Then, facing the glittering wall of bronze, he heard something else. A cry, a deep hoarse blare of wrath. Some of his men glanced round.

'Hold your places,' the Jackal snapped. Now the terror had sunk into the ground; the sandy soil vibrated, a barely-felt shudder under their feet.

'God.' The Fox licked dry lips. 'The bloody scribe's made an earthquake.'

'Not him, I think.' The Jackal grinned. 'Something much larger.'

He stepped forward quickly. 'Ice men,' he yelled. 'Go

back now! Before the god sends his revenge down on you all!'

They didn't stop but the line became ragged, as if the trembling in the ground rose into their limbs, made the shields heavy, the swords unsteady. The war beat faltered. Then the Jackal drew the two bronze blades from his shoulders and turned, pointing them.

'Behold!' he yelled. 'The sacred creatures of the god!'

The Northmen stopped dead. Because down the track the elephants came pounding, maddened by heat, raging for freedom. Their riders, almost invisible between the great ears, urged them on but it was the sea that drew them, its delicious expanses, the smell of its cool depths. Their vast wrinkled bodies dehydrated and crusted with dust, their hides itching with fleas, the Emperor's elephants thundered into the invading force with a scream of fury, trunks high, ears wide.

The mercenaries fled. Flinging away shield and spear they leapt into the sea; others, mesmerised with fear, rolled and scrabbled aside and were instantly torn down by the thief-army. The elephants ran over them, and as the foremost passed him, the Jackal saw its small red eye as intelligent as if a god lived in it, and then the remnants of the shield wall were down under the trampling grey beasts.

In all the noise Fox was at his elbow. 'Seth?'

'Seth.'

They could see him, running down the track. As he

raced up, winded, Prince Jamil cried, 'I wonder you did not ride, scribe! What a triumph! What pride I feel in the beasts! How my uncle will laugh at this!'

Seth crouched, dragging in air. He felt neither pride nor delight but a sour anger, a disgust. The mercenaries that had not swum were dead; the thief-army stripping them mercilessly, cutting throats, searching for weapons. Turning away, summoning a desperate courage, he gasped, 'Listen. I have to tell you about Chryse.'

But the Jackal was not listening. His gaze was hard and intent, and he was staring across the blue water to the broken bridge opposite.

Ingeld stood there, a massive figure, the bronze of his helmet gleaming, his ice-blue eyes clear through the slits. And in front of him stood a woman, plump and grey haired, wrapped in a black cloak.

Seth caught his breath. 'That's her! Manto.'

The Jackal didn't answer, it was the Fox who growled, 'We know her.'

The woman came to the edge of the water and called out. 'Your ruse was clever, thief-lord, but will gain you only pain. It's been a long time since my people saved your life. Do you remember that night, Lord Osarkon? How I stole from the King of Thieves?'

She held up her hand. In it was something so small they couldn't make it out; it glittered like gold. 'I have them all here. The clippings of your hair, your nails, your skin. I will return them if your rabble leave the Island. If not, I begin my spells.'

'She has these things?' Jamil's voice was grave.

The Jackal nodded, bleakly.

'This is serious. A witch's hatred.'

'Won't change anything.' The thief-lord's voice was quiet, but steady. He walked down to the spars of the broken bridge and gazed across at her.

'It's too late, sorceress. Once I might have feared your malice, but not now. Things have changed. The Jackal has somehow become Lord Osarkon again, and he has drunk from the Well of Songs. Perhaps that will protect me.'

Ingeld muttered something; Manto shook her head. Her voice was edged with scorn.

'It won't. Your death will be long and painful. Nothing will be gained. We will keep attacking until we win, and then every man and woman on the Island will be slaughtered, the Temple renewed and the god appeased with honey and gold. I will be Speaker and mine will be a new regime. And don't think the god will reject me, because gods are fickle. You know that.'

For a long moment he held her gaze. Then he turned away. 'Do your worst,' he said.

The Sixth Gate
Of the Punishments

People play games. Do they think gods never do?

People fool themselves, lie, make up stories.

The world is my story. I make it of hopes and desires and water and mud, and I roll it through the sky.

The stars gather round and watch. Mermen rise from the sea.

But the way is long and even gods get weary, so I turn the world into an orange and peel it. It smells delicious, and drips with juice. All down my fingers.

Does he think his love is enough?

On the far side of the river the land was dry and sandy.

As Mirany scrambled up the bank she felt soft holes collapse under her feet, burrows of martins or tiny chinchillas. She grabbed handfuls of the sparse grass. On top, a warm wind blew.

Oblek called, 'Don't go too far.'

Then Argelin snapped, 'What's up there?'

'Grass.' She turned. 'A great plain of grass.'

It stretched as far as she could see. No hills rose in it, no trees grew. Above it the sky was blue and remorseless and the sun burned like a disc of gold. In the breeze the grass was never still; it rippled and flowed with the softest of hisses, its mesh of stems bending and flattening,

Frowning, she looked back.

Argelin had the sword at the old man's throat. 'The disc. I want it back.'

Unafraid, the Archon laughed. But he handed the sun-disc back, and the light was gone from it. Argelin slipped it inside his breastplate, and released him.

'There was no need for threats, General. I, for one, am already dead.'

But Argelin was already scrambling on to the shore; hastily Oblek lifted Alexos out of the boat and turned back.

'You next, old friend.'

The old man smiled sadly and shook his head. 'Ah no, Oblek. This is as far as I come. The road to the Garden is not for me yet. I have my orders.' He took the oars in his hands and pushed off clumsily.

Oblek said, 'But are you just going to strand us here?'

'I am. You won't be coming back this way, I'm afraid.'

Oblek watched the eyed prow drag through the poppies.

'It was good to see you again,' he said quietly.

'Remember me, Oblek. When you sing and when you play.' The boat moved slowly out over the blood-red surface, diminishing into mist.

Argelin called after it. 'Old man. Whose orders?'

The voice came back faintly over the splash of oars. 'The Rain Queen rules here, Lord Argelin. She watches you come into her realm. Beware her anger, my lord.'

For a moment he was only a shimmer among red flowers. Then there was nothing there at all.

Argelin sheathed the bronze sword with a click. 'Does *my* anger count for nothing?' he snarled.

Oblek turned to face him. For a moment, eye to eye, they glared at each other. Finally the General said, 'You and I also have a long feud to settle, fat man. Once you thrust a knife at me, and only the breastplate turned it. Perhaps we should finish things here.'

Oblek folded his arms. 'You'd like that, wouldn't you? Kill me and have the girl and the Archon unprotected.' He grinned, sweat gleaming on his forehead. 'Besides, why should I bother breaking your neck? We're all in the land of the dead already, and I doubt we'll ever get out.'

'This is silly.' Alexos had climbed up beside Mirany and was scuffing his heels impatiently. 'You could fight each other until the end of the world and neither of you would like each other any better, so can we just get on? The Garden is a long way off, Lord Argelin.'

For a moment Mirany thought the men would not move. Then Oblek gave a great bark of laughter, turned his back and clambered awkwardly towards her up the sandy bank. Argelin watched. For a terrible second she thought he would draw a knife and plunge it into the musician's back; instead he climbed after him, gloved hands deep in the slithering land.

Oblek heaved his weight to the top and groaned

upright. 'Hell's teeth. *This* is the Underworld? No wonder men fear death.'

Alexos was already running waist-deep in the swishing grasses. 'It's lovely, Oblek!' he called back. 'There are butterflies!'

There were. They rose in clouds about him, small yellow and blue and white flutters, and as Mirany waded into the stiff stalks she laughed at the sudden release of colour. In seconds the sky was adrift with bright wings. Oblek grunted. With one glare at Argelin, he followed.

They walked across the plain for hours. At first the space and light were exhilarating, but Mirany soon realized that the constant trudge through deep grass was tiring; hidden holes tripped her and the fear that unseen snakes might lurk among the roots made her cautious and slow, parting the stalks, watching where she put her feet. When at last she paused and looked up there was a dull crick in her neck; to her surprise she saw the river of poppies was far behind, a miasma of scarlet light. In the eternity of emptiness ahead, something shimmered.

'What's that?'

Alexos was riding on Oblek's back; he shaded his eyes with one hand.

'A door, Mirany.'

As they slowly came closer they saw it rise up, a grey structure all alone in the grass. If it was a door, Mirany thought, it must be wide open, because between its uprights the same plain shimmered on for ever. She wished she knew more about the Way of Guidance. Seth must have copied it out tens of times; he would remember all that it told about the road to the Garden. She thought about the anguish of his cry. *Don't go without me! Wait!* It had shaken her. She had turned to him; nothing had been there but the wall of dark-red stone.

Did he think she hadn't wanted him here? That wasn't true. She glanced across at Oblek's trudging bulk and then at Argelin. Seth knew how to deal with people. She didn't.

'I wish he was here,' she whispered. The god, if he heard, did not answer.

When Argelin finally came to the structure, she saw him stop and gaze up at it. He reached out a gloved hand; Alexos' squeal was loud and frightened.

'Oh, don't touch it! WAIT!' He leapt down from Oblek's back and ran. Mirany scrambled after him.

It was a lintel and two pillars. No doors closed it. The pillars were twin images of a tall man, sword in hand, and each of them had Argelin's face.

'She mocks me,' he hissed.

'I'd call it a good likeness,' Oblek growled.

It was made of blocks of grey matter; they seemed like stone, but the wind weathered them strangely, their edges drifting and gusting away, eroding even now.

'What is it?' Oblek muttered.

'Ashes.'

For a moment they gazed at it in silence; then Mirany asked the question no one else would.

'The ashes of what?'

Alexos touched the edge of a block with his frail forefinger. A shiver of dust slid down; grey clinkery stuff.

'Not everyone has mummies, or tombs. I can remember times when heroes were burned on great pyres.' He turned quickly, and behind him Mirany saw tiny specks, high in the sky, that must be birds. They were flying very fast, a flock that split and swooped. Dark small birds, like crows or swifts, they circled overhead.

'Spies.' Argelin's voice was tense. 'Her spies.'

'They can't hurt us.' Oblek turned back to the twin images, walked all around them, stared up at their height. 'What's the point of this? It guards nothing, leads nowhere.'

The birds karked. Like a sudden cindery fall, they came down and perched on the bending grasses, a circle of eyes and wings all around the travellers. Mirany turned, facing them; behind her the others did the same.

Argelin slid out his sword. 'These are not birds.'

Their eyes were shards of glass; their wings metallic. The sheen of their feathers made a perfect oily iridescence in the sun. One screeched and took off, whipping past Oblek's head, so that he ducked with a curse and fell against the blocks of ash. Mirany gasped, grabbing him.

'I'm all right.'

'No! Your arm! Look!'

Where Oblek's arm passed beneath the stones his hand vanished, as if cut off at the wrist. At once, as if the second of disbelief was a signal, the birds swooped back, a metal hail of beaks and talons.

Alexos gave a wail of dismay and Mirany ducked. 'We have to go through!' she screamed.

'No! We don't know where it leads.' Argelin beat wings off; something sliced through his sleeve with a savage rip.

She turned. 'Archon? *Alexos?*'

A blow knocked her into the grass. Crouching over the pain in her chest she dragged air into her lungs, yelled. 'He's gone, Oblek! He's gone through!'

Without waiting to see if they followed her she took one step under the grey lintel, and as if an edge of fog filled it she dissolved instantly. Oblek roared and grabbed at her but his hand met nothing. He fell full length, in the grass, scrambled up, whirled round. His heart turned cold.

There were no birds.

There were no twin statues.

Argelin, sword out, circled warily.

All around them, in every direction, lay nothing but grass. And out of it, cautiously, a small head of dark hair rose.

'Where's Mirany?' Alexos whispered.

★ ★ ★

Mirany picked herself up. 'It's just the same' she said. 'Except—'

The colour. Here the crop was golden. Great ears of corn sissed and danced, and over them the sky was heavy with dark clouds. Distant lightning flickered, silently.

She looked round. 'Archon?'

Then she saw the Gate had vanished. Not even a trace of it remained. She swallowed.

'Alexos, please, don't hide from me.'

He would be crouched, watching her. Or tying his sandal strap. Playing games. He'd jump up, any minute, say something calm and annoying.

But the cornfield stretched for miles, faintly swishing out from her waist to the ends of the earth, as if it was some great skirt she wore, and the knowledge came to her coldly and surely and over slow minutes that he wasn't here, that she had come through the door alone.

'Bright One?'

No answer. Maybe there was no god in this place. Maybe there was no one but her. Quickly she stepped to where the door had been, looked round, knelt. Gouged in the ground, so that the corn grew in its dip, was an ancient furrow, as if something vastly heavy had rolled here or been dragged through. She straightened, following it with her eyes, seeing how it led west across the plain.

She hesitated. If she went on, what if Oblek and the others found a way through? And yet to stand here until the sun sank and the night crept over her was terrifying. She bent and tore a tiny strip of white linen from her hem and tied it to a stalk; then a little further, another. It would give them the direction. There was nothing else she could do.

Walking the golden plain exhausted her. At first it was ripe corn, but then as she waded on and on, hot and desperate with thirst, her mind drifted into waking dreams. She felt the corn liquefy, become a plain of molten gold that rippled round her waist and wrists, that slid and dripped in warm unwet droplets, hardening into bracelets and bangles, knobbled fringes on her tunic, rings on her fingers. When she wiped sweat from her face, gold smeared her; a metal pollen that made her cough and dusted her hair. She tasted it on her lips. It was sweet as honey.

Stumbling, afraid of falling and drowning in the viscous crop, she looked up and saw the sun straight ahead, barely above the horizon. But against its scarlet glimmer was a darkness, and her heart thudded. Perhaps it was the twin statues, and she had come back to them. Putting her hand up to her eyes she waited, letting the sun's orb sink into mists and vapours.

With the suddenness of the desert, night fell.

She saw a rise in the land and on the top, a mysterious shape.

Was it a building? She thought not, but had no idea what else it might be. Quickly, she hurried on.

In the darkness, the sea she walked in became water,

rippled with phosphorescence and the flicker of fish shapes beneath its surface. Cupping some in her hands she brought it to her lips, but then opened her fingers slowly and let it drain away.

If she drank she might never escape.

Gradually the ground rose, and step by step the water level was lower. It sank to knee high, and then ankle deep, and when the moon climbed behind her she turned and saw the whole plain lying below, the silver track of light across its surface as if it was a road she had walked.

Turning back, she shivered. Her wet tunic clung to her legs.

Ahead, on the hilltop, was a grove of trees.

They were low and twisted, an olive grove maybe, untended and ancient. Deep among them there was a spark of redness, as if a small fire burned among the gnarled trunks. Cautiously, she came closer. There was a breeze up here; it brought her the crackle of the flames, the hiss of sparks. And it spun the masks.

They hung on all the branches of the grove, silver and ebony and birch bark and emerald. In the moving air their faces turned from side to side, as if they listened, and the gaze of their vacant eye-sockets wandered across her. She recognized them. Speakers' masks, the masks of Bearers and Embroideresses, of long dead Tasters-for-the-god. Thousands of discarded faces, generations of the Nine. Some from long ago ages when the Oracle was barely known, when the Rituals were unformed, mere papyrus slitted with eyes; right up to the ornate feathered mask that had been Hermia's, delicately incised on the cheekbones, its drift of gold discs clinking and tinkling.

Unsteadily, Mirany put out a hand and held it still.

The face was open-mouthed.

It breathed, *Mirany*.

She jumped, leaping back in shock. Released, the mask twisted, turning away and back.

After a moment, she summoned courage. 'Is that you?'

That depends on what you mean by you.

She rubbed dusty hands together nervously. 'Bright Lord?'

Ah. No. When I spoke through the mask the words were always mine, remember.

She knew. It was a woman's voice, irritated and cool. Familiar. Just to be sure, she whispered, 'The Rain Queen?'

You seem to have lost some of your courage, Mirany, all alone here. Without the scribe and the god, what are you but a scared girl, after all? It seems I was right about you. As for the Rain Queen, this whole realm is hers. She watches you approach. As do I.

Mirany glanced round. The wind was rising, turning the masks away, their eye-holes slits of darkness.

She said, 'Hermia, where are you?'

Tell him. He must go back. No mortal can pass the Nine Gates and return. Does he really think his love is enough? That he's

267

some hero, who cannot be harmed? Tell him it's not love but pride that torments him. He killed me. What more does he want?

Cloud was gathering, piling up from the east where the moon had risen; great swathes of glimmering storm, lit by lightning flashes. Mirany glanced round anxiously. The fire lay a little deeper in the grove, but there would hardly be any shelter even there. She reached out to snatch the mask down, to take it with her, but the voice cried, *NO!*

Too late. As her fingers jerked away from it, lightning struck it. The eye-holes softened and drooped, instantly running into droplets, as if they wept golden tears. The mouth sagged; the metal hung with a molten heat, distorting, dissolved. Thunder rumbled.

Mirany said, 'Hermia, wait! Where do I go? *What do I do?*'

Out of the ruined lips, a sigh issued. The words were twisted and choked, vowels incoherent.

The sun . . .

'What? Tell me!'

The scarab . . .

And then there was nothing before her but a dribbling gargoyle, its beauty gone, the gold discs tinkling and falling from melting wires. Mirany stepped back; glancing up she saw the lightning flash a second before the thunder rumbled, a great echoing roar that seemed to sweep across the plain. As the gale hit her it whipped out her hair and dress. The trees groaned and bent. Rain raked her face like fingernails.

Instantly she turned and ran, deep under the tangled branches of the olives, a network of small gnarled trees, stuffy with fallen leaves. The downpour crashed through, and she gasped with the shock of it, the hissing monsoon power. It was hard to see; the firelight seemed no nearer, and as she stumbled over roots and snake holes the trees turned and watched her pass, gnarled dryads with hag-sharp faces.

Then, scrambling under a low branch, she looked up and saw him.

He sat by the fire, his back to her. He wore a dark cloak and when he turned the snout of his jackal-mask seemed to smell her panic, the red eyes bright in the flamelight.

'I'm worried, Mirany,' he said. He slipped the mask off and she saw the white glimmer of his face. 'The Northern men have breached the Second Level. They are into the tombs.'

Fear is what she feeds on

'It's certain.' Seth paced the room. 'They've stopped digging on the north side and concentrated all their men on that patch of desert by the rock outcrop, just under the Wall. And that's bad.'

He looked up, waiting for the Jackal to ask why, but the tomb-thief was irritatingly silent. It was Fox who said, 'Spill it, pretty boy.'

Seth sat on the table. 'It's just about where the tomb of Acheroes is. Old and near the surface. You know it?'

'I believe,' the Jackal said languidly, 'we once stripped it bare. Ingeld will find nothing there.' He sipped water from an ebony cup.

'But there are tunnels leading out from it. Mostly false, with dead ends, but behind the sarcophagus is a secret door to the galleries of the Third Level. If they find that there's no stopping them.'

Fox swore. 'We never found it.'

'We were in and out in a night, Fox.'

'There must be traps.'

'Ingeld will send slaves in first.' The Jackal turned to Chryse, who sat demure in the windowseat. 'Lady? How is progress at the Oracle?'

She rubbed dirt from a glossy fingernail. 'Well, since your men fixed up that stone-shifting thing it's a lot easier, though Rhetia will be furious when she finds out they've been up there.'

'Her anger,' the Jackal said mildly, 'terrifies me.' He sipped again. Seth noticed the Fox glance at him out of the corner of his single eye.

'So it's getting clear.' Chryse shrugged. 'But it might take weeks!'

'We haven't got weeks. We've got until the Day of the Scarab.' The tomb-thief glanced across the room to the open terrace. 'Lord Jamil?'

The Pearl Prince leaned on the white arch, staring out at the fleet. He turned his dark face to them.

'Thief-lord, I'm just a prisoner. You know my desire. Get me a boat and let me sail to the fleet. The Lady Rhetia has obviously failed. Once there I will lead my men in;

271

we'll sweep these barbarians into the sea, and the Oracle will be free.'

The Jackal smiled. He clicked his thumb against the black cup. 'Ah yes. How simple it all seems.' Pushing the cup away he stood up and walked over to the big man. 'But what would happen then? The people of the Two Lands are weary of tyranny, my lord. If not Argelin, then Ingeld. If not Ingeld, then the Emperor. Is this the price we pay for our weakness, for being without any army, and any power but the words of a god? Once we ruled ourselves; my father was one of that Council until his head decorated the Gate of the Port. The Oracle will be free, you say. But with a satrap in the Archon's palace and a new army in the streets.' He grimaced. 'And my head, almost certainly, on the Gate.'

Seth glanced at Chryse. She was watching him from under her lashes. He swallowed, then said bluntly, 'I think we should concentrate on the Oracle. Everyone should be working there, not just the Nine.' He made himself smile at her. 'With respect, Holiness, the Nine are . . . not the strongest of people. We have a few tough men . . .'

Chryse looked haughty. 'I'll have to discuss it with the others.'

He wondered if she would even tell them. The desire to blurt out to the Jackal what she was, was so strong it almost hurt. Instead, he nodded.

The Jackal turned and poured more water into the cup.

His delicate fingers shook slightly on the wood. He said, 'Discuss it quickly, Holiness.'

She stood up and swept out, her pleated skirt tickling Seth's arm like a teasing draught. As soon as the men had escorted Jamil after her he turned on the Jackal, but before he could say a word Fox pushed him aside and grabbed the Jackal's elbow. 'Sit down,' he growled. 'Before you fall.'

Guided to a chair, the thief-lord crumpled. His skin drained of colour; he rubbed his face with shaky fingers. When he spoke his voice was hoarse. 'Lock the door. I don't want anyone coming in.'

Seth ran over. There was no lock, so he opened it and looked out. The corridor was empty except for an image of the Rain Queen gazing at him through a curtain of crystal drops. Inside, he wedged a chair against the door and hurried back. 'Is he ill?'

Fox glared up. 'It's Manto. She's begun.'

Seth shuddered. For a moment the smell of the woman's room came back, that miasma of potions and mummified creatures. 'Is it possible—'

'He can't eat.' Fox poured more water. 'Vomits it up. Nothing since yesterday.'

'That could just be—'

'It's her, scribe, believe me.'

'Will you please stop talking about me as if I'm already dead!' The Jackal sat upright, with an effort. His skin was clammy with sweat. 'If she doesn't kill me you will, Fox.'

He sipped the water and then coughed. 'Fear is what she feeds on.'

There was silence. In the blue open spaces of the sea a gull swung by, crying. Seth sat. After a moment he said bleakly, 'Will you surrender?'

'Never.'

'Without you we have no leader.'

'Nonsense. For a start, there's you.'

'Me?'

'Why not?' The Jackal managed his cold smile at Seth's discomfort. 'Or I'm sure Rhetia would be delighted to take over. But I'm not ready to die just yet. In two days it will be the Day of the Scarab. You say the Archon will return then. If we can hold out that long, that crazy little boy might yet restore the world.'

For a moment Seth wondered if he was slipping into fever. Then he said, 'Listen, I have to warn you about Chryse . . .'

The Jackal laughed painfully. The Fox spat.

'You know?'

'I have never trusted that pretty little cat, and never will.' The Jackal sipped the water and took a deep breath. 'Tell him, Fox.'

'We made enquiries. She spent two months with Manto. The woman is her mother's sister.'

Seth said, 'And she knows where my father is. I need to—'

'No.' The Jackal's narrow eyes watched him, intent. 'No, Seth. This is a trap. None of us leaves the Island until we can crawl down through the Oracle itself. You'd be far too useful to them – you know the layout of the tombs. They want you to make some foolish rescue attempt.'

He leaned over, his voice hard. 'Promise me you won't even try.'

'But think of that woman getting hold of Telia!' He shuddered, jumped up, unable to bear it. 'That whore-mistress. That witch!'

The Jackal and the Fox exchanged a look.

'Your father can look after her.'

'He's an old man!' Furious, Seth turned. 'I've left him on his own too long! I should be there, with them!'

In the tense silence Fox muttered, 'I could take a small team—'

'NO.' The Jackal's command was terse. 'We give no more hostages to Manto. This is about more than your guilt or Chryse's spite, or my death. The future of the Oracle and the tombs depends on us.'

Seth marched to the door and dragged it open. The chair fell with a smack. He was hot with shame and anger, but he managed to keep his voice to a low snarl of self-disgust. 'There are only bones in the tombs. Telia matters more than all of them.'

★ ★ ★

All afternoon he worked at the Oracle. He stripped to the waist and laboured there with the girls and the men Persis allowed up, hauling the stones out, dragging their weight, scrambling into the pit and fastening the great ropes around rubble and debris. There were scorpions, but at first he was too angry to care, until one ran over his foot and he leapt back in sudden stabbing terror. After that he was more wary.

Sweat gathered and ran down his back; the sun burned his face and shoulders. He let it, taking a perverse pleasure in the discomfort, the flies that bit him, the swarms of mosquitos. Despite the breeze the pavement of the Oracle reflected heat; as he straightened once to ease the strain in his spine he saw the blue sea shimmering through mirages of quivering air.

He should have brought them. He knew he had only just got out of the Port alive, but to leave them there . . . Closing his eyes against the glare his father's scorn washed over him, worse than ever because for a moment there had been something else. An understanding. He remembered how Telia had loved the monkeys . . .

'Seth?'

Chryse. He waited for a moment, then turned. She was holding an amphora of water and a cup.

'Thirsty?'

He nodded; watching her pour it, he noticed the careful manicured whiteness of her hands. When he gulped the water his throat hurt with the coolness. He handed the empty cup back to her. Very gently, he let his hand brush her fingers.

Chryse giggled. 'I suppose you want more?' She poured out a tiny drop and held it out; this time he closed his hand over hers and she let him. But her voice was cool.

'You're all sweaty, Seth. Some girls like that, but I don't.'

He turned and sat on the step. Glancing over at the workers, she sat beside him. 'So you've decided to be nice to me.'

He drank, then balanced the cup on a rock. 'It seems wise, Holiness.'

'That's right. It is. I always liked you, Seth, even from the start. Though Mirany said—'

'Don't talk about Mirany.'

Chryse smiled. 'You think she'll come back, don't you?'

'Yes.'

'But no one comes back from the Underworld. It's impossible.'

'She has. Once before.'

'Well, I don't want to talk about Mirany either.' She licked a drop of water from her thumb. 'Seth, is the Jackal ailing yet?'

Cold, he said, 'No.'

'Well, he will soon. Manto has begun her spells. And when he dies – because they always do, you know, horribly

– you and I will be able to give her the Oracle. And then we can leave, if you like. We can find your father and go anywhere, because she'll give us a ship, and jewels, and gold. Or we could stay, and . . .'

He reached out and took her fingers, rubbing his rough thumb over them. 'How do you know that she's begun?'

Chryse looked pleased, and coy. 'I told you. The scarab.'

He shook his head and pushed her hand away. Although he deliberately didn't look, he sensed her pout.

'It's true!'

'I'm not a fool. How can a tin beetle—'

'It's gold. And besides, it's . . . well, look. I'll show you.' She reached deep inside her dress and drew it out, a scarlet and blue jewel on her hand. Curious, he took it and turned it over, saw the gold pin, and under that the oldest hieroglyphs he knew, sigils of pre-Dynastic age.

'The winged beetle,' he said. 'Sign of the Sun's rebirth. Does it really fly?'

She giggled. 'Yes. And it lets me see anyone I want.'

He scratched his dry skin. 'Show me,' he said hoarsely.

For a moment he thought she wouldn't. But her lips curled in smug satisfaction, as if she knew he was hers now, that he was begging her for help. As if she couldn't resist that.

She took the beetle and placed it on the stone, then took the cup and poured water into it, very slowly, murmuring soft syllables. The water was clear and fresh; two bubbles rose and plopped on its surface.

'Now. Watch.' Her fingers picked up the scarab; very gently she slipped it into the water, laying it in the bottom of the cup.

Soft ripples distorted it. He said, 'So what's supposed—'

Then he saw Manto.

A choked gasp; his own. Chryse hugging his arm. 'Quiet, Seth. She mustn't hear us.'

The woman had her back to him. But the mirror hung before her and in the mirror he could see what she was doing. She was sitting at her table of spells in the room with the latticed windows. Slants of sunlight fell across the floor, striped the silver box she was opening. He recognized it; it was the box she had threatened the Jackal with, across the Bridge. Fascinated, he stared as she took out a glass phial and unstoppered it, and then, very gently, with a pair of gilt tweezers, lifted out a twist of hair. Fair hair.

'He's down there,' Chryse whispered.

Seth looked up. The Jackal had come out on to the Terrace of the Upper House; from here they could just see him, a thin figure leaning with both hands on the balustrade.

'We'll be able to see it working!' Chryse sounded thrilled. He wanted to pull away from her. But in the water, Manto was burning the hair.

She was holding it in a flame and instantly it frazzled black, twisting and coiling on itself.

Seth leapt up. The Jackal cried out. He bent slowly, as if fighting the pain, his arms wrapped round his chest, and then he crumpled on to his knees as if his strength had given out. One moan escaped him.

'Stop it!' Seth hissed. 'Make her stop!'

'Oh, I can't, Seth.' Chryse looked up at him calmly. 'It's up to her. She could kill him now, if she wanted.'

Voices. The Fox, others, running.

He couldn't bear it. He wanted to kick the cup over, stamp on it, crush it with his heel, let the water steam on the hot stones. Chryse smiled.

'I'm surprised it upsets you. I thought you'd do more than this to be someone, Seth. That's what Mirany said.' She reached out and caught his hand. 'Was it all pretence then?'

'No.' He stepped towards her, pulled her to her feet, put his arms round her. 'I was . . . it's just a little strange.'

She looked pleased. 'We can be so powerful, Seth. You and me. We can be just like Hermia and Argelin.'

He held her tight, looking over her shoulder at the knot of men round the Jackal, fear churning in him, the despair he dreaded.

And then, far out on the Port wall, a syrinx wailed. In the water, Manto's head jerked up. She flung down the burned hair and moved out of vision, as if to the window. And looking over the blue sea, Seth saw the boat. It was tiny and its sail flapped awkwardly, but it was heading swiftly for the Island. And standing in the stern was a tall figure he knew well.

Chryse saw it too. She pulled away from him with a howl of anger, stamped her foot, screeched with fury.

'Oh this is so unfair! She always spoils everything!'

Below, the Fox helped the Jackal stagger up. The tomb-thief could barely stand but he looked out at the boat, and the girl at the helm waved at him.

Seth breathed out, a long shaky sigh of relief.

It was Rhetia.

Instantly he turned and kissed Chryse. A long kiss, his lips on hers. When she pulled away she was red, her hair askew.

She put a hand to her mouth. 'Oh, Seth,' she breathed, and turned and ran, giggling, down the stairs of the terrace.

Ignoring the Fox's stare of disbelief, Seth watched her go. When she was out of sight, he opened his fingers.

On his dirty palm, blue and gold, and wet, lay the scarab.

A man who struck down her images

'It's not Mirany.' Oblek peered through the darkness gloomily.

'Something's there.'

'I can see that, General, but it's a lot bigger.' He raised himself on both hands and crept a little closer to the top of the dune. Black sand slid under his stubby fingers.

Argelin scowled. 'And I had thought bringing a god would be some use.'

Alexos just sniffed. His face was wan in the dimness and his eyes were still wet and puffy. Since Mirany had disappeared he had been disconsolate, sobbing that it was all his fault, having to be carried through the plain of green crop. Now, with darkness falling, the crop had petered out into a black desert, and a single figure ahead, strangely swathed.

'It's too still.' Argelin narrowed his eyes. 'Another statue.'

'We should be careful . . .'

'Why? The Rain Queen's traps are nothing to me.' Abruptly he scrambled over the top of the dune and strode on. Oblek watched him grimly.

'A man insane from drinking too little.' He laughed, gruffly. 'What an upside-down place this is, old friend.'

But Alexos was already running after Argelin, and Oblek heaved his bulk up hastily and followed. He wished with all his heart that the girl was still with them. The girl had sense. Even that upstart Seth could read and knew things, but what use was he, Oblek? Except for the songs of course. He, alone here, had the songs.

The figure was huge. As they approached it they saw it was overgrown with ivy and tangled hop bines so that almost nothing could be seen of it; a hand as big as Alexos jutted out, the toe of a brazen shoe.

Alexos stared up, his head bent back. 'It's a giant!'

Argelin sheathed his sword in disgust. 'It tells us nothing. Let's go.'

'*Wait.*'

He turned, and for a second they saw the agony that was consuming him.

'I can't wait! We must find Hermia! I don't know why I'm dragging you along anyway—'

'General.' Oblek's voice was wary. 'That wasn't me. I didn't say a word.'

For a moment they exchanged glances, then each looked at the boy. Alexos gave a wail of surprise. 'Well, it wasn't me!'

'*I spoke.*'

For a second then Oblek knew it was the god, and he fell on his knees in the shingle, shaking in terror. But did the god speak aloud like that, in a voice of metal?

The General turned on the statue. Looking up he was silent a second, then his old asperity swung back. 'Are you alive, bronze man?'

'*I was, Enemy-of-the-gods. Now, I am dead.*'

Alexos was hopping with excitement. 'What happened to you? How did you get all covered up like this?'

'*Clear my face, little being. Let me breathe, and I will tell you.*'

Quickly, before Oblek could roar, Alexos jumped up into the ivy. He climbed quickly, his deft fingers grasping tangles and knots of branch, sending small scatters of hops and berries and dead leaves falling into the musician's upturned face.

'Archon! Be careful!'

'It's all right, Oblek.' The preoccupied answer was almost lost in branch rustle. 'A bit gnarled. I can reach easily, look.'

Branches snapped and fell. A bunch of dark grapes hit the ground and spattered. Out of the webbed vines a face began to emerge, ear and eye, great lips of bronze, a nose smooth as obsidian.

A breath. It was drawn in, a gust of the Underworld's still air. Dust flew up; something stirred in the sky like a storm.

The giant creaked open one eye.

With a gasp of surprise, Alexos slithered back.

'*Fear me not, little god. I am grateful to you.*'

The eye was white as ebony, its iris blue as lapis. It stared into the darkness.

'*It has been centuries.*'

'Come down, boy,' Argelin said. 'We need to get on.' He took two swift steps, stopped and then turned. 'The road to the Garden. Are we on that road?'

The giant looked at him, askew. Heavy bines wrapped its face, knotted its closed eyelid. It said, '*The Garden lies to the west. Free me. I will lead you there.*'

'No.' It was Oblek who said it. He moved cautiously to the giant's foot. 'Archon, come down. Right now.'

'No one makes my decisions for me.' Argelin stepped aside as the boy leapt down in a shower of leaves.

'Then maybe they should, General.'

'King. I am king now, fat man, king and Archon, and I will do as I wish.' He drew his sword and slashed swiftly at the roots of the smothering growth, great thick trunks that twisted out of the rocky ground. Sap and resin seeped from the wounds.

Oblek grabbed Alexos, pulling him back. 'Argelin! Think!'

The General slashed again, the sharp blade hacking through bines. Great lengths of tangled creeper crashed down, so that the ground seemed to shudder. One finger of the giant's hand unfurled.

'You! Bronze man!' Oblek's voice was a roar of tension. 'Why did she do this? What did you do against her?'

'*Nothing.*'

'Liar!'

'*A small thing.*'

The resin oozed; it ran in sticky trails across the shingle. Argelin tugged one foot from it, then hefted the blade and cut again.

'Tell us,' Oblek yelled. 'Or are you afraid to?'

'*It is my fate to tell those who ask. I was a man who struck down her images. I replaced them with my own.*'

'Argelin! Are you listening to this?'

He had slowed. Now he turned and gazed up at the bronze giant. Its lips creaked.

'*For this, she made me a man without skin or bone, without heart or liver. I have stood like an image for countless aeons. Forests have grown over me and decayed, and grown again. Without you, I will never reach the Garden.*'

For a moment Argelin paused; then he drew back the sword to strike again.

Oblek grabbed him. 'It's a trap!'

'He can get us there.'

'You fool . . .'

'We could wander here for ever, fat man. And I will . . . Not . . . Wait!'

With the last three words he made three mighty cuts. The giant's hand sprang free, opened, flexed. The bronze elbow bent; the vast fingers grasped masses of greenery and tore them away.

Alexos backed. 'Oblek. I don't like it any more.'

'I never liked it, old friend.' The musician snatched the boy up. 'We run. Come if you want.'

He only managed three steps before the ground shuddered and heaved. Falling flat, Oblek squirmed round, saw the bronze foot strain. Vines snapped like taut cables. He grabbed Alexos but the boy wailed, 'We can't leave him!'

'Just watch me, Archon.'

'But, Oblek! *He's stuck!*'

With a skidding of sand, Oblek turned.

It was yellow as amber, sticky as glue. As Argelin struggled, it stretched from the soles of his boots, hardening into spindles and pinnacles. His sword was clotted with it; as Oblek watched in horror the stuff went stiff; Argelin yelled and swore and tugged but the blade was held fast to the branches.

'*My fate was to stay here, until someone took my place.*' The bronze lips cracked wider; the hand ripped away vines. '*A man as proud, and as deluded.*'

Argelin flung the sword away. Or tried to. As he knew

his hand was stuck to it, he gasped, tugged back, twisted, his one foot held tight.

Across the black desert he stared at Oblek, and Oblek stared at him.

'Help me,' he breathed.

'Well, if you ever need a job I'm sure we can find you one. Pickpockets and scribes need the same deft fingers, it seems.'

The Jackal was white with the aftershock of the pain, but he sat upright and waved away the Fox's anxious attentions.

'Eat something, Chief. There's a box of—'

'Shut up, Fox. But there are spells, you say. And you don't know them.'

'Yes.' Seth tried not to look too smug but it wasn't easy. 'She had to learn them by heart – I suppose Manto taught her them. But that's because she can't read.'

He turned the scarab over. They saw the wedge-shaped letters cut into the gold, circling round in a tight spiral.

The Jackal said, 'Not hieroglyphs.'

'Much older. Pre-Dynastic.'

'And you can decipher them.' He held his side and breathed out, unsteadily. Seth saw the sweat flush his pale skin.

'Just watch me. Get some water, Fox.' But when the one-eyed man brought it the Jackal put his long hand over the top of the goblet swiftly. 'Are you sure this will work? I have no desire to put anyone else into her power.'

'I know, but there's no choice. She'll kill you.'

The Jackal looked up ruefully. Then he said, 'She's here.'

For a fearful moment Seth thought he meant Manto, and spun in fear, but it was Rhetia who was running up the broad white steps, Rhetia in a corselet of finest chain mail, silver-bright.

Breathless, she said, 'Where are the others?' Then she saw them racing down from the Oracle, and stared in dismay at their dirty, weary faces, the bindings on their hands. 'Is the Oracle cleared?'

'Not yet.' Persis came up to her. 'What does the Emperor say?'

Rhetia straightened. Turning to the Jackal she said, 'Jamil must hear this.'

While they waited for him the girls drank thirstily, and Gaia poured a little of the precious water into a glass bowl, sprinkling it with myrrh and rose petals. They each washed their hands and Seth turned his gaze away, because Chryse smiled over at him coyly. She hadn't found out yet, then. He wasn't looking forward to her fury.

Two of the Jackal's men escorted Jamil in. He was hot from the climb and beckoned for water; the Fox poured it out with a sour look.

'I'm not your slave, Prince.'

'Just as well.' Jamil took a grateful sip. 'Your ugliness would get you sold.'

Ignoring the thief's sharp bark of laughter he turned his

massive bulk to Rhetia. 'Holiness. You have seen my uncle's messenger?'

She nodded. Aware that every eye was on her, she pulled up a small gilt stool and sat in the centre of the group.

'It took two days for the message to come back. These are the Emperor's terms. Jamil and the elephants are to be handed back. Then the Prince will command the fleet, jointly, with the Speaker. The tombs will be defended, and the Port relieved. The barbarians will—'

'Be driven into the sea.' The Jackal gave Jamil a dark look. 'I seem to have heard this little scenario before. And after our wonderfully generous rescue? A satrapy?'

Rhetia smiled. 'No. The god will rule through the Speaker.'

The Nine were silent. It was Seth who said, 'But someone will have to command the army, run the Port . . .'

She seemed a little reluctant. But she lifted her chin and looked at him straight. 'From now on, the Speaker will command everything.'

A small breath among the girls. Seth looked at the Jackal. They both knew she had made some agreement with the Emperor, that he would never have agreed to leave the Two Lands without a hold over the Oracle.

'It seems to me,' Jamil said slowly, 'that the Lady Mirany would not make a great—'

'Not Mirany.' Rhetia stood, tall. 'We have to face the fact that Mirany is not coming back. No one comes back from the Underworld. Neither she nor Argelin, nor the musician will ever return.'

'And the Archon?'

She shrugged. 'The first thing I – we must do is find a new Archon, of course.'

They had all noticed the slip. Their silence told her that. Finally Persis said, 'Why should it be you?'

'I'm the oldest, the longest served, the most fearless.' She looked round at them, challenging. 'Because at a time like this the Oracle needs a Speaker who isn't afraid of her own shadow. Who's willing to take risks.'

'Oh, you take risks all right,' Chryse breathed sourly.

The rest looked at each other uneasily.

'Well?' Rhetia snapped. 'Do you all agree, or not?'

Persis looked at Seth. Then, scraping the soil out from under one fingernail she said anxiously, 'I'm afraid things have changed a little while you were away. We needed to consult the Oracle, Rhetia. We convened the Nine, and a Speaker was chosen. At least . . . That is . . .' Catching Rhetia's eye, she stumbled into silence.

'The Holiness means, the god chose and spoke to one of those assembled,' the Jackal said pleasantly. He seemed to enjoy saying it.

Rhetia was pale with fury. 'Who?'

Seth realized they were all waiting for him.

'Me,' he muttered.

She seemed not to understand, just for a moment. Then

her astonishment overwhelmed her; she stared at him, at the others, laughed weakly. 'A scribe? A *man*?'

'Apparently,' the Jackal sounded unperturbed, 'in an emergency . . .'

'It's totally ridiculous!' She glared at Persis. 'What were you all thinking of?'

Why ridiculous?

The voice was so soft Seth barely heard it; it made his heart leap, and yet unexpected relief flooded him.

'The god asks, why.' Over the girls' rising argument his voice was harsh.

Rhetia spun. 'The god! You have such a nerve, scribe!'

Ask her why she wishes for power so much. Tell her that power is a scorpion; that it can sting itself to death.

He licked his lips. 'I can't say that!

Speak my words. If you are the Speaker.

He had no desire to. He knew to say any such thing would instantly make her his enemy; that it would make the whole situation a battle between her and himself. Gods were supposed to be wise. Was this the choice Mirany had made? But when he opened his mouth the words came out anyway.

Holiness, beware. It is the god who chooses the Speaker and no other. I the Bright One, Rider of the Chariot of the Sun, Mouse Lord, Giver of Gifts, say this. Do not wish for power because it will destroy you. Do not wish to hold the sun in your heart, because it will burn you. The ways of gods are strange and beyond all mortals. You are brave, Rhetia. You are strong. Let that be enough.

The words rang in the loggia and white rooms of the Upper House. All down the terrace the marble figures of the Speakers seemed to hear them, sitting rigid in attention. Far out in the bay they called a school of dolphins out to leap and splash, and a small brown snake flicked from a crack and slithered over the Fox's foot.

Rhetia stood. She was pale with anger, but her dignity was frosty. She walked to the door and no one else seemed to breathe, but at the door she turned.

With a terrible calm she said, 'The Emperor's agreement is with no one but me. If you want his help, I must be Speaker. That's your choice. While you delay, hour by hour, the barbarians are stripping the bodies of the Archons.'

When she was gone, Seth collapsed on to a bench. A breath of release went round the room; Chryse said, 'That bitch,' and Persis looked at the Jackal.

'We'll talk to her. But she won't—'

He held up his hand. 'Try, Holiness. Just try.'

The priestesses drifted out, Chryse last.

The Jackal put his head in his hands and groaned. 'Seth . . .'

'He *made* me! You don't know how it is! He's so . . .'

Powerful, the voice supplied slyly. Seth was silent.

'Yes, well. I suppose at least this means we must carry out your plan.' The tomb-thief sat back.

'Watch the door, Fox.' He tipped the dirty water on the floor, poured clean into the bowl, and looked at Seth.

Seth took out the scarab. It glittered, a blue and red insect. For a moment he thought it would fly away, so he gripped it tighter.

'What is that?' They had forgotten Jamil was still here; the Jackal frowned.

'Sorcery, Prince. I trust it doesn't trouble you.'

Jamil stared. 'You are ill, Lord Osarkon.'

'Yes.' The Jackal rubbed his face with one shaky hand. Then he said, 'Do it.'

Seth dropped the scarab into the water. As it floated down he chanted the words he saw on its back, the strange murmured syllables, wondering if the god approved or disapproved, whether he would be struck down for this. But if the god was still here he said nothing, and the words hummed and bubbles rose from the scarab, and when Seth came to the name in the cartouche, he altered it.

The water blurred. He saw a small room, lit by a single oil lamp. A figure came through the doorway, paused, and stared in amazement at a brightness in the air, blue eyes wide with disbelief.

Seth smiled, wryly.

'Yes, Pa,' he whispered. 'It's me.'

The Seventh Gate
Of the Crocodile

It is true that men disobey the gods, though it seems foolish that they think they could know better.

All my long lifetimes I've heard stories of those who did this, and were punished. In the marketplaces people listen to the tale-tellers, and nod and are satisfied, and pay their coins to the chained monkey in its velvet coat. Then they go home and disobey the gods.

I am not vengeful. A being of light and youth does not brood. And my brother in his darkness dreams of silence and a world that contains nothing, which a god can never know.

But the Rain Queen.

She is water and soil and anger.

She is different.

Dying before their eyes

'How did you get here?'

'I guard the tombs.' Kreon smiled at her sideways. 'And the tombs lead only here.'

'Is the Oracle—'

'The way is still partly blocked.'

She noticed how he kept his eyes from the flames. Now he turned their paleness on her.

'Mirany, you must come back. The Oracle is threatened by more than barbarians.'

'But I can't.' She glanced up nervously at the moon through the tossing trees. 'How can he get to the Garden without us?'

He shrugged. 'The Queen's ways are a mystery, but

Argelin will never persuade her to release Hermia. You must see that. His madness is a gift from her; she draws him down by it. It will destroy you all. Find Alexos, Mirany, please, and make him bring you back.' And then he added quietly, 'Or come alone, now. With me.'

She knotted her fingers together and stared into the fire. She wanted to go. She was Speaker, and she should be there, and she was worried about Seth, and the Jackal, and Manto. But she could never leave the Archon, and besides . . .

'It's just that the god told me to come. I asked him—'

'—to break down the walls of the world.' Kreon smiled his crooked smile. 'Never ask a god for things, Mirany. He may give them in a way you would not wish.'

'But surely it must mean there's a chance.'

'To have Hermia alive again as Speaker? All as it was before? You would want that?'

His voice was kind but sharp. She felt a despair in it, and wondered, because if the gods despaired, what could mortals do?

'Men have always had this dream of returning from death.' He looked away from her into the moonlit grove. 'This is why they preserve the bodies of the Archons, wrap them with jewels, fold them in linen and natron. Because one day a road might be found, a way back from the Garden. But the road does not return, Mirany, and if it should, the whole of time would unravel, the monsters be loosed and Chaos fall on us again. Argelin must not succeed. If you stay, this must be your task. Do you understand? Not to help him. *To stop him.*'

'The god . . .'

He smiled sadly. 'My brother is young. He will always be young. He loves the sun and the bright animals and the sparkling sea. What does he know of fear, Mirany, and the descent into darkness, of age and decay? What does he know of pain? That is my realm.'

'People know,' she said, thinking of the sword slash, of the blood when Hermia fell, how it had run over Argelin's hands, his choking anguish as he had tried to staunch it.

'Then perhaps people know more than the gods.' He turned. 'Have you decided?'

She knew she had, but not how. 'I have to go on.'

'You feel for this man.'

She shrugged. 'I never thought I would. He destroyed the Oracle. But perhaps the Oracle is something inside us. Even inside him. How will he find the Garden, Kreon? Where is the road?'

He looked up into the gusty branches, his white hair drifting. Then he said, 'Do you still have the gold scarab?'

For a moment she had no idea what he meant. And then she remembered the tiny beetle Manto had given her. It was still pinned in the folds of her tunic; feeling for it now she remembered how it had betrayed her at the gate. She pulled it out.

'This? But it's the witch's—'

'So she no doubt thinks. Put it down, Mirany.'

She laid it in the litter of dead leaves. Kreon leaned over and touched it with one white finger. At once it shrivelled, glinted, moved. It grew to fist size, a heart-scarab, was turquoise, then gold, then a coppery brown. Briefly it spread wings, tucked them under the heavy carapace. With a rustle, it ran into the dark.

Kreon's eyes turned to her. 'Follow its tracks. They are the tracks of the sun. As you go on they will become easier to see. Do not turn aside, not for any reason. Do what you must, even if it means none of you return. Even my brother.'

She shook her head. 'I don't know if I can stop Argelin.'

He did not answer. When she turned back to him, no one was there.

'Kreon?'

She stood, looking round. Had he ever been there at all? Had it been her own shadow she had spoken with, because there was no one else alive but her, in all this empty land?

The night was black. In the east the disc of the moon hung, and the great plain beyond stirred and murmured. She shivered with loneliness.

Then, running out from her feet, she saw a mark. It was a tiny furrow, as if a child had rolled a ball through mud, but it led west between the olives and as she kicked debris aside from it she saw it headed straight out of the wood. She walked along it. At the grove's edge she looked back at the fire.

Shadows flickered its margins.

'I'll do my best,' she whispered.

'Pull!' Argelin yelled again.

Oblek swore bitterly, changed his grip and heaved. The General's hand came off the sword with such force that they both nearly fell; Oblek clutched Argelin's armour to stay upright. Above them the giant snapped its bonds. One great arm snatched at them, missed, swung again. Oblek hauled the General towards him, the yellow resin dragging at their heels. A gobbet splashed Oblek, gumming his fingers.

'The sword!' Argelin swung back.

'Leave it!'

'Don't be a fool!' He went to grab for it.

Oblek heaved him away. 'Touch it again and you're stuck there for ever! I take the boy and go!'

For an instant pure hatred consumed them; then Argelin tore his foot out of the resin and swung away.

Oblek stopped in horror. 'Archon! *Don't!*'

The boy stood on the toe of the bronze man, staring up. A rain of greenery fell around him; his beautiful face was calm. He said, 'I can free you, if you want.'

The giant went quite still.

Oblek groaned.

'*How can a child free me?*'

Alexos laughed happily. 'Like this.' He reached out and pushed his small hand through the knotted bines, shoulder deep, till he must have found the polished surface of the great foot. Then he began to sing. His voice was high, tuneless, shrill as a bird's whistle. The song had no words. Instead it had warmth. Even from where he tugged himself frantically out of the amber resin, Oblek felt it creep into his bones and body, a heat that comforted at first, and then grew fierce and burned. He backed off.

'Old friend—'

Stay back, Oblek. And then it won't hurt.

But it did. Radiance stung tears to his eyes; he put a hand up to cover them, heard Argelin gasp. Their shadows streamed behind them, because the heat was a glow now, the giant's body a shimmering copper. As they watched, it intensified to red. Bushes burst into flame around them; they saw a molten man, towering above them, a colossus of fire. One drop of hot metal as big as a boulder splashed from his fingertip.

It hit the desert beside Alexos and bounced, eerily slowly, the globules wobbling, hardening, thudding into the shingle. Small spheres of bronze rolled down the dunes.

'It's melting.' Oblek hardly recognized Argelin's croak; then the General came up to his shoulder. 'Look at its face.'

White-hot, the giant had become a god. Its incandescent features burned as if the sun inhabited the spaces of its body; it became a solar creature, an Archon wrapped in the ceremony of gold and pure light. The bines ignited round its brow; it lifted both hands to its face and they moved like flesh moves, easily as a man's hands, and it stared down at Alexos through wide eyes.

'There will be others,' it said.

'I will release all of them. Tell her.'

The giant sighed. 'She knows.'

'And Mirany. Can you see Mirany?'

'The marsh.' But the words were twisting too, sounds coming loose and running down, the fire inside it breaking out through rivets and seams, through fingernails and ears, so that before their eyes it became in seconds a white blaze standing wide armed to the moon, and then a hissing, crumpling, tumbling mess of fiery pieces crashing to the sand.

Argelin pulled Alexos back, clasping his hand.

'That's what I did to her statues,' the General said.

The boy looked round in surprise.

'That was revenge. This is release.' He looked down. 'Let me go now please.'

Argelin's hand closed tighter. 'Not until we get to the Garden,' he said, his voice taut.

'You heard. Let him go.' Oblek's rumble came from behind. Instantly Argelin turned and brought the weight of his fist thudding into Oblek's stomach, then on the back of his neck, hard. With a retch of gasped air Oblek crashed down. He hit the sand and never moved.

Alexos turned to run but couldn't. He tugged and fought and kicked, but the General's hand and his were sealed together. Argelin pulled him close and grabbed him.

'Stop struggling, Archon. You're with me now.' He lifted their clasped hands; from the palms resin oozed, already clotted hard. Sheathing the sword he pushed the boy in front of him. 'Walk. Now.'

'But what about Oblek?'

Argelin didn't look back. The moon caught his haggard face, the dry cracked lips. His voice was edgy with unreason, his mood grim.

'We're all already dead. You. Me. Even Hermia. When I find who killed Hermia . . .'

He paced quickly, and Alexos trudged beside him, looking up at him, warily. 'But that was you, General.'

Argelin stared ahead. 'She drove me to it,' he whispered.

They were mice.

At first she had thought they were rats and that had terrified her, because once at home on Mylos they'd had a plague of rats and that still made her shudder.

But no. These were the god's creatures.

As she climbed down the rocky track she felt them scuttle out from holes in the land, from rocks and stones. Behind her, over the clifftop, a great glow was lighting the horizon, growing around her from ruby red to a misty shimmer. The air was damp; she could taste moisture on her lips. Had the sun risen? Had she already walked a whole night in the Underworld?

The mice were hard to see. Brown and discreet they ran in small packs, their tiny claws rustling in the litter of leaf drift. As the light paled, its quality puzzled her. She was clambering down into a vagueness that her eyes could not penetrate, as if mist had gathered in some vast hollow. Swirls of it came up to her, tendrils of opaque air. Slipping on the steep rock, Mirany reached out and caught hold of leaves, fleshy and thick, their edges studded with tiny polyps that her fingers crushed. The scent they released made her sneeze.

The mice had stopped. She could still hear their squeaks, but they were no longer moving with her. They had stayed up in the rocks, and now she began to wish she had, because the mist was rising over her, and as she climbed down into it, as if into cloud, it was impossible to see the furrowed track, or anything.

She stopped.

Pearly light surrounded her. There was no up or down. There was only vagueness. It smelt of mildew; as she spread her hands out they were silvered with droplets. Her tunic clung to her. She shivered.

Then, with a creaking of wings something splashed and took off and fluttered close over her head; she gasped, ducked, took a step forward.

And sank into swamp.

It was warm and steamy; she gave a stifled scream and flung out her arms, terrified for a sickening moment that she would topple under the surface. The muck rose to above her waist until she felt something solid underfoot; floundering she struggled for balance. But this was not water, it was clogged by ferns and floating algae, a soup of greenery. Panicking she tried to turn, scramble out, but the moon was hidden and she had no idea now which way she had come. As she turned, the marsh lapped, slicking her sleeves against her skin, rising and falling in thick waves that slimed her arms.

With a great effort she began to wade; something swam against her side and she gasped, but the oozing muck under her feet shifted and squelched, and with every step she was sure she was sinking deeper. 'Where are you?' she thought, and then called it aloud, demanding.

'Where are you?'

Nothing answered but mosquitos, a haze of them in her hair, biting her face.

Mirany slapped them away, shuddering. She felt as if she had come to some depth that could never exist, that she would never escape from. It was hard not to panic; she wanted to scream and flounder and yell out for help, but the mist was ominous with silence.

Then, from her left, came a splash. A slithering ripple.

As if something heavy had slid into the swamp.

★ ★ ★

He was burning with fever. As Jamil's physician stood back and shook his head, Seth muttered, 'You must be able to do something!'

'Alleviate the symptoms. The cause is beyond my art.'

The Jackal's skin was clammy with sweat; he lay doubled up in agony on the bed, clutching the flimsy mosquito net convulsively. Fox held him as the spasms worsened.

'This is sorcery,' he spat. 'Filthy spells.'

'We have to keep him alive.'

Through the window the sound of the renewed attack rang; the smack and reek of flaming pitch souring the air. Seth glanced out. Moonlight lit the Port like a great mirror, small lights here and there winking in its ruined houses, the stars a vast backdrop over the desert. Across the black waters of the harbour a sliver of brilliance ran right up to the Island, right up to the window, as if this was the road of the dead, and the Jackal's ghost had only to rise from his body and walk down it, and go.

In the dim room bowls of myrrh and sandalwood smoked, columns of incense rose. Most of the Nine seemed to be there, Persis praying before a broken image of the Rain Queen, Gaia and Tethys wiping the sick man's face and arms with some cooling potion that smelt of lemons. Rhetia paced impatiently. 'This plan—' she hissed.

'—will work.' Seth held her eyes steadily. 'I know it will.'

'Oh, really. I suppose the god told you.'

Her sarcasm sent chills of fear down his back. The god had said nothing.

The Jackal choked out a shuddering breath. He was beyond speech now, dying before their eyes. Seth was wracked with guilt. The plan had been his idea. Maybe they should have surrendered, played for time . . .

A flash of flame exploded in the Upper House garden. Artemisia crackled, a pungent burning of branches. Sweating, the Jackal cried out, his head flung back.

'Come on,' Seth urged, his teeth set with tension. 'Come on . . .'

But under the Rain Queen's heartless moon the Port lay silent. It was too late. He had failed. The Oracle would be taken, the thief-lord would die. He had failed the god.

And then the door was flung open, and Chryse raced in. Ignoring Gaia's 'Hush!' and Rhetia's startled stare, she crossed the room in two steps and slapped Seth full in the face.

'You scum!' she screamed, 'you hateful, low-bred, arrogant *scum*. Where is it? How could you *dare* do this to me!'

A swamp of delirium

Manto lit another oil lamp, and placed it carefully in the dark alcove. She drew her black mantle over her head and turned.

'Go below and guard the door. If men come for the other girls let them in, but no one else. Don't disturb me again tonight.'

The hetaira nodded and backed, relieved. The room reeked of sorcery.

Manto looked around. Everything was ready. The darkness was heavy with the man's agony. After years of practice at these rites she could almost taste it, a salty sourness like sweat that was not a smell or a sound but something of both. He was fighting her, but his despair was clear. Pain and fear were her weapons, and they never failed her.

'He's near the end,' she said quietly.

'Yes, but will they surrender the Island to save him?' Ingeld leaned by the latticed window looking out into the shadowy alley. A group of his men loitered down there, the moon glinting on their armour and stolen gold.

Manto shrugged. 'Probably not.'

'And you do not care, do you, sorceress? You will torture him in any case.'

She smiled, and turned. 'Are you afraid of me, Ingeld? Of my deep magic? Does the hero fear a woman's arts?'

He would have killed anyone else for even suggesting it. For a moment he thought about killing her, but the dread of being hag-ridden by her ghost for years held his hand. Perhaps she was right. He grunted and stood up.

'I have divided my men. The majority ride with me tonight, to raid the City of the Dead. Word has come of a breakthrough into a tomb – empty, but tunnels lead from it.' He nodded. 'I will do Argelin's evil for him.' Then he looked at her closely through the darkness. 'You are certain that he will not return?'

Manto shrugged. 'Who returns from the Underworld? The Rain Queen has beguiled him into her secret realm; she'll have her own revenge on Argelin. Forget him, Ice-lord. He was broken before he went.'

She crossed to her crystal box and opened it. He saw

how her plump fingers hovered over the glass phial of hair and skin, how they caressed it lightly. Suddenly all he wanted was to be out, to breathe air that had no stink of death. He strode to the door, pulling on the bronze helmet, but as he passed behind her she said, 'The rest of the men?'

'Ready for you. When the Island is taken, a messenger will come. You will be escorted to the Oracle, and you will be Speaker. As we agreed.'

In the mirror she watched him leave and then smiled at herself, a pleased, secret smile. When the Northerners had all the gold they wanted she would have to devise some holding spell, some forgetfulness of their homes to keep them here. She would need forces to stand against the Emperor, though her real power would lie in fear and the threat of sorcery. And the voice of the Oracle.

She looked down. In a small tray of basalt inlaid with silver scorpions, a tiny fragment of fingernail lay in the corrosive liquid she had mixed from oils and acids and the venom-sacks of snakes. Carefully, using a pair of silver tongs, she lifted it out and examined it. Almost gone now. The merest sliver of dead cells, and yet here she held a man's life, all his thoughts and memories, his spirit, his very self. With a small sigh she placed it back in the black mess, wiping the tongs on linen.

Ingeld had been right. Death was no longer enough. For several years she had required more, she had needed to be cruel. Slaves and girls were all very well, but the torment of a man, a man like this one, thrilled her with pleasure, slaked her dark thirst. Wetting her forefinger she ran it over her curved eyebrow, examining in the mirror the blackness of her eyes, her smooth skin. She looked plump and sleek, younger than her years. Her hair was grey but she liked it shorn; it set her aside from the foolish girls, the scathing fishwives of the Port. No one was like her. And with the Jackal dead she would rule both the Island and the thief-world, the living and the dead.

She had nothing personal against him. She had held no hatred for Argelin either. They were men and they were in her way. After this one, there would be others.

For a moment she stood in the dimness listening to the door below, the low voices of the clients as they climbed up into the rooms of the hetairas, the distant wail of Marta's baby. Then she reached into the box and took out the phial.

With the tongs she extracted another hair. One would do. He could not survive more and the longer it took the better. Carefully, she lowered the hair towards the venom.

A muffled sound.

It came from behind her and she glanced up, alert. The bronze mirror reflected the dark, distorted room, a concave shadowiness of furniture, flimsy curtains, the stack of amphorae, the shelf of scrolls with their eye-tags hanging.

She looked back. Very gently, the hair touched the poison. She settled it in.

Then she said 'How did you get in here?'

He stepped out from behind the leopard couch and she saw him, a small, scrawny-looking man, his hands gripped in fists.

'Up the stairs. I told them I wanted a girl.'

'The doorkeeper should have recognized you.' Wiping her hands, Manto turned. 'As I do.'

Pa nodded. 'You've had my house watched. Why? What do you want?'

'Because of your son, why else?'

Pa frowned. She smiled to herself to see how nervous he was, how afraid.

Quietly, he said, 'Listen, woman. Seth is nothing to me. For years now. Everything he does he does for himself, not us. I don't want my girl hurt because he's mixed up in some crazy rebellion. We've got nothing to do with any of that.'

He had stepped closer. She thought about calling for the slaves, but what threat was he to her?

'Ah yes, your little girl. What a pretty child she is.'

Pa looked down. When he glanced up his face was anxious.

'Look. I have something to say about her. I'm not young. I won't live much longer. I want Telia to be looked after. Do you understand?'

Manto raised an eyebrow. 'I'm not sure.'

'I want her somewhere she'll be alive, and protected. I don't ask for anything else – a girl without family must live as she can, in these times.' He shrugged, hopeless. 'As you say, she's pretty.'

The hetaira considered him coolly. 'You are a different man than I had expected,' she said after a moment. 'Is the girl with you?'

'No. Not yet. Not till I . . . well, she's too young yet.' He came forward, closer to her.

'She will be safe? Rumours are about that you are to be Speaker. If she could come to the Island with you. If she could be one of the Nine . . .'

He was around the couch. She had not realized how lithe he was. She stepped back.

Like a cat, Pa leapt. He swept the table with his hands; as she screeched and grabbed at him everything crashed to the floor; bowl, mirror, crystal phial. Shards of glass crunched underfoot; poison drained into the cedar boards. Manto yelled, then he had his thin hand over her mouth; she squirmed for the dagger in her robe but his grip was tight. Both her hands were dragged behind her, the dark cloth of her own mantle whipped around her face. Staggering against the shelves they brought down a cascade of amulets, curse tablets, eye charms, ankhs. Feathers of wryneck and silver wheels drifted and bounced around the room. Fearfully, Pa struggled to keep the woman silent, wrench the dagger from her hand.

His fingers closed on the corded grip; he forced her wrist back, she screeched a muffled screech.

Then he had the point up to her eye.

'Not a word,' he gasped.

Crocodiles.

Mirany was certain of it. She tried to keep totally still but she was shuddering, creating tiny ripples, making the swamp lap around her. To her left something powerful surged; she closed her eyes, imagining the long snout streaking towards her, the terrible jaws clamping on her legs. A shiver of movement slid past her waist; she wanted to scream and scream, but instead she managed a plea.

'Don't leave me here. This is the farthest place I've ever been from you.'

He didn't answer.

But strangely, quite suddenly, she knew he was here. The terrible loneliness she had felt since Kreon vanished, left her. She opened her eyes; they were wet. Beads of moisture glinted in her hair. The light was growing. She leaned down into the water, and touched his hands.

There was a green place, a swamp of delirium. The Jackal swam up from it, kicking his legs hard because the algae and growth clung to him and long-jawed aquatic monsters snapped at his heels. Breaking surface was a huge relief, and he gasped in air, pushing the long hair back from his face. All around him glass shattered, spattering the surface; a rain of slivers, crystal rainbows in the sunlight, lead curses, wryneck feathers, eye charms.

Through the downpour he saw a triple face looking down at him, a snouted mask crowned with the sun-disc, a scorpion and a shadow, their dark eyes watching him struggle.

'Is that you?' he breathed.

It reached down, and took his hands.

The physician looked at Jamil. 'I'm sorry, prince. This is the end.'

They knew that.

The convulsions had stopped; now the Jackal lay quiet, slumped, the Fox watching his shallow breathing intently. All the tomb-thief's vigour had sunk, Seth thought, had been drowned in the fever that had exhausted him.

Rhetia stood up, and the rest of the Nine did too, as if death was coming like a potentate, to be honoured. Fox leaned over and kissed his leader on both cheeks and stood back, grim with grief and anger.

The Jackal did not move at all. Even the terrible heavings of his chest were stilled; only Seth saw how his left hand closed slowly on the rough blanket. As he watched, Seth felt something crawl from his own tunic; glancing down he saw the scarab open its metal wings, take off and fly.

Persis gasped; Rhetia stared.

The beetle flew once around the Jackal's head. Then it fell on the floor and the Fox stamped his foot on it, all his hatred in one metallic crunch.

Rhetia bent over the bed. 'He's not breathing,' she said.

They were silent. As if their silence could bring him back.

His hand was cold and strange and wrong. A god should not be touched, she thought. She knew if she pulled he would rise up to her out of the water, that she might see him, but the thought filled her with terror.

'No. I can do this on my own.'

Are you sure?

'Yes. Please, let me.'

Then let go of your friend's fingers.

With a shudder of understanding she opened her hand, felt the grip loosen. 'Is it Seth? You wouldn't have brought Seth here just to help me?' She was angry and shaking. 'You wouldn't do that?'

He must have been smiling; it was in his voice. All he said was, '*Look. The Temple.*'

It rose out of the swamp, a pale facade shimmering as if made of mist, but as she stepped forward, her tunic dragging around her, she saw it was real, a half-drowned complex rising from shallow green staircases, columns of carved granite, pylons of stone cut with figures of gods.

Wading closer she realized the place glittered with dragonflies, they clustered on its edges, and lichens of yellow and gold matted the images. On each side of her, long snouts rose from the swamp, a double row of stone faced crocodiles, their eyes barely above the water, algae greening their carved scales. As she struggled on, the wash she made slapped against them, sending dragonflies skitting with deft, alert zigzags of wings.

But there were real beasts here too, sliding and nosing between the stone ones, their tiny eyes surfacing and watching her. Once, one of them opened its vast jaws in a yawn, slapping back into the swamp with a treacly splash. Mirany held her breath.

When she reached the steps she climbed slowly. Rising from the water made the tunic plaster itself to her legs, the moist air steaming with heat. Midges annoyed her, and brushing them away she saw the dark rectangle of the doorway ahead, its black emptiness ominous.

She crept up to it.

It rose above her. As she peered round, tiny against the mighty stones, she saw the hall inside was immense, painted on every wall with colourful frescoes of water-lilies, columns of hieroglyphs, great figures carrying jugs and robes and staves in an urgent sideways procession.

In the centre, ten steep steps rose to a great throne, wavy-backed like water. On the throne, a being sat. Hands crossed, it stared down at her, carrying a flail and a crook like the Archons of old, its white robe bound with gold thread around waist and knees. A great head-dress snouted like a crocodile masked its face, and between its ears a sun-disc gleamed, of purest gold.

In the black slits, living eyes watched her approach.

The giant had been right; there had been others.

It had been a plain of punishments, but Argelin had dragged the boy across it, never stopping, despite his shrill protests.

A man lip-deep in a lake of wine, the sweet dark liquid receding whenever he tried to drink from it. A sobbing woman carefully building a house of wet sand that dried and crumbled as she worked. An ancient couple invisible to each other, both struggling to push a rock along a path, each working against the other and taking no notice of Alexos' anxious explanations. Now a scribe working on a vast scroll that lay across the sand like a road, scribbling and muttering to himself.

'What are you doing?' Alexos called, pulling Argelin closer.

'Translating.' The man did not lift his nose from the hieroglyphs.

'Will you finish soon?'

He blinked. Then, as if astonished, he looked up at them both. His eyes seemed weak, palest blue. Small lights like stars moved in their pupils.

'I daren't stop. If I stop the world ends. Don't you see, this is the story of the world.'

Despite the reckless haste, Argelin said, 'She told you that?'

'It's true.' The scribe turned back to his scroll. They could see parts of it were lost, eaten by beetles. Ragged holes devoured cartouches bright with ancient names.

'What did you do to her to deserve this?'

For a moment he did not answer. The stylus wrote swiftly.

Then he said, 'Diverted a gift of gold. from her temple to my family's coffers.'

Argelin laughed harshly. 'A hard punishment for a petty theft. What horrors will she have in mind for me?' He tugged the boy away.

'Come. You can't release them all.'

'I could.' Alexos trudged after him, dispirited. 'But it would hardly please her. And you don't want her angry, do you? Have you thought about what you'll do when we get there? Just asking her will be no use. And you have nothing to bargain with . . .'

'I have you, crazy boy.' He looked ahead, at the dark plain. 'And I have something else.'

'What?' Alexos sounded avid to know.

The General stared grimly ahead. 'Love,' he said. 'A burning fever.'

★   ★   ★

The voice was distorted.

'*He's coming round. He's waking.*'

There was a taste in his mouth that he recognized, the taste of the water he had drunk at the Well of Songs. Someone was holding it to his lips; he sipped it and remembered the crystal handful he had gulped down hastily there, that had dissolved some tight inner knot in him, that had taken away the nightmares of the dead, the twisted self-hate that had filled his nights.

He looked up at the god's triple-faced mask. 'Is that you?' he murmured.

But it was no god; it shivered and burst in his eyes; it was sunlight in a room, and Seth and Rhetia and Fox all crowding him.

The Jackal licked dry lips. He felt sick and weary and shaky all over but he wasn't going to let them see that. With a great effort, he managed his cold smile.

'It seems I'm not dead then,' he whispered.

The masked face looked down at Mirany. 'Come no closer.'

'Hermia?'

'You know who I am.'

She knew. The long fingernails dripping water, the blue dress shimmering like the waves of the sea. Mirany shivered, despite the muggy warmth. The Rain Queen gazed impassively down.

'This isn't the Garden . . .'

'This is not the Garden. You've been there. You know that.' The crocodile face lifted slightly; the Queen's voice darkened. 'This is the place where you will stop Argelin.'

Mirany's voice shook, but she said boldly, 'How? By killing him? We're all already dead, aren't we?'

The Queen laughed. There was a quiver in the building; the shallow pools of swamp on the marble floor rippled. Dragonflies settled on Mirany's dress.

'There are other ways. You will make him forget.'

'Forget?'

'Hermia and her death. Use this.'

One hand uncrossed; its wet fingers held out the flail. Mirany swallowed, then began to climb the steps. Her wet sandals left a trail of algae and weed. At the top she reached out, and as she took the thin wand her fingers touched, just for a moment, the Queen's. The flesh was cool, and as non-existent as water.

Mirany looked at the flail. It was striped gold and black, the ceremonial cords knotted and threaded with faience beads. 'How can he ever forget her?'

'Touch him with it. Then he will wander here for eternity, seeking the reason he came, and you and the Archon can return and take the fat man with you. There is a war awaiting you, an Oracle to be kept open, because the god must be heard by his people. Argelin is mine now.'

She lifted her head; the masked eyes gazing out at the swamp.

'He comes. Do as I say, priestess. Or my anger will fall on you, too.'

Mirany turned.

She hurried down the steps.

The road runs through light and through darkness

He was unsteady, but walking. Fox hovered anxiously.

'You should rest.'

'No time.' The Jackal looked pale, his skin still clammy, but the old cold amusement was in his eyes. He made himself stand tall, eyed his paleness in a silvered mirror. Then he said, 'The old man has done what he promised, but if she's made him pay, Seth, I swear I will take revenge for both of us.'

'I don't want revenge.' Dully, Seth sank into a winged seat. 'I want Pa here.'

He was chilled with fear. Had Manto killed Pa? And where was Telia?

The Jackal said, 'Things will move quickly now.' He turned to the Nine.

They had put Chryse on a small stool by the window, Tethys and Gaia keeping a close eye on her. She was still smouldering with temper, her flushed face held away from them all, and when the Jackal said, 'Holiness,' she didn't even turn.

The tomb-thief reached over and took her chin in his hand. Rhetia snapped, 'Don't touch her,' but he relentlessly turned Chryse's face to him.

'I don't blame you,' he said coldly, 'for your family ties. But you must know we can never trust you again.'

Her eyes red, Chryse sniffed back tears. She spat deliberately on the floor in front of him, then wrenched her face away.

A burst of flame crashed outside the window. The Temple parapet crashed in splintered stone. Rhetia leapt up. She faced the Jackal.

'We must act. Now, or we're lost.'

They confronted each other, a tall man and a tall woman, in an instant of bitter decision. Then the Jackal stepped back, spreading one long hand.

'I agree. Neither you nor I can dispute the choice of the god, lady. Seth remains Speaker. But you are the Nine and the care of the Oracle is yours. This is the time for you to resume it.'

He turned to Jamil at the window, looking down at the

barbarians swarming across the blue channel. 'Prince, you are free to go. Here and now, I release you. Rhetia, send your signal to the fleet. Bring them in.'

She stared at him. 'What signal?'

He smiled. 'Oh, come, Holiness, don't insult my acumen. You will already have arranged something.'

For a moment she seemed too shocked to move. Then she turned.

'Persis, Tethys, with me.' With one glance at Seth, they had gone.

Seth stared at the tomb-thief. 'What made you change your mind?'

The Jackal shrugged. He rubbed his neck with his hand and looked down at the fingers as if they were wet. 'I don't know,' he said.

She could hear them. They were wading and splashing through the swamp, a quiet glooping sound. Once or twice she caught Alexos' excited whisper, a growl that might be Argelin or Oblek. Then, as if they had gained the stairway, the sounds changed, a shuffling, the snick of metal, squelching steps.

Mirany crouched in the darkness at the side of the doorway. Her wet hair dripped down her back and her skirt was plastered to her knees. In her fingers the flail felt light; a wand of balsa wood, its cords making tiny rattling noises if she moved. Carefully she closed her fingers over it. What magic did it hold, this talisman? How could it make a man forget the one thing that drove him on, the last obsession he had left? And if it worked, what sort of man would he become, without the shame and the relentless urge to find Hermia? Without his destroying love, would he even be Argelin any more?

In the doorway, shadows moved. She watched them lengthen, as if it was lighter out there, the shadows of a man and a boy, hand in hand. In a scatter of dragonflies they approached the opening, and in the high spaces of the roof above her tiny rustles sent dust down, as if the coming of the Archon woke insects and bats, mice and scorpions,

Mirany tensed.

Argelin stepped through the doorway.

She saw how he glanced up and round. In the pearly light his face had lost much of its smoothness; he was older, his beard untrimmed, the dark eyes weary.

Behind him Alexos was unchanged, his beautiful face turned up in awe. Mirany waited. No Oblek. Was he waiting out there in case of ambush?

Puzzled, she leaned one hand on the wet floor.

The General had no sword. His hand clasped Alexos' fingers tightly. He looked up at the figure on the throne.

For a moment they were both still. Then Alexos whispered, 'Don't be afraid, General. She isn't real, she's a statue.'

And looking beyond them Mirany knew that he was

right, that what had been the Rain Queen was nothing now but stone, lichen-furred and weathered, the dark eye-holes in the snouted mask a lacing of cobwebs.

Argelin muttered, 'Stone or flesh, she won't stop me.'

He came forward, and Mirany saw how he dragged the Archon after him.

She stood up. 'Alexos!'

'Mirany!' His screech of delight sent beetles scuttling. 'How did you get here?'

'The same as you. Through the swamp.' She stepped forward, leaving a wet trail. 'Where's Oblek?'

He frowned, his dark eyes glancing up at the man. Argelin's voice was hard.

'We dumped the fat drunk. He was a liability.' His gaze slid to the flail. 'What's that?'

She walked right up to him. She was so close she hardly needed to reach out; her fingers trembled on the frail wood. He glanced across the hall, suspicious.

'You took it from the statue? Why?'

He sensed danger. She had only to touch him with the goddess's wand and their whole crazy quest was over; Hermia would stay for ever in the Garden, and she and Alexos could find Oblek, and maybe a way back. It would be better. For them and for him.

She knew all that.

And yet she couldn't do it.

Don't blame me, she thought. It's all he has.

She smiled at Alexos.

'This? It's nothing.' Sick at her own weakness, her stupid folly, she turned and flung the thing away, high and hard into the darkness of the roof; it spun, circling, the cords flailing with a whoop of air, and Alexos gave a shout of delight, because as it turned the flail burst into flames of gold and scarlet; long streamers of fire whirled around it, peeling away and searing down. Sparks spat on the paving. The building trembled.

Mirany staggered and overbalanced. Sprawled on the wet floor she glanced up at the roof, and saw it was opening like lacework, like the dark pools of a flood evaporating away. In a blue sky the sun burned, rolling back down on them, the air around it crackling like a vast winged beetle.

The walls shuddered. Alexos screeched, a shrill terror, as under his feet the floor cracked in a rapid zigzag of blackness; he toppled backwards. Argelin was jerked back too, yet he still gripped the boy's hand, heaving him closer.

Spilling fire on their hands and faces the sun sphere descended; its heat seared them as they lay curled, its weight crackling just above them, crisping the ends of Mirany's hair, lighting Argelin's breastplate and the grubby tunic Alexos wore. Into the deep crack in the floor it rumbled, and the world opened to receive it, a great thundering progress into the darkness of the earth. And for a moment she was sure she saw the beast that rolled it, a carapace black and shiny as basalt, pincers, the folded wings of the scarab.

Steam rose from the pit. A smooth, melted track led into it.

From the sky, a thousand tiny sparks tinselled down on them.

The torch bobbed towards them up the steps. Rhetia had every slave and priestess she could find carrying kindling and running with logs. Now the fuel was stacked on the platform of the Oracle, and even before the girl had reached the top she had snatched the guttering torch from her, and thrust it in.

Far over the sea the sun was rising, hours too early, as if, on the eve of the Scarab, the very rhythm of night and day had shattered. It steamed through mists, and in the rosy dawn gulls and terns woke and cried in dismay.

Rhetia circled the beacon, thrusting in the torch. Sparks leapt; the barely visible flame charred into the heart of the wood, the heap shifting and crackling.

'Will they see it?' Persis sounded anxious. 'At this distance . . .'

'They'll be watching. I told them to watch.' But Rhetia smudged soot from her face, flung the torch in and stared out too, her hair lifting in the sudden dawn wind.

The horizon was a line of fog, the sun nailed on like a

copper rivet. The birds went silent; flapped away. Eeerie stillness hung over the Island.

Then, out at sea, the world rippled.

As the Jackal and Seth ran up the steps behind her, Rhetia gasped, 'Earthquake!'

Everything shifted. Seth grabbed wildly at nothing and fell into a thicket of artemisia, the pungent smell dizzying him. He crashed to the dry soil, a lizard darting into a hole beside him, and for a moment the whole of the Two Lands were moving apart, a dislocation of the living and the dead.

Rocks crashed. As he dragged himself up, dust erupted from the pit of the Oracle, a gasping cough, a throat-clearing. All the debris collapsed in; the crack yawned.

For a terrible moment he balanced on the lip of darkness.

Then the bush and the edge and the lizard's hole slid in. He yelled, grabbed. And with a howl, fell after them.

On her hands and knees, Mirany stared into the tunnel. 'We have to follow this.'

Argelin's face was cut; he wiped blood away savagely. 'No!'

'But it's the way! *The gateways through which the beetle rolls the sun.*' Impatient, she caught hold of Alexos and tugged him toward the darkness.

Stretched between them, the boy cried out, 'I can't, Mirany! I'm stuck!'

Amazed, she realized their hands were gummed

together with a yellow resin; she pulled, but Argelin held the boy tight.

'It's a trap,' he snarled. 'Do you think I don't know she was here, before we came? Do you think I can't smell the slime of her? What plans did she scheme with you? I won't be dragged into some filthy hole to rot for eternity, priestess.' He turned, looking up at the lichened image.

'Do you hear me?' he yelled. 'If I have to tear the Underworld apart, I'll get to you!'

'Quiet.' Alexos turned. 'Listen.'

Something slithered. Soft at first, then a rattle, a slap. Mirany whirled round. Beyond the door, up the steps, dim scraping shapes were dragging themselves, scales rasping against marble, heavy tails working from side to side. The ominous gait of awkward creatures, heaving out of the swamp.

'*The crocodiles.*' She looked at him, appalled. 'You have to come!'

Instead, Argelin faced the door. Furiously, he tried now to free his hand from Alexos', put the other to it and tugged, desperate. But the fingers stayed entwined.

'Do something!' he yelled viciously at the boy. 'You're the Archon! Release yourself! Now!'

Alexos shrugged miserably. 'I'm scared,' he whispered.

Argelin swore. He scrabbled left handed for a weapon, found a small knife, swore again at its utter uselessness.

'Pick up stones! Anything.'

Alexos looked at Mirany; she didn't move.

'We're going into that tunnel,' she said stubbornly.

The doorway teemed with sleekness; small eyes glowed. The crocodiles were emerald, gem-studded; their haunches dragged slime and weed, their out-turned claws scraped the paving. One opened wide jaws, revealing yellow razor sharp teeth.

Argelin dragged Alexos close; held him across the chest. He had the small knife, and only as it sliced down did Mirany realize what he meant to do with it; she yelled and threw herself at him, the crocodiles slithering into the hall, a green wave.

Alexos screeched and struggled; Argelin hacked with the blade at the boy's wrist; blood spurted, the knife skewed. Then Mirany had it; she shoved him back with a scream of pure anger and he slammed into the parapet of the statue and lay still.

Breathless, she scrabbled to her knees and held out the knife, a slow semicircle.

Gleaming, the snouted beasts closed in.

The Jackal tied a rope hastily around his waist. Behind him, Fox yelled, 'Seth?'

The mouth of the Oracle breathed dust and silence. Beyond it the beacon blazed, a snapping inferno of flame.

'It's no use. If he's still alive, he'll be hurt.' Tossing the end to two of his men, the Jackal backed into the pit, took one look down, and then gazed up at Rhetia.

'I leave the Island to you now, lady. The Jackal must re-enter the tombs.' He frowned. 'My people will stay and fight with you. Good luck.'

Rhetia drew herself up. As he abseiled into the crack she said, 'Don't worry about us. The god will never let this place be taken.'

Muffled, his voice came up. 'He didn't stop Argelin.'

She snorted. 'I wasn't Speaker then.'

'*Nor are you now, Holiness.*'

Warped and echoing, his words rose out of the Oracle. For a moment they hung strangely; some of the Nine turned, Gaia glancing at Persis, eyes wide. Rhetia stared at the scorched, sulpher-stained lip of the Oracle.

'What did you say?'

The pit was silent. Instead, Jamil gave a cry and pointed. 'Look! Holiness!'

Far out at sea, a ship's prow broke through the mist.

Then another. And another.

'Drag him!' Mirany had her arms under Argelin's shoulders, but he was too heavy. Fumbling with fear and terror she said, 'The breastplate. Get it off him.'

One-handed Alexos helped, sobbing and bleeding as the Rain Queen's creatures closed. The buckles were leather and stiff; Mirany sawed at them frantically with the knife and they snapped, and she tugged the breastplate away, but they could still barely move him.

Teeth snapped at her leg; she gasped, stabbed wildly.

'Leave me!' Alexos screamed.

'No! Never!' The smooth tunnel was so close; cool draughts rose from it.

'You have to, Mirany! They're too close! Look!'

She looked.

Beyond the dimness she saw flame.

It rose like the sun, came to the top of the steps, was carried high by a heavy figure, a man with a crooked bronze sword and a fearsome yell, and the dark beasts panicked before it, scattering and snapping.

Oblek kicked his way into them. He thrust the torch at their jaws, screamed curses at them, his anger ferocious and terrible, and Mirany's relief was strangely chilled at his fearlessness. Once through, he looked sourly down at Argelin, and they saw the bloody weal across his bald scalp. Without a word, he gave Mirany the torch and Alexos the sword, bent, and put his arms under Argelin's shoulders.

Like a beast with its prey, he dragged the General into the darkness.

The Eighth Gate
Of the Balanced Scales

Once I fell, down and down.

I think that was dying. Or perhaps it was being born. I remember thinking there could be no fear, because I could only fall into my own hands.

It's the same for them, only they don't know it.

She will make her stand

'More rope. It's narrow but there's no bottom.' He heard his own voice echo around him. His hands slid on the crumbling rock.

'Only an armspan left.' High over his head, Fox's grunt sounded anxious.

The Jackal frowned. He was still weak, and they had been climbing down for too long. After the rope had been dropped from above they had paid it out twice more to the end of its length. Now, feeling with his foot for the cracks in the shifting debris, he wondered how much deeper he could go.

Seth was dead. That, unfortunately, must be true. No one could have fallen this far and lived.

'The walls are closing in. Take the strain.'

His whisper hissed in invisible space. Trusting to Fox's strength he hung from the rope, swarming down hastily. A slab jutted out of darkness; he grabbed at it. Under his fingers he could just see figures and hieroglyphs, tilted and smashed.

The Oracle had once led to Kreon's kingdom, but he was no longer sure that was true. The earthquakes had split the original fissure; maybe in this blackness he had passed some slot to it, or it had been blocked. He felt that the world had moved in its very depths, and that nothing down here would be recognizable.

Dust drifted in his eyes; he looked down, felt for a foothold.

His foot touched something soft.

Cloth.

It was fine and felt like linen. As he caught his breath the scent came and he recognized it, sweet unmistakable natron, the unguants of the embalmers. Carefully, his fingers moved along the cloth. Swags of it hung across the shaft like cobwebs, snagged on rocks, torn. Kreon must have set it up as some sort of stone-catching device. Might it have caught Seth?

'Seth?' he whispered.

Carefully he climbed through the webs till the rope jerked him still. Then he touched something else.

Bones.

They were disturbed, the wrappings broken. His hand groped over an eye–amulet, and jerked away.

As if he sensed it, Fox's whisper echoed down. 'Is it the scribe?'

The Jackal wiped his dry mouth. 'A body, but not Seth's. The sarcophagus is smashed, the chamber in pieces. Come down, Fox.'

It was certainly an early tomb; by the time Fox had grunted and shuffled his way down the narrow chimney the Jackal had lit an oil lamp and held it out, finding only dark space and sparsely painted walls. The colours were furred with a strange fungus; behind its mottled green, kings and Archons and slaves bowed before the gods, the texts of the Way of Guidance spilling over doorway and lintel.

Feeling the thief–lord at his back, Fox turned. 'Well?'

'Second Dynasty. Maybe even earlier.'

Fox coughed. 'But where's Seth?'

Before the Jackal could answer, a low sound rumbled. Far off, it sighed at the edge of hearing, faded into a murmur of cool air. They had both heard it many times before.

'The Shadow walks.' Fox laughed sourly.

The Jackal was gazing up. 'I think the scribe may have lived after all. These swags of cloth would have broken his fall; maybe even held him.' He edged past the ruins of the burial to a small doorway and ducked under it. 'Someone has come this way. See the marks.'

Footprints disfigured the dust; two sets, one a little blurred, as if dragged.

Fox said, 'Kreon?'

'Who else? We have to find him. The mercenaries will be inside by now.'

As he moved, a lithe black shape slid from a hole in the wall and streaked past him; Fox had a knife out instantly. 'What the hell was that?'

The Jackal smiled wearily. 'A cat.'

They had lit a fire in the cave, because that was what the tunnel had become, a cavern too big to see roof or walls. Mirany had gathered scraps of kindling, and Oblek had lit them with the torch. Now the pine-scented wood snapped and cracked, sending sparks into the darkness. Bats flitted up there. Mirany had no idea whether it was night or day, or whether those words even had meaning any more. Sucking one of the sour figs Oblek had emptied from his pockets, she listened to their story of the bronze man in amazement.

'And the others.' Alexos shifted. 'I should have helped them all.'

'Keep still, Archon.' With the small knife, Oblek was chipping delicately at the resin; the boy's wrist was bandaged and Argelin still lay silent. He had not moved since they dragged him in.

'You don't think I've killed him?' Mirany asked nervously.

'If you had, so much the better.' He levered out a chunk of the yellow amber, tugged experimentally at the boy's hand.

'Nearly, Oblek,' Alexos said.

She wondered what he would say if she told him about the Queen's flail, the chance she had thrown away. Maybe Alexos knew. Glancing at him sideways she wanted to ask, but the boy and the big man were absorbed in their task, the knife scraping gently in the hush.

'Where are we, anyway?' She wanted to walk to the cave walls, to get some idea of the dark space, but the tiny warmth of the fire held her close. She felt they were the only living things in a vast blackness; that whatever lay beyond could be changed by how she moved or what she said.

'I can't say how glad we were to see you.'

Oblek grunted. 'No one gets rid of me so easily.'

'Oh, yes, Oblek!' Alexos looked up, his eyes bright. 'Like in the desert, remember. You showed them then.'

'I showed them, old friend.'

After a moment Mirany asked quietly, 'Is that why you don't drink any more?'

He stopped work then, and glanced at her. In his ugly, creased face his eyes were small and shrewd. 'Lady, each of us has his secrets and shames. Let's just say the songs quench that thirst now. The water of the Well was sweet and dark, and once you taste it, no other drink comes near.'

He bent back to the resin. 'We should have brought a flask back for that lunatic. Steady now, Archon.'

The blade slid in against the skin; he prised, and the boy gave a laugh of relief. 'It's broken, Oblek!' He pulled his hand free and waved it wildly in the air; then he jumped up and ran round them, and turned a cartwheel in the dark.

Oblek sat back. 'Thank the god. Only just in time.'

Argelin was stirring. He groaned and muttered and rolled over; Mirany took the flask of water to him.

'Drink this.'

For a bleary moment he let her put it to his lips, but as soon as its coldness touched him he seemed to convulse; he flung it aside and the precious liquid spattered into the dust. Annoyed, Mirany grabbed after it; the General scrabbled away.

'I won't touch it,' he breathed. 'Don't bring it near me.'

She stared. For a moment all his steely defiance was gone; this was a terrified man adrift from everything he knew, lost in an Underworld he had always ignored. Now it held him; it played with him and teased him; its innumerable creatures crawled out and tormented him. She knew the feeling she felt for him was pity.

Perhaps he sensed it. Something shut down in his face; he rasped a hand down his beard and glared at Oblek.

'So,' he said hoarsely. 'The drunkard is back.'

'Believe it, Lord King.' Oblek folded his arms and stared

at him. 'Back, and holding the only weapon. This expedition has a new leader.'

'You!' Argelin laughed icily.

'Me. We stay together and I watch you like a hawk, because you would have cut the boy's hand off. I couldn't care whether you find your woman or she stays dead, but if the only way out of here is through the Gateways, I intend to get the Archon back to the world of the living. Mirany too. God knows what's going on without them.'

The General drew himself up. A bruise was darkening on the side of his forehead; his tunic was filthy, and without the breastplate he seemed uneasy. He turned, and his dark eyes met Mirany's.

'Surely the leader should be you. *Speaker*.'

'I . . . I think we are all bound together.' She frowned. 'What do you think, Archon?'

There was no reply.

'Alexos?' Oblek stood, quickly.

In the darkness of the cavern nothing moved.

Then, very quietly in Mirany's mind the voice whispered, full of joy.

Come and see what I've found, Mirany!

The ships burst out of the mist in ranks and squadrons. Great quinqueremes and triremes emerged into solidity, caravels and transports loomed, their decks crowded with benches of oarsmen, the thud of their drums a muffled boom across the waves. Prows carved like elephants, like sirens and open-mouthed gorgons, cut through spray, flying fishes leaping out of their wakes. As Rhetia ran after Jamil down the steps she saw white sails billowing taut, the ropes hauled, men swarming in the cross-trees, bizarre artillery being assembled. The fleet was brilliant with banners, the Emperor's white stallion and Jamil's own device of the horned bull glinting from the flagship. And these were not just foreigners either; she could make out emblems of the islands fluttering in the strengthening light, of Mylos and the Cyclades, the argosy of Temlos, the seagirt kingdoms of Krios and Herpelon that owed ancient allegiance to the Bright god of the Oracle. Spearmen from Mykene had come, and the bronze-thighed hoplites of Zanthe, and women warriors from tawny Arge, where the land grows crops of dragons and the mice are winged. Behind the warships a flotilla of fishing boats filled the waves, netsmen and lobster haulers and pearl divers racing to the defence of the Island.

Rhetia grinned as she ran down, the wind whipping out her tunic, the bow on her back humming. In the Port she could see people on rooftops; among the wreckage of the sacked town they ran down to the harbour, faint shouts rising, a rattle of metal as they tried to drag the great chain to the shore.

Breathless, she slammed into Jamil. The Pearl Prince was elated; he raised his hand and laughed.

'My people have come for me, Holiness! Now we will sweep Ingeld and his barbarians away!' But she was already looking over his shoulder, her joy gone.

'Then they'd better hurry,' she snapped.

The Northerners were on the Island. The Bridge swarmed with them; the remnants of the Jackal's men already pulling back, breaking under the relentless attack. Bodies lay on the sacred shore.

Jamil turned her to face him. 'I will go to my fleet. You, Holiness, must form the elephants into a last defence at the base of the road, and everyone, slaves, thieves, the Nine, must flee to the Temple and barricade themselves inside.'

She laughed. Her odd happiness startled him.

'Do you really think I would do that, Prince? Slaves, fugitives, yes, I'll make sure they're safe. But I will make my stand at the Oracle, and the rest of the Nine will be with me.'

For a moment he stared at her in dismay. 'Seven girls? Pampered priestesses?'

'We can fight, Prince.'

He shook his head, heavily. 'These men are animals, lady. Your lives are worth more than—'

'What? A hole in the ground, is that what you mean?' Rhetia stared him down. 'That may be what it is. But it is also the Oracle, the mouth of the god. It's everything, Lord Prince. And if I have to, I will die defending it.'

He nodded, sombrely. Then he pressed her arm and turned, his servants racing after him.

For a moment Rhetia stood unmoving in the wind. The sun was higher; its rays struck the Temple and the people streaming in there, and as if the heat shrivelled it, the mist was gone, and all of the sea a mass of ships.

She turned, yelled orders. Persis ran up.

'We're with you. But what about Chryse?'

Rhetia laughed sourly. 'Bring her.'

'But—'

'Bring her! She's one of the Nine. She dies with us.'

'And there's a boat. Just come from the Port. To the secret landing.' Persis ran off, calling the others.

Puzzled, Rhetia climbed to the terrace and looked over the balustrade. A tiny blue fishing boat bobbed below the cliff. And she could hear someone climbing up, their gasps, the slither of soil on the thread of goatpath.

Stealthily she pulled out her bow, fitted an arrow to the string, and drew it back. She lined the arrowhead up to a notch on the path.

The breeze was salty and brought faint cries from the battle. She waited, untiring, until a head bobbed up, a small, dark head, its hair loose in the breeze. It looked up at her and stopped, and wailed. 'Oh no! Don't shoot!'

Rhetia didn't waver.

The small girl waved a monkey toy. 'The others are coming. It's us.'

Behind her, a woman toiled up, hot and red faced. A bulky, older woman, grey haired and irritated. Rhetia stared at her in astonishment. Last of all, armed with a rusty sword, a thin man.

He said, 'You know me, Holiness.'

Rhetia carefully lowered the bow.

'You're Seth's father,' she said.

As Mirany raced through into the next cave, the sight of him brought her up short. Oblek came wheezing behind her; she heard him stop, appalled.

He gasped, 'Oh god! Don't move, Archon!'

The chariot was huge and ancient. Its wheels were bronze-riveted and painted red, the central pole heavy. Alexos had climbed up on to the wicker platform, he had untied the reins and was knotting them carefully about his waist.

Mirany couldn't breathe.

The four horses were magnificent and powerful and restless. Black and glossy, more than mortal, they stamped and shook their manes, the intricate harnesses clinking and shifting. One turned and looked at her, its eye intelligent.

Argelin came to her elbow. 'Get down, boy! Those beasts will—'

'Do you think I can't control them?' Alexos smiled; they saw his face was alight with joy. 'I've driven them before, Lord General. When I was Amphilion and Ramsis I hunted for days at a time in the desert; I tied the reins like this and shot geese and duck, leopard and lion. When I was Sostris my war-chariot hung with flailing chains, I sped faster than the wind!'

The horse on the far left snorted and reared; Alexos' thin arms tugged at the leather straps. Oblek pushed past Mirany, careful to move slowly. He walked round in front of the horses and caught the harness of the nearest. It was taller than his head.

'You were a man then, old friend.'

I was the god, Oblek. I am the god still. Stand aside.

The musician paused, his face lost colour; he licked dry lips.

'Archon . . . you may be . . . that is, yes, you are the god-on-earth. You are also Alexos, and I do not want your bones broken.'

Stand aside.

'You are a boy and I am your guardian. No one else but me.'

I could ride over you. I could trample you for this.

'You won't do that, old friend. You know you won't.'

There was a tense silence. Mirany saw the boy's eyes fill with tears.

Finally he said, 'I want to drive the horses, Oblek.'

'And so you shall, old friend.' He didn't move, just glanced over at Argelin. 'But the General will take them now. The General is a soldier. He knows about chariots.'

Mirany thought for a second that Argelin wouldn't respond. Then he came from behind her and climbed warily up on to the wicker platform, took the reins from the boy's waist, and gripped them tightly in his gloved hands. She realized she was barely breathing. She unclenched her fists.

Oblek wiped sweat from his face. 'That's better, isn't it? Much better.'

He exchanged one unreadable look with Argelin, then came swiftly round and beckoned to Mirany. 'Since we've found it, we'd better use it.'

As he put his hands round her to help her up, she whispered, 'The god is fickle. You were in danger. For a moment . . .'

'For a moment I heard him, knew who I was talking to.' His fear chilled her. 'I never thought I would argue with a god, Mirany.'

His weight made the chariot dip; the horses moved, restless. He put both arms round the boy.

Alexos looked up. 'I love you, Oblek. Even if you are so stubborn.'

'And I you, little one.'

Argelin snorted in disgust. He shook the reins and the four horses began to pace, their chests glossy, their eyes bright. He shook again, and they were galloping. Their hooves were thunder. They shed sparks, like lightning.

She rides in the chariot of the sun

Seth opened his eyes.

The first thing he realized was that his whole body ached. Though he was lying on his back on hard stone he felt crumpled and sore, and as he pulled himself up on one elbow he hissed with pain.

He was in complete darkness, almost certainly in a tomb chamber. He remembered falling into the Oracle, being snagged in the webs of cloth, tumbling from one to another, into hands, into blackness. The hands had been firm and real. He whispered, 'Kreon?'

Silence.

He was on some sort of slab. Swinging his legs carefully off, he stood unsteadily on gritty paving. He needed light.

The albino may not but he did. He had to find out where he was and how long he'd been out, so he shuffled forward, arms stretched, until he touched something like a wall and groped along it, looking for a door. Plaster crumbled under his palms, he fingered patches of brick; the wall was painted, and desiccated. He came to a corner, felt up and down it, turned it, and stumbled on. It took long minutes to be sure that the second and third walls were blank. Bumping into the fourth he scowled and swore aloud, just to hear something and because this was typical, that he should have chosen to go the wrong way in the first place.

He patted his way anxiously across its surface.

Another corner.

His heart-thud was so loud he felt it throb in the deep chamber. There must be a door. *There had to be a door.* Unless of course he'd somehow been lowered into the chamber, or brought up from a trap in the floor.

Trying to keep panic out of his voice he yelled, 'Kreon! I'm awake. Don't leave me here!'

The flat rebound of his own words scared him. They were absorbed into the walls, with no distant echo, as if the chamber trapped even sound. He rubbed his dry, dirty face. It wasn't the darkness so much, he was used to darkness and after a while it got to be normal – no, it was the silence that got to him. The terrible, unfillable silence of the dead.

It was worse because he knew there were rooms on the plans like this. Four-walled, sealed, their contents unguessable. Some were marked with odd hieroglyphs; signs that meant *deadly* or *infected*; sigils for *lair* and *creature*. The scribes had running jokes about what was locked in them; silly humour that seemed sick to him now. These rooms had self-slamming doors to trap thieves, panels that slid and would never open again. They were places where an intruder could be imprisoned for ever, dying slowly of thirst, his corpse desiccating on the floor, to bones and then even to dust, without anyone knowing what had become of him, his soul wandering the corridors for eternity.

This was such a chamber. And he was inside it.

He made himself laugh, a hollow defiance. He was Seth, wasn't he? For a start, he could try climbing.

Finding the slab again took ages; finally he crashed his knee against it and swore; then he kicked it. Hauling himself up on its dusty surface he stretched upwards, reaching as high as he could, feeling for rope, the ceiling, a hanging ladder, anything.

All there was was stale air.

He sat on the slab, and hugged his knees. After a while he found he was rocking himself back and forth, humming a tuneless, monotonous note. When he heard it, it seemed to have been going on for minutes, so he stopped abruptly. Minutes, or hours? He had to get a grip.

But dread had crept into him; he had opened some trapdoor and like a shadow it was in, making his skin clammy, prickling goose-flesh down his spine. The silence had become solid, an intense unliving presence pressed all round him. He barely breathed so as not to break it. A sound, any sound, would be a crack of pain, would shatter him in pieces.

But he was Seth, and he would stay Seth, so he lifted his head and made himself whisper, 'Are you here?'

The answer came in moments. *I wondered when you would remember me. It is usually only in the darkest places.* The voice sounded resentful. In his utter relief he didn't care.

'Why the hell didn't you speak to me! I'm worried sick here . . .' His voice hummed in the enclosed space, made a rustle, as if plaster had fallen.

Gods prefer to listen. To speak is to interfere, and that is always tiresome. You can manage on your own.

'Fine.' He scrambled off the slab. 'Tell me how to get out of here.'

The voice sighed. For a tight second he thought no answer would come, then a whisper drifted.

My brother is anxious and he needs you. The Northern men have lit torches in his darkness. They shout and the tombs echo with noise and fear. They rip jewels from the bodies of the Archons.

'Then tell me!'

You need to bend, Seth. You are too proud. Feel the currents of the air.

He took a step. His boot clunked against something

that tipped; fumbling hastily for it, he found a crust of ryebread and a dry scatter of olives. There was no water. Kreon must have left them, but a lamp would have been more use.

'Is this all you meant?'

But the god had gone. He was beginning to know when it happened, to recognize that emptiness in the air. It dismayed him; he tried to tear the bread with his teeth, then sucked an olive. Kreon wouldn't have been able to wait. Not if Ingeld's men had broken in. He spat out the stone, threw the bread into the dark, turned away. And then stopped.

Behind him, something was eating the crust.

His whole skin tingling with terror, he heard a rustle, the crunch of sharp teeth.

He couldn't move, couldn't breathe.

Something else was with him in the tomb.

'Why did you bring her here?' Hands on hips, Rhetia stared coldly at the sorceress, who stared coldly back.

'I suppose I thought she might be useful,' Pa muttered. He was waiting for Telia to finish the cup of water; as soon as she did, gulping it down, he filled the cup and drank himself, as if his thirst was unbearable. Then he said, 'The Jackal?'

'Alive.' Rhetia snapped. She smiled spitefully at Manto. 'Your magic seems to have failed.'

The woman seemed unconcerned. 'I have other powers, even here.'

Rhetia turned. 'You'll all have to go in the Temple with the others. Keep her under guard. You should be safe if—'

'No one will be safe,' Manto said, in a voice calm with certainty. 'Ingeld's men are ruthless. They intend to kill you all.'

'They're terrified of the elephants,' Rhetia snorted.

'For a while. Until they find the elephants are also terrified. Of fire. Of artillery. Then they will slaughter them and overrun your holy Island, priestess, and your friends in the fleet will not get here in time.'

Rhetia was white with fury but Pa could see she had no answer, and would not bluster. She turned.

'We'll see. But maybe you should be at the Oracle. At least we'll have a hostage. Bring her.'

She strode ahead, head high, Telia running after her.

Pa nudged Manto with the blade; she lifted her hems out of the dust. 'Ah,' she said softly, 'the Nine will not be so haughty when I'm Speaker.'

They hurried along the terrace and up the road. Everyone else was running the other way; slaves, fugitives, some of the Jackal's army, children, beggars, con men. Pa took Telia's hand; they pushed through the frantic crush until Rhetia ducked under the broken lintel of the stone door to the Oracle. She ran ahead, climbing the smooth worn steps. Manto puffed up and Pa followed more slowly, his legs aching and the coldness of his fear making the sun's heat a weight on his sweating back. It astonished him that he should be entering the precinct of the god – him, a man, and such a man too! Dirt poor, of no family. It was unheard of. It was as if the world had turned upside down.

The riven platform and its terrible dark crack shocked him with terror; he had never imagined such a darkness, such dust swirls that rose from its wide mouth. He wanted to kneel and bow his forehead to the hot stones, but the girls were here, the Nine, all talking, all frightened, their masks piled on the floor.

He stared round. 'Where's the Jackal? Where's Seth?'

They bit their lips and looked away. He knew then it had happened again, that his son had gone ahead of him, that he had failed to catch up. It had been happening for years.

The blonde one, Chryse, turned on him spitefully, pointed a white finger at the Oracle.

'He's fallen in there. And that means he's dead, old man.'

She exchanged a single glance with Manto, and the sorceress smiled.

To his surprise, Chryse burst into tears.

Mirany had never ridden in a chariot before; it was wild and fierce and exhilarating. Alexos whooped with joy, and Oblek clung on to him tight, as the horses ran with a thunder that might have been the shifting of the earth;

Argelin urged them on, yelling and flicking the whip at their necks as if speed eased the pain in him, and the balsa and wicker structure creaked and bounced on the smooth track.

She gripped the rail with both hands, her hair streaming back, her tunic rippling like some nike figure on the pediment of the Temple. Ahead of them the track was wide, it spilled out of the cave and became a road, flawless, grooved across the Underworld. It ran on sand first, smooth and yellow, and above them swifts darted and swans creaked in V-formations, and then the grit under the wheels darkened and the sky clouded, and the way led uphill. Mountainous, the road zigzagged up cliffs where tiny lemon trees sprang from crevices; it crossed chasms on bridges that sprang without buttresses from crag to crag. Looking down, she felt giddy. Birds nested on ledges far below; tiny fields were pale with crops, and as the chariot roared round a turn she saw olive groves down there, a tiny house, a white scatter of goats, their bells clanking in the heat.

Argelin slowed the horses. 'Look there.'

The sun hung low ahead of them; it was setting, as if the day was ending.

'That can't be,' Oblek growled. 'What's wrong with the bloody time in this place?'

'And what's more, how can we follow it?' Mirany whispered.

Myrtle trees crowded the path; as the horses' flanks brushed them their scent rose, clouds of fragrant pollen with the bees lazily buzzing in it. The road narrowed; it stopped zigzagging and headed west, straight into the setting light, the sky before them deep blue with twilight.

Argelin beat gnats away. He shook the reins.

'Faster!' Alexos cried. *Run, my horses! Spring, Summer, Autumn, Winter!*

As if they heard him, the black stallions looked back. They shook their heads and arched their necks, and then, together, they ran. Along the road, straight towards the sun they thundered, over grit, over stones, over scrubby grass, and Mirany screamed and Argelin swore, dragging savagely at the reins, because before them the road ended in a sheer cliff. Feeling the curb, the horses reared up, neighing and kicking; then they plunged on, and before Oblek could think of throwing the boy out and leaping after him, they had jumped from the cliff-edge into the blue emptiness.

Mirany had both hands over her mouth.

She couldn't breathe.

Because the road still ran, and they were driving on it, across the sky.

Seth kept still.

Whatever it was, it was alive, that was clear. He backed, one step.

The sound stopped. The creature had lifted its head.

He waited, in the silence. After only seconds he was no longer sure where the sound had been, if the thing had moved, where the slab was. He slid his foot back for another step.

Then he felt it.

A drift of air, a coolness about his ankles. Instantly he understood that the doorway was incredibly low; that he had passed above it in his exploration of the room. He turned, dropped on hands and knees, groped desperately for the opening, touched plaster, brittle wood, a space!

Behind him, faint sounds padded close.

A tiny breath tickled his leg; a prickle of whiskers. A black smoothness butted him.

He breathed out, hissing relief through clenched teeth. He still couldn't see it, but as the muscled fur rubbed his shoulder he caught a glint of gold; carefully he reached out and the lithe body purred under his hand. He felt a fine collar, a gold earring.

One of the Tomb cats. The Shadow-cats.

It walked straight into the wall in front of him. Far ahead, it mewed.

Draughts cooled his face.

'Lead on,' he muttered, and crawled after it. The tunnel sloped down, scraped his back, then turned left abruptly and became a steep ramp, running deep into the dark. As he straightened and walked his feet crunched bone, small fragments of dropped pots, the flowers of ancient processions. The cat ran ahead; sometimes where it passed under shafts to higher levels he glimpsed its muscled fur, the glint of gold.

He was in the Tombs, and they were a labyrinth. In one wide hall the walls must have been mother-of-pearl; they reflected a faint lustre that showed him his own face, stubbly and tired. By the pale glimmer he tried to read the hieroglyphs, but only found a list of the victories of an Archon so ancient his name was in none of the histories. Padding on, Seth breathed dust and the exhalations of stone. He was deep, deeper than he had ever been, the Sixth or Seventh Levels perhaps. These were tunnels of which the plans had long been eaten by beetles, desiccated to scrolls that crumbled if you pulled them out of the racks.

He began to panic again, to fear that someone was walking behind him, that the dead were slipping out of chambers as he passed them, crowding after him in the black corridors. Twice he stopped, crouching down and holding on to the solidity of the wall for comfort, because his terror had become too much for him, had stolen his breath. The black silence was heavier with each step, a curtain to push through; if he let it, it would smother him. To distract himself he began to count, chanting numbers aloud, fiercely, so that the cat came back and poured its slinkiness against his ankles.

Mirany must have felt like this, that time in the tomb.

'Where are you now?' he asked her. 'Are you here, in the darkness? Is the Land of the Dead like this?'

Through pillared halls and antechambers, he followed the slither of the cat, round heaps of treasure, under slabs propped on a few precarious stones. There were grooves in the grit; he began to understand this was one of Kreon's private pathways, the secret haunts of the Shadow.

Then he came to the stairs.

They led into darkness, and the cat streaked up them and was gone.

Breathless, Seth climbed.

One hundred, two hundred, three. His legs were shaky with fatigue, his chest heaved for breath. Dragging himself up, he knew he must be coming to levels he knew. This might even be the Stairs of Mesehti, the mad Archon who had tried to conquer the Underworld itself, who had led an army of ten thousand down into the darkness. None of them had ever come back.

A faint murmur. He stopped, realizing he had been hearing it for some time under the gasping of his breath. Distant noises, dim crashes. It was sound, and he thanked the god for it, but it worried him. He climbed on.

After another fifty steps there was an alcove in the wall; eagerly he put his hand in and found the expected lamp, a tinderbox wrapped in oiled cloth. That meant he had reached the Second Level at least. His hand shaking, he struck a spark, amazed at its brilliance, then another that caught. The tiny flame steadied and he lifted it and cradled it in both hands.

With light came colour; warm terracottas, blues and yellows, the elongated figure of the Rain Queen, her winged arms wide, welcoming him to the top of the stair. He held the lamp up in tribute, then caught his breath as the flame flickered.

Another crash, ahead.

He walked quickly round the corner straight into a figure that came out of a side tunnel with a hand over its eyes. It said, 'Put that thing out.'

'No chance.' Seth's voice was hoarse with disuse, but the old desire to sound assured kept out relief. 'Where are they?'

Kreon pulled him to the wall and slid a tiny hinged circle aside. 'There.'

Putting his eye to it, Seth saw Ingeld.

In a chamber acrid with flaming torches he was wedging the tip of his sword into the slit between the top and bottom of a sarcophagus; as Seth watched he heaved it open in a crash of dust, some of his men coming in to help him. They worked quickly, grabbing the heart scarab, the jewelled collar, the gold pectoral from the wrappings of the corpse. Subdued, their voices muttered.

'I'm surprised they can do it!'

The Shadow beside him nodded. 'Greed conquers many

fears.' He turned. 'But that doesn't mean the fears have gone, Seth.'

Two lights were coming down the tunnel towards them; one high, the other lower. Seth saw how they lit the Jackal's pale hair, his long eyes. Behind him, Fox spat, 'So the boy's still pretty.'

A cat ran between Seth's legs and vanished. 'What kept you?' he said.

Kreon stepped back from the spy-hole. 'Now. My army is all assembled.'

'Army?' the Jackal said.

'Oh yes, thief-lord. An elite force of guile and expertise. And with it, we attack.'

The end of the world

The sky-road was blue and wide and arced over the sea.

Far below them, tiny islands made archipelagos of atoll and coral, their paler lagoons crescenting around crag and pinnacle. On some, minute buildings gleamed.

Alexos laughed aloud, turning in Oblek's relentless grip. 'Look, Oblek! All the world is down there.'

The big musician was sweating. His eyes were fixed straight ahead, and through his teeth he said, 'I'll take your word for it, old friend.'

Winds whistled around them, zephyrs and breezes with hollow notes. Mirany watched geese fly at the horses' heads; one of the horses snapped at them irritably and they flapped ahead, honking in scorn.

She said, 'We must be riding on something. It feels hard. It sounds like glass.' The hooves were clattering, and now and then sparks flew, vivid as meteors.

Argelin wrapped the reins around his gloves. 'Fast enough for you, crazy boy?'

'Oh yes, General! This is fantastic.'

Oblek groaned.

The chariot shone in the setting sun. No longer wicker, it gleamed with gold; sunbursts adorned its sides. The harnesses glinted as if diamonds were studded in them; the horses' black flanks creamed with sweat.

Leaning over, Mirany saw they were galloping lower now; a school of whales swam in the green depths, dolphins leaping out around them. As the chariot raced down the sky its shadow darkened water like an eclipse; she saw mermen on a rock slipping under in alarm, and once, far down in the underwater chasms, a whole drowned city, its temple askew, weed and fishes in its houses and tombs.

Ahead, the sky was scarlet and flame.

'She must know we're coming,' Mirany said anxiously.

'Let her know,' Argelin yelled. 'I shout it to the winds! Argelin is coming, Rain Woman! Despite anything you can do! Do you hear me?'

Far ahead, deep in the sunset clouds, lightning flickered in reply.

'Bloody fool,' Oblek said sourly.

★　★　★

'It was nothing.' Sword in hand, Ingeld turned in the treasure chamber. 'An underground draught. Soil shifting.'

It didn't reassure them, he knew. Flames made the room a flickering deception; the crumpled wrappings of the ancient king, or god, or whatever these people called these desiccated packages, spilled a sweet, faintly sickening scent.

'Listen to me. Take what you can. Fill those sacks. Unlef, bring the gold boxes, you two, the carved leopard couch between you. It will look very fine in the meadhall at Hreimsfell.'

He knew their nerve was going.

Breaking in had been fine, a savage swooping through dirty corridors, scribes and slaves fleeing before them. They had torn through rooms of paper, labyrinths of files and pigeonholed plans, and if they'd had time, would have torched them for the blaze. But as they'd gone deeper the men had quietened, and breaking through the cedar doors of this chamber, the gust of foul air, the unflinching gaze of enamel-eyed statues, had dampened their recklessness.

'Move,' he snapped.

They were loaded with treasure. Some could barely carry the heaps and sacks and furnishings. And now these noises had begun.

Faint at first, barely heard behind smashing and searching. Then, when Wiglaf called for silence, they all heard it. A soft slither, magnified. A low throb, barely at the level of hearing.

The slave they had dragged in to show them the way fell on his knees in terror.

'The Shadow,' he breathed. 'The Shadow is coming!'

Ingeld kicked him. 'Silence!'

The murmur whispered into dust and stillness.

'A worm,' someone murmured.

'There are no dragons on this treasure.' Ingeld had swung round angrily. But whatever he said, it was creeping under their skins. The time had come to get out. He hauled the scribe up.

'Lead us to the stairs, before I cut your fingers off, one by one.'

Sobbing in relief, the scrawny man hurried to the chamber door and ducked through it. Ingeld stepped after him.

Then he stared in alarm.

The corridor was empty. Astonished, he turned, but the slave had vanished, and all that he saw was the long line of torches the men had left to mark the trail back up to the surface, gusting and flickering in the draught.

His men came crowding out. 'Where did he go?' one roared.

Ingeld snapped, 'Forget him. We don't need him. Follow me.'

He took one step. The furthest lamp went out. Then the next, and the next.

All down the corridor, inexorable, unstoppable, the darkness of the dead was rolling towards them.

★ ★ ★

Fire rained now, a new deluge. It came down like a storm and the elephants trumpeted in anger; they trampled their frail tethering ropes and broke the line, turning to attack spark and pain. Their panic chilled Rhetia; the cold war-whoops of the Northmen, the clatter of their swords on the bronze shields made her shiver with fear and an exhilaration the others could never understand. Slithering back through the bushes, she thought suddenly that the only one who might was Mirany, the girl she had despised at first, the mousy one. That had been a bad misjudgement. She would proably have to apologize, when they were both in the Garden.

Racing up the splintered steps she found them all at the Oracle, the rest of the Nine, Telia holding Pa with one hand and the monkey toy with the other, the witch Manto sitting calmly at the very edge of the pit. Seeing Rhetia's face, they fell silent.

'The elephants are finished.' She crossed the paving and picked up her mask, the mask of the Bearer. 'They'll be here as soon as they ransack the House.' For a moment then, she looked round at them all.

'There might still be time for anyone who wants to to get down the cliff. There's a boat at the secret landing. Take it, and go. Wherever there is left to go.'

None of them moved.

For a moment she sensed their uncertainty; then the

moment was gone and she knew, with a glow that was something like joy, that they would stay.

She turned to Chryse. 'What about you?'

The blonde girl pouted. 'You'd like that, wouldn't you! Chryse the coward. That's what you'd say.'

'You're staying because of that?'

Chryse was silent. Then she marched over and snatched her mask from Persis.

'I was Mirany's friend,' she said. 'And you never were, until you had to be.'

It was hardly a reason, Rhetia thought, but there was no time now to argue. 'And you?'

Manto rose, with dignity. She drew her dark robe around her. 'I will stay,' she said quietly. 'I have the protection of the Scarab. Ingeld's men know me, and will not harm me.' She folded her arms. 'Of course, even now, a truce could be made. My terms are simple . . .'

'Stuff your terms.' Rhetia pulled on the mask, and picked up her spear. She nodded to the rest of the Nine; each did the same. It was hopeless, she knew, but despite that, she was amazingly, impossibly happy. This was all she had ever wanted, and had never known, the certainty of this, the finality.

A circle of armed girls surrounded the Oracle, their bronze smiles facing out, the feathers and discs of the masks rippling in the wind. Behind them the beacon flamed, collapsing now, its heart a bed of embers.

Below, the first ships had reached the Port.

Out at sea, a storm was brewing.

They were lost. Ingeld knew that, but he strode on. Wulfgar was missing, and the twin sons of Uthecar and their men had argued furiously with him at the last fork in the tunnel and then taken the right-hand corridor, hot-headed and reckless. There had been a crash, a cry. When he had gone after them, nothing had remained but a trail of staters to a solid brick wall. Now he wore his bronze helmet, and all the men with sense had dumped much of their gold. The darkness teased and tormented them; shapes loomed from it that seemed horrors but were just walls, pillars, a room of hateful mummified baboons all sitting in jewel-eyed rows.

They had crossed vast spaces that could have held armies, crawled through knee-high slots, twisted round curved passageways. Twice pits had opened in their way, once a metal grille had fallen, trapping six of the men behind it. They had spoken boldly, their laughter loud and defiant, boasting to beat the rest to some exit. The darkness had swallowed them. He thought it almost certain their throats were already cut.

Because someone was doing this. Not the dead, but someone alive, someone rich in cunning. Unless, of course, Manto's sorcery was over and the Jackal's vengeful ghost had entered the tombs. Ingeld's eyes narrowed. That was not a thought that he should think. It was a crack to let in fear.

Now he groped round a corner into a dead end. Swearing in wrath he said, 'Turn. Turn back.' The dwindled war band crowded together. Then a voice said, 'Look. There.'

Eyes.

A small pair of emerald green eyes watching them in the dark.

The group halted. Ingeld pushed his way to the front. 'A cat,' he snarled. 'Nothing more.'

The men loathed the cats. There was talk that the animals were the wandering souls of the Archons, and besides, some fool had strung one up in the Port and nothing had gone right since. Whispers echoed behind him. He could smell their fear.

He strode forward and the cat's eyes vanished. The paving slid under his feet; with a yell he leapt back just as a whole section crashed open, slabs plummeting to unguessable depths. Far down, something splashed.

Breathless, he knew they were lost and would never get out. This was the world below, a place where bizarre punishments were enacted, where endless battles were fought. He lifted his chin.

'Shadow! If you are mortal, hear me! Let us out, and we will come to terms. Show us the way and we leave the Two Lands for ever. Do you hear me, Shadow?'

No reply.

The men shifted. Armour clinked. Istan said, 'The dead make no terms.'

'Fight me!' Ingeld roared, stung to sudden, shaking fury. 'Come out and face me!'

In the trembling echoes he waited, sword in hand.

More eyes.

The cats seemed to come out from the walls, from cracks in the floor. They formed an avenue down the tunnel to the right, sitting or crouching like the stone gods these people built. Head high, he led his men through them, into a chamber so vast its sides and roof were lost in darkness. He knew his challenge had been heard; as the tunnel came to an edge, and he saw the bronze scales, vast as a palace, suspended from the roof, he knew this was the place.

Turning to Isgar he said, 'If I die, burn my body on the cliff, in the open, under the sun. Take what men are left, and go home.'

Then he stepped into one giant pan of the scales.

Slowly, as if on perfectly maintained machinery, it descended.

Waiting for him below, his yellow hair tied back and an Archon's sword in his long hand, was the ghost of the Jackal.

They rode into cloud.

Black as soot it loomed up and around them, fleeting

snags of mist that blurred them from each other. The chariot jerked, leaned sideways.

Mirany wouldn't scream. Instead she gasped, 'Look out!'

Crows floundered out of the storm, a criss-cross tumble of them. Thunder rumbled, long and ominous, and as she crouched the lightning cracked, a white, unbelievably brilliant spark that made Oblek yell and Alexos screech. The air stank of sulphur; it tasted of metal.

'Get us down,' Oblek yelled. Hurling the Archon towards Mirany he grabbed the reins from Argelin, trying to heave the horses' heads back. Furious, Argelin fought him off.

'Be careful!' Mirany screamed.

The horses plunged. As if the sky-road was gone, or as if it careered steeply down, they raced into the storm, through cloud and sudden showers of icy hail, through needle sharp flashes of cold.

Soaked, terrified, Mirany flung her arms round Alexos. Oblek had Argelin half over the side; the rains trailed and she leapt to grab them. As she struggled to hold the mighty horses, Alexos was there; together they gripped the reins and slowed the beasts.

Cloud turned to grey, slashes of white.

'Oblek!' Leave him!' The Archon's order was tiny. Then, above the crack of the hooves, it roared, enormous. *Leave him!*

The big man's fist still drew back. Argelin watched him,

379

unmoving, his spine bent over the gold rim, below him the sea deep as night.

'Obey your god, fat man,' he hissed.

Oblek breathed hard. He saw the lightning crack over miles of sky, saw distant mountains, a vision of the road turning gold in the sunset. Then he hauled the General back.

Mirany yelled, 'Help us!'

Before he could step towards her, the cloud broke and they saw the sun.

It was a sphere of secrets, a falling star, a ball of gold. The air around it was dark, a pincered, beetle-backed darkness, winged with night, and at the storm's edge the sphere rumbled under the Gates of the Underworld. As Oblek stared and Argelin laughed in harsh joy the horses followed, under the gate of Skulls, of Ashes that crumbled and fell on them. The chariot lurched through the vast gate of Devouring, formed like a locust of enormous green agate. The sharp sides of the Gate of the Crooked Sword planed slices from the wheels, snicked the ends of Oblek's tunic. As they rumbled under the dark arch of the Triple Dog a puppy barked at them from its top, and Mirany laughed, suddenly unafraid.

'He remembers you!' Alexos screeched in her ear.

Then the chariot slewed, and they all gripped tight as the Gate of Punishments loomed up, a slot of darkness that she knew they could never fit through, an impossible, needle-thin slit. Arrowing towards it the horses ran headlong; Mirany closed her eyes, squirmed from the crash, the terrible scrape along the sides, but only a flash of darkness cooled her face, and when she looked again they were through, and Argelin was staring back in astonishment.

Now they were low over the sea; the sun's heat was terrible, the gold of the harness softening, gems falling out, the fiery glow unbearable on their faces. Through the open jaws of a Crocodile the beetle rumbled its burden, and the chariot swooped after, a hollow rumble in the tunnel of bone and fish scales. The stench of weed wrapped them; they burst out into a red sky, and saw the Eighth Gate like a double pylon ahead, a pair of perfectly-balanced scales trembling above the wide open doorway.

Once through, the road became a wooden bridge, an explosion of noise under hooves. Argelin grabbed the reins back from Mirany. 'Slow them!' he yelled, and she pulled with him and the horses were dragged to a reluctant, skidding stop under the last Gate, pure gold, completely circular, a sun-disc of unbearable pain, the beetle suddenly tiny, its sphere a ball of dried dung rolled into a crack.

And beyond the end of the world, green and calm and trickling with streams, they saw the Garden of the Rain Queen.

The Ninth Gate
Of the Reborn Sun

I have brought many mortals here.

Some hold my hand, some are dragged, some find their own way.

There are many roads to this place, which is just as well, because people seem to think whether they come or not is up to me.

The truth of course, is quite the opposite.

And who will tell them that the Garden is not the end of the journey?

That beyond it lie realms and kingdoms?

The scales are balanced

Exhausted, the horses stood trembling, breath steaming from their nostrils in the damp air. When Mirany was lifted down she felt as if the ground was still buckling under her; her legs were shaky and weak, and she wanted to collapse. Behind, Argelin dismounted warily. They stood all three in a row, with Alexos peering from under Oblek's firm arm.

'It's the Garden,' the boy whispered.

'I can see that, Archon.'

He slipped out, suddenly bold. 'Come with me, Oblek; all of you. You needn't be afraid. Mirany's been here before, haven't you, Mirany?'

They stared at her, and she straightened her back. 'Not like this,' she said softly.

The Ninth Gateway's smoothness amazed her; as they ducked through the small circular opening in its centre she let her fingers trail across the warm gold. Then her feet sank in mossy grass.

How could she have forgotten the beauty of the Garden? Its trees were enormous, green with summer leaf, heavy with fruit. She saw quinces and lemons and pomegranates and apples; species she had no idea of grew wild, and from all of them dripped a rain so soft she could barely feel its whisper on her skin. Birds of a hundred colours whistled among the laden branches. Alexos smiled up, his eyes dark.

'I always like coming here,' he muttered.

Underfoot, as they walked, the grass was long and wet, the earth saturated with water. Water was everywhere, rainbow-glinting in spray and fountains, tiny in dew-drops and crystalline beads of moisture that rolled from great leaves. It trickled in springs from rocky hillsides, ran in perfect channels through groves where deer and zebra waded; splashed in pools, thundered down waterfalls.

Alexos ran to drink, kneeling and plunging both arms to the elbow, and Mirany realized how thirsty she was; she crouched beside him and dipped a hand in.

'Should we?' Oblek muttered.

She had no idea. But the water was cool and clear; dragonflies skitted over its surface and as she raised it it dripped through her fingers. Silently, she drank.

Oblek gulped a handful too; then he looked up. 'Drink, man. You must be crazed with thirst.'

Argelin looked away. He looked as if he had entered a landscape of nightmare; his hands were clenched, his body tense against the drifts of rain on his skin, the tap and trickle from the trees. Already, like all of them, his clothes were wet, his hair dark with moisture, clotted against his scalp. The Rain Queen was all around them, Mirany thought, scrambling up. Like the god, there were no defences against her.

Alexos led them down a path where frogs hopped into the grass, under stone arches hanging with emerald lichen.

Argelin glanced at Oblek. 'The sword. Give it to me.'

'What use is a sword against gods?' Oblek growled. 'Can you cut water? Will death bleed?'

The General was grim. 'I'll worry about that. Give it to me.' But when Oblek drew it out the bronze was green with corrosion; water dripped from the blunted blade. Argelin took one look and threw it in the grass. His face was cold and set.

Alexos ducked through a grove of olives and then stopped. He came running back and took Mirany's hand and dragged her after him, to where the path opened into green light.

'Look, Mirany!'

It was a courtyard of magic. All around, fountains played from stone dryads and satyrs, from horns and spouts and mouths. The paved floor ran with moisture, and as a backdrop a great sheet of water fell smoothly into a pool silver as the moon, a throne of blue stone dripping in its centre.

Argelin looked round. 'Is this her judgement seat? Then where is she?'

He turned, raising his voice, and it was hoarse, and weary, and bitter. 'Lady, I've come. I've travelled far, through pain and death. I deserve more than silence, Rain Woman! Come out, and let this end.'

Nothing at first but birdsong, the patter of the rain. Then a glimmer of notes from a lyre, ominous and low. Mirany turned, expecting a procession, some ceremony, but Alexos' wet fingers touched her wrist. 'There, Mirany,' he whispered.

She came through the waterfall. Through it and from it, one hand first, the fingers long and delicate, and then as she stepped out the water formed into the rest of her, so that her blue robe ran and shimmered, her tall body was transparent and formless and then firm flesh, her dark hair in its elegant curls tied with silver.

She sat on the throne and her dress was the blue-green of the sea on a hot day; small waves of light rippled in it as she moved. Her feet were bare. Bracelets of pearl and coral slid on her wrists, a gold snake climbed one arm.

Her face was Hermia's.

Argelin was rigid. Then he took a step forward.

'Hermia?' His voice shook with joy and anguish. 'Is it you?'

She did not smile. 'Who else did you expect, General?'

'But you're not—'

'Am I not?' She smoothed her dress. 'I am the Queen here, that's all that matters, and you – all of you – have broken into my realm.'

'Hermia,' he breathed. 'It's me. Argelin.'

She raised an eyebrow at him. 'I know my murderer,' she said. Small hummingbirds, orange and emerald, flashed and hovered above her shoulders, darting into white flowers that opened to receive them.

Looking past his haggard face, she said, 'You, priestess, were given a command; it has not been obeyed. And as for the musician, he won't play his way out of death so easily. The only songs here are my songs.'

Mirany shivered. Though it was steamy in the Garden, a cold touch moved down her spine.

Oblek said stubbornly, 'Where the Archon goes, I go, Holiness.'

'Touching.' She glanced down at Alexos. 'And you. How many times I have seen you enter my gates.'

He was sitting on the steps of the throne, playing with a frog on his palm. His answer was preoccupied.

A thousand lifetimes, Lady. In every generation.

Hermia nodded. She looked at Argelin. 'Make your request.'

'To you?'

'There is no one else.'

He was bewildered. 'Hermia . . . does she imprison you?'

Hermia shrugged. 'No more than I was imprisoned by your love, my lord.'

'Even here,' he said, 'you torment me.' He stalked forward on to the steps, and his voice changed. 'Listen to me, if you are Hermia. Come back with me to the Land of the Living. I sent you here, and that was my mistake, and for every second of every day since I have repented it. Come back with me. Let everything be as it was.'

Mirany caught Oblek's eye; he frowned.

'Why should I?' Hermia said quietly.

'Because I love you. You know that.'

'I thought I knew it.'

'Hermia . . .' He leapt up the steps, but she held out a hand flat against his chest and stopped him.

'It's not that easy, General. There are rites that must be performed. You must be judged.'

Mirany turned, quickly. She saw girls walking in behind her, bare-foot. They carried fans and scented boxes, rattles and small drums that they beat and shook rhythmically. Two had metal frames which they struck to create soft shimmers of sound. As the last walked past the girl glanced at her, and Mirany took a silent intake of air, because it was

Alana, the girl who had been Bearer before her. The girl who was dead.

Two men came too, carrying a metal chest on legs. They wore leopard skins, and their shaven heads glistened with damp. Placing the chest down, they drew the purple cover from it, revealing a wooden box painted with water-lilies, and Hermia rose and came silkily down the steps and opened the lid. She took out delicate gold scales, swinging on tiny chains from the central pivot. Red petals fluttered out with it, a scent of musk and sandalwood.

Hermia looked at Argelin over the scales. 'You must be judged now, Lord General. Your life and deeds must be weighed.'

He took one step back. Water dripped from his fingers.

Seth gasped.

The Jackal was down again; for the second time Ingeld's weight had been too much, the blow crashing against his blade. Now the tall thief ducked and scrabbled as the sword struck sparks beside his head; with one lithe turn was on his feet again, winded.

Seth said, 'He's finished.'

'Not him,' Fox growled.

The fight was ferocious. The men were well matched, Ingeld heavier, the Jackal lean and fast, and the clang of their swordplay rang in hideous echoes all over the underground hall. Seth ran down the spiral stairs and leaned over, watching the breathless stagger of the men, their weary lunges, the heavy weapons whipped up in clumsy parries. Both were tiring. The Jackal looked white and gaunt. Sweat slicked Ingeld's beard. Through the helm-slit his eyes were blue as ice.

From the ledge in the roof, his men yelled and encouraged him, the harsh syllables of their words distorted by distance. For a moment he staggered back, the fight paused, and Seth muttered, 'Where's Kreon?'

'Not sure.' Worried, the Fox fingered the sharp blade in his hand. 'I swear, if this one kills the Chief, I'll take him myself.'

Seth said, 'He should be here. Things may have gone wrong.' He turned.

'Where are you going?' Fox yelled.

Swordclash broke out again, desperate and savage.

'To find out!'

The cries from the House were nearer; Rhetia glanced around. 'They're coming up. This is it.'

Smiling behind the mask, she held the spear tight to stop her hand trembling, and whispered, 'Bright One, take our sacrifice. Protect the protectors of your Oracle.'

Bronze, a clash of shields. Men were running up the Processional Way, their swords aglint in the sun, their voices muffled by helmet and heat.

Rhetia levelled the spear, seeing the other weapons in

the ring swing up, hearing Pa's sword stop sharpening on the stones.

Manto said swiftly, 'This is foolish. Let me call out to them. Let me send the Scarab.' She sounded uneasy, at last.

'Shut up.' To their surprise it was Chryse, her voice tight, her teeth gritted. 'Shut up, *shut up*.'

A man appeared round the turn of the path. Shimmering in the heat mirage, his armour seemed to glow. His face helmed, he stopped and looked up at them, then yelled down.

'The god be with all of you,' Rhetia muttered.

The soldier approached up the path. He came out of the shimmer and was mortal, even small; came steadily and relentlessly until his gorgon-headed breastplate was inches from the lethal tip of Rhetia's spear.

Smiling mask and bronze helmet faced each other.

A word emerged from his mouth, distorted and harsh.

It sounded like, 'Holiness?'

Crawling down the passageway, Seth thought, 'Are you sure?'

This is the way. Quickly.

Jewels studded his hands and knees like grit; opal and jasper, shards of chalcedony. From some reflected light ahead he saw the walls were faceted with diamonds; they scraped his back and sliced his palms. If the Norsemen ever found this . . .

This is it, Seth. The sun-disc. I showed it once to Mirany. I told her that all the world fits into its brilliance. Yet in all of you there is a sun like this. Even in Argelin.

'Argelin?'

His head emerged into the chamber. He saw the underground sun.

It was gigantic, suspended from the roof, swinging gently in the draught, a thin smooth perfection. How it could have been brought down here he had no idea. Standing below it, looking up at the brilliance as if it held no pain for him, was Kreon.

The albino turned. 'The Jackal?'

'It's even.'

Kreon lifted his face to the beaten metal. In the golden light his white hair shone, his pale skin seemed almost to glow.

'Then we wait for my brother. And for Argelin.'

She laid a feather in the scales.

A small white feather, which she took from the box. It was so light it lifted in the wind, but the scales sank swiftly under it.

Hermia looked up. 'Now, Lord Argelin. What can you set against this?'

Tormented, he muttered, 'Hermia . . .'

'Your virtuous life?' she said sweetly. Turning, she went back and sat on the throne, crystal drops shining from her fingernails. 'Your ruthless rise through the army? The bloodshed and purges? The murder of most of the Council, the families of your enemies, the children that might one day grow to usurp you?'

'None of that bothered you once.'

She smiled. 'Or perhaps the women you destroyed? Your desire to control the voice of the god himself? Not to mention the murder of the Archon . . . both Archons, if you'd had your way. Blackmail, intrigue, the buying of an alien army, which of these will you set in the scales, Lord General?'

He kept his face set; but Mirany saw the lines etched deep in his skin.

'We were friends once, Hermia. More than friends. You were my partner in these crimes.'

'I'm glad you confess them as crimes. To crown yourself king with the circlet of the god. To call yourself Archon. To throw down my statues and turn your face from my power, my life-giving rain.' Her voice trembled with anger. Even Alexos looked up at her, and for a moment Mirany saw the terror and fury of the Queen glimmer through.

Argelin did not flinch. 'Set those in the scales, but also set this. My love for you.'

'Love!' She leapt up. 'You murdered me!'

'I struck in anger and not at you. I would never have hurt you.'

Her laugh was harsh. 'You would have cast me aside at any time. I was Speaker and had power, but when you'd had enough . . .'

'No!' He leapt up the steps, caught her hands. 'No, I swear it, Hermia. That would never have happened, because in all my life I have never loved anyone, not even myself. Only you. Between us there was more than conspiracy, more than guilt. We were the same as each other, our joining was deep and real and can never be separated, not even by death. We won't let it be! You know that! I will take you back with me, in the face of the Queen's hostility, in the face of all the gods, if it causes the world to end and Chaos to fall, I will be with you, Hermia. And always, what I want, I get.'

In the silence, only the waterfall splashed. Mirany bit her lip, watching the woman's face, her manicured eyebrows, her red lips. Was it Hermia, or a mask of flesh the Queen wore?

Hermia smiled, uncertain. 'We can never know what you would, or would not, have done.'

'We can. Come back with me.'

'Impossible. Unless . . .'

He touched her hand, her arm. 'Unless what?'

'There has been a death, Argelin. My death. If I leave, someone else must stay here. The Queen demands her sacrifice.'

Argelin laughed, a choked, brittle laugh. 'Then she'll

have one!' He spun round. 'Shall we give her the fat man, my assassin?'

Oblek scowled. He folded his arms, but his voice had no bluster. 'Not so easy, General.'

'Well then, the priestess.' Argelin came down and stood by Mirany. He said softly, 'It was you my blow was aimed at. Perhaps I should finish what I began.'

She looked up at him, and his eyes were dark and steady, but she knew that her fear of him had long gone. 'I don't think you'll do that,' she said softly.

'No? Then, the boy.' He turned. 'The Archon, who must die for his people.'

Alexos laughed, and the frog jumped.

Mirany said, 'Not him either.' She moved in front of him again, so he had no choice but to look down at her.

'We all know, General, whose life you must offer the Rain Queen.'

He was silent.

'The sun-disc is the only way out of here, and you have it. Give it to her.' Mirany's voice was quiet; she glanced at Hermia and saw the strangeness of her smile.

Argelin said, 'You've long planned my death.'

'No.' Mirany shook her head. 'I've only wanted the Oracle to be free. The people to be free. You can do that, too.'

'If I do it, none of us may get back.'

'I know. But I've learned to trust the god. However things seem.'

'But do the gods love the creatures they torment?'

She said, 'I think so.'

For a long moment they looked at each other. He glanced round at Alexos, at Oblek. Then he took the sun-disc out of his tunic, and placed it on the other pan of the scales.

They watched it sink slowly downwards.

Do not turn

Darkness.

Seth was swallowed by it as the light of the sun-disc went out. For a moment he was sure it had been eclipsed by giant fingers, lifted by a god's hand out of his view. He stared up, afraid that impossible terrors were beginning, that Chaos was intruding into the world, stealing light and warmth, plunging them all into dissolution. The creak of a million insects slithered down the wall.

He said to the god, 'Is this the end?'

This is the end and the beginning, someone answered, and he knew it was Kreon, standing close to him, but there was a note of triumph in the albino's whisper that bewildered him. He was grabbed by the arm, hustled into the low passage. Ahead, in the tombs, the clash of swords stopped with a yell of pain.

Someone had won.

'Holiness?'

Rhetia stared as the man's armour glistened in the dawn mists. He put both hands to his head and dragged the helmet off, revealing tousled greying hair and an expression of intense anxiety.

'Holiness, forgive us being here. I know it's wrong but we felt . . . we couldn't let this happen . . .'

As he gabbled out the words she recognized him; he was Argelin's optio, and the men gathering in apprehension behind him the remains of the army of the Port. The Jackal's men, traders, fishermen with knives and nets.

She silenced him with a gesture. 'The Northerners?'

'We have them surrounded at the Bridge. As they goaded the alien beasts they overlooked our crossing; we took them in the back and routed them. My men are gathering those left alive.'

A whoop from Persis behind her. An out burst of voices and hisses of relief. Chryse giggling hysterically. Slowly Rhetia took the mask from her face, and lowered the spearpoint. She stood upright, very tall; the optio hastily knelt, his forehead to the ground, his men following.

She looked down at them. She should be triumphant, but she felt nothing but a strange numbness, a stupid reaction of dismay. There would be no attack on the Oracle now. And this was not relief. It was almost disappointment.

Pa came up beside her. 'Listen,' he muttered.

They heard it in the silence, a rising murmur of sound, ominous and faint.

Hastily he pushed past the soldiers to the edge of the platform, and she came after him and looked out, and saw, from the Port, from the City of the Dead, along the white road through the desert, from gateways and houses and hideouts and ruins, the people of the Two Lands, hundreds upon hundreds of them, streaming towards the Island.

Hermia stood.

'The judgement is complete,' she said formally. 'The feather rises, the sun rises, the Day of the Scarab dawns. Today the Bright One, the Scorpion Lord, the Rider of the sun, must bless the people of the Oracle.' She looked at Mirany. 'The Speaker will open her lips, and breathe his words.'

'But that's you,' Argelin said urgently. 'You are the Speaker.'

'Is it me?' Her poise wavered, just for a moment. She became doubtful, suddenly human.

Then, as they stared, Hermia stepped towards him out of herself, and what was left behind had no shape and no form, it was a creature of water, her eyes gleams of light, her hair dark wetness, her robe a crusted velvet of pearls and shell.

Impassive, she watched as Hermia ran down the steps to Argelin. She smiled, then rose, and Mirany stepped back in fear as the wash of her movement splashed them, as the Queen paced downwards and faced Argelin and smiled at him, her smile as cold as the abyss, as deep as drowning.

No one leaves my Garden, she said, in a voice of liquid. Even now, he would not step away.

One arm round Hermia, he said, 'She comes back with me.'

You are persistent in your demands, you who have destroyed my images.

He looked into the shifting light of her eyes. 'They say you once loved a mortal. You must know how I feel. I don't ask you, goddess, because asking is not enough. We are enemies, but even enemies can show mercy to the defeated. *I beg you, Lady*. I, Argelin, beg for her life.'

Slowly, as if it crippled him, he knelt and bowed his forehead to the wet paving.

The Queen watched. Then she said, *What you will take is this.*

She lifted from among the watery ripples of her dress a small figure, carved perhaps of ivory or whalebone. As she pressed it into his hand Mirany glimpsed it; the image of the Queen herself arms wide, her tunic shining with water, studded with crystal drops.

I will have my image rise over the Port again. As for the woman you say you love, she will follow you. She will always be with you. Where you walk, she will walk. When you reach out for her, she will reach out for you. But do not look back to see her, do not turn, for he who gazes again into the dark land is swept away in my revenge.

She withdrew her hand; small drops spattered from his fingers.

As he lifted his head and stared up at her in astonishment, she turned to the scales. Lifting the sun–disc she held it out to Mirany, and reluctantly Mirany came and took it. It felt slightly warm, perfectly smooth.

The Rain Queen leaned close.

When you were made Speaker, you did not learn the god's secret name. Here and now, I reveal it.

Glancing at Alexos, who stood and watched the frog hop away, she breathed the syllables into Mirany's ear. They were cool sounds, they meant nothing, and yet Mirany shivered as she heard them, they soaked into her, and she was at once so happy she laughed, not knowing why, and Alexos came and held her hands and swung her round and laughed with her.

As for you, the Queen said to Oblek. *What gift can I give one who has drunk from the Well?*

'None, lady,' he said proudly.

Except this. That water will never drown you. Never will you be sucked down into its depths. No liquid will submerge your soul again.

Acknowledging his grunt with a sideways tip of her head, she climbed the steps and sat on the throne, leaning forward, spreading her hands.

The Journey of the Scarab is ended, and begins. The people wait for you.

They saw, opening through the green of the Garden, a corridor. It was high and wide and intricately painted, every inch bright with images they recognized from a hundred tomb paintings, from temple rolls and scripts. Archons and Princes and Speakers walked in an endless procession; above and around them the texts gleamed, cartouches of blue and gold enclosing their names.

Mirany turned the sun-disc in her hands, and it shimmered into light.

Argelin glanced at it, then scrambled up. 'You promise me this?'

The Queen said, *The gods keep their promises.*

He grabbed Hermia's hands. 'I'll be waiting for you at the Oracle.'

She smiled. 'If I come. Once I swore I would not be used by you, and that still holds.'

'But you love me,' he insisted.

She raised an eyebrow. 'Did I ever say so?'

'Hermia, will you never stop tormenting me?' He took her hand, kissed it slowly, then turned and strode under the painted lintel.

Oblek said, 'Archon. Are you coming?'

Alexos turned to the Rain Queen. Hands on hips he smiled up at her; she reached out and lifted his chin with one wet finger.

Be careful among the mortals, Bright One. They will steal your innocence away.

He nodded.

But they are my dream, and my adventure, lady.

He ran lightly down the steps in front of Oblek; then, walking backwards, he waved at her. For a moment, Mirany gazed around at the Garden to hold it in her memory, its sweet smells, the beauty of its trees, the endless ripple and splash of its fountains. Then she followed Argelin, already marching grimly ahead, never turning, never looking back.

After only a few paces, the colours on the wall faded. Mould spread like green dust over the painted procession; slabs of plaster began to fall, crumbling away the faces of slaves, the fans and doves, the words of the Way of Guidance. The corridor sloped upwards, a dark incline, and only the light from the sun-disc lit their way. Argelin walked rapidly, and Alexos ran ahead; at Mirany's shoulder Oblek loomed, his heavy footfalls cracking through bone and ash, splintered plaster.

Behind them, the corridor was silent.

The Jackal was bleeding from the arm, but it was Ingeld who was down.

As Seth raced into the hall he heard the roar of the Northmen as they swarmed down the great chains of the scales, howling for revenge.

'Is he dead?'

The Jackal was breathless; it was Fox who whipped out a knife and said, 'Not yet.'

Seth pulled off Ingeld's helm. The Northman bled from nose and mouth; the wound that had downed him a slash in the side.

Seth turned in panic. 'They'll kill us all.'

'Face them.' Fox threw him the knife and swung round. 'Back to back.'

There were too many of them. Gripping the sweaty hilt, Seth knew he was finished, that there was no time, that he would see the Garden himself any second, but even as he breathed a desperate prayer to the god, the first man hit the ground and they saw how he buckled, how he crumpled and lay still. Another, and another slid down into instant sleep; in moments the remnants of the war band lay silent on the floor of the dark cave, one round shield rolling away and falling.

Very quietly, the Jackal turned his head. His stillness made them see what he saw.

The throne of the Shadow was without light, and the creature on it was a darkness crowned with a crown of nightshade and cobweb. Its voice came from a snouted mask with red eyes; a voice that was the whisper of dust falling through centuries in deserted chambers, the slow desiccation of bone. It was both Kreon's and a hiss that knew nothing of time or growth or the sun, making Seth crouch with dread, the Fox fall prostrate and whimper.

They will sleep, it said.

The Jackal was the only one left standing; his answer was a hoarse murmur, but Seth was amazed he could speak at all.

'And us?'

Leave the tombs to me now. My brother awaits you.

Slowly, with a grating shudder that made Seth grip the swordhilt tight, a round stone rolled away in the wall. They saw light out there, the stairs up to the City. Without waiting for the others, Seth picked himself up and ran. It was panic, he knew, but Fox was close behind him and even more terrified, and together they sped up the steps, their breath gasping as the sounds of the world flooded back, the crispness of scrolls, the smell of paint and papyrus. Only when Fox fell over a cleaning woman's bucket, and spilled out into the air with an oath, did they stop. Doubled over, Seth gasped for breath. By the time his pulse steadied, he was chilled with a faint damp.

The City of the Dead lay silent in the dawn mist. In the wide plaza's centre the mass of the Ziggurat rose, its bulk ominous among the nine Houses of Mourning. A few scribes maintained a watch on the battlements, dwarfed by the vast stone Archons. Everything was shuttered and barred. Far out at sea, soft thunder rumbled.

The Jackal came up the stairs calmly, and walked straight past them.

Seth ran after him. 'Are you hurt?'

'Not much.'

'But . . . down there, why didn't you . . .'

'I had words to speak to the Lord of the Dead.' He leapt up on the first step of the Ziggurat, climbing quickly. 'Words I should have said long ago. I'm no longer the Jackal, Seth. All those nightmares are over.'

Together they climbed into the rosy sky, the three of them in a line till Seth's legs ached and his breath was a pain, and they reached the platform where the Archons began their journeys to the Garden. A gale was blowing; they turned to meet it, and Fox gave a roar of wonder. A vast fleet of ships tossed on the choppy sea, crowded the harbour. Already the gates of the Port were open; the desert road was massed with people running to the Island, clutching offerings and livestock, carrying their children on their shoulders.

'It seems Jamil has relieved the Port,' the Jackal said drily.

From the Oracle, the pale smoke of the beacon rose. Seth stared at it.

'So the Emperor rules. But how many of the Nine are left alive?'

The Jackal looked down. Near the gate the Northerners'

horses were stalled, rare beasts, uneasy in the misty dawn.

He smiled. 'I don't suppose you know how to ride, Seth?'

Argelin stopped for the third time, his breath a catch in his throat. In a broken whisper he said, 'There's still no sound. Is she really there?'

'I don't know. I daren't look back.'

'I have to. I have to know.'

'No!' Terrified, Mirany grabbed his arm. 'If you do, you'll never see her again.'

'The Queen is treacherous. What if there's nothing behind us, Mirany, what if we walk out of this world into the air and it was all for nothing.' Tormented, he stared ahead, at the far opening, the shimmer of light.

She was tense with fear. 'Alexos will tell us. He can look.'

'Can you, boy?' Rigid, Argelin watched him.

'I suppose so.' The Archon turned on his toes. His gaze moved past Oblek's shoulder, into the distance. Then he looked at Argelin.

'Tell me!' the General snarled.

Alexos glanced down, tapping his toe on the stones. 'You've not always been very kind to me, General.'

Argelin tensed. For a moment Mirany knew he would grab the boy, squeeze his throat. Oblek shoved past her.

But the General unclenched his gloved fists. He

whispered, 'Please.' The syllable fell among them like an icy drop.

Startled, Alexos looked at Mirany and she saw he was on the verge of tears, his face red, his eyes filling.

'She's there,' he whispered. 'She's just behind you, waiting for us to walk on. But don't look back, General, please don't, or the Queen will make her disappear.'

Argelin did not move. 'Are you telling me the truth, boy?'

Alexos nodded.

For a moment they thought it would not be enough; then he abruptly strode on. Oblek swept the boy up, and hurried after him.

Left in the silence, Mirany listened.

There was no step, no breath, no rustle of a presence. She was certain the corridor behind her was empty. 'Are you there?' she whispered. 'Hermia?'

No one answered.

But as she walked after them, the sun-disc grew. It opened in her hands, shone, deepened. Its shape flexed, became a bowl, a wide, shallow bowl that she recognized with a murmur of dread and relief, a bowl incised with the ship of the Rain Queen, heavy and cumbersome, that she had to clasp with both arms.

In its depths, shaken and crouched, rode a single, tiny scorpion.

He steps off the Road

They rode at a gallop, Fox on a dappled horse, Seth clinging behind the Jackal on a half-wild white stallion, people scattering before them.

At the Bridge the Jackal leapt down; a boat was speeding from the fleet, and he waved and yelled at it urgently. As its prow turned Seth saw Jamil, wearing chain mail, and a sword. He was surrounded by armed men.

'Taking no chances,' Fox said drily.

The Jackal jumped aboard. 'Are they alive?' he gasped.

Jamil looked grave. 'I have no idea. But the elephants are.'

As the boat approached the Island, Seth saw he was right. The beach looked as if a battle had raged across it; trampled

413

pieces of armour and snapped arrows littered it. But the mighty beasts were content; they were knee-deep in the sea, their riders caressing them and washing their gashes, adorning their necks with laurel and bay hastily snatched from the overgrown gardens of the precinct.

The Jackal raced up the road with Seth close behind, dodging strewn remnants of plunder. Bushes and walls had been shattered by flame bombs; in places small fires burned, scorching lavender-scented smoke into the sky. The day had dawned, and as Seth gasped up the last few steps to the Oracle the sun blinded his eyes, and he put up his hand against its splendour.

'Seth!' Telia screamed in delight. She broke from Pa and came and flung her arms round him, dropping the monkeys. He saw Rhetia with the optio, and then Manto.

The witch stood, and the Jackal faced her.

For a moment neither spoke. Then she said coldly, 'You escaped me.'

'This time.'

She nodded. 'You are wise to say so, Lord Jackal. And not through any craft or strength of yours, but through the slyness of a scribe and an old man.' She was looking at Pa and Seth now, and her face was twisted with spite. '*Watch how I repay them.*'

She spoke one syllable. Telia screamed. The monkeys opened their eyes. Their paws unlinked, they grew, screeched, howled and attacked. Before anyone could move the creatures were all over her, tearing her hair, clawing at Seth as he beat them off her, the brother and sister lost in a vicious biting, scratching assault.

The Jackal was slashed at; Rhetia's spear shattered on their backs, Pa howled in terror. And then a clear voice snapped out a word, and the monkeys clattered on the ground and were toys again, broken, and Telia was peeping in terror from Seth's arms.

Manto turned, astonished. 'After all I've done for you!'

Chryse folded her arms. 'Well, I never wanted any of it. I hate you! You've ruined everything! I never liked you, not even when you taught me things. And now I never want to have anything to do with you again.'

Manto seemed lost for words for a moment. Then she nodded in cool appreciation.

'Always on the winning side, Chryse. I approve, sweetie, I approve.' Looking at the girl hard, she said, 'I think you'll go far.'

Telia pulled away. 'What's that?'

It opened from the sun, a tunnel of light, and from the depths of the Underworld they saw Argelin stalk, grim and haggard, and Alexos running after him, and Oblek, and last of all Mirany, carefully carrying the Bearer's bowl of bronze, anxious not to trip.

Cold with relief Seth pushed past Oblek and grasped the bowl.

'Oh, be careful,' she gasped. And then, 'Seth?'

'Who else.'

Dirt was smudged on her face; she was wet to the skin. She glanced round, at the Oracle, at the others. Then as he smiled back, her face darkened.

'Is there anyone behind me?' she whispered.

He looked over her shoulder. There was no tunnel, and the sun was far on the horizon. In the hush of new light thunder rumbled, closer. Even the gulls seemed muted.

'No,' he said.

Argelin's choked cry froze them both. The General stood on the pavement of the Oracle, looking back at the sun. He was rigid in the brilliant rays, his face haggard and drawn.

'She lied,' he breathed, disbelieving. 'She lied to me.'

Oblek moved close. 'Wait. Something may happen.'

Rhetia whispered, 'Wait for what?'

'Hermia.' Mirany's voice was low. 'The Rain Queen promised him she would come.' She hefted the bowl; quickly Seth took the weight of it, glancing warily at the scorpion.

Argelin looked round at the Oracle, the ruined Precinct, the fleet, barely registering the Nine in their armour, Manto cold and furious by Pa.

'You would have been better doing things my way, General,' the sorceress mocked. 'At least I keep my promises.'

With a clank of armour and laboured breathing Jamil ran

up the steps, waving to his men to stay below. Seeing Argelin's face, he stopped.

Lightning flickered.

Gently, the Jackal muttered, 'It will never happen, General.'

With a great effort, Argelin focused on him. 'Osarkon.' Something seemed to fall into place in his mind; he stared at the Jackal's hair, his eyes.

'You,' he said, dully. 'All the time, it was you?'

The Jackal smiled ruefully. 'A painted prince, General. Who could not forget his mother's agony, or how the fountains of his house ran with blood. For years I have dreamed of telling you this to your face.'

Argelin nodded, as if he could barely remember. 'And does it satisfy you? My humiliation?'

The Jackal was silent. Then he said, 'No. It does not.'

Alexos had climbed the smoking beacon. 'Look at me!'

The sun was behind him. For a moment he was translucent with its brilliance; he shone, his beauty hurt Mirany's eyes, his hair in the breeze shocked her with joy, and she saw him as she had never seen him, the Bright One whose light made her own shadow long and thin behind her, and the Jackal's, and Argelin's.

She's behind you, General, just as the Queen promised. She always will be.

Argelin turned. On the paving before him a shadow lay long, but it was not his. It was a tall woman's, stretching from his feet, her hand raised as he raised his, reaching out as he reached out. She was joined to him. Untouchable. Silent.

He stepped forward, and the shadow moved away. He could never come closer to it. For a moment he stood still. Then he gave a strange, brittle laugh.

'Clever, Queen. Ingenious. True to your word, exactly.'

Seth whispered, 'General . . .'

Argelin didn't move.

'Listen to me. No one can defy the gods. Not even you. Accept it, General. Hermia is dead. The Emperor's fleet is here. Join with us. We need you.'

Slowly, Argelin raised his head. He looked round at them all, at the Jackal, at Rhetia, Mirany, Jamil. When he spoke, his voice was quiet.

'You don't need me. The god will guard his Oracle from the Emperor, from whoever he wants. He always could. He has played with us like figures on a board, Seth. Our fears, our madness, our desires. What do the gods know of love, of shame? We know, you and me, these standing here, that thief-lord, that blonde girl. For all her power, the Queen never will. For that she envies us and torments us. But here, it will end.'

Seth met his eyes. The madness was gone; he saw a man worn thin with suffering, with only a brutal pride left. Silent, he stepped away.

Argelin pulled out the whalebone image. Chilled, Mirany said, 'Don't . . .'

'You were wrong, lady. For me there is no forgiveness.'
Close to her, his eyes were dark and deep. 'But then, neither do I forgive.'

Suddenly he lifted the small statue, yelled, 'Rain Woman! See what I do with your precious image!'

He flung it, hard and high. It sailed up over the cliff edge, falling in a great arc down and down, a white glimmer, a tiny plink and splash in the blue waves. A gull swooped, disappointed over the ripples. Then even those were gone.

Mirany gripped Seth's hand. Breathless, each of them waited for her anger, for the earthquake that would overwhelm them, the roar of the tidal wave that would sweep the Island away.

And it came.

With a deep rumble, the sea-bed heaved. Lightning cracked the sky; bubbles broke surface. The waves erupted, became slick and slanting, and with a terrible roar the earth shifted, a deep tremor that threw everyone off balance and sent tiles thudding from the Temple roof.

Scrambling to hands and knees, Mirany pushed hair from her eyes. She stared out at the sea.

The ocean burst wide. A fingertip rose through it, a great hand thrust up from under its surface, a hand of purest marble, white and snagged with weed. With a roar like the thunder of storms, the outspread arms of the colossus lifted from the seabed, her face calm and implacable, her carved eyes stern. Water dripped and poured from the crevices of her dress; the uprush of her coming dragged crabs and anemones with her; sucked shoals of fish to gasp in the curls of her hair. From the surge and thunder dolphins leapt, gulls screeched; on the shore the people threw themselves down, screaming as the ground rippled and cracked.

High in the stormy sky, a goddess knee deep in water, the statue rose over the harbour, arms wide to the rising sun. Foam slid down her shoulders. Great waves slapped and washed the hems of her tunic, swamped the harbour, overturned ships, men leaping in terror from the tilting masts.

Mirany stared. Sky and sea seethed with a goddess's fury. Tidal surges swept the wharves clean, pounded the lower streets. The ships clashed and splintered. She turned on Argelin.

'What have you done!' she screamed.

Thunder drowned her words, the gale whipped out her hair and tunic. Staggering, Argelin turned and faced the Port, saw the Rain Queen's wrath tear chunks from its walls, burst gates and houses, demolish artillery.

He laughed, cold. 'She demands her sacrifice,' he said, so low that Mirany barely heard him. He glanced at Alexos, clinging to the remnants of the beacon. *'And it is the duty of the Archon to die for his people.'*

Terror seized her. 'No!' she screamed, grabbing at him. The Jackal's sword whipped out; but it was too late.

Argelin had already reached the boy; they were locked

in a struggle, soaked by a great wave that flounced down, spilling Oblek away, drenching Mirany. Alexos staggered back; then he snatched the bowl up and held it between them like a shield. Argelin came right up to it, let its edge rest against his chest. As the scorpion scrabbled up the soaked metal he looked at Alexos, the boy facing him across the ring of bronze, as if they held the world between them.

'The next statue in the row of Archons will be mine,' Argelin said quietly.

Thunder rumbled.

Defiant, he thrust his hand into the bowl.

Alexos was trembling, his eyes flooded with tears. 'You don't have to do this.'

'Exactly.' Argelin did not wince as the scorpion's raised tail stung his fingers. 'I take my own way, Archon. I step off the road. Now I go to seek revenge . . . She and I . . . Hermia . . . we will seek it together.'

He stayed standing a moment, then collapsed; as Seth and the Jackal got to him he shuddered; retched out spittle, gave a faint gasp of release. The bowl clanged and spun to stillness.

Carefully they lowered him to the wet stones, spray lashing them, the Jackal jerking back as the scorpion scuttled into the Oracle. In the terrible silence the wind died; it sank to barely a breeze, hushing through branches. Rhetia knelt and felt his pulse, her fingers on the dry skin of his neck. Then she straightened. She said nothing.

Waves lashed the cliff, spray slapping high, but as she looked out, Mirany saw the waters recede, slacken, turn oily-smooth. In the grey storm clouds, light grew. Gulls wheeled, screaming. There would be no flood.

It was the Jackal who moved; he strode to the edge of the platform and shouted, his voice strong and clear. 'The Archon has returned! The god has returned to his people!'

The massed crowds on the road roared as they deciphered his words. He turned, beckoned. 'Quickly. Come and let them see you.'

Shy, Alexos went forward. The roar increased, flowers were thrown up at him, drums and rattles broke out into sudden rhythms, and he swallowed his tears and waved back, smiling.

In Mirany's ear, Seth whispered, 'They must see the Speaker too.'

'I haven't got a mask.' Stupidly, she wanted to cover her face, because it was hot and red and she felt as if sobs would choke her.

The Speaker's mask was pushed into her hand, and as she stared at it Rhetia tutted, turned her round and adjusted it. 'There. Get up by him.'

Through the eyeslits, Mirany saw the girl standing tall before her. She wanted to speak, but there was nothing to say. She felt as if she would never speak again, as if the death of a man she had learned not to hate had silenced her, and as she turned, she saw Oblek lay a borrowed cloak over Argelin, spreading its folds gently.

When the crowd saw her, the roars increased.

'All very well,' the Jackal muttered. 'But when they realize the Emperor has power here . . .'

'That can be discussed.' Jamil looked down at the people.

'Maybe the god doesn't want to discuss it.' Seth gripped Mirany's elbow. 'Does he?'

His hand was hot, and tense. She knew what he wanted. She raised her hands and slowly, reluctantly, the crowd fell silent. A baby cried, a gull wheeled. Everyone stared up at her, waiting. And she waited too, because he did not speak and she had no words of her own.

'Tell me what to say,' she breathed. 'Don't let me be like Hermia, making the Oracle speak my own wishes. Let me tell them the truth of the god.'

The answer was the breeze in her ear. *How do you know, Mirany, that Hermia's words were not also always mine? You mortals are so self-centred.*

'And you're not?'

He laughed, but she didn't wait for his answer. Instead she spoke his words.

People of the Two Lands, hear the words of the Oracle! The Mouse Lord, the Bright One, the Son of the Scorpion, says this. The Archon has returned and the Emperor will bow before him. There will be no more war and no oppression. No fleet will rule here, no mercenaries despoil. From this day the

Council of Fifty will speak for my people and the Nine will be the guardians of my voice. There will be an end to drought and an end to plagues, and water will run free for all who wish to drink. I have said this. I have spoken my desires and my power will bring them about.

She paused, breathless. Over the clash of spears, the drums and the cheers her final words were quiet. Only Seth and the Jackal heard them.

And perhaps I will learn from you about love.

The Procession was hastily formed, the men carrying Argelin's body in a rough litter. Casting aside their spears, the girls tore down flowers and garlanded their hair; Chryse made a circle of hibiscus for Mirany, and put it on her carefully.

Mirany said, 'Thanks. What about Seth?'

Chryse glanced at him. Her voice was strained. 'Persis is making one for Seth.'

Seth frowned. 'Thank you, Holiness.'

She blushed, hotly. 'I really don't know what for.'

As she took her place, Mirany muttered, 'What was that all about?'

'I'll tell you later.' Seth moved back, out of the Nine, and they streamed past him, masked, Telia giggling and holding Tethys' hand proudly. The god's absence was already a desolation inside him. To hide it, he said, 'She looks as if she's already one of them.'

'Not as Bearer,' his father muttered. 'I won't have that.'

'You're never satisfied.'

To his surprise, Pa grunted out a sour laugh. 'Today I am.'

'Seth!' Oblek yelled. 'Get over here.' He and the optio and the Fox were shouldering the Archon's litter; Alexos hopping from foot to foot impatiently.

'Come on, Seth! You're going to carry me in the Procession.'

'Am I?' Seth sighed. He looked at the litter, then lifted the fourth pole and hoisted it on to his shoulder. It was heavy. He thought of the wet road in dismay.

'Wait till I get in,' Alexos said, half-muffled. The litter dipped. Seth groaned.

'Get a grip, scribe,' Oblek muttered. 'We drank from the Well, remember. We're strong.'

Working into the rhythm, Seth gritted his teeth. Sweat was already dripping into his eyes; his back ached. 'I'm just a scribe.'

'Then you should have kept to your place,' the Jackal said acidly from the back of the white horse. 'We all should have. Because things will never be same for any of us after this.'

Behind the soldiers he rode and the litter followed, through rows of cheering people, over hastily-thrown lavender, crushed sprigs of rosemary. Behind them came girls strewing flowers, and then the Nine, their tunics grimy, their bronze masks smiling out at the people, Rhetia and Chryse stiffly side by side. At the back, alone, Mirany walked, her sandal rubbing her heel.

'Did I say it right?' she whispered.

But the god did not answer, and she gazed steadily ahead, down the long road to the City of the Dead.

As the cheers died away, the storm clouds shimmered. The Island lay quiet, a breeze murmuring in the mouth of the Oracle. Deep in its heart darkness moved, and after a while the small scorpion climbed out and lay basking on the paving in the sun, its tail raised over its back.

Far in the desert, rain fell, the drops plopping deep in the sand, one by one . . .